INTENSE
BENEATH THE BLAZE

LUNA MASON

Author's Note

ABOUT THE AUTHOR

Luna Mason is a USA TODAY and Amazon top 12 bestselling author of dark and spicy romance. If she's not writing, you'll find her with a cup of tea and binge watching her favorite shows.

To keep up with Luna's chaos, find her on social media:
Instagram: @authorlunamason
Her FB Reader Group- Luna Masons Mafia Queens
Sign-up to her newsletter here- https://bit.ly/3SShFuW

And if you want signed books, store exclusives and all the *naughty art,* you can purchase directly from my store:
www.lunamasonbookstore.com

For the wild ones who thought choking was enough.
*Congratulations, you've unlocked the deluxe package: **a psychopathic doctor, a live snake necklace, and a blood kink so filthy it'll make your therapist quit.***
Are you ready for your appointment?
Because Dr. Quinn will see you now.

P.S. Your safe word won't save you...

PLAYLIST

SPOTIFY PLAYLIST!

- Into Hell - I Prevail
- Psycho - Asking Alexandria
- Counterpart - Take Luck
- Gods - Sleep Token
- People Are Strange - The Doors
- Him & I (with Halsey) - G-Eazy, Halsey
- Put It on Me - Matt Maeson
- Die With A Smile - Lady Gaga, Bruno Mars
- Euthanasia - NXW TIME
- Believer - Liam St. John
- Psycho Killer - Talking Heads
- You're Gorgeous - Babybird
- Delusional - Visenya
- Ego - Sarah Kennedy
- i lied - Cheyanne, Ex Habit
- In Your Fantasy - ATEEZ
- Out of the Black - Royal Blood

- Snake Oil - Foals
- Never Fight A Man With A Perm - IDLES
- Eternally Yours - Motionless In White
- Jenny - NOTHING MORE
- Take Me Back To Eden - Sleep Token
- Medicate Me - Rain City Drive, Dayseeker
- Figure It Out - Royal Blood
- Closer - Kings of Leon
- Creature In The Black Night - Dayseeker
- Outro - M83
- The Gravity of You - Mourn
- Masterpiece - Motionless In White
- The Drug In Me Is Reimagined - Falling In Reverse
- Specter - Bad Omens
- can u see me in the dark? - Halestorm, I Prevail
- Will You Love Me When I'm Dead - Amira Elfeky
- Gethsemane - Sleep Token
- Careful What You Wish For - Bad Omens
- Control - Halsey
- Smile Like You Mean It - The Killers
- over me - Camylio
- Dance With The Devil - Breaking Benjamin
- Miracle - Bad Omens
- Zombie - YUNGBLUD
- Fire - Kasabian
- As the World Caves In - Sarah Cothran
- My Demons - STARSET
- The Worst In Me - Bad Omens
- Marry You - Bruno Mars
- pretty poison - Nessa Barrett

- Chokehold - Sleep Token
- Madness - Ruelle
- The Offering - Sleep Token
- Sin- Ash to Eden
- Infinite Baths, Sleep Token

PROLOGUE

STEPHANIE

Two years ago...
Song- Infinite Baths, Sleep Token

No matter how many lives I save, I'm constantly haunted by the parts of myself I lost to get here. Lost isn't even the right word. They were ripped away from me.

I've always been proud of my achievements, like they validated my pain. I let them hurt me so I could be successful in my dream job.

And I was at peace with that. Until today, when the devil rested on my shoulder and whispered at me to kill a man on the operating table.

And for a split second, I thought about it. I wanted him dead, and I wanted to be the woman to kill him.

But I can't. I'm well respected. I work with charities. I'm the second-best surgeon here, knocked off my top spot by the sudden appearance of an asshole by the name of Dr. Quinn.

As I go to take the syringe from my surgical gown to hide

in my locker, the door creaks open. I freeze, the air shifting to ice cold.

And I know whose heavy footsteps they belong to.

"Good work today, Dr. Miller." Finn's deep Irish drawl makes the hairs on my arms stand on end.

"Thanks," I whisper back in an attempt to hide my sadness.

I can never show that side of myself to Dr. Quinn.

Today's operation hit me harder than anything before in my career. Coming face to face with a monster of my past.

"What's the attitude about?" he asks, resting his back against the door with his arms crossed over his chest.

The only reason this patient is still alive is because Dr. Quinn was assessing me the entire time.

"Nothing. Long day," I tell him, grabbing my jacket from my locker.

I'm not a monster for having these murderous thoughts. Am I?

I shake my head and stop in front of Finn. His huge, tatted biceps tense. He doesn't move from the door.

"Can you move?" I can't hide my irritation.

His jaw twitches, and his pale grey eyes lock on mine. There's something sinister behind them.

It'd be easier to despise his existence if he wasn't such a fantastic surgeon. It would be even easier if he wasn't so damn attractive. Like he's just walked off the page of a romance book, smothered in tattoos and a delicious accent.

"Are you going to tell me why you're so damn snappy with me all the time?" he asks, his eyebrow arching.

I huff. I'm fighting a moral dilemma right now. I wanted to kill a man. Not a man—an abuser.

"Because I don't like you, Dr. Quinn," I tell him matter-of-factly.

He snickers.

"But I respect your talent. And the fact you now basically own this hospital, and my career is in your hands." I fake a smile.

He won't fire me. Because this department is in shambles other than me and Dr. Quinn.

He shrugs, like he's completely unaffected by my statement. He slowly pushes himself off the door and moves out of my way.

"Do you still think I bought my way in? Do you think you're a better surgeon than me, Dr. Miller?" His tone is laced with a threat.

"I bet I got higher grades than you. I know I nearly killed myself to be here. That this is my passion. But no, I'm not better than you… yet. Although I might not be now, but one day I will be."

He chews on his lip, pulling out a small black notebook from his pocket, and starts scribbling in it.

"Hmm," he mutters, deep in thought.

I shake my head and go to open the door, he steps right behind me. I can smell him. Feel him all over me.

"I don't like you much either, Stephanie."

He leans in closer. I hold my breath as his heat settles against the shell of my ear.

"Perhaps find another place to hold your passions. Because today, you saved the life of a sex trafficker, Dr. Miller. Not everything we do is gratuitous nor right. If that were me, I'd have made sure he didn't wake back up from that operating table."

He backs away, and my chest almost closes in on me.

I shake my head and turn to him. A menacing grin is on his lips. My eyes are wide.

"W-what?"

He lets out a deep chuckle.

"I'm fucking with you. I'd never break our sacred code. But seriously. There is more to life than work. And a lot of these patients don't deserve our sacrifices."

He has no idea how right he is.

"Anyway, good work saving the life of a complete cunt today." He winks at me and strolls past, straight out of the room and whistling as he goes down the hallway.

Every single interaction I've had with him over the last four years leaves me either furious or confused.

But his words hit me deep.

As I walk down the hallway, I stop outside Mark's room. Taking a deep breath, I peer in through the glass. A single tear slips down my cheek, thinking about the eighteen-year-old Stephanie. And what I'd do now to protect her. What I could do to protect other girls like me.

As if on autopilot, I walk in.

I stand at the foot of his bed, the potassium syringe still hidden in the sleeve of my gown. I took it earlier during surgery. Why? I don't know. It felt right.

He's alive because of me.

I swallow hard, the memory of the pre-op consultation crowding out everything else.

He smiled at me. Sat there in the too-small gown with his chart in his lap and looked me dead in the eye like he knew exactly who I was. Like he knew he'd wrecked me and was curious to see how much was left.

The same smile he gave me when I was eighteen and too desperate to leave to notice he was never going to let me go.

My chest tightens until I can't breathe.

I saved him. I fixed the heart that has always been black and hollow. I did my job because everyone expects me to be the surgeon who saves lives, no matter who they belong to.

But standing here now, I can't bear the thought of him opening those eyes again. Of him walking out of this hospital with a stronger heart, free to hurt another girl the way he hurt me.

I step closer, my hands shaking so badly I nearly drop the syringe.

He doesn't deserve the life I gave back to him.

He doesn't deserve a second chance.

I slide my hand under the sheet and find the port. My fingers are slick with sweat. For a moment I just stand there, looking at his face. The sedation makes him look harmless. Almost peaceful.

But I remember everything, even if it was over thirteen years ago.

The back hallway. The smell of bourbon on his breath. The way he told me it was time I learned what men were willing to pay for.

A sob claws up my throat, but I swallow it.

Beep.

I press the plunger down slowly.

Beep.

His rhythm skips.

Beep.

And then the monitor screams.

Beeeeeeeep.

My heart is beating so fast I think I might faint, but I don't look away. I want to see the moment he's gone. I want to feel it.

I'm numb on the outside.

But inside, I'm alive. I'm free. Like a weight has been lifted.

He's dead. He's gone.

I'll never get justice through the legal system. I just tried to forget. Who was going to believe a young stripper desperate for money over a rich predator? No one.

But none of that matters. My sacrifices paid off. I have the career I always dreamed of.

And now, I can serve justice myself.

Maybe, I've worked hard to get to this moment. My true calling.

Because it wasn't just Mark who hurt me. There's a trail of them littered around Pennsylvania.

And they all deserve to die.

CHAPTER 1

FINN

Present day...
Song- Psycho Killer, Talking Heads

Taking another drag of my cigarette, I lean on the railing. Eyes fixed on the target.

Currently he's on floor ten of this high-rise. Doing some kind of home workout in his boxers.

Blinds up. Lights on. Fucking idiot.

You never know who is watching you from the shadows.

Should I let him finish working out or dancing? Whatever the fuck he's doing, before I kill him?

I often wonder about my last moments. I'd want mine to be with my brothers, drinking a beer in Dublin. Not prancing around in my boxers at midnight on a Wednesday, trying to burn some calories, like this asshole is.

I check the time on my Rolex.

Go to fucking bed, buddy. I have a life to get on with.

"Are we going in yet?" Rowan asks from beside me.

"Not yet."

"What, are we letting him finish his routine?" Reggie, Rowan's identical twin brother, grunts from the other side of me.

I used to work mainly on my own. But these two dipshits have become like the extended family I didn't ask for. And they're exactly as you'd expect of Irish twins. Reggie is the serious one, and Rowan, the batshit crazy one.

"Yeah. I need him asleep for what I have planned this time."

"Right," Reggie says.

Their preferred method of killing is more of a spectacle. Brutish. Mine? More methodical. Evil. I've spent years training to save lives, but it's also meant I can perfect the most painful deaths.

And these cunts deserve it.

Flicking my cigarette into the water, I stand, securing my flat cap.

"Does he seem like a mafia boss to you? Or a leader of any kind?" I ask the twins, already knowing the answer.

Something seems off.

Rowan frowns, looking back up at the dancing man in the window.

"Not really?"

"Hmm."

Drago, our hacker and man behind the scene, is certain this is our last target. Following on from my brother, Conan's, Decadence Chase, we have located and killed the first eight targets easily. But this one was fucking hard to find and landed us in Ohio of all places.

"You think it's not him?"

I grunt.

"He is the man who entered Abigail."

But is he The Preacher? The man Abigail warned me about as she set off for her new life.

"He will never let me go. He's evil. I'm not safe in the United States." That's what she told me, breaking down into hysterics. Enzo has contacts in Italy, so we made an agreement with him to have her sent to Italy to live.

But her words have bothered me ever since. 'The Preacher' didn't appear on any of her paperwork. We can't find shit about him.

She showed me her brand, the italic PR carved into her forearm. That fear in her eyes—it was real. As I look up at this balding, dancing man, I know it ain't the leader of whatever organization she was a part of. Something deep in my bones tells me it's something far bigger.

"What you thinking, Finn?" Reggie asks.

"That, we have to make sure this death doesn't come back to us. I'm not sure about this place."

I rub my stubble on my jaw. I got a bad feeling about this, and I never ignore my gut. I did that once, and that ended up killing me at age ten.

I shake my head, not wanting to remember that time of my life. I buried it with them.

Rowan nudges me. "Hey, the light's gone off."

I shoot him a look, warning him not to touch me. It makes my skin fucking burn. Only my brothers can get away with it, but only just barely.

He takes a step back.

I keep my eyes fixed on the building, watching my prey, waiting to pounce. When the lights don't turn back on, I know it's time.

A buzz spreads through my body. This is my true calling in life.

"Remember the rules. You stay outside and keep watch,

just let me do my job, aye?" I flick my eyes between the twins.

Rowan grins. "Yeah, yeah. We know, Dr. Finn."

In the thick of the night, we make our way to the building, and I slip on my leather gloves and pull down my hat.

"How the fuck we getting in?" Reggie asks as I approach the keypad.

Pulling out the white card from my jacket pocket, I hold it between my fingers and roll my eyes at Reggie.

"While you two were busy stuffing your faces with burgers, I was being productive."

I slipped it out from one of the resident's pockets while having an exchange with them about what kind of fucking horse I should buy next for my nonexistent ranch.

Swiping the card, the door clicks and I push it open, heading straight for the elevator. We squeeze inside. All three of us are bulky and over 6'3".

"Well, this is cozy," Rowan chuckles.

"I heard you two sleep in the same fuckin' bed still?" I tease, arching a brow.

Reggie sighs.

"Jesus fucking Christ. We don't fuck each other, that would be disgusting. We simply fuck the same woman. Our dicks do not touch," Reggie clarifies.

"Yeah, I don't even look at his cock!" Rowan exclaims.

I chuckle.

"Great. Thanks for clarifying. So you prefer the Eiffel Tower situation?"

They both shrug.

"Lots of different positions we can use," Reggie tells me, deadpan.

I've had my fair share of threesomes. Normally with two women, though. And never, ever, with one of my brothers.

But the twins, the dynamic? Reggie the dominant, scary one, and Rowan the cheeky, probably sub. I can see why women are into it.

"Who has the bigger dick?" I bite back a grin.

I know this whole sharing thing is a joke between us all and that it riles them up, particularly our grumpy Reggie.

"Me," they say in unison.

"I know for a fact, identical twins doesn't always mean dick size. I'm a doctor, remember?"

Rowan rolls his eyes. That makes me clench my fists.

"Fine. Reggie has a bigger dick, lengthwise. Only just. Mine is girthier. And pierced."

My own cock shrivels up. Ouch. I have a freakishly high pain threshold, but that doesn't extend to my cock.

The elevator pings open on the tenth floor, and I rush out. I don't particularly want to be thinking about them two fucking someone while I kill a man.

The twins get into position on either side of the door, and I start to pick at the lock, jabbing the metal into the hole until it clicks.

"See ya on the other side, fuckers," I whisper to them.

The room is silent as I step inside, closing the door behind me. It's modest. Clean. Boring. Only confirming my suspicions. This is not The Preacher. Merely one of his lackeys.

But Enzo wants him dead, so Luke Taylor will be dead. Rules are rules. Any man who enters a woman into our Decadence games dies. Luke entered Abigail into Conan's Chase. So here I am, like I am for every kill.

They enter these women thinking it gives them a chance to become part of the elite in the mafia world. Little do they realize, all it does is send me into their homes in the middle of the night to kill them. Poetic in a way. They do get a new life, just in hell.

I wait, leaning against the doorframe to his bedroom. He's sprawled across his mattress, mouth slack with sleep, a faint wheeze rattling in his throat. Pathetic. I stand there a moment, taking him in—how ordinary he looks, how easy it is to end a life that once thought itself untouchable.

Because he did believe that, that's why he tried to use Abigail, his damn girlfriend, as a sacrifice to get a ticket in to Inferno.

I draw the syringe from my pocket. Rocuronium. It's rapid and reliable. I step beside him, my gloved hand presses against his jaw, tilting his head just so. He doesn't even stir when the needle breaks skin, only exhales a sleepy sigh as if he senses nothing.

But he will.

I watch the seconds count down in my mind, my pulse steady. When the drug takes hold, it's not like he jolts awake. No, it's subtler. His eyes flutter, then widen with a clarity I savor. I relish this part.

He tries to draw in a breath, but the muscles refuse him. I hear it—the hitching, the ragged choke of air caught somewhere he can't reach.

I know what this feels like, being so vulnerable at the hands of someone more powerful than you and not being able to do a single thing about it.

I kneel beside the bed, my face inches from his. I want him to see me. To know.

"You're still here," I murmur, my voice low, almost kind. "That's the curse of this one. Fully awake. Nothing you can do."

I tap his cheek and grin.

His pupils blow wide, fixed on mine. His chest jerks in shallow spasms, diaphragm locked in paralysis. I can feel the panic rolling off him. He tries to scream, but there's no sound. Only that wet, futile rattle.

Air hunger. The most primal terror there is.

I rest a hand over his sternum, feeling the weak flutter beneath. He's drowning in the open air, and I am the only witness. His heartbeat thunders, then falters. His lips go purple. His eyes, pleading for a mercy I don't possess.

I slit his throat with a single, clean stroke. A ritual more than a necessity—a small mercy, I suppose. And I make sure to do it while the heart is still pumping so the arterial blood splashes across the sheets, stark against the dull beige. I work quickly, pressing the fentanyl patch to his skin, letting the overdose soak in. Insurance for the coroner's report.

And for good measure, I give him matching slices across his wrists, leaving the blade in his limp hand.

I stand back to admire my work. There's an elegance in this artistry.

He never really knew how close death had been. Not until it was too late to beg. Not that it would have helped his cause.

I don't believe in second chances.

CHAPTER 2

STEPHANIE

I'm rushing toward the exit, yanking the stethoscope from around my neck, when I slam into something solid.

My hands fly out to brace myself.

I freeze.

"Dr. Miller. Somewhere important you need to be?"

That Irish drawl makes my heart thud like it's trying to escape.

"Sorry," I murmur, stepping back as fast as I can.

He brushes my touch from his pristine white shirt like I've contaminated him.

"Well? Normally you only run toward the O.R., not the exit."

He tilts his head, eyes narrowing, reading me like he always does—too well.

"I have somewhere I need to be. If you'll excuse me."

I throw in a fake sweet smile for good measure. Dr. Quinn is still my boss, even if he's a walking migraine.

He checks his watch, then flicks those cold grey eyes back to me.

"Your shift doesn't finish for another thirty seconds."

I hiss out a breath.

"Are you being serious?"

His eyebrow arches and his eyes darken.

"Deadly."

He's cruel. Always has been. Gorgeous, brilliant, and emotionally bankrupt. Dead behind the eyes. It would almost be fascinating if he didn't anger me so much.

I plant my hands on my hips, tapping my foot like I'm not moments from snapping.

"No small talk today?" he presses.

With him? No. Never.

I count the seconds in my head like I'm in surgery.

He smirks. "Looking forward to the award ceremony?"

My scowl deepens.

Three years in a row. Same painful circus. Where cardiology departments across the state gather just to bow down to the almighty Dr. Quinn.

Because no one ever wins that award except him.

He paid his way to the top. Of course he wins. That's why I call him rich boy.

We're just there to applaud him.

"I can't go," I lie flatly.

"It's not an invitation you simply reject, Dr. Miller. It's classed as a working day. No excuses."

I roll my eyes so hard they might detach.

"Don't you think the patients need us more than you need to hold that damn trophy?"

His jaw twitches.

"Our shifts are covered. Adequately. It's two nights. You are expected to be there."

Translation: he wants to watch me lose. Again. He wants

to see the disappointment crawl across my face when his name gets called.

Again.

"Fine. My thirty seconds are up. Please move."

I say it as sweetly as I can muster.

He steps aside. Barely.

"Have a lovely evening, Stephanie. I'll see you bright and early."

"Yeah… bye."

I race to my car and whip out my phone. My second life is calling.

Ever since my last club burned to the fucking ground, I've had to move to a new one. The manager there, Paulie, is a dick, but he's strict, and that works for me. One night a week. Just enough to do what I need.

It's how I scope out my next victims.

Because the men who preyed on girls when I was eighteen? They still haunt these places.

And now, I haunt them back.

It's my favorite game.

It's also the only time I get to stop being Dr. Miller.

When I'm on that stage, I'm Angel.

Bright red hair. Brown contacts. Heels like weapons. There, I have power, and my rage is disguised in rhythm.

And every dollar they throw? I send straight to the women's shelter downtown.

Heaven and hell. I like to strike the balance.

I rid the world of monsters. And help the girls clawing their way out of the dark.

My Mercedes hums beneath me as I fly through the streets.

Paulie's name flashes on the dash.

"Fuck."

I press the answer button on my dash.

"Angel, where the fuck are you?" he barks.

"I'm on my way. Got caught up at work."

He sighs hard, like I'm the bane of his existence.

"You wanna keep this gig? Stop being late. I'm already doing you a favor letting you work one night a week. This isn't a fucking part-time hobby. Women would kill for this slot."

"I know. I'm trying. Okay?"

I try to keep him sweet. The same as I did with my last boss, Ben. It seems to be the trick of being a woman in this society: pretend to be nice to men. And it's a damn sight harder than it should be.

But there's only one other place I've heard about I could move to.

Inferno.

Elite. Hush hush. Invite-only.

A playground for the worst of the worst.

A fucking paradise for someone like me. But how you get in, or where the hell it even is, is still unknown to me.

I pull into the parking lot, cut the engine, and grab my duffel. Head down, fast steps, no eye contact, I quickly make my way to the dressing room.

I can't let anyone here see me as Dr. Stephanie Miller.

She doesn't exist in here.

Only Angel does.

And tonight?

Angel's got work to do. It's been a while since I've had some fun and let some revenge out of my system, and that needs to change.

CHAPTER 3

FINN

I wasn't planning on being here tonight.

Not when I have an operating room to dominate in eight hours and a list of patients longer than most hitmen's body counts.

But then Drago called.

And when the Russian brainiac calls, I answer. And he's been busy digging on The Preacher. It's all hearsay at this point, but it's got me intrigued. And what we've found so far ain't good.

He said one of The Preacher's men, those twisted, Bible-quoting traffickers, drinks here. Every Friday night. Same booth. Same drink.

I couldn't let it go, not after what Abigail said. Not after killing that man, Luke. I want to know who our enemy is. And knowing one of these bastards has been stepping foot in Quinn territory makes me sick.

But tonight's not about confrontation. It's recon.

Get in. Watch. Identify. Get out.

That's it.

The bouncer eyes me like I don't belong here. Maybe I

shouldn't have worn a designer suit, but I flash the card Drago slid me. He nods and lets me through.

Inside, it's the usual chaos.

Velvet seats. Stale sex in the air. Music vibrating in my spine. Half-naked girls twisting on poles or wrapping themselves around men who don't deserve the attention.

I hate places like this. Inferno is where I belong. It's made to our tastes. It's clean, pristine. Not like this. And our women are protected, looked after.

I order a whiskey, neat, and slide into the booth Drago flagged. It's dimly lit, with a perfect line of sight across the main floor.

Then I see him.

Booth six. Fat ring fingers. A flat nose that's clearly been punched into his face. Finished off with a designer watch that doesn't fit his cheap suit. Here we have it; it's our guy, Troy Barnes. The Preacher's logistics man.

He's not alone.

A woman straddles his lap.

Red hair. Tight black corset and a red thong.

She's facing him. Grinding. Rolling her hips with the kind of lazy rhythm that drives men to madness.

Barnes looks like he's in heaven. His hand slides to her ass and she grabs his wrist, hard enough that he freezes.

Even from here, I see her lips move.

She lets go, leans in, and whispers something in his ear that makes him turn pale.

Then she stands.

Turns.

And walks off without taking a dollar from the man.

Like she came for something else.

Like she's not here to be seen, but to see. That's what I

do. I always assess in a room of people. I like to read them, probably better than they can read themselves.

But now? I'm frozen in place. My brain is fucking glitching.

Not because of him.

Because of her.

That kind of control… that kind of power… it's rare. And dangerous.

She's not like the others. She doesn't move like them. Doesn't perform for the crowd.

She moved for him.

And owned him.

I take a sip of my whiskey, forcing my pulse to calm.

Who the fuck is she?

My mind races, trying to place her. The hair's too red to be real. The body. God, that body is sculpted like temptation, but there's something about her posture. Her command.

A whisper in my brain tells me I've seen her before.

But I brush it off.

My grip tightens around the glass.

Whoever she is… she's playing a dangerous game with monsters.

And I can't decide if I want to protect her or pin her to the wall and demand answers.

Either way—I need to know her name, so I'll be back.

Because a woman like that doesn't just disappear.

She leaves a mark.

And I've already got the first one.

Burned into my memory.

For now, I have to sit and watch this ugly fucker get hard over women he could never have and try to figure him out. That's what I'm good at. Assessing people better than they know themselves.

CHAPTER 4

STEPHANIE

"**S**teph, wait up!" I call out to Kia. God, it feels wrong shouting my real name at another girl. But it's her stage name, and I'd never go around shouting her real name for any of these monsters to hear.

She spins on her heel, brushing her platinum blonde hair over her shoulder. She pulls a wad of money from her bra.

"What's up?"

I nod toward one of our changing rooms, and she follows me in.

"Oh, gossip time? Have you heard from Ben? He completely disappeared after the place went up in flames," she rambles on.

She's always been obsessed with Ben. I couldn't give a flying fuck. He was an asshole—well on his way onto my hit list.

"No. Probably ran away from all his debt. That guy in booth six—did he say anything weird to you?" I ask.

He gave me the creeps, and when he touched me, I nearly smashed his glass and sliced up his face.

I've seen him here a few times before, but never danced for him. But tonight, he requested me personally.

And then he told me to meet him outside after my shift, which I politely declined. But that evil glint in his eye? It worried me.

I know men like him. The ones who don't take no for an answer.

"Umm. Not really. Just the same as the rest of them. Fucking pervs."

I tap my chin. Something isn't sitting right with me. He's not from round here, he has some kind of drawl to his voice.

"Okay. Just keep an eye out. Let me know if he comes back or asks for me again," I tell her.

Her eyes narrow.

"Are you okay?" she asks.

I give her a smile.

"Yeah. Of course. I just... don't want to find myself in a similar situation to when I first started dancing."

Nearly all of the girls here carry stories like mine. Young. Naive. Dazzled by the fast cash. I might have had a scholarship into med school, but it wasn't the full ride. I had to find a way to live. And with both my parents in jail, it was up to me to figure it out.

And so I did. In a club much worse than this.

What you don't see is the dark side of this job. When you're desperate to secure your future, your present becomes chaos.

I gave away something I can never get back. Let a man of my past persuade me to become more than a stripper.

Something I never wanted. Something I'll never forgive myself for.

And no matter how many years go by, I can't help but mourn what I lost. I can't change my past, but I'll be damned if I let predators like *him* take something from the next girl.

"I will. Go home. You look exhausted, Angel," she whispers.

After a ten-hour shift and five hours here, she's right. Luckily, tomorrow is my day off.

As I head to my car, I pull my jacket tighter, quickening my steps.

The dull streetlights make everything feel more sinister.

With one hand wrapped around the pepper spray in my pocket, relief washes over me as I unlock my car. But then I spot a small white slip tucked under my windshield.

I pick it up, holding my breath. A messy handwritten note, with a PR stamp on the top.

EXPECT A PHONE CALL, DR. MILLER.

My heart practically leaps out of my chest. It has to be that guy from earlier.

They know my real name. My job.

What the hell does he want with me?

And what the hell does the PR stand for?

I'm kicking myself. I knew there was something off about him.

I jump in the car and lock the doors, my pulse racing.

And then my phone rings.

Unknown flashing on the screen.

I hit accept and stay quiet, trying to calm my breathing.

"Dr. Miller." A distorted voice fills the line.

Well, fuck.

"Who is this?"

"That is none of your concern. We have a task for you. If you wish to live, you'll stay on the line and listen to our proposition."

My fist clenches.

What do they know about me?

I'm careful. Always. No kills in the club. I follow them home. I make it look clean. Undetectable.

There's no way I slipped.

"Stephanie?"

"Y-yes. I'll listen."

"Do you recognize the name Mark Fisher?"

My stomach drops.

My first kill. The man who shattered me. Who brokered my body to his men like a fucking commodity.

"I think I know the name vaguely," I lie.

The voice laughs.

"Knew. But we know what you did. Very naughty."

My nails dig into my skin.

"What do you want?" I ask, practically whispering.

"For you to do it again, Dr. Miller. But don't worry, your secrets are safe with us. You won't take the fall. We just need you to set it up."

I rub my palm across my collarbones.

"And what happens if I say no?"

The voice scoffs.

"You'll end up just like your parents and die a murderer in the public eye, Dr. Miller. That'll make quite the tabloid, don't you think?"

There's a drawl under the distortion.

"What proof do you have?"

"Enough to burn your career in twenty seconds. Mark was a very good friend of mine."

"I'm not apologizing."

He chuckles.

"I don't expect you to. I'm impressed, really. He had it coming. Surprised it took that long for karma to catch up.

That's why I'm asking you. You're the only one who can pull this off seamlessly."

I pause.

"Who would I be killing?"

"A patient at your hospital."

I feel sick.

"Too risky."

"That's a you problem, Dr. Miller. I'll send you the patient details. Just get it done. We'll take care of the rest."

I shake my head, trying to process everything.

"If I'm not getting the blame, who is?"

I swear I hear him smile.

"Your favorite attending surgeon."

Dr. Quinn.

Fuck.

Think. Think.

There has to be a way out of this.

"You have twenty-four hours to decide. Just know—if you decline my offer, you better have your burial plot picked out. If you accept, we'll vanish once the job is done."

I blow out a breath. Before I can respond, he cuts the call.

Fuck.

CHAPTER 5

FINN

"**D**r. Miller. A word?" My tone is clipped.

But I'm furious.

The past couple of days, she's been acting differently. Less confrontational, which, to most, would be a good thing.

To me? It means something's up.

And the fact she nearly fucked up a cardiac bypass in there, something I've seen her do on many occasions over the years, is unacceptable.

It's not like her.

She follows me into the locker room. I shut the door behind her, but she doesn't turn to face me.

"What the fuck was that in there?" I hiss.

She turns and frowns but stays quiet. I don't like this version of her. I like the spunky, sassy, nothing-held-back Stephanie. That one keeps me on my toes.

This quiet, reserved version?

Makes me livid.

Over the past nearly six years, I've become accustomed to

many versions of Stephanie. All of which seem to hate my guts, but all equally fascinating versions of her.

"Oh, come on, Dr. Miller. I know you can speak. Tell me."

I step in front of her, and she slowly looks up, into my eyes.

"I'm just exhausted."

"Go on vacation then. Don't offer to do a surgery when you clearly can't concentrate."

She scowls at me.

"What would you have done if I wasn't there to save your ass, Stephanie? Seriously?"

She rolls her eyes, and I have to physically stop myself from pinning her against the lockers. I can't fucking stand when someone rolls their eyes at me.

"Dr. Quinn is always there to save the day." There it is, that spite on her tongue.

She's returning. And that stirs something inside my chest.

"Someone has to be, clearly. Whatever's going on, get it fixed. If it starts to impact your work, I'll have no choice but to write you up."

Her eyes go wide.

Ah, there it is—fear. That rare flicker I barely ever see from her, but when I do?

I bask in it. And threatening the one thing she loves most in the world seems to bring it out.

"It won't happen again, Dr. Quinn."

I shake my head.

"Don't make promises you can't keep, Dr. Miller."

She scowls at me, like I'm the worst person in the world to her.

Just as I suspect I have been since day one.

I made myself her enemy without so much as opening my mouth the day I joined the cardiology department.

And every day since, I've studied her.

She is my favorite patient to assess.

When she bites her lip, my eyes zone in there.

There's a fine line between lust and hate.

And we dance it like it's second nature.

I allow her to despise me, because it keeps us both sharp. Keeps her at my level.

It's a dance I want to keep doing.

I pull out the black marker from my pocket with a grin.

"Really? Now?" she snaps.

"You know damn well it's time." I hand her the marker.

She huffs and stomps over to the whiteboard.

Week four hundred and eight.

Total tally: Dr. Quinn, three hundred. Dr. Miller, one hundred and seven.

She puts a line under this week's chart. Make it three hundred and one.

I can feel the anger rolling off her in waves. It's silly really, a tally chart that I completely fix every week. It can be something as mundane as a decent joke or as raw as bringing someone back from the dead. These lines on that board mean nothing and everything.

"Good work, Dr. Miller," I tease.

I can't help it. Any opportunity I get to rile her up, I take it. It's a habit now. Even after she flawlessly saved my brother's life, I still can't help it.

If I wasn't who I am, I would have let her win that entire leaderboard for the rest of our careers for giving me Conan back. I can never really thank her enough for that.

I knew making that call to have her do the surgery was a bold move. I thought I'd never live it down.

Yet, much to my shock, she doesn't throw that one in my face too often. Maybe that is her limit with me. She's the only one who has seen me almost fall apart.

I think she knew. And chose to stay silent. As if she likes this power play between us. Perhaps she thrives in it as much as I do.

Maybe we need it to survive here.

I've spent most of my life pushing people away.

Yet with Stephanie, I push and I push, and she never moves out of my orbit.

She stands her ground.

Maybe that's why I gravitate to her.

"I really don't like you," she says, almost sweetly, as she tosses the marker at my chest.

I catch it with a smirk.

"Really? I had no idea," I say, sarcastically.

She darts around me. I watch the sway of her hips as she heads for the door—like being near me sucks the life out of her.

"Go get some rest before the award ceremony. I'll see you on the airstrip!" I call out.

She swings the door open.

"Fucking rich boy," she whispers under her breath.

I pull out my phone when the door slams shut and note this interaction down, chuckling to myself.

She hates failure. But hates needing help even more.

Her constant obsession with independence might just be the thing that breaks her.

Dr. Miller feels a lot. She is quite the opposite of me. I'm numb on the inside. She isn't. She's a fucking ball of fire waiting to erupt.

CHAPTER 6

STEPHANIE

I promised myself I'd stop.

That my first kill was my last. Well, at least inside the hospital. My endeavors have continued after hours. In the dead of the night, when only the predators come out to play.

Yet, one phone call, from a distorted male voice, changes everything.

I have my orders, and I don't have a way out. I'm used to ending lives, for myself. Never under the command of another, especially not from a man. I'm not an assassin. I kill for a good cause, I kill for vengeance, and to save other women from having to go through the pain of what I went through.

I close the door behind me, sucking in a breath as I look at the sleeping man. It's like I've stepped back in time.

Except, for all I know, this man could be innocent? Doubtful, seeing as I'm being enlisted to kill him by god knows who.

Men like this, men who end up as my targets, rarely are.

But I suppose I'll never really know.

And in the end, it won't matter.

Dr. Quinn just saved his life yesterday.

And Dr. Quinn will be taking his life. That's how my blackmailer has assured me it will appear. The CCTV will be wiped. The systems have been hacked.

Right now, Dr. Quinn is standing here, not me. Or that's what the police will believe. I am merely a ghost.

I cross the room in measured steps, my gloved fingers brushing the IV line threaded into the back of his hand.

He shifts in his sleep, a tiny groan escaping his slack mouth. My heartbeat doesn't even quicken. This part of me—this precise, clinical part—has always been terrifyingly steady.

I draw the syringe from my pocket. It's not filled with any poison, but it's just as deadly.

I pause at the bedside, scanning the readouts. No one would question me if they saw me checking his vitals.

I press a button on the cardiac monitor, bringing up the settings menu. My gloved finger hovers just long enough to confirm that the alarms are active, then I toggle them off. The screen freezes. No more beeping. No more witnesses.

The silence feels enormous. Ominious.

I detach the pulse oximeter from his finger and tuck it under the folded blanket near his hip. No alarms to announce the moment his oxygen drops to nothing.

He shifts against the sheets, eyelids fluttering. A faint, bewildered sound in his throat. He's waking just enough to know something's happening.

Air. What we need to survive can also kill us just as easily.

I pull back the plunger until the barrel is filled with emptiness. Four, five, six milliliters. Enough to shatter the illusion of safety.

He exhales in a sigh that sounds almost content as I ease the needle into the line. I watch his face as I depress the plunger.

One moment, he's dreaming.

Next, his body knows something is catastrophically wrong.

His eyes snap open, confusion bleeding into horror as he tries to suck in air that won't come. His chest bucks against the sheets, pupils dilating in primal panic.

An air embolism. So small, so efficient. The bubble travels straight to his heart, a silent saboteur. I can almost imagine it racing through his veins.

His hands scrabble weakly at the tubing, trying to claw it out, but it's too late.

I rest my palm over his sternum, feeling the stuttering rhythm sputter, then seize. His gaze locks with mine, glassy with terror and the dawning realization that nothing will save him now.

Thirty seconds, maybe less.

His lips part around a wet, broken gasp. His last breath.

Then silence.

I wait until I'm certain the last flicker has gone out.

Then I pull the syringe free, I reconnect the pulse oximeter to his finger, and tap the monitor back to life. It will alert the team.

That's what my blackmailer wants.

I slide the spent syringe into my pocket and exhale. Leaving the man as he is.

Out of all the lives I've taken, this one is the worst.

Because I didn't just take his.

I've also taken Dr. Quinn's. My boss. My rival.

I should be elated at the end of his reign. No more tally charts every week to prove he's better at his job than me.

No more losing to him at our award ceremonies.

No more of his smug grins or cheeky winks to annoy me.

I should be happy.

Except I'm not. I wanted to beat Dr. Quinn fair and square with my skill and my work ethic. Not like this.

This feels like I'm cheating.

I don't know if I prefer the devil that walks the hallway of this hospital to the one blackmailing me.

As I slink out of the room and calmly head back to my office, I see Finn racing back down the hallway. Our eyes lock, and I swear time freezes.

His stare is always ice cold, yet it burns me from the inside out.

Knowing my luck, he probably will bring the dead back to life and royally screw me over.

Because if I fail this.

I die.

CHAPTER 7

FINN

Four contestants. Or, as I like to call them—test subjects.

Their applications are all sitting in my inbox.

Except I'm too busy scrolling through the social media feed for the strip club.

Who the fuck was that woman?

Perhaps I should be more interested in the fact we lost three patients last night. None of which come as a surprise in their conditions. But it doesn't look good for our stats.

There's a light knock on my office door and I grin. I like to start my day with an interaction with Stephanie.

"Come in," I call out.

The door opens slowly, and I see a message pop up from Conan.

I can't hide my smile as I open the picture of little baby Liam. Born this morning.

God, he looks just like my brother.

Before I can text back, Dr. Miller clears her throat.

I look up and freeze.

She's standing in front of three police officers, looking like she might pass out.

I rise with a smile that's all teeth.

"Officers. How can I help?" I ask.

Inside, I'm burning.

We have a deal. This is my fucking place of work.

And Stephanie looks seconds from collapsing.

"We need you to come down to the station, Dr. Quinn."

My jaw clenches.

"Dr. Miller, you're good to go."

I flick my eyes toward the door.

She nods and flees like the room's on fire.

I don't recognize any of these cops. That's the first red flag.

"Am I under arrest?"

They glance at each other.

I tut.

"Look. I need to make a quick phone call. I have someone very important at home that needs feeding. Then I'll come willingly. No handcuffs. No issues. Okay?"

The one at the front swallows.

"Uh. Yes. Okay."

I hit dial on Rowan's number.

"Finn. Where are you? Reggie said the cops came sniffing around earlier."

I let out a breath.

"Yeah. They're here. Don't worry. Get hold of Drago for me. I need a favor."

"Sure. Anything."

His chirpy attitude grates on my nerves.

"It's feeding day for Nyx. Everything you need's already been defrosted—it's on the counter. Just toss it in for her."

He coughs.

My men aren't scared of anything… except my fucking pet python.

"Just open it up, like fully? What if she gets out?"

I pinch the bridge of my nose.

"She's not a fucking jumping frog, Rowan. She's a snake. A docile one. Drop her food in and walk away. Okay? And call Drago."

"Alright. Alright. Good luck."

I let out a sarcastic laugh.

"Yeah. Thanks."

I cut the call and turn my attention back to the officers.

"Ready when you are."

I gesture toward the door.

With one officer in front of me and two behind, we head for the exit.

I spot Stephanie in the corridor.

Pale as a ghost.

Frozen.

Watching.

She looks like she's been sucker-punched instead of wanting to celebrate something. Interesting. I must note that down.

When our eyes lock, she flinches.

"Fill in for my shift, Dr. Miller," I call out.

Whoever is responsible for this bullshit is going to feel my wrath.

The second this is cleared up, I'm coming for blood.

CHAPTER 8

STEPHANIE

I've never wanted to run out of Finn's office so fast in my life. Seeing him being arrested, yet even then, no cuffs, no drama.

Just a smug grin on his face. Like he knows he is going to be walking out of that police station unscathed.

They're taking him.

And I'm the reason why.

I stand there, frozen, while the man I betrayed walks out of this hospital surrounded by cops like he's nothing more than a case file waiting to be buried.

But he's not.

He's everything.

The chaos. The storm. The addiction I can't name. Who will I become if I'm not constantly rivaling him?

My chest feels too tight, like my ribs are trying to strangle my heart. My hands won't stop shaking. Not from fear. From the crushing weight of knowing I did this.

I let them take him.

I signed the fucking dotted line with my silence.

I did what they asked.

Set him up. Let them believe he's the monster.

Because it was him or me.

And I told myself I could live with that.

But now that he's gone—I'm not so sure.

His voice echoes in my skull. *"Fill in for my shift, Dr. Miller."*

No bite. Just cold. I bolt for the stairwell the second the doors close behind them. I can't breathe. I need to scream, to cry, to undo this somehow. But I can't. It's done.

He's gone.

And maybe he won't come back.

I slide down the wall and dig my nails into my palms, my knees pressed tight to my chest. There's a tremble in my spine that won't stop. My mouth is dry. My thoughts won't slow down.

This was supposed to be the end of it.

They said once he was arrested, I'd be free. That my debt would be paid.

And fuck, there's relief in that. There really is.

No more threats. No more notes on my car. No more distorted voices at three AM telling me what patient to kill next.

I did it.

I chose the devil I knew and threw him to the wolves to save myself.

So why do I feel like I'm the one bleeding out?

Why does it hurt this much?

Maybe because for all the hell Finn Quinn has put me through, he's never lied to me. He's never blackmailed me. He's never forced me to become someone I'm not.

He's an asshole, yes. But he's the devil I know. The devil I poke.

The guilt slithers through me like a blade under the skin,

slicing deeper with every breath. If he doesn't come back… If they bury him…

What does that make me?

But if he does…

If he finds out what I did…

God help me.

Because even if there is a part of me that screams it wasn't worth it, my freedom is worth more than any man.

CHAPTER 9

FINN

I don't even knock. I just storm into the Commissioner's office and let the door crash against the wall.

I've already sent Drago home to update my brothers on the situation. I should have been meeting my baby nephew, Liam, today. Not be here in this shithole dealing with bullshit charges.

Arrested for murder. In my own fucking hospital. Like hell would I be that reckless, to kill at my place of work.

It didn't take them long to release me. But I'm pissed.

"Dr. Quinn." He pushes himself up to stand, using the table for balance.

He's a heart attack waiting to happen.

"Tim." I glare, slamming the door shut behind me.

He's wary of me. Always has been. For good reason.

Keeping calm, I pull out the chair opposite him and sink into it, leaning back, resting my foot on my knee.

"Sit," I order.

He clears his throat and does as he's told.

"Finn. Look—"

I hold up my index finger to silence him and his piss-poor excuses.

"I've just spent nearly three hours locked up in a questioning room, Tim. For crimes, shockingly, I didn't commit. Who gave the order to arrest me?"

Sweat beads on his forehead.

"I–I, I—" He stumbles over his words.

"You did?" I snap.

He shakes his head, face paling.

"No. God, no. You think I have a death wish?"

I chuckle.

"I don't know. Looking at you, maybe." The smirk on my lips sharpens.

"Now. Give me the name."

"It was our Sergeant, Peter. He got an anonymous tip. Evidence came in. He had to act on it—for the sake of the precinct. I would have stopped it if I knew. I didn't find out until after the order was given."

I scoff.

"Evidence? That shit wasn't real. And a heads-up? Where the fuck was that?"

He clears his throat again, voice thinner now.

"We know it was all bullshit. Hence why you're walking out of here. I'm sorry, Finn. It won't happen again."

"Hmm. So do I need a word with Peter?"

I lean forward and tap my fingers on his desk.

We have a deal with the department—and enough blackmail to end most of their careers.

He shakes his head.

"He knows now. I've spoken to him."

I roll my eyes.

"You gonna find out who tipped them off? I need to know

who my enemies are to keep us all fuckin' safe, Commissioner."

My tone drops.

That's part of the deal.

I remove the problems in this state.

They keep the cleanest record across the U.S.

In return, they turn a blind eye to our business.

But this arrest? Fucking bullshit. And he knows it.

"Was it a British man?" I ask.

"We don't know, Finn. We're working on it."

Arthur Bowen is the first suspect to my mind. A family vendetta that dates back to our fathers. Conan killed their youngest son, James, in an underground cage fight before we moved to America. And now their eldest, Arthur, despite murdering my father, is still out for blood. Which is my issue to resolve.

I swore an end to the Bowen family in London years ago. And maybe, this is his fucked up way of proving he can still get to the Quinn brothers. Even if we have gotten rid of every man he has brought into our state.

Tim pulls out a brown folder from his drawer and slides it across to me.

"Everything we got is here. The best we can find right now is a link to Ohio."

I scratch my jaw. Hmm. I was wrong. It's not the Bowens. Arguably this is worse.

I fucking knew this wouldn't be the end of it.

That killing Luke was only fueling the fire with The Preacher—who, as far as I can tell, is a ghost.

I open the folder and shake my head, staring at the grainy, clearly doctored images of me 'killing' my patient. I look closer. I remember him; I did his surgery. It was his last chance for his failing heart. What I do remember most is that he had a watch on worth a fucking fortune.

"He died from complications after surgery. In my field, it's kinda common," I say nonchalantly.

My mind is racing. I'm dealing with someone who can hack hospital systems.

"I suppose the hospital CCTV went down, conveniently? It's just this one still image of me walking in a hallway around the time of death?"

He nods.

"You arrested me on these fucking grounds?" I can't hide my anger.

"I–I'm sorry."

I blow out a sharp breath. They're sending a message.

They can get to me. They know who I am.

And that—ain't fucking good.

"You think anyone at the hospital was involved?" I ask.

He rubs his neck.

"I don't know what to tell you, Finn. We got nothing. And I'm not sure you want us to be the ones doing the digging."

His body language is screaming he wants to leap out the window and away from me.

"Dr. Quinn," I correct.

He's damn right. I have my own team who can dig, not the cops.

I stand and he holds out his hand. I hesitate, then give him a firm shake. I have to keep the cops on my side. Especially now.

"You know I don't kill my patients, Tim. I have a reputation to uphold."

He swallows. I tighten my grip.

"Well, Dr. Quinn. Just keep an eye on your hospital. Keep the records clean. I'll give you a heads-up if anything else comes in. I'm not sure how much I can bail you out of if this continues, though. Clearing the streets of mob violence is one thing—killing patients in our hospitals is another."

I arch my brow.

He's talking shit.

And we both know it.

Because as long as he's on our payroll, he'll bail me out of anything.

"I'll take care of it. Leave it with me."

Translation:

Keep your nose out of my hospital.

"No problem."

Before I leave, I straighten my jacket and grab my flat cap from my pocket, pulling it on as I head out into the fresh fuckin' air.

I turn back.

"What do you know about a guy called The Preacher?"

He frowns.

"Finn. Leave that well alone."

I arch a brow.

He's piqued my interest.

"No one knows who he is. But rumor is—it's like a cult."

Makes sense.

The mark.

The girls.

The ownership.

"Like a cult, or is a cult?" I question.

He shrugs. "Depends who you ask."

Now I know for sure, my kill in Ohio wasn't The Preacher.

"You know where I can find him?"

Tim laughs.

"If anyone knew, he'd be getting the death penalty right now, Dr. Quinn. Leave it alone. Don't bring him here."

What a fuckin' baby.

"Fine," I scoff and head out.

Being in this place too long makes me itch.

The rain pours down.

I tip my head back and close my eyes, letting the droplets fall across my skin.

Fucking cleanse me.

It's been one hell of a year.

My brother nearly died in my arms.

I became an uncle again—twice.

And me?

I'm stuck living two damn lives.

Heart surgeon by day.

Serial killer by night.

And hopefully, if all goes to plan, I'll be leading a war to London to finally take down our lifelong enemies.

To get revenge for my father's murder.

Nothing is going to stop me from ending the Bowen family.

I've had this vendetta since I was ten years old. But, it seems like we have another storm brewing here in Pennsylvania.

Pulling out my phone, I call Reggie.

With my brothers, Declan and Conan, both having newborns, I can't expect them to drop their lives to help me.

I'm more alone now than I've ever been.

Which is fine.

I've always tried my damn best to keep them safe. But I need my brothers by my side.

"Dr. Quinn. Would you like a rescue party now?" Reggie asks.

"Yeah. Straight to a fucking bar."

An engine roars to life in the parking lot, and I grin.

"Come on then!" Rowan shouts, hanging out the passenger window with a wild grin.

He revs the engine and I head for the car.

Before I get there, Rowan hops out and opens the door for me, then slides into the backseat.

"Glad to see you managed to survive feeding Nyx," I say to Rowan.

He blows out a breath.

"Yeah, I actually think she quite likes me."

I scoff.

"She's probably waiting for you to return so she can strangle you to death."

"Well?" Reggie asks as he hits the accelerator.

"Ohio's catching up with us, it appears," I say coolly, lighting a cigarette.

"We going to head back there?" I can hear the anticipation in Reggie's voice.

I shake my head, exhaling smoke out the window.

"No. We need to pull Drago in for more digging. And wait for Theo King to tell us when we head to London. One enemy at a time."

This is how my life has always been.

You kill one, another takes its place.

It's never calm.

Never peaceful.

Only death and destruction follow me.

Reggie's lips curl into a sickening grin.

"I can do one better than going for a beer. How about spilling some Bowen blood?" he says.

"You got him?" I ask.

The last fucking Bowen in our state.

Reggie nods.

"Yep. Tied him up in Decadence, ready for you. Thought you'd need a little treat."

I don't often go into our chocolate factory, Decadence, my brother uses it as the base for his games, but since they've ceased existing, his designed rooms do come in rather useful for holding hostages and torturing. No one would expect such a thing to happen in a goddamn chocolate factory.

The perfect cover for all of our operations. Bringing in drugs and arms, disguised as cocoa? Perfect.

Cracking my knuckles and releasing some of the tension in my neck, my mind is easily made up.

"The perfect way to end a fucking disaster of a day," I tell the twins.

CHAPTER 10

STEPHANIE

I'm on my second glass of wine, and nothing is calming me down.

What if they didn't get rid of the CCTV?

What if they kept copies to keep blackmailing me with?

God, I feel sick. I check my phone. Still nothing from the blackmailers. But, I'm still alive.

And the wine isn't helping me either.

All different scenarios play out in my head. Most end with me bleeding out in bed while I sleep. With people like this, I doubt it matters that I've locked my door. Or that I even have security.

At the end of the day, I'm still a woman on her own.

Flicking back onto the news channel, I watch it on loop.

Unsure what I'm expecting to flash up—his mug shot? I bet even that would be sexy.

Surely a top surgeon being arrested for murdering his patient in the hospital would make the news.

It's been hours. I've even checked my emails. Nothing to say he's been suspended.

Something isn't right.

I should be celebrating his departure.

But this nagging feeling inside tells me this isn't the last time I'll see Dr. Quinn.

I pull the blanket over my legs and knock back the rest of my wine.

All I can picture is his stone-cold face as he was escorted out of the building.

And all I can feel inside is fucking dread.

If I'm not careful, I'm going to land myself in a cell next to my parents.

Or perhaps one right next to my boss. I suppose that's better than in a grave.

CHAPTER 11

FINN

The sweet aroma of chocolate floods my airways. The place is crazy with our workers, creating America's favorite flavors.

They're paid a lot to turn a blind eye.

And no one except us has access to the back of the building.

Where our drugs and guns get delivered.

Where we play our games.

Where I now torture my victims to death, but in this case, I don't have the energy for a long, drawn out spectacle. He won't provide any answers to us that we don't already have about Arthur. He just simply needs to die.

Pressing my finger up to the scanner and entering the passcode, the door unlocks, and I'm through to my torture chambers.

I step into the white room. Bright lights overhead. The floor is flawless—no cracks, no drains, just marble that gleams like bone under the fluorescents.

A pool sits in the center with a golden fountain, filled with warm, rippling chocolate. The crown jewel of our factory's tour lies on the other side of hell. No one suspects what's beneath it.

He's already here. Tied to a metal chair, barefoot, shaking, eyes wide like he's finally realized he won't be walking out of here.

I'm glad Reggie didn't sedate him. I want him awake. I want his fear. I fucking thrive on it.

"Evening," I mutter, rolling up my sleeves.

He jerks in the chair, the ropes creaking. He recognizes me now. That makes it sweeter.

This man blindly followed Arthur Bowen to his death.

"I've been thinking," I continue, pacing in slow circles around him. "There's no satisfaction in slicing you open while you scream. That's too easy. Too clinical, and you see, I do enough of that at work. I want more. I've had quite a day."

His lip trembles. "Please—"

I snap.

With one hand, I grip the back of the chair and slam it to the ground. His skull cracks against the marble, and I crouch beside him, watching him bleed.

"You will give me something," I whisper, "because I need to feel it too."

I untie the ropes. His wrists are raw. His hands tremble as they realize the mistake, that freedom isn't coming.

The same fate the rest of the Bowen men had. After this man, it's just Arthur himself left to kill.

"Get up," I bark. He doesn't move.

So I grab him by the collar and lift him like a rag doll, shoving him upright. He stumbles and tries to swing at me.

Good.

I take the hit. A weak punch to my jaw. It hurts more than I thought it would.

But not enough. Not nearly enough.

So I return the favor. My fist cracks into his ribs. Again. And again. Until his knees buckle and he coughs blood onto the marble.

"This," I snarl, hauling him back to his feet, "is for my brother." I slam my fist into his nose.

His screams are music to my ears. His blood spatters across the floor in bursts of red. Still not enough.

I grab him by the throat and drag him to the edge of the chocolate pool.

"Tell me the truth," I whisper in his ear, breath heaving. "Was it worth it? Giving your life for a cause that is worth nothing?" I seethe.

He wheezes, blood bubbling at his lips.

"I—I don't know what you're talking ab—"

I plunge his head into the chocolate. He thrashes violently, arms slapping the edge of the pool, fingers scrambling for purchase. I. Don't. Let. Go.

His air is gone. His screams are muffled. His fear… now that is delicious. I don't have a sweet tooth really, but I do have a deadly one.

I count the seconds. One. Two. Three. Four.

On five, I pull him up. Chocolate clings to his face in thick drips. He gasps. Chokes.

I stare into his eyes, waiting for something. Pain. Panic. Remorse for nearly killing Conan.

But there's nothing. Just empty pleading. It disgusts me.

I shove him under again. Harder. Longer. This time, I don't pull him back.

The bubbles rise, slow and erratic. Then stop. The room is quiet again.

I toss him out onto the floor, and he just lies there still. My fists ache. My chest heaves.

And still—I feel nothing.

No redemption. No clarity. Just silence.

I sink to my knees, hands stained in crimson and cocoa, chest hollow.

And then I laugh. Just once. A low, broken sound that echoes across the white walls.

"I wish that lasted longer." I sigh, dragging myself up to my feet.

I'm still the only monster in the room.

Reggie cracks open the door like he's afraid of what he'll find.

"You good?" he asks.

I nod once.

He steps in further, holding out a phone wrapped in a cloth. "I took this before you had your fun. Figured it'd be fucked in that chocolate if I left it."

A chuckle escapes my throat. I wipe the mess from my hands onto my pants and take the phone from him.

"You unlocked it?" I ask, rotating it in my palm.

He shakes his head. "Nah. Can't take credit. Drago hacked it. Said it was amateur shit."

"Of course he did." I blow out a breath and unlock the screen.

These stupid fucks never learn.

No aliases. No burner numbers. No effort.

Just Arthur's name sitting at the top of the contact list, like an open wound begging to be cauterized.

So I press it.

It rings twice before the voice on the other end answers.

"Albert, fuck. Are you okay?"

Arthur.

I smile, letting my Irish accent come through sharp as a scalpel.

"Arthur. Nice to speak to you again."

There's a beat of silence.

"Finn," he spits.

"The one and only. You don't sound thrilled to hear from me, pal."

He exhales like he's trying not to choke on his own fear.

"What do you want, Quinn?"

I click my tongue against my teeth. "Nothing you don't already know. I'll be seeing you soon. And I've got a bullet with your name on it."

His laugh is forced.

"Not if I see you first, doctor."

But his voice gives him away. That pitch—I know he's bluffing. He knows what I'm capable of. What I do with my hands when I'm not saving lives.

He hangs up.

"I can't wait to slit that fucker's throat," I mutter, handing the phone back to Reggie.

He grins, running a hand over his jaw. "Yeah. I think we're all waiting for that day to arrive."

CHAPTER 12
STEPHANIE

Song- People Are Strange, The Doors.

I'm in the middle of a conversation when I feel it. The staff room goes silent, and the atmosphere shifts to ice. I know exactly who has just graced us with his presence.

Dr. Finn Quinn.

Shit. Shit. Shit.

A shiver runs down my spine as I look up and lock my gaze into those icy grey eyes.

He just stands there like he owns the damn place.

Which, apparently, he does. He practically owns this hospital now, like it's just another trophy he snatched out of someone else's hands.

We are all under Finn's rule.

And I hate it.

I hated it the first time I ever laid eyes on him, back in our final years of residency. He breezed in from Dublin with that delicious accent and flawless record and took everything I'd been working toward without even breaking a sweat.

My fists clench just thinking about it.

The years I'd sacrificed and the horrors I had endured to get to the top of my field—gone. Erased when this asshole decided America needed to be the next place he conquered.

And I was stupid enough to think I could take him down. And I tried, in the worst possible way, to do so, and he still remains victorious.

His eyes scan the room. We all remain still, like we're the ones about to be interrogated, like none of us dare to even breathe too loud in his presence.

Fuck that.

I stand, plastering on a smile so false it feels like it's going to crack my face.

"Dr. Quinn. What a pleasure to have you join us for lunch."

His jaw twitches, the corner of his mouth curling into that contemptuous little smirk.

"Is it?"

He steps toward me, and my heart pounds, hating itself for noticing the way he moves. The way he carries that lethal confidence.

I wish he wasn't so damn handsome. I wish he were balding and puffy and middle-aged so I could hate him without this dull, traitorous ache in my chest.

But no, he has the brains and the looks.

The perfectly black, swept-back hair. The chiseled jaw, the white teeth. Tattoos crawling up the side of his throat, even around his ears, like vines choking out anything soft that might have lived in him once.

Again, no one else could get away with that as a surgeon.

Yet here he is.

His rules. His kingdom.

"Yes. Would you like a coffee?"

A smirk dances on his lips, and then he squints, closing the distance between us until I can feel the heat coming off him.

"Why are you being nice to me, Dr. Miller?" he says in that low, mocking tone, pitched for me alone.

"I was planning on spitting in it," I whisper.

"I'd poison yours."

The threat slides between us like something intimate.

"I could get you fired for threatening me," I hiss.

I look up into those glacial eyes, and I swear I stop fucking breathing. He knows exactly how to get under my skin. And he simply doesn't care.

"If you'd like to lodge a complaint, email me and I'll do my best to rectify the situation. Although, the wait time is up to three years. And hopefully, you would have found new employment by then."

He rolls up his sleeve and checks his watch, as if I'm nothing more than an inconvenience wedged into his schedule.

"How's your brother?" I ask, biting back a grin I know will infuriate him.

I bet he hates that he had to call me to save Conan's life. The best heart surgeon in the state didn't have the balls to operate on his own brother. But I saw his pain. The one time I've seen Finn vulnerable. And I didn't like it. So I don't tend to bring this moment up unless he pushes me to.

He scowls, his jaw tightening almost imperceptibly. Almost.

"He's doing well." He pauses, like it pains him to say it.

"Thanks to you." He winces as the words leave his mouth.

I smile brightly, shoving the moment down his throat.

"Good. I'm glad."

"Why are you here?" I ask.

We don't like Finn joining us. He doesn't just intimidate, he drains every room of any scrap of goodwill. He scares most of his staff senseless. Everyone except Hallie and me.

But Hallie isn't on my side anymore.

She was always his little pet project. The only one he ever smiled at. The only one he ever bothered to protect. And now she's married to his damn brother.

"Investigating, Dr. Miller."

My palms go clammy. I force myself not to step back, but my body betrays me with a slight flinch.

"Investigating what? Is it to do with your arrest?" I ask, keeping my tone as flat as I can manage.

He taps his finger against the side of his nose, infuriatingly smug.

"None of your business, is what."

I roll my eyes, refusing to give him the satisfaction of seeing me unnerved.

He leans in, and I hold my breath.

"I was never arrested, Stephanie. Just erase that encounter from your memory," he whispers.

"Whatever you say, wizard," I mock, rolling my eyes again, knowing that it irks him.

"I hope you're looking forward to this weekend." He winks, as if he doesn't already know he's going to win.

Smug bastard. He knows how much I really don't want to go.

"You mean a free trip to Vegas and to be forced to spend even more time around you? Yeah. I can't wait," I say sarcastically.

I wish I didn't care. I wish I could let him win and not sulk about it. But it's every. Single. Time.

Promotions—always him.

Awards, still him.

Even after that, he has to keep the competition going, like it's a game only he can win.

My eyes form slits as I watch him come up with his next little jab at me.

"Do you like losing? Is that why you're still here?" he asks smugly.

"You think I'd make it that easy for you, Dr. Quinn, and just leave? Not happening. I get far too much enjoyment out of making you work for your position."

"Hmm. I'm glad it keeps you entertained. To me, it's more like having gum on my shoe I can't get rid of. But, to each their own."

I swallow the lump in my throat. I can just imagine smashing my palm across his cheek to wipe that smug grin off his annoyingly gorgeous face.

"At least I don't get arrested at work," I spit back.

His face remains stoic.

"Touché. Have a point for that comeback, Stephanie. Well done. You really hurt me there." He places a tatted hand over his chest.

"Whatever," I scoff, heading back to my seat next to our new junior, Poppy.

He scans the room one last time before turning on his heel, and the door slams behind him. I let out a breath the second he's gone.

Every interaction with this man both excites me and exhausts me.

"Is it always so tense between you two?" Poppy asks.

She's young and full of life.

She doesn't understand.

"Yes. Always," I mutter.

CHAPTER 13

FINN

"Drink?" Declan asks before I even take a seat.

"Large one."

As I drop down onto the couch, his wife, Charlotte, appears with a sleeping Noah in her arms and little Isabella trailing behind.

"Uncle Finn!"

"Come here. I need a hug." I open my arms and she barrels toward me, launching into my lap like she's been waiting all day.

"How was jail? Did you have to pick up any soap?" Charlotte smirks.

I knew I wouldn't live this down with her.

"You're a wicked woman, Charlotte."

"Heartbreaker, are you picking on my brother again?" Declan steps in with two whiskeys, kissing her cheek as he hands me one.

"Always," she purrs.

They're sickeningly sweet. Both of my brothers are married, trying to be softer versions of themselves. They've found peace in places I can't even look too long without flinching. They're just like Mom and Dad used to be.

And me? I'm still the jagged piece that doesn't fit the family frame. Watching love from the outside, pretending like I don't want it, like it wouldn't burn straight through me if I ever tried to hold it.

But then Isabella curls her arms around my neck and presses her head into my shoulder. Her weight anchors me. Calms the rage always simmering beneath my skin.

She's, so far, the only person alive who can do that.

"Please don't leave us, Uncle Finn," she whispers.

I pull her tighter and kiss the top of her head.

"Like I could ever leave my niece and nephews. I love you too much."

"Come on, Isabella. Drago's waiting for you!" Charlotte calls.

"Tell Drago I'll be stopping by his later."

Charlotte flashes a knowing smile. Drago's her best friend. Her savior, really. And I know she's happy we're accepting him in the family. He's proven to be useful. Loyal. And the only one in the room right now who can handle my kind of chaos.

When they leave, Declan slouches into the chair across from me. I take a sip of Dad's whiskey and let it scorch its way down my throat.

"I need filling in, Finn. I know you like your secrets, but we've gotta be on the same page now."

I nod. He's not wrong. He's the eldest. The boss. But even bosses get tired of blood on their hands.

"What do you want to know?" I ask.

"Why were you arrested?"

I shrug.

"Until I speak to Drago, I can't confirm. My gut says this is retaliation for killing one of The Preacher's men in Ohio."

Declan's jaw tightens. "The Preacher?"

Exactly my point. He doesn't know. Not yet.

"Yes, brother. The Preacher. One of the contestants in Conan's games—Abigail— warned me. But I had no choice. Enzo gave the name. You know the rules. So I took Reggie and Rowan, made it look like suicide. But who ever got me arrested? They wanted me to know I'm not untouchable. That they can find me anywhere. Even at work."

Declan spins the rings on his fingers, processing.

"And you don't think it's Arthur?"

I shake my head.

"Arthur's neck-deep in war with the Kings. We've already wiped out all of Bowen's men here. This… this is different. We've got more than one enemy now."

Declan swallows hard.

I rest my foot on my knee, letting the weight of my body lean into the conversation.

"What do we know about this Preacher?" he asks.

"Look, Declan. I love you. But right now? I don't have the full picture. I just need permission to act on behalf of the family."

I stare him down. Waiting.

His jaw ticks, eyes meeting mine. There's still steel in him. He hasn't gone soft, not entirely.

"I trust you, Finn. Just keep me in the loop, okay? And if you need me, I'll be there."

I scratch at the stubble on my jaw.

"Your kids need their dad, like we needed ours."

He narrows his eyes.

"That isn't how this works. I'm not stepping down. I'll fight to protect this family—which includes you. So yeah, you've got my permission to deal with Arthur and The Preacher. But you're not getting yourself killed. We do this together."

I tap my thigh, absorbing it.

"Okay. Then first, I'm going after a man in Pennsylvania with links to The Preacher. I want him tortured. If he talks, great. If not, he dies. But I need to see what Drago found from the hospital. The patient I'm accused of killing? Died from surgery complications. Still, the CCTV was wiped. I need to know who has the skill to do that."

Declan nods.

"Keep pressure on Theo King. As soon as he gives us the green light to go to London, I'll head there with the twins. Settle that score once and for all. Then we focus on this cult."

I pause.

"If we kill Arthur… Conan has to come with me. After what they did to him and Hallie, he deserves it," I tell him.

He nods in agreement. We all hate the Bowens, but Conan needs this to heal. And that's all that matters to me, that my brothers are safe.

Declan sighs. "This is gonna get messy, isn't it?"

"When has our life not been?"

We were born into this. Raised in fire. Survived off of grief.

Declan nearly lost everything. Conan nearly died. I saw what no child should ever see—and did what no child should ever have to do.

Still, the memory haunts me. The girl, whose name I can't even say. Her throat slit. The blood. The scream caught in my lungs as I bled for her. As I killed for her. As I became the monster that's still hiding under my skin.

I shake my head, trying to shove it back down.

"Well, maybe we should try for a future that isn't messy,"

Declan says, his voice softer. "Wouldn't it be nice to live in peace?"

"Peace sounds boring."

I knock back the rest of my drink, just as the door swings open and Conan storms in looking like hell but happier than I've ever seen him.

"Finn!" There's panic in his voice, under the grin.

"Worried about me?" I grin.

"Damn right. I'm usually the one getting picked up by the cops, not you."

"Ha-ha." I roll my eyes. "How's Liam? And Hallie?"

"They're both doing amazing. Just napping. So I thought I'd check on my favorite brothers."

"Only brothers," Declan laughs.

Conan looks between us, suspicious.

"You two better not be plotting without me."

I arch a brow.

"Shouldn't you be playing happy families?"

"Finn," Declan warns.

"Easy," Conan growls.

Hallie softened him, yeah. But under it all, he's still fire. Still the fuse. The killing machine that we need.

"I was just filling him in. Now sit."

He does, grabbing the whiskey.

"Well? Now it's my turn," Conan says.

"Declan can catch you up. I've got lives to save. But when we're ready to go after Arthur, I assume you'll be joining me?"

Conan's eyes flash.

"Fucking too right. That cunt won't be identifiable once I'm done with him."

I nod, standing.

"Good to see fatherhood hasn't dulled your edge."

He punches me in the arm and I clench my jaw.

"You know, some of our guys think you're a psychopath, Finn," Conan says.

"They're probably not wrong." I flash him a smile that doesn't quite reach my eyes.

"Oh—and go take a nap. Drink some electrolytes. You look like shit," I order him.

It's habit now, worrying about him. I've never really stopped. Even now, I still see his blood on my hands every time I scrub in.

That moment of helplessness will never leave me. I couldn't save him.

No amount of training can ever get you ready for that moment you have to use it on your own family.

"How's work? With the doctor that saved me?" Conan asks.

I groan.

"Still as painful as ever. I lost points on the leaderboard for her saving your ass."

"Leaderboard?" Declan asks.

"Yeah. We've got this weekly tally. Points for complex surgeries, comebacks, whatever. Keeps her riled up. Motivated."

What I don't say is that the leaderboard is our version of foreplay.

Because watching her fury when I win? It's the only thing that makes me feel alive during the week.

And when she gains on me, those rare, rare moments she does? It's chaos. Beautiful, addictive chaos. She glares like she wants to slit my throat, and I can't help the smirk that always comes after.

Every point I take from her, I get just a little deeper under her skin.

Every loss stings for her and for me.

Because I'm not just addicted to beating her.

I'm addicted to the game she doesn't even realize we're playing.

"Ooo, does Finn have a crush on a co-worker?" Conan teases.

I smack him in the back of the head. Hard.

"Shut the fuck up. No."

Declan and Conan exchange that look—the one that makes me want to flip the table.

"Oh, fuck this. I'm out." I flip them off as I head to the door, their laughter following me like a curse.

"Tell her I said thank you!" Conan shouts.

God, I knew I'd regret asking her to save his life.

Because now she owns that win. She has power over me, and I handed it right to her.

"Oh, I'm heading to Vegas tomorrow," I throw back over my shoulder.

"Vegas? What for?" Conan asks.

"To win some awards," I say bluntly. Then I'm gone.

CHAPTER 14

STEPHANIE

"Nice jet," I tell Finn sarcastically as he steps beside me on the tarmac.

I resist rolling my eyes. His presence next to me is already grating. There are fifteen of us waiting to board, yet he chooses to stand right in my personal space.

Close enough for me to smell his maddeningly delicious aftershave.

"Thanks. It's mine and my brothers'."

I cross my arms over my chest, keeping my eyes locked on the sleek black jet.

Not the man beside me.

"Fancy. Is there caviar on board? Champagne for the rich boy?" I tease.

I know he hates it when I call him that. Yet, he has never offered me an explanation as to why I'm wrong.

"Whiskey and nachos. I'm not your typical boring billionaire, Dr. Miller."

I turn my head to face him. His tight black shirt is rolled up to reveal inked forearms that should be considered sinful.

He's right. There's nothing normal about him.

"Billionaire. Hmm. And why is it you decide to still work?"

I tap my chin as he smirks at me.

"So I can irritate the fuck out of you every day. And make sure you never get Head of Cardiology."

My mouth drops open.

This prick. A thorn in my side that just won't leave. Even jail time didn't work.

"You're an asshole, you know that, right?"

His eyebrow arches, those pale grey eyes darkening.

He pulls a small notepad from his pants pocket, along with a tiny pencil, and starts writing.

"What are you doing?" I frown.

I've noticed he does this around me more and more.

"Just noting down everything that gives me a case to fire you. I'm sure the director would love to hear."

I scoff and squint at him.

"You wouldn't dare."

As I try to grab the notepad from his hands, he lifts it above my head.

"Wanna see?"

"No," I lie.

He shoves it back into his pocket and stares off into the distance.

"Maybe I should start my own journal of all the stupid shit you say. Hell, the whole department can."

Actually, I doubt it. He's not the chattiest man you'd ever meet.

He doesn't react. Bruce, our medical director, smiles at Finn as he approaches.

Thick as thieves.

This really is a man's world.

"Good luck at the ceremony tomorrow, Stephanie. May

the best surgeon win," Finn says under his breath as he walks off to greet Bruce.

Leaving me reeling.

"You okay?" Poppy whispers from behind me, making me jump.

"Yes. Fine," I seethe.

She is our newest junior resident, and I kinda feel bad. I remember what it was like. Even if I rose through the ranks fast, it wasn't as quick as Dr. Finn.

Being a woman here means you have to work twice as hard for half the credit.

"Sorry," I whisper, shaking my head.

She gives me a soft smile.

"I get it, Dr. Miller. He's hard on you."

"That doesn't bother me. Don't let them get to you."

She frowns, glancing over at Finn.

"He is very distracting, though."

"Poppy," I warn. "Whatever you do, do not go after our head of department. Do not give them ammunition against you. In fact, don't fuck anyone at work. Okay?"

"Like he'd ever be interested in me," she sighs.

I place my hand on her shoulder, trying to offer some semblance of comfort. I understand how she feels, I guess.

"Only because he's not interested in anything other than himself. Followed by trying to ruin me. It's not you." I pause, taking a deep breath.

"Never let a man define your worth, Poppy. There's a reason why we all choose the bear." I give her a squeeze.

Women have to stick together to survive.

"You're a great boss. I won't let him ruin you." She smiles.

"I appreciate that. But we're under Dr. Quinn's rule here, there isn't much we can do to fight back. I've tried."

I shake my head and step back. I just have to suck it up and deal with the fact my boss is a dick, in the hopes that one day, all these years of being an arrogant asshole catch up with him.

As we board the jet, Poppy joins Josh, our other resident.

Finn is talking quietly to the pilot at the front.

The pretty flight attendant hands me a glass of champagne.

I grin as I take it and thank her. Turning back to Finn, I hold it up smugly.

"Is the caviar up next?" I ask.

He scowls at me.

My heart races as he excuses himself and strides over. The whole plane falls silent. He takes the drink from my hand and knocks it back in one gulp before turning to the attendant.

As his eyes bore into her, she goes bright red.

"Can you get Dr. Miller a whiskey, please?" he asks.

She nods and rushes off, returning with two glasses of amber liquid.

"Thank you, Amber."

She chews her lip and bats her lashes.

Apparently, any woman would drop to her knees for this man.

"Better, your highness?" he asks quietly.

"I had no issue with champagne. You are the one who did. Don't like being called rich boy?" I ask.

He blinks at me. Shit. He's so hard to read.

"No. I don't."

He pulls out the damn notepad again and scribbles something down. I wonder if he's actually been making notes to fire me this whole time?

"Sit," he orders, pointing to the two chairs behind us, with a solid gold table in front of them.

All the other seats are taken, except those.

He leans in and goosebumps race across my skin.

"Yes. I'm just as pissed off I have to endure your company for the entirety of this flight," he whispers.

"It's fine. Just don't talk to me, and I'm sure we won't want to kill each other before we land." I give him a fake smile and take my seat next to the window.

He sits next to me, his thick thigh brushing mine.

It makes me shift uncomfortably. I pull out my headphones and bring up my audiobook. Can't beat a bit of alien smut being read to me by a delicious man in my ears.

"Who is that?" he asks.

I turn to look at him.

"Who is who?"

Oh.

He's looking at the sexy guy on the cover.

"My boyfriend, James. We're so in love. Isn't he drop-dead gorgeous?" I tease.

His jaw ticks. He glances back down at my phone.

"I suppose. I didn't have you down for dating a model."

"And what the hell does that mean?"

I cross my arms over my chest, clenching my fists.

"Nothing against you. Moreover, they would never be able to handle a woman as intelligent or powerful as you."

Before I can reply, he's on his phone typing away frantically. And just like that, I'm invisible again.

Shaking my head, I shove my headphones in and let this man's glorious accent calm me enough for my eyes to close.

Hopefully I can nap.

That'll kill time.

I stay behind in the casino at the front desk while the rest of my department are shown to their rooms.

With a whiskey in hand, I glance around at all the people gambling their money away like it's nothing.

"Dr. Quinn," a deep Russian voice booms from behind.

I turn, coming face-to-face with the masked Mikhail. His dark eyes cut straight through me.

I hold out my hand and he shakes it firmly.

"Mr. Volkov. Great to see you again."

"Same goes to you."

He hands me a white card.

He's the King of Vegas, owning nearly all of the casinos and hotels. They're also part of the same organization as us through Enzo.

We help them get their drugs and arms in—and vice versa.

The Volkov family is a good contact to have in your back pocket.

"Penthouse suite. 20th floor. Stunning views. Stocked bar. If you need anything, call either Jax or Alexei."

I nod.

Jax, I know well. He helps Conan with his MMA training. Alexei, I've only met briefly. He's fucking hilarious but half mad at this point. Still, he's loyal to the death for the Volkovs. He reminds me of the twins.

"I don't expect any issues. We're just here for an award ceremony."

As I finish my sentence, I spot her. A flash of silky black hair in the distance, and that's enough to anchor my gaze.

Her hair is twisted up in a messy bun, those bright red lips, and sinful thighs are poured into tight leather pants.

Fuck.

She might test me to my limit, but I can't deny she's stunning.

Mikhail chuckles. "I never know what trouble you Irish might drag with you to Vegas."

We've been dragging him into our messes lately. Though he's had his fair share of shit to deal with, just to cement his place here. Mafia life never comes cheap.

"Not me, Mikhail. I'm the quiet one." I smirk.

His eyes crinkle at the corners. The mask is clever. I've heard it's to cover the burns on his face. I think it runs deeper than that. But, unless I can prove myself to him, I doubt I'll get to see his scars.

Because no one will ever see mine either.

"The quiet ones are the most deadly. I should know, I am one."

He has a point.

"Drink later? I don't have any plans until the awards tomorrow," I say.

He nods, checking his watch.

"Let me speak to my wife and brothers. We can show you how the Russians do it, yeah?"

I laugh.

"Sounds like you're the one bringing trouble."

He shrugs.

"We all need a little fun sometimes. And in my home, we can do whatever the fuck we want."

Once we wrap up talking, I head over to the elevator for the suite.

"Oh, rich boy gets his own elevator too." Stephanie's voice makes my body tighten like a bowstring.

"Jealous?" I ask, not turning around.

"Nope. I'm happy it means your room isn't near mine."

Oh. That makes me spin on my heel. The sight of her makes my chest tighten. What the fuck? That's something new.

Those dark winged eyes make her blue eyes pop like a shot to the ribs.

Those red lips. Fuck me.

"And why is that? So you don't accidentally creep into my room in the middle of the night?"

She rolls her eyes.

I clench my fists by my side. I have to remind myself—do not grab her by the neck.

"No. So you can't see who and what I'm doing in my room." She winks and steps back.

"Why would that bother me?" I keep my face expressionless.

But she frowns, like she's confused.

"So you don't have anything else to write in your silly notepad?"

I grin at her, stepping closer.

"Oh, is that what you meant? I've got eyes everywhere, Dr. Miller. Remember that."

Right on cue, my elevator dings and I step inside.

When the doors close, she's already stomped off. I get my notepad out and write the next page.

LOOKED GORGEOUS IN VEGAS.

Bratty as hell.

Still hates my guts. I sensed a hint of jealousy? Or was that me?

It's not that I hate her. Not even close. I get enjoyment out of being a dick and seeing how far I can push her.

Like an experiment, of sorts. At what point does she throw in the towel and move hospitals?

How far do I have to go for her to slap me?

Why do I hate it when she ignores me?

It's a lot of unanswered questions that I'm trying to figure out.

Hate is an emotional response. Usually, you have to like someone first to then hate them.

In this case? From day one, I felt her dislike. It seeped out of her pores like venom.

And me, being me, decided I liked that poison.

I wanted more.

I need to see how deep this can run.

I like games. And this one keeps me inspired.

I flip the pad closed.

Maybe I'll keep writing notes on her in here and wrap it up for Christmas.

But she can never, ever, see my other ones.

CHAPTER 16

STEPHANIE

I'm the last one to arrive at the bar and the party's already in full swing.

Sliding into the booth beside Josh, I scan the room. Poppy's letting her hair down, dancing with a couple of the other girls from the Chicago hospital.

It's a shame Hallie couldn't come, but she won't be back for another couple of months after the birth of their son.

Which, I guess, makes him Finn's nephew now.

Speaking of…

"Is Dr. Quinn here?" I ask Josh.

He clears his throat. I follow his gaze, straight to Poppy.

"I've already warned her not to fuck anyone at work, Josh."

He straightens his tie and sits up.

"I—I don't."

I hold up a hand to silence him.

"She is your junior. You are training her. That, Josh, is an abuse of power that'll get you fired. Leave her alone. Or, if you really want to pursue her... quit."

"Jesus. We're not at work now."

I pinch the bridge of my nose.

"I'm your supervisor. I'm always watching."

Christ. I sound like Finn.

"What's up your ass, Steph?"

My eyes go wide.

"A fucking butt plug? Why?" I try to sound serious.

"Nice."

He knocks back his drink and turns to face me.

He's a pretty boy—dark hair, dark eyes, designer clothes.

But he's not my type.

"So does that mean, because you're my boss, the power is balanced now and we can…" He trails off, wiggling his brows.

I open my mouth, but before I can speak, electricity bolts down my spine.

A man clears his throat behind us.

Shit.

I cringe internally, plastering a smile on my face as I cross one leg over the other.

"Dr. Quinn. Nice of you to join us," I say, turning to face him.

He's glaring at Josh.

"Yeah. Glad I came."

He takes the chair next to me and sits. Josh looks at us like we've both grown horns.

"Please, continue what you were about to say, Dr. Miller."

I scowl at Josh. Like I need more ammo for Finn.

"Fine," I say lightly.

"No, Josh. It's still a no. Anyone with an asshole that works in the department is a no-go. Sorry."

Josh taps his fingers on the table.

"You got it."

I swear Finn growls under his breath.

Josh excuses himself and heads to the bar. I keep my mouth shut.

"Very professional answer, Stephanie. I'll be sure to jot that one down. Cannot fuck anyone with an asshole in the cardiology department."

My cheeks burn. I feel his stare like it's dragging heat down my spine.

"Asshole covers men and women. Thought I'd cover my ass. Literally."

He chuckles. A real laugh. Not sarcastic. Not cruel.

Like he actually finds me funny.

That's new.

So I look at him to confirm.

Yep. Laughing.

"What?" I smile.

"I think I'll pass that new rule to HR. It's a very vivid description."

"Gets the point across. 'Don't fuck your colleagues' also works."

Finn's gaze drops to my lips, and my heart races.

"Rules can be so…"

His eyes flick to mine.

"Boring. Really sucks the fun out of life."

I nod.

"Well, some people need them," I say.

"Hmm."

"Or they need to be better at hiding when they break the rules."

He looks back to the dance floor, where Poppy's now in Josh's arms, swaying to the beat.

"Or some men just need to learn to keep their dick in their pants," I counter.

"Yes. Some men don't understand the word 'no'." His voice is dry. Too dry.

We sip our whiskeys in a very uncomfortable silence. Until a group of men walk in, like something out of a movie. Their skin inked, their eyes dark. They're trouble.

One of them is covering his face with a balaclava.

And holy shit, they're walking straight toward us with their eyes locked on Finn.

"Uh. Finn?"

He places his palm on my thigh, and I nearly shoot out of my chair. He snatches it back, like my skin burned him too.

"Shit. I'm sorry. I—I strangely got comfortable with you there. Won't happen again. Trust me."

Is the infamous Dr. Quinn… stumbling on his words?

I smile. Loving this.

"I'll jot it in my own notepad. Dr. Quinn touched me," I tease.

His eyes burn into mine, and my breath hitches.

"I would never touch a woman without her consent. Not like that. Never." His voice holds fury, but his face is expressionless. Still, any light behind his eyes dies right then.

"I was joking," I whisper.

He exhales and nods, steadying himself.

"I mean it. I'm sorry. I don't like being touched. I shouldn't have done it to you either."

I lean forward, resting my chin on my hand.

He doesn't like being touched?

Is this cold, hard-as-nails man… damaged?

It explains a lot.

"Noted. Don't touch Dr. Quinn. But can you protect me from that scary group of guys heading our way?"

He smirks, nodding toward them as they approach.

"Well, piss me off enough and they might become your problem."

I frown as he stands. But then he leans down, and my body is on fire.

"Don't forget to take your butt plug out before bed."

I ignite like a furnace. Of all the things my boss could have caught me saying out loud, this one will go down as one of the most embarrassing.

"You jot that one down, and I will punch you so hard in the throat that you won't be able to do a speech when you win tomorrow." I smile sweetly as I deliver my threat.

He chuckles. This time not with me, but at me. His eyes darken as he leans in.

"If you're going to hit me, you're going to want to make sure you knock me the fuck out so I can't come after you for punishment," he whispers.

My mouth drops open. The punishment I want makes a blush spread up to my cheeks. I shake my head, willing away the filthy images of me and Finn in my brain.

He strides away, greeted by the four scary-looking men. Tattoos. Killer eyes. And not a single person in this club stepped foot near them, except Dr. Quinn.

Somehow, our Head of Cardiology fits right in, like he belongs with them.

Maybe there's more to this man than I thought.

But right now? I need another drink to forget the burning pulse still radiating from where he touched me.

CHAPTER 17

FINN

My cell vibrates in my pocket. Sliding it out, I see Declan's name on the screen. I drank far too much with the Volkovs last night.

"Brother. I'm five minutes from going to an award ceremony. What's up?"

I can hear his new baby, Noah, crying in the background.

"I've got a meeting set with Theo and his brothers. Looks like next month we can go to London and fix this Bowen issue."

I swallow.

"Next month? My Trials?"

Every year, we each host our own Decadence games. Our own spin on it. Mine is the Decadence Trials.

A science experiment in human limits and kink exploration.

How much pain can a person endure and still get off?

How far will the body go for freedom?

It's fascinating.

My Trials are kept under lock and key. Only Reggie assists me—he's the only one with a stomach tough enough.

My brothers? They've distanced themselves from the games. Hell, they've abandoned them completely since they found love.

Me? I use mine.

Because while we're weeding out the disgusting fuckers in society, the ones willing to sacrifice a woman to us, to make her property—

We free them.

After probably fucking with their heads. But I like to think of it as freeing them from evil.

They just have to earn it.

Just like we all have had to do to get somewhere in life. There is always a sacrifice.

My brothers aren't bad. They're not villains.

I, however, have always been the one called to do the shit no one else can.

I'm numb from it.

After having your humanity stripped from you at ten...

After witnessing what I did.

A child used for the gratification of adults.

I can't say I possess the same humanity Declan and Conan do.

They have good hearts. Mom always said so.

Mine got cut out, stomped on, and buried with my abusers.

The real Finn Quinn died twenty-five years ago.

What's left is the shell.

So no, my Trials don't have the same level of grace.

Sexually—consent is always there. That's non-negotiable.

I don't touch them. No one does.

But what I make them do?

That's the shit I'm going to hell for.

I was told to make the Trials believable.

There are rules. Challenges. It's real life.

You have to earn your place in this world. It's an initiation into true freedom for them.

"Look, Finn. I'll speak to Enzo. We can delay your Trials for a few months?"

I hiss. That man's name sparks a rage in me like no other. To everyone else, he's a fucking god that we have to bow down to. I see through him. The way he uses people. Hell, he's smart. But he's also conniving. I don't trust him.

And quite frankly, I'm happy to keep pushing him out of the gates of Decadence.

We needed him once, we paid for our sins, six years is long enough. And gradually, it's working.

But I'll keep my games going to please him. Everything's set. Ready to go.

Four women. Four rooms.

It's about who can survive in their own head.

"Fine. We can delay. I'll need to figure something out at work if I'm going away and doing the Trials."

He sighs.

"You do know you don't have to work, right? You've got billions sitting around."

I shake my head, smoothing out my white shirt.

"You don't understand, Declan."

No one does.

If I quit, I tip the balance.

Into pure fucking evil.

While I'm working, I'm saving lives that matter.

That keeps me level. It stops me from thinking.

This mafia life was injected into my veins as a child. Doesn't mean I want it to consume every part of me.

Medicine is my passion. It's the only thing I won't give up. Not for anyone.

"Maybe if you let us in, we would understand, Finn."

I tut and shake my head.

"Sometimes holding back the truth is to protect, Declan."

They don't need to know what happened.

I'm not sure I could find the words even if I wanted to.

"Holding it in will kill you eventually."

"I'm a doctor. I'll be fine. I've got it sorted."

So long as I don't sleep too deep.

Don't get high. I made that mistake before.

Don't let myself think for too long… I'm fine.

Distraction is key.

It's harder speaking to Declan than it is Conan. Declan remembers more from that day.

He saw the shift.

The Finn after the incident wasn't the same boy.

So Declan had to grieve the loss of a brother, I suppose.

But I think it's safe to say he still loves the man I became.

Conan, though?

He's a little away with the fairies. We gotta keep him in check, make sure he doesn't explode.

For me, that's another distraction.

But I love them both. To death. That's never changed. Never will.

I'm only here because of them.

My brothers are the last living piece of me.

Well, them and my niece and nephews now.

We lost our parents.

Lost our home.

And we rebuilt it into something unbreakable.

And if I'm the one who has to take the hits to protect it, then so fucking be it. I'm the one with nothing to lose.

"I'll send you the dates once I have them, okay?"

"Okay."

"Have a good night. I hope you win… again."

A smile tugs at my lips.

"Yeah. Me too."

It sends a thrill through me, thinking about Stephanie's face when I collect that trophy.

It's always a picture.

I wish I had a year-by-year collage of her expressions. Pure hatred. Absolute loathing.

It really drives me to do better.

Maybe she's another distraction.

Or more like a drug.

An addiction.

One that's probably going to fight back and kill me.

But I keep going back.

Her anger fuels me.

Or maybe… It's the sparkle in her eyes when she tells me to fuck off.

I don't know.

It's fun.

For me, anyway.

I do a final spin in the mirror, making sure my ass looks good. This dress is tight as hell, to the point I'm scared that once I eat, I won't be able to breathe.

But it's worth it for how good I feel. I've been strict this week on cutting out any snacks. Drinking so much water, I can't stop peeing. It worked, though.

I pair the dress with a pair of gold strappy Jimmy Choos and my serpent necklace; I look good enough to eat.

I trail my hands along my chest, down the very low-cut neckline that dips between my breasts. You can see the tail of my tattoo sneaking up in the middle.

My snake. I call her Raven. Beautiful and deadly. Just like how I feel tonight.

The tattoo represents power. How something smaller than you can still kill you.

There's a knock at the door. I swipe up my purse and down my champagne.

A smiling Poppy greets me.

"Wow, Steph. I mean, Dr. Miller."

I laugh.

"Steph is fine, Poppy. You look beautiful," I tell her.

The baby pink dress, filled with sequins, makes her look like a princess. It's very her—cute and sweet.

"Thank you. Is it too much?"

I shake my head. I need to work on her self-confidence. Especially if she's going to make it as a heart surgeon.

"No matter what you wear, it's never too much."

"I swear, I'm not normally this bad. It's just… you're so, so cool, Steph. I aspire to be like you."

That makes my heart stutter.

No. She doesn't want to be like me. Maybe my work self. But not who I am underneath.

I do horrible things. Even if I believe it's right, that doesn't mean it is.

"Come on, let's go watch Dr. Quinn win all the awards and rub it in my face," I joke, hiding the sting that comes with it.

Just another thing for him to be smug about.

By the time we get down to the lobby, all the guys are already at the bar drinking. Finn is assessing the room with a whiskey in hand while the other men laugh beside him.

His eyes lock on mine the second I walk in, then drag down the length of my body.

I walk straight past him and order my drink at the bar.

"You're late," his deep voice rumbles behind me.

I ignore him, taking the champagne from the bartender.

"Write it in your notepad if you're bothered. You might get me fired by the end of the year if you carry on."

"Hopefully."

I spin to face him.

Holy shit.

The black tux. The slicked-back hair. The tattoos. That goddamn smirk.

"I'll need something new to write in if you carry on with this attitude."

His eyebrow arches, and I take a long, slow sip of my drink.

"Write a book or something, Dr. Quinn. Go make yourself even more money." I wink at him.

That's how he gets through everything in life. Just more and more money.

He tilts his head, staring into my eyes. Like he's trying to read my soul.

"You scrub up pretty well, Dr. Miller."

"Jeez, thanks. What a compliment." I roll my eyes and scoot past him, half expecting him to follow. But he doesn't. By the time I get to the table with Poppy and Josh, I don't need to look over to know he's still watching.

The double doors open to the grand hall.

Everyone rushes in to get to their tables. As I tip my head back to finish my drink, I sense someone next to me.

"Dr. Miller. Lovely to see you again."

I go still and cringe internally.

Jesus. I forgot he was going to be here.

The one-night stand that won't fucking die.

This is why I have the *never sleep with someone in the same industry* rule.

Because it comes back to bite you in the ass.

I turn to face him, plastering on my professional smile.

An attending cardiology surgeon of New York State Hospital is looking me up and down like he wants to devour me.

"Hey, Zak. It's been a while," I greet him.

He opens his arms for a hug. I frown. Wait. I'm probably making it weird. So I step uncomfortably into the hug.

"Too long, Steph."

I quickly pull away, blowing one of my curls out of my face. He still looks good. Those blonde curls, that navy suit—he pulls it off.

"We're busy people, Zak."

He nods.

"Well, if you transferred over to New York, you could be less busy for me."

"I've already said no. I like it where I am."

He chews the inside of his cheek.

"There is always tonight?" he whispers.

"That isn't a good idea, Zak." I give him a tight-lipped smile.

He's a good guy.

Scratch that. He was a good guy. Now he's engaged. Baby on the way. Word gets around.

So maybe he's just another piece of shit with a stethoscope.

"It doesn't need to be any different from last time."

When he leans in, I step back.

"Oh, Zak. Can I borrow your phone?"

Amidst his horny haze, gazing right at my cleavage, he hands it over—unlocked.

Men can be so fucking stupid.

With a sinister smile, I pull up his messages. It's easy to find his fiancée.

"Now, Zak. Should I call Elsa and explain how the love of her life is trying to fuck his one-night stand from two years ago—again—at a work conference in Vegas? I'm sure she'd want to know what kind of douchebag she's marrying."

His mouth drops open. I hit dial.

He moves fast like a fucking ninja, but I duck out of his way.

"You're being a bitch."

I let out a chuckle and toss the phone across the floor.

"Go on. Get on your knees and crawl to get your phone, you fucking dog," I hiss.

He shakes his head and steps into my space. His nostrils flare.

I tip my chin up.

"I'm not scared of men like you," I whisper.

"I'll have you lose your job for this."

I shrug.

And then he's pulled away from me.

I come face-to-face with a furious Finn, gripping Zak by the scruff of his neck.

I glance around; thankfully, everyone has filtered into the ceremony room.

"Stay the fuck away from her," Finn hisses and throws him to the floor.

Zak scrambles away, leaving just the two of us.

"Uh… Thank you?"

I tug at the hem of my dress. I guess I better keep up the damsel-in-distress act.

"You're welcome." He nods, straightening his bow tie.

If he really disliked me that much, why would he step in like that?

"Like I'd let that asshole have you fired. If anyone gets to be responsible for it, it's me. Good luck tonight." He smirks and strides away without another word.

Ah. There it is.

Asshole.

Sometimes I wonder why I'm still into men.

I guess it must be their dicks.

Because I've yet to see what else they've got going for them.

CHAPTER 19

FINN

I don't go straight into the ceremony room. Not yet. I hide in the shadows. My pulse picks up as Stephanie stomps past me without so much as a glance.

I need a minute.

My hands are still clenched from grabbing that smug fuck by the collar. I should've done more than throw him to the ground. Should've knocked out a tooth or two. Left a mark. Something permanent.

He touched her.

Looked at her like she was something he could pick off a shelf and play with.

And even though I have no goddamn right, I'm the only one who gets to fuck with her, push her buttons. I don't own her. But something about it made my vision go red.

She didn't need me.

She had it handled like the calculated, venomous force she is. But still… I stepped in.

Because men like him never learn until another man teaches them. And no one teaches harder lessons than me.

I step into the hallway and pull out my phone, scrolling

through the notes I keep on her. Lines she throws, reactions I provoke. A study of hatred disguised as obsession.

The notepad in my suite—she thinks I started on this trip. She has no idea I have years of phone notes on her.

I open a new one and type:

SAVED HER FROM A SEX PEST. SHE WAS FIRE IN A DRESS. LOOKED ME IN THE EYE LIKE SHE'D SET ME ALIGHT TOO.

WOULD LET HER.

Actually, she never needed saving. She had him on the floor like a dog. Very naughty.

I lock the screen.

By the time I walk into the grand hall, the lights are dimming and the host is rambling on. Champagne flutes clink. A few people glance over, nod, and murmur.

I don't care.

I'm already scanning for her.

She's sitting in the front row. Legs crossed. Chin high. The snake tattoo teasing from beneath her neckline like it's daring me to come closer. I must add this little snippet of information to my notes. This tattoo intrigues me; was it a personal choice or aesthetics? Or does she love the creature as much as I do?

She hasn't even looked at me yet. Which means she knows I'm watching her.

I take my seat on the edge.

They call out a few names before mine. Runner-ups. Special mentions. All white noise in my ears.

Then—

"And this year's recipient for Cardiac Surgeon of the Year… Dr. Finn Quinn."

Applause erupts around me. I don't even blink. I stand slowly, button my jacket, and start toward the stage.

Her gaze follows me the whole way.

I don't look at her until I'm at the podium.

Then I do. And this time my heart hammers.

Right before I speak.

And fuck, I wish I had a camera to capture the way her lips purse and her jaw clenches. You'd think by now, she would be used to this.

Because, much like many parts of our industry, I rigged these awards. In fact, this entire bullshit award ceremony was created and funded by me to purposely piss her off three years ago. I was bored. I wanted to assess how she'd react.

If it's the rivalry that gets her so angry. Or something else about me.

I'm starting to figure out it's both. But she thinks I'm a typical rich boy with high-class parents that got me here. Wrong.

My history is actually far worse. More of a horror story than anything. But yes, she's right. I forced my way to the top. Blackmail, threats, money. A fuck ton of money. Because it keeps up impressions for us here. The award-winning doctor could never be involved in the mafia. Could never host games that take women from their abusive families and give them new lives.

He would never, ever, sneak into men's homes and kill them as they sleep.

I wonder what she would think of me if she really knew the truth.

"This award means a lot," I start, eyes still locked on hers, "but I'd like to dedicate it to someone very special in the room tonight."

A few heads turn.

Her brows lift a fraction.

"Dr. Stephanie Miller," I say smoothly. "Your constant…

motivation has pushed me harder than anyone else. This is as much yours as it is mine."

I let that sink in.

Then I wink.

A few people laugh politely. The cameras flash. I hold the trophy high with one hand and press my palm to my chest with the other, all while my eyes never leave hers.

She doesn't smile.

She's too pissed.

Perfect.

I step down from the stage, award in hand, and make my way toward the bar instead of my seat. I need another whiskey.

And maybe the distance.

Because if I stay close, I'll say something I shouldn't.

Or kiss her.

Or both.

And I'm not sure which one would make her hate me more.

But God, she looks beautiful when she's seething.

What the fuck is wrong with me? What is this temptress doing to the cold, numb Dr. Quinn?

CHAPTER 20

STEPHANIE

The motherfucking audacity.

Heat floods my cheeks. Not the flustered kind. The kind that comes right before I throw something heavy across the room. And right now, I'm picturing myself with super strength and launching that asshole off the stage.

And yet, I still don't look away.

Because part of me, some clearly deluded, masochistic part, likes that he said my name in a room full of people and made it sound like a fucking power play.

Because it was.

One day, I'll wipe that smug grin off his face.

He turns, trophy in hand, and walks off stage like he just sealed a deal with the devil.

And I'm the fucking fine print.

Josh leans toward me, whispering, "Are you okay?"

I don't answer. I just grab my champagne and knock it back in one gulp. I need something way stronger than this.

Champagne makes me horny. I need vodka. Tequila. Something industrial-grade.

"Dr. Quinn's speech was… flattering?" Poppy says from across the table, trying to read my face.

Flattering?

If by flattering, she means a public humiliation wrapped in praise, then she's dead on.

"He's insufferable," I mutter.

But my thighs are clenched under the table.

And I hate myself for it.

I glance toward the bar. He's there. Whiskey in hand. Smirking. Watching.

Like he knows.

And maybe he does.

Because the bastard didn't just win the award.

He made sure I knew I'd lost.

And somehow… somehow that stings more than I'm willing to admit.

I stare off, trying to simmer down the violent urge to commit a felony.

I let out a groan and roll my eyes as Zak approaches me.

He's really brave.

He leans down, that smug little grin carved into his face.

"I see how it is. You won't entertain me because you're too busy fucking your own attending. Classy whore."

My nostrils flare. I stand, ignoring the gasps around the room, and pull back and slap him across the face.

The sound cracks like lightning.

He grabs his cheek, eyes blazing.

"Come near me again, and I swear I'll cut your heart out and mail it to your fiancée."

He laughs and backs away.

"Tell Finn I said good luck. You're a fucking psycho."

Fuck him.

And Finn.

Without looking back, I storm out of the room, the doors crashing shut behind me. The lobby's buzzing with people, but I need space. I need air.

I spot a hallway and dart for it. First door I find, I push open and slip inside.

Of course. A fucking storage closet.

The smell of bleach hits me in the face.

Before I can close the door, a tattooed hand catches it.

"Fuck off," I spit.

"No." His deep Irish lilt slinks down my spine.

He shoves the door open, steps inside, and lets it slam behind him. He doesn't speak. Just stares.

Always assessing. Always calculating.

"What do you want? I just need a breather. And I'd rather not have an asthma attack from your aftershave."

No smirk. Just a frown.

"What did Zak say?"

"It doesn't matter. I handled it."

He steps closer. I don't move.

"It does matter. That was one hell of a slap—I heard it from the fucking bar. I need to know if he's getting fired before he even gets on the plane."

I rub the back of my neck. I know that tone. When Finn Quinn wants answers, he gets them.

"Fine," I huff. "He said I wouldn't fuck him because I'm fucking you. Then wished you luck. Called me a psycho."

Finn laughs, and it's almost feral.

"Us?" He gestures between us. "He thinks we're sleeping together? Wow."

My jaw tightens.

"Why is that so funny?"

I take a step forward, closing the gap.

"You wouldn't fuck me? How rude."

His laughter dies instantly. His face like thunder.

"I would if you kept your mouth fuckin' shut."

Oh. That makes my heart race.

"Well, I can't do that. Not possible. I've never shut up a day in my life."

His brow arches.

"Trust me. I know, Stephanie."

The way he says my name—it should be illegal.

As should the fact that I'm turned on by this arrogant, controlling bastard.

"Anyway," I step back, needing space from him. "I wouldn't fuck you if you were the last man on earth. I'd wait for the aliens to arrive and fuck one of them instead."

His fists clench and release.

"Make your feelings known, Dr. Miller. Glad you finally let it out."

He turns, reaching for the door.

"I'll leave you to it. Have a good night."

But something inside me snaps.

"Why did you dedicate that award to me? Do you do things like that just to upset me?"

He turns slowly to me, eyes narrowing.

"I upset you?"

"Yeah. I think so."

He chews his lip.

"Upset..." he whispers, like he's tasting the word for the first time.

"Angry. Hurt. Pissed off. Inferior. Never good enough."

His gaze darkens.

"You are good enough. You're fucking fantastic at your job."

I nod.

"I know. But you like to remind me that your rich ass is better than mine."

He clears his throat. The click of the door lock is deafening.

"You have no idea who I am, Stephanie."

His voice is sharp enough to cut.

"I've worked with you for nearly six years. I've seen how it's gone down. What was it? Daddy's money? Bought your way to the top?"

"That's what you think?" His voice drops an octave.

I open my mouth and nothing comes out. I'm not even sure what I think of him. I don't think he ever opens up or shows anyone the real him.

"This is what I mean. You never know when to shut up," he mutters.

He storms forward. I back up until I hit the shelving unit, knocking a bottle of bleach to the floor.

"Rich boy doesn't like it?" I tease.

He's in my face now. Towering. Eyes burning. Jaw tight.

"You just can't face the fact you aren't as good as me."

Ouch.

I press a hand to my chest.

"No. I'm pissed that you stole my job. That you walk around like you own the damn place. Covered in tattoos. Wearing your stupid black shirts and rings. You think any of us could get away with that? No. Because you're special. And it's bullshit. You're just another cold, entitled asshole."

I stare him down. Daring him to fight back.

A wicked grin spreads across his lips.

"You're brave, you know that?"

His voice is a threat and a promise.

"Why?"

"Because next time you lock yourself in a room with me

and talk like that—” He steps closer, breath hot against my ear.

“I'll bend you over my knee and cut that attitude out of you. I'll make you bleed for it.”

Jesus.

My core clenches so hard I forget how to breathe.

“You wouldn't fucking dare.”

He runs a finger down my arm and I shiver.

“You. Have. No. Idea. Who. I. Am. Love. Do not push me any further. I'll allow this outburst, once. But this is your one and only pass.”

I try to steady my breath as he backs off.

“I—I…”

He shakes his head.

“Don't you dare apologize. Own your fucking words. You meant them, didn't you?”

I stare into his eyes. Searching for something. Anything. But, as usual, there's nothing there.

“Yes.”

“If you hate working under me so much, leave. I'm not stopping you.”

There it is. The dagger to the gut. The part that always makes me feel disposable. Just like I always end up feeling in the end.

“Maybe I will.”

He nods.

“Good. The whole competition is getting boring. I'm tired of winning.”

Smug bastard.

I hate how much I want to slap him and kiss him all at once.

“I lost by one point last week,” I say through gritted teeth. “And we both know I deserved more. What about saving

Conan? Didn't that count for something? I should have won the entire year for that."

I'll never admit it, but I was terrified.

Terrified I'd lose his brother. Terrified I'd lose myself.

"You're just desperate to beat me, aren't you?" he says.

I shrug, biting back a grin.

"Maybe."

He huffs.

"Fine. What about tonight?" he suggests.

I frown.

"What? Find someone to operate on?"

He looks confused for a second. Then rolls his eyes.

"No. A drinking game. We're in Vegas, after all, Stephanie."

I blink.

"What kind of drinking?"

He closes his eyes, visibly restraining himself.

"Water. Let's drown ourselves in hydration," he says, dripping with sarcasm.

I snort.

"Real drinking. Shot for shot. Whoever's standing wins. Beat me, and I'll give you the chart win for the week. Hell, I'll put a plaque over your office door."

Victory. I'll take it.

"Deal."

He laughs, a deep, wicked sound that makes me regret it immediately.

He pulls the door open and motions for me to leave.

"Ladies first. And don't ditch me for any alien dick tonight."

I spin, walking backwards to face him as I grin.

"I'm not missing out on monster dick if the opportunity arises."

He shoves his hands into his pockets.

"You already are."

He winks and turns down the corridor.

Of course Mr. Perfect has a huge dick. Even that's annoying. He just has to be the full package.

That's the least of my problems.

Drinking with my boss is probably not my smartest move.

But if it gives me a win?

I'm all in.

And what's worse is I'm thinking about the size of his cock now.

CHAPTER 21

FINN

I shouldn't be doing this.

Drinking with her. Letting her bait me. Humoring her fire.

But here I am.

Because she challenged me. I didn't think she'd bite, to be honest. She seems to flip between emotions rather quickly. That has always intrigued me about her. I keep my emotions locked up tight. But she doesn't.

But I never fucking walk away from a challenge. Especially not when it comes from her mouth.

We push through the crowded hallway, back into the main bar. Music is thumping. People are laughing, drinking—celebrating my win. Not that I give a shit.

The only thing I'm focused on is the way her ass moves in that dress and how close I came to bending her over a shelving unit ten minutes ago.

She slides into a booth, and I hesitate, ripping off my bow tie before it strangles me. Fuck it. What harm can a few drinks really do?

So, I join her.

"Two tequilas," I tell the server before she even opens her mouth.

"And just keep them coming."

"Bossy," she mutters, stretching out her legs under the table, letting one of them brush against mine.

Not an accident.

Not from her.

"You'd hate me if I wasn't."

"I already hate you," she says sweetly, flashing me a smile that could cut glass.

"And yet, here you are."

The drinks arrive. She downs hers without hesitation.

I follow.

Round one.

Her lips press together, brows pinching for a second before she breathes out and flashes me that smug look again.

"Please don't tell me that was your idea of a challenge."

I lean forward, resting my elbows on the table. "Love, that was foreplay."

Her pupils flare. Just for a second.

But I clock it. And I will be noting that down. Because this is a side I haven't unleashed from her before.

Round two.

The burn hits harder this time. She blinks fast, steadying her breath, but I can see it—her tolerance isn't low, but it's not mine. I've trained for pain with poison. She's running on spite and champagne.

That can only get her so far.

"How many rounds till you fold?" I ask, waving down the server again.

"I don't fold. Every damn day of my life is a battle."

There's a hint of sadness in her voice. A real side of her.

"And yet, I'm the one with the trophy," I say, low.

She smiles, but there's something beneath it. Something jagged.

"You dedicated that trophy to me. Which tells me it meant more than you'd like to admit."

She's sharper than people give her credit for. Too sharp. She's fuckin' dangerous.

Round three.

We drink. No words this time.

She exhales, slower now. The kick is catching up to her.

"Feeling it yet?" I ask.

She rolls her neck like she's about to swing at me. "I could do this all night."

"Is that an offer?"

"Only if you're ready to lose."

Her leg presses fully against mine now. The heat is setting something off inside of me I've never felt before.

I should pull away.

Instead, I press back. Everything between us is a play of power. Even down to a touch.

The tequila's rising in my blood. But that's not what's making me reckless. It's her. Her laugh. Her mouth. The fire in her eyes every time she talks back.

She looks around, then leans in.

"I'm serious. If I win, I want that plaque. On my office door. In gold letters."

"And if I win?" I ask, voice dropping.

Her breath catches.

Then she recovers.

"I don't know. You tell me."

Bad idea, sweetheart.

"I want a page from your journal," I say quietly. "The one I know you keep. You're too tightly wound not to have one."

She blinks. Hard. Like I hit a nerve. I knew she'd have one.

"No one reads my journal."

"Then don't lose."

She drinks.

Round four.

I can see the buzz crawling under her skin now. Her lips are redder. Her cheeks flushed. She's blinking slower, trying to focus.

But she won't back down.

Neither will I.

She knocks back round five and sways just slightly, hands gripping the edge of the booth. I reach out instinctively, fingers brushing her wrist.

She yanks away like my touch burned her.

"You don't get to touch me, remember," she says. But her voice cracks slightly.

"Then stop looking at me like you want me to."

Our silence is charged.

A beat passes between us, and she lets out a laugh that throws me off guard.

"God, I hate you."

I grin.

"No, you don't."

She opens her mouth, probably to argue, but the server returns with round six and cuts her off.

I raise the shot in salute.

"Ready to fall, Dr. Miller?"

She lifts hers. "You first, Dr. Quinn."

I think she might be right.

We drink.

This one makes her wince. Just slightly, but I notice. I always do.

She pushes her curls back from her face. Straightens her spine.

But I've already won.

She won't admit it.

But I can feel it.

Not the tequila.

Her.

I could taste her victory and her downfall in the same breath.

And I'm starving for both.

"Shall we go somewhere, maybe where our colleagues aren't?" she asks, her eyes roaming the busy room.

"Yeah. Sure. I know some good places my friend owns. Can get us in anywhere."

She rolls her eyes, and I tap my rings against the table.

She really needs to stop doing that to me, because the more I drink, the more likely I am to jump across the table and grab her throat.

And then who fucking knows what will happen between us.

A bloodbath or an incredible hate fuck.

Or something worse.

"Of course you can. Friends in all the right places," she winks.

She thinks her words hurt me.

They never could.

Because I've felt pain most couldn't bear, let alone live with.

CHAPTER 22
STEPHANIE

Song- You're Gorgeous, Babybird.

We stumble from bar to bar, and for the first time in a long time. I forget everything. I am just enjoying myself.

And with the most unlikely companion.

My rival.

My rich boy boss.

"Suits you," I tease him.

He holds up his cocktail in a coconut with a little pink umbrella.

"I think so too. Fuck. I could use a vacation."

He stretches his arm above his head.

"You're a busy man, Dr. Quinn."

I take a sip of my own sweet liquor. We needed a quick break from the shots before both of us vomited.

"You have no idea. Gotta keep busy to keep distracted." He taps the side of his head.

The more he drinks, the more he's losing his calm and collected exterior.

He's becoming… a yapper.

"Lot going on up there?" I ask.

I'm intrigued to see how his brain works. It really is a mystery.

But I'm so damn drunk, I'm struggling to keep up.

"All the things, Stephanie. All the damn things," he sighs, and then drinks the cocktail in one go.

"Go on, your turn. Shot. It."

His bloodshot eyes meet mine, and they don't falter as I do the same.

He leans in and wipes a drip from my lips off with his thumb and sucks it clean.

"If my brothers could see me now, I'd never fucking live this down."

He leans back in his chair, the first time I've ever seen him relaxed.

While I almost combust from the heat of his movements. His touch.

"Shall we take a picture?"

He pouts and sits up, resting his elbows on the table.

"So you can blackmail me?"

I blush. He thinks so highly of me.

"Yes."

He shrugs. Wrapping a strong arm around my shoulders, dragging me next to him, I bring up my camera and take a selfie.

"Wow. We look so drunk," I giggle.

He chuckles beside me, his arm still heavy on my shoulders.

His finger brushes over me in the picture.

"You look cute when you're drunk, Stephanie."

"So do you. Aw. Look at us being all sweet."

I'm not sure how I feel about it. But I have to keep my

victory in mind.

"Next place?" I ask him, sliding my phone back in my purse.

"Yep. You gotta lose soon."

He helps me out of the booth, and I smile.

An actual real smile at Dr. Quinn.

CHAPTER 23

FINN

Song- Marry you, Bruno Mars.

She's losing.

But she's too stubborn to say it.

Round seven hit her hard. I saw it. The tremble in her hand. The unfocused blink. Her spine's still straight, but her soul's sliding sideways.

I'm not much better. I'll admit that.

But I've danced with worse poisons than tequila.

She finishes her drink and slams the shot glass down like it offended her mother.

Although, I shouldn't bring up her parents. I know they're in jail for a homicide. Probably an awkward conversation topic. And I don't know how I'd deal with a crying Stephanie.

"I hate losing," she mutters, voice rasped.

"Good thing you're used to it," I reply, lips curling into a grin.

She glares at me like she's about to lunge across the table. "You are such a smug, self-absorbed, egotistical—"

"Careful," I cut in, lifting my glass. "You're starting to sound like my therapist."

She laughs. A real one this time. Unfiltered. Unpolished. Like she forgot how to be angry for half a second.

It's the best sound I've heard in months.

"I should've known you had a therapist. Makes total sense. Even sociopaths need someone to talk to," she says.

It was a complete lie. There is no way in hell I could let a shrink dive into my subconscious. My brothers are right, I would end up in a padded cell and have to kill everyone in there to escape. Although, that does actually sound quite entertaining.

"You want his number?" I ask. "You could use a session. Or twelve."

She holds up two fingers and signals for more shots.

I raise a brow. "You trying to impress me, Stephanie?"

"I'm trying to forget I've been professionally humiliated by a man who wears rings like a mob boss."

I chuckle. "Don't knock the rings. They have more personality than half our department."

The shots arrive. She pushes one toward me but then picks mine up, with a naughty glint in her eye.

"Have you ever done body shots before, Dr. Quinn?" She wiggles her eyebrows.

I chuckle.

"Stephanie, I don't have the energy to fight every guy in here if you strip and lie on that table," I tell her.

She shivers at my words and then, without breaking eye contact, places the shot glass between her breasts. I swear to fuckin' god, I'm salivating looking.

I shouldn't even be admiring her tits like this. But, fuck, I can't help it.

Grabbing the salt, I lean forward, reveling in the fact her

breath hitches the second my tongue connects with her shoulder. I lick slowly before pulling away and shaking some salt. As I sit back, my cock twitches.

Picking up the lime slice, I place it in front of her mouth. Her pillowy lips open, and she bites down on the skin.

"Atta girl," I wink.

With one hand on her thigh, I lick up the salt and then put my lips around the shot glass. But I don't move; I stay, just for a few seconds.

Knocking my head back, the tequila burns its way down my throat, but that ain't nothing in comparison to the heat radiating from Stephanie.

Our eyes lock, and the fire blazes as I lean in and retrieve the lime from her mouth, sucking it dry.

Without a word, I pick up her shot and hand it to her. Her fingers are trembling, and I can't help but smile.

"To Vegas," she says, taking the shot without the salt or the lime.

As if she's desperate to calm the inferno within her.

She wipes her mouth and leans back in the booth, eyes half-lidded, legs tangled with mine beneath the table.

"You know what we should do?" she slurs.

I tilt my head. "Can't wait to hear this."

"We should get married."

I choke on my drink.

She grins wide. Drunk yet still deadly to me. "Come on, Finn. Let's do it. It's Vegas. Isn't this what people do? Get married on tequila and bad decisions?"

"You think marrying me would be a bad decision?"

"I think it'd be the worst decision I've ever made. Which is why it fits perfectly with tonight's theme."

I bark out a laugh, leaning back, completely wrecked.

"Fine," I say. "But only if I get to file for an annulment before sunrise."

"No prenup," she adds. "You lose half your fortune and your spot on the surgical board."

"And you'll have to deal with the emotional turmoil that you were my first and only wife."

She pretends to think. "Worth it."

There's a lull then.

"Wait. You never actually want to get married?" she asks.

I shrug. "Never crossed my mind before."

She frowns. "Yeah, me neither actually. Maybe that life isn't meant for us."

That sadness is back in her voice and I chew on my lip. I think actually, she's wrong about herself there.

"Looks like we better tick that off the list and get married then."

She gives me a naughty grin that makes my cock twitch.

"Really?"

I nod slowly. I might regret this. But I'll do it just because of the way she's looking at me in this second. I want to grasp onto this feeling. Even if it is alien and hurting my fucking chest.

Her eyes drift toward the dance floor, where couples sway under string lights and pop music.

She blinks.

Then turns back to me.

"Dance with me," she says.

My brows shoot up. "Now? I don't dance."

"Why not? Come on, Dr. Quinn. Show me you've got rhythm."

She grabs my hands and bolts of electricity sizzle. She bats her lashes dramatically and pouts. Fuck. Turns out I'll do whatever this woman asks without a second thought.

Is she… making me weak? Or is it all the alcohol?

"Please, Finn."

Fuck. I can't say no to those eyes.

"I could perform open heart surgery with one hand, Stephanie. Of course I have rhythm."

"Prove it."

She stands on wobbly legs, yet still looks hot and fucking electric in that dress. She holds out a hand, but I hesitate.

She notices.

"You scared?"

I grit my teeth and take her hand.

"Let's go, future Mrs. Quinn."

Her eyes go wide. "I'm not sure that suits me."

I smirk. "Too late. Vows will be legally binding. Non-refundable."

She's wrong. It sounds fucking perfect.

We make it to the floor, and I pull her in by the waist, her body flush to mine. And fuck, it feels good.

She laughs again; the sound makes my heart race.

"I hate you," she whispers.

She rests her head against my chest, and I don't flinch. I don't do comfort. I don't do cuddles. I don't let people touch me.

Yet, here she is, with her hands all over me and her face snuggled against me.

I'm drunk. But I'm not sure if it's from the tequila or her.

"I know," I murmur. "But right now, you're wasted enough to forget why."

She pulls back and starts spinning like an idiot, dragging me with her.

We're a mess. Laughing, stumbling, and colliding on the dance floor, but something in the chaos feels good.

Like breathing. Like not just surviving for once.

Just living.

And for the first time since I was ten years old, I let myself do exactly that.

Even if it's only for a single song.

CHAPTER 24

STEPHANIE

Song- Careful What You Wish For, Bad Omens.

I try to open my eyes, but the second I do, bile climbs up my throat.

My stomach gurgles violently, and I sit up way too fast.

The room spins.

Pulling my knees to my chest, I run my shaking hands through my hair, eyes locked on the unfamiliar white sheets.

"Morning."

Finn's husky voice slices straight through my skull.

My stomach drops.

I launch myself off the bed and race for the bathroom—except it's not where mine is.

Fuck.

Am I in his suite?

"Over this way," Finn croaks from the bed.

I spin and dart into the bathroom, barely making it before I throw up the five thousand gallons of tequila we drank last night.

I don't stop until my throat's raw and my dignity's in hell.

I run the cold tap, splash my face, and steal some of his toothpaste. Looking in the mirror, I see the mess that's my face. I wipe the smeared eyeliner so I don't look like a panda and drag my fingers through my tangled hair.

Good enough.

When I open the door, he's still sprawled in bed, one arm behind his head, watching me like I'm a show.

"Why don't you look like shit?" I rasp.

He laughs, but it turns into a cough.

"I don't know. Because I feel like it."

My eyes scan the tattoos. He's shirtless. Inked to the gods. Broad as hell.

Wait.

Wait.

"Finn," I say warily.

"Yes?"

"Did we fuck?"

He lifts the blanket, glances down.

"Uh, no. I'm still in my boxers. You got your red lace panties on?" he says with a mocking tone.

My heart skips into panic mode.

"Yeah. But that doesn't mean…"

"Stephanie," he cuts in, smirking. "You'd know, drunk or not, if I'd fucked you. You'd be covered in cuts and bruises. You wouldn't be able to walk. And you sure as hell wouldn't be questioning it. Because you'd feel it. I'd still be dripping down your thighs. So no, we did not have sex."

I grip the doorframe to stop myself from collapsing.

"Jesus," I hiss.

That's... vivid. Cuts? What the hell is he into? And why does that burn me from the inside out? The pain, the trust. Fuck, that would be exceptional.

"So I just crashed in bed with you?"

"Yeah," he says casually, sitting up and stretching, revealing abs and arms I didn't need to see.

"But," he adds, "you might wanna sit down."

My stomach coils.

"Why?"

He motions me over with one finger. And like the moron I am, I obey—sitting at the edge of the bed.

"Give me your left hand."

I frown, confused, and let him take it. He turns my palm down, and my heart stops.

There, glinting under the Vegas sunlight, is a massive diamond on a silver band.

"Finn. Tell me we did not—"

Memories come crashing in.

Joking about getting married. Laughing. Drinking. Dancing.

No. No. No.

He pulls his hand out from under the covers.

A platinum band sits proudly on his tatted finger.

I slap a hand over my mouth.

"Finn. You're fucking with me. You just... put these on for a joke, right?"

His expression is stone.

His eyes, dark fire.

"No, I really didn't." He pauses. "Mrs. Quinn."

He smirks. Like he just won the goddamn lottery.

"No. No. No." I jump off the bed, pacing like a lunatic. "Finn! What have we done?!"

"Stephanie, calm down. It's fine."

"Fine?! *Fine?!* They're legally binding marriages here, you psycho!"

I yank at the ring, but the second I do, a growl erupts

from him.

"Dr. Stephanie Quinn."

His voice is sharp and commanding.

He stands, stepping toward me like he's stalking prey.

I forget how to breathe. Fuck, he's sexy.

"That ring stays on your finger."

"Are you still drunk?" I snap.

He leans in. Close enough to smell. Dangerous enough to destroy me.

"No. You lost the challenge. My reward... is you."

My hangover evaporates in an instant.

I shove at his chest, but he doesn't move. Just grins, infuriatingly smug.

"Annul our marriage, rich boy."

He runs a hand over his stubble. And then he just fucking shrugs.

"Nope."

He hops back into bed and pulls the blanket over him like this is just another Thursday.

"You coming back in to sleep this hangover off or what?"

My jaw drops.

"Who are you, and what have you done with Finn?"

"I'm a married man now, Stephanie. And your husband needs a nap."

I grab a pillow and hold it over his head.

"Say you'll annul it, or I will smother you."

"Good one," he grunts, eyes already closed.

"I'm serious."

"Oh, I know." He doesn't even flinch.

"'Stephanie Quinn' has a nice ring to it, don't you think?"

A fire erupts inside me.

"No. It sounds horrible."

"Now get up, and let's sort this out."

He snuggles deeper.

"No can do. I'm a busy man."

He fucking yawns as he talks.

"Stop being a dick, Finn."

"Stop being a brat, Stephanie."

I toss the pillow at his face and stomp toward the door.

"Where are you going, wifey?" he calls out.

"Back to my room. Then to figure out how to divorce your ass."

He sighs dramatically.

"Well, that leads to storage, not the door for your dramatic exit. But good luck. I'm not signing shit. I won this fair and square. I won you. If you could also track down the chapel we went to and get them to send me the footage, I'd love to savor the moment that I claimed you."

I turn slowly, rage vibrating in my bones. Putting my fingers to my plump lips, I freeze. Did we kiss?

Fuck. It's so annoying I can't remember anything.

"I'm going to kill you."

He beams.

"Not before our honeymoon, love."

CHAPTER 25

FINN

Spinning the ring on my finger, I sigh.

I'm disappointed she doesn't remember our first kiss. I can still feel how soft her lips were against mine. I was wasted, yeah. But I'm never wasted enough to completely lose control.

Especially not around her.

Pulling up my phone, I click play on the video.

My chest tightens as it starts.

The way she's looking up at me, smiling like that. Almost sweet.

A stark contrast to the viper who just slammed my door on her way out.

But she made a grave mistake this morning.

She showed me her new button.

And I'm going to press it until she breaks.

I have fifty different scenarios running through my head, all the ways I can use our new bond to test her.

To punish her.

To ruin her.

Maybe if I push hard enough… I'll end my obsession.

Or maybe, I'll drown in it.

Can I really make this woman hate me?

Is that even what I want?

I'm not sure anymore.

Because when she kissed me—drunk or not—

My entire world fucking stopped.

When the video hits the moment our mouths collide, I pause it and take a screenshot.

A keepsake. Stephanie Quinn is mine.

And by the time she's done begging for a divorce, she'll know the truth.

This intense friction we have? It isn't hate. Not really.

It's something more. Something dangerous. Something raw and consuming.

It's intoxicating. Possessive. A disaster waiting to happen.

Her touch burns through my skin. And she's the first woman that I haven't wanted to sever from me.

No. With her, I want to sew her into my fucking skin and never let her go.

It didn't feel like being haunted by my past.

It felt like I was setting fire to my future.

And that is why the ring stays.

Until I figure out what the fuck this all means.

Until I know how deep this obsession runs.

If one drunken kiss has my mind spinning. What would her complete submission do to me?

Kill me?

Maybe.

I guess something has got to one day. Perhaps she should have smothered me with that pillow, because that's the only way I can see her getting out of this.

"Wait, we still have one more passenger," I tell the flight attendant as she goes to close the door.

She turns to me with a frown.

"No. This is the full count."

I turn to Poppy and Josh; they seem to be the closest to Stephanie in our department.

"Where is Dr. Miller?" I ask.

They exchange a look.

"She left late last night."

I swallow, making sure my face remains emotionless.

"Right," I reply sharply.

"Go ahead. Wheels up, I guess."

The door shuts with a thud, and I pull out my cell.

ME

> And why did my wife leave me without so much as a goodbye?

I see the three dots appear and disappear. I need to change her contact name. She isn't Dr. Miller any longer. Dr. Quinn. Or Temptress would work. Because that's what she is to me. A temptation.

STEPHANIE MILLER

> I have no idea what you're talking about.
> You have a wife?

A smile tugs at my lips.

ME

> You know very well I do.

Her reply is lightning speed, just as I change her name.

TEMPTRESS

Who was dumb enough to marry an
arrogant asshole like you? What's her
number? Maybe I should text her and tell
her you let me crash in your bed on a work
trip.

I clear my throat to hide my laugh.

ME

Did you just call yourself dumb, Mrs. Quinn?

I shouldn't enjoy calling her that as much as I do.

TEMPTRESS

I'll pay you ten thousand to annul the
marriage.

I have enough money to last ten lifetimes. But a marriage I can use to rile up my wife for the rest of my life? Priceless.

I have no intentions of being married twice in my life, so I guess this is it.

Her or no one.

I might as well have some fun with this—before we kill each other.

ME

There is not a price on our union, temptress.
I'll see you tomorrow.

I don't have long to put phase one of my plan into action. I've already got Reggie and Rowan on the arts and crafts portion.

TEMPTRESS

I'm already engaged to someone else.

My heart stops for a moment. If she is, then it's quite simple; he will need to go.

ME

You better end it, fast. I won't be sharing you. You're mine now.

I turn in my chair to Poppy, who immediately sits up straight. She's scared of me. I thought I'd actually been rather pleasant to her.

"Does Dr. Q–" My mouth snaps shut. "Dr. Miller, have a fiancé?" I ask.

She frowns, and her mouth pops open.

"No. Maybe a secret boyfriend? But none that I know of."

I nod and turn back around.

ME

Your lies will be punished.

She doesn't reply. I wonder what she's doing right now. Is she pissed off? Turned on? Hmm. She is fascinating. And fucking distracting.

CHAPTER 26

STEPHANIE

Song- Delusional, Visenya

"Morning," I say to Josh as he walks past me.

He offers me a strained smile in return.

Weird. Maybe he's still hungover from Vegas.

But then I round the corner into reception, and the two nurses behind the desk just… stare. No words. Just blinking, like I've grown a second fucking head.

I frown, pulling out my phone and opening the camera.

No mascara smudges. No lipstick on my teeth. My hair's fine. I don't get it.

I keep walking, shoulders stiff, eyes forward, pretending not to care while my heart thuds like a warning shot in my chest.

As I reach my office, I grab the door handle—then stop.

Something's off. Viscerally wrong.

And there it is.

A new plaque. Bright, gold, and sickening.

Dr. Stephanie Quinn

My stomach twists. Rage flashes hot and white in my bloodstream.

How fucking dare he.

I dig my nails under the edge of the plaque, trying to rip it off, but the damn thing won't budge. I'm seconds from causing a scene, so instead, I shove the door open and storm inside.

The first thing I see is the black box on my desk. Beside it —an envelope.

My breath catches.

He has to be kidding.

This has gone too far. Way too far.

Rivalry is one thing. I can take the snide comments, the surgical pissing contests, even the damn leaderboard. But this? A whole-ass marriage? With that egotistical psycho?

Not happening. Not in this lifetime.

Even if he does make my heart skip and my skin flush and my brain glitch when he so much as breathes near me. Still. No.

I open the box with trembling fingers.

Holy. Shit.

That is not just a ring. It's a goddamn statement. The diamond alone could buy my apartment building. It's flanked by a band covered in smaller diamonds, gleaming like gilt.

There's purpose behind it.

This isn't a spur-of-the-moment Vegas gimmick.

These rings are a warning.

I don't even know how he pulled the Vegas ones off, let alone this. What strings he yanked. What rules he rewrote.

And I've ignored him since we landed. Not one reply to his texts. I thought if I left the city and pretended it didn't happen, we could go back to what we were. Enemies. Rivals. The cold war we waged daily in the OR.

I was wrong.

So fucking wrong.

No one can read Finn Quinn.

I pick up the letter with fingers that won't stop shaking.

> *Mrs. Quinn,*
>
> *I know you dared to come to work today without your rings, and I thought to myself, you probably deserve to have something more of a statement to show off our marriage. So, your first gift from your husband.*
>
> *Wear them, or else.*
>
> *Once you have them on, please come to the staff room. Your presence is required for a very important meeting.*
>
> *P.S. I hope you like your new plaque, as specifically requested by yourself.*
>
> *And yes. HR knows about our marriage, and it has been signed off on.*
>
> *Love your doting husband,*
>
> *Finn*

I want to scream.

My hands ball into fists. I press one to my mouth to keep from letting the sound out. Rage floods every nerve ending, but underneath that—beneath the fire—is something worse.

He's doing this for me.

Not for attention. Not for applause.

He's doing this to get under my skin. Because he knows it'll work.

And the sickest part? He's right.

A sliver of me finds it funny. Another horrifying part? Flattered.

He's always cold. Always composed. Never a man for spectacle. Yet, here he is, loving the fact he's trapping me in a legally binding nightmare.

One minute I was worried he wouldn't come back. That he'd vanish—arrested and gone for good. Now, I want to throw him into a wall.

I haven't heard a word from the people blackmailing me. Not since I handed Finn to them on a silver platter. I guess my part's done.

But I'm not dumb enough to believe it's over. They'll be back. Blackmailers don't like loose ends. And now I'm married to my biggest liability.

I toss the note aside and snap the ring box shut with a hard click.

Like hell I'm wearing those rings.

Finn needs to annul this circus now before I commit murder.

Fueled by fury, I storm toward the staff room. My heels strike the floor like gunfire. Heads turn, but I don't care.

I slam the door open.

Balloons. Streamers. Confetti.

And front and center, a giant banner that reads:

"Congratulations, Mr. and Mrs. Quinn."

The room spins.

A sea of faces, but I only see his. That smug, self-satisfied grin.

My breath lodges in my throat. I can't even move. My body forgets how.

What the fuck is this?

Finn Quinn doesn't throw parties. He doesn't even like people. He makes that abundantly clear.

And yet here he stands, center stage, celebrating a joke that only he finds funny.

I move through the room like a woman possessed. People whisper congratulations like I'm a fucking bride instead of a hostage.

Poppy catches my eye, confusion etched across her face.

This is the most humiliating moment of my life.

I stop when I reach him.

"What in the actual fuck do you think you're doing?" I hiss.

"Celebrating my wonderful wife." He smirks.

I shake my head, barely containing the scream building in my chest.

"Do you want me to make a scene?" I snap.

He tsks, snakes his arm around my waist, and pulls me close—his lips brushing my ear.

"Where are your rings, wife?"

"I'm not wearing them. This wedding isn't real. Do we need to send you to the psych ward? This is insane. Even for you."

He chuckles, but it's warm, not patronizing. Too intimate. Too real.

"I thought you'd appreciate the effort."

I wrench away from him and spin, hands planted firmly on my hips.

"Take it all down. And leave me the hell alone. I am not your wife."

His lips curl at the edges. He's enjoying this too much.

But then his expression falters. Concern flickers. Genuine, maybe.

"Steph, are you okay?"

And that nearly breaks me.

Because if he cared, he wouldn't be doing this. He

wouldn't be dragging my name, my work, my whole fucking life into his twisted idea of love or revenge or obsession.

Tears burn behind my eyes. I blink hard.

No one sees me cry. No one has ever stayed long enough to deserve that piece of me.

I back away. Silent.

Someone bumps into me, but I don't stop.

I don't go to my office. Not when that plaque is still on the door, laughing in gold.

I run.

Straight to the only place in this hospital no one thinks to look.

Where I can breathe.

Where I've cried more tears than anyone knows.

Where life and death hang in the balance every goddamn day.

The hospital roof.

I find my secret spot, hidden in the corner, and find my stash of cigarettes behind the planter.

Lighting one, relief washes over me.

I know I shouldn't. How I preach to my patients not to.

But, damn. They do work for stress. And today has been awful.

I nearly fucking cried in front of a room of people.

I promised myself I'd never become a man's property. Or allow a man to control me. I forged my way in this industry on my own, in spite of them.

And then in waltzes Finn, just like he did six years ago.

Storming in and taking over.

And now, that includes me.

The door clicks in the distance, and I close my eyes.

Here we go.

Round two.

And I want to throw him over the railing. Maybe watching his body splat on the concrete below will bring me some sort of satisfaction.

No. Killing my boss, and now my apparent husband, would be a bad idea. And what's worse, I could never do that to him.

Sighing, I keep my gaze fixed on the ground, hoping that, if I don't look at him, he won't come over. That he will just let me have a minute.

But, no.

His shiny black shoes soon appear in my vision.

Blowing out an exhale of my cigarette, I lift my head.

His eyes are like daggers. There is no remorse for what he just did to me. How he humiliated me, like I am some pawn in his game, only there for his amusement.

I toss my cigarette on his sparkling rich boy shoes, and he growls. I might as well have spat in his face by the sound of his reaction.

I stop breathing as his hand snatches my face, dragging me up to him like I'm nothing but a rag doll made for punishment.

His crazed eyes don't just stare; they consume.

They track every inch of my face, dissecting me.

Assessing me. Breaking me open.

And I can't hide. Not from him. Not now.

The tears have already betrayed me.

"Your tears won't have the desired effect on me, love."

He leans in so close I can feel him in my bones.

"They have quite the opposite, actually." His fingers slide from my cheek to my throat, coiling tight.

"But this isn't the real you. Is it?" His voice dips into something darker. Hungrier. "You're like me. We don't break. We don't show our weakness in front of people."

My bottom lip trembles.

Wrong move.

His grip tightens, jaw twitching with disdain.

He tuts like I've failed some unspoken test. "I thought my wife could take a joke," he says coldly. Like he doesn't care. Like this game means nothing to him.

But it means everything to me.

"That wasn't a joke. That was humiliation in front of all of my colleagues in a career that means everything to me. You have no fucking idea what I've had to do to get here." I spit the words with fire, but they burn me on the way out.

His eyes go narrow. A storm brews in the space between us.

"You really think you know me, huh? Rich boy this, rich boy that. You think you're the only one here who has felt real pain?"

Then he drops me.

Like I'm disposable. Like I don't matter.

And that hurts more than anything.

He steps away, shoving his palm against his chest.

"You think my life was a walk in the park? Do you believe I was always this fucking ice cold?"

He looks like he wants to tear his own skin off.

"You don't get this fucked up for nothing, temptress."

Suddenly, he's in my face again. So close I can taste the fury on his breath.

But instead of striking, he drags the back of his hand across my cheek. It's so soft compared to the fury radiating from him.

"I don't hide my crazy. I am who I am. But you? You're trying to conceal it, like I can't see straight through you. Like I haven't spent the past six years analyzing your every move.

I know you, Stephanie. Now how about you fucking show me?"

My head shakes before I can stop it. He doesn't know me. Not really.

Not the parts that still wake up screaming. Not the girl who crawled out of hell just to prove she was worthy of the title doctor.

"No, Finn. Just fuck off."

He cackles.

"Words are pointless to me. People lie. You can never trust what comes out of someone's mouth. Actions are the only thing I believe. So, I dare you, show me how you really feel about your husband. Not with tears, not with venom on your tongue. Fucking show me."

My fist clenches at my side. Heat coils in my gut. It's a mix of rage and desperation. It's how I've always lived, the only way I know how.

Everyone always leaves. My parents got sent to jail for fucking murder when I was twelve. Leaving me in a foster home until I was eighteen. No funding for college. No home. Nothing. The two people in the world who were meant to protect me were too busy trying to fund their schemes to even think about me. I'll never forgive them.

I don't even think. My body moves on instinct.

Before I know what I'm doing, my fist collides with his throat. Hard.

The sound that leaves his mouth is half-choke, half-growl.

His grin spreads slowly and twistedly, like he's been waiting for this.

"There she is. The real Dr. Miller," he taunts, eyes gleaming.

He claps; it's so loud it makes me flinch.

My hands tremble at my sides.

I just throat-punched my boss.

On hospital grounds.

"Oh, come on. I'm not going to get you fired. You think that's what I want? If I wanted you gone, I could have done that years ago."

I swallow the lump in my throat, my whole body shaking with the weight of it all.

"What do you want from me? Why do we keep playing these stupid games?" Now I'm practically yelling at him. Great, throat-punching and yelling at my boss. All in the span of two minutes.

His eyes soften, but only a fraction.

He steps forward, brushing his thumb along my lip. My breath hitches. My knees weaken.

I think Dr. Quinn is making me lose my mind.

"The answer isn't quite that simple."

"But you hate me," I say.

"And you hate me."

It's quite clear that isn't the truth from either of us. His hand drops to my hip, curling into the soft curve there like it's his. Like he has every right.

"Do you believe that lust and hate can't walk the same line, temptress?"

My skin erupts with shivers. My lungs seize.

His breath ghosts my mouth.

My whole body screams with want. With conflict. With everything I've spent years burying.

He's taking over everything.

And then—

"Kiss me and find out," I whisper breathlessly.

He's done it. He's broken me.

And I know the second his mouth meets mine…

There's no going back.

CHAPTER 27

FINN

She whispers it like a sin, like an invitation to her downfall.

That's all it takes. That one breathy dare and my restraint snaps like a fraying wire.

I crash my mouth into hers, swallowing the fury, the fire, the broken parts of her soul she hides behind sarcasm and scalpel-sharp precision.

Her lips part with a gasp, and I take everything.

Every fucking sound. Every tremble. Every ounce of power she thought she still had.

I grip the back of her neck, dragging her closer, crushing her body against mine.

Her fists ball into my shirt, like she's trying to push me away but can't commit.

Because deep down, she wants this just as badly as I do.

She tastes like rage and ruin. Like the first thing I've ever needed more than I needed control.

And I hate it. I hate that I can't stop. That my hands are already traveling, one tangled in her hair, the other gripping her hip like I'm staking a claim.

Like I own her.

Because maybe I fucking do. She is my goddamn wife.

Her moan breaks into my mouth. That desperate, wrecked sound that makes my cock throb behind the zipper of my pants.

I could fuck her right here. Against the rooftop wall.

Bend her over the ledge and brand her with every brutal inch of my obsession.

Let the city watch while I tear her open and put every lie to bed.

But I won't.

Not yet.

Because this isn't about lust. This is war, perhaps the one going on in my head. I pull back just enough to look her in the eye.

Her lips are red and swollen.

Her chest heaves against mine.

And her pupils are blown wide, begging me for more. Tempting me. Just like they did the first time I ever saw her.

"You kissed me back," I whisper.

My voice is low.

Her mouth opens. Closes.

No witty comeback. No sass.

Just her. Laid bare for me.

I drag my thumb across her bottom lip, smearing what's left of her lip gloss.

"That's what I wanted. Not tears. Not lies." My thumb hooks beneath her chin, tilting her face to mine again.

"That is the truth between us, Mrs. Quinn."

She shakes her head like she's trying to deny it.

But her body tells a different story.

I feel her chest rise against mine.

I feel her thighs tremble where they press into me.

I feel the war she's trying to fight—but I've already won.

Because I've seen it now. The one thing I was yet to assess in my notes about Stephanie.

The way she falls when she's not pretending to hate me.

The way she needs me to ruin her.

And I will.

But on my terms.

When I decide.

Where I choose.

I lean back just an inch and let my breath hit her lips.

"Are you going to deny it again?"

Her silence is everything I need.

And nothing I expected.

Because Stephanie Quinn just stopped fighting.

And now? Now I have no intention of letting her get back up.

With a chuckle, I step away and wipe my lip with a grin.

"You taste good, Dr. Quinn. Now, get back to work." I give her a parting wink and head towards the stairs.

CHAPTER 28

Today has been one of the longest days in history. Replaying that damn kiss in my head all day until I finally dragged my ass to the club. A distraction is what I need before Finn consumes me.

"Oh, I thought you'd quit," one of the girls says as I put my bag down in the changing room.

"Nope. Just been away," I say politely.

I'm still technically one of the new girls. I haven't quite been fully accepted in this club.

But I'm not here to make friends.

I'm here to keep them safe.

And to scratch the itch the only way I know how.

The other dancer, Steph, creeps up behind me.

"That guy, the one who you weren't sure about, he's here again. Same booth."

I swallow. "Thanks," I say quietly.

Fuck.

The girls all leave, and I stare at my reflection in the mirror before popping in my brown contacts for the night.

Who am I?

I look... lost.

I think I have been for a long time.

I've never really found my place.

I thought the hospital—that was my calling.

But then Finn happened.

And after yesterday, I can still feel his lips claiming mine.

The way his hands owned me.

And I can't stop thinking... what if I went after more?

What if I stopped denying that I crave him in ways I shouldn't?

I think he was right. We are similar. Maybe that's why we clash so hard—two bombs in the same room.

But I can't help wondering... what the fuck happened to him?

That pain in his eyes I felt it deep in my core, like I'd lived it with him.

We're both hiding who we are.

What if we dropped the act?

Maybe I am meant to be more than this.

I sigh, picking up the brush and running it through the soft red strands of my wig.

By the time I'm ready, I have a face full of makeup and a thong that shows off every inch of my ass. And as always, the snake tattoo that runs down through my breasts is covered completely.

I'm hot.

But I'm not Stephanie.

I'm Angel.

I'm a fucking monster.

No one would understand why I do what I do.

Why I need it.

The door cracks open.

"Angel, you're up."

Nerves tingle through me.

That guy—the one who I think blackmailed me into setting up Finn—is back.

What does he want now?

To frame Dr. Quinn again?

Kill more people?

I'm not a hitwoman for hire. I'm a surgeon. And I'm now someone's wife.

With every ounce of confidence I can muster, I walk out into the room with my head held high and move straight to the main stage.

Eyes track me as I grip the pole, swinging my hips in circles, pushing my ass back as I squat low to the floor.

Cash starts to rain around me.

But this heat crawls up my spine.

Like I'm being watched.

Not by strangers.

By the one man in the world I can't face. It's like I can feel Finn here, even if I can't see him.

No. It's not real.

It's my mind playing tricks.

As I climb the pole and bend backward, I tug my bra playfully, biting my lip.

Slowly sliding down, I grab the pole and split my legs.

Fuck, I'm getting too old for this.

It was easier when I was eighteen.

Thirty-three?

Not so much. I'll be paying for this tomorrow.

But the longer I'm up here, the safer I am.

The less likely that blackmailing creep will summon me; my boss doesn't let anyone off the stage mid-shift.

I dance for maybe forty minutes before I'm beckoned over to the bar.

That same gnawing tension is still there.

I scan the room through the haze of lights and shadows.

But when I glance at booth six, he's gone.

Three men rush past me, brushing my arm, and my world stalls.

That smell.

As I look up, their heads are tucked under flat caps. One of them, wearing leather gloves, is pushing my blackmailer toward the staff exit.

"I'll be back, just need a tinkle," I tell my boss.

I slip through the back door, heart hammering.

The cold air bites my skin.

And there, in the dark alley behind the club, he's got my blackmailer pinned to a brick wall.

A knife glints at his throat.

The guy in the long coat turns his head slowly, blade still in place.

Even in the bad lighting, those pale grey eyes hit me like a bullet.

That smirk.

That fucking smirk.

He presses a finger to his lips to silence me.

I stumble, the door slamming behind me, echoing like a gunshot.

My lungs squeeze tight.

He's going to kill him.

And my boss, my husband, Dr. Quinn, is doing it at my fucking club.

I don't breathe.

I just run.

Straight back into the changing room.

Locking the door and pressing my back to the cold wall.

This can't be real.

This can't be happening.

My boss—or husband, or whatever the hell he is— is about to murder someone on my turf.

And I don't know who the bigger monster is anymore—me or him.

But one question burns in my veins… What the hell does Finn want with the man blackmailing me?

What does he know…

Who is my husband, really?

As my little watcher runs, I carefully make my mark on my next victim's face.

The blade slices clean, and blood trickles down his cheek.

I bite my lip. I could fight him, break his ribs. Take his teeth out one by one, just how my brothers would.

But I prefer mostly to assert power in other ways.

"Shove him in the Range Rover and take him to mine. Don't touch anything. Just tie him up and shut him up."

If he is—as Drago's confident he is—high up within The Preacher's cult, then he ain't going to speak.

They're loyal.

Just like I would be for my brothers.

Our secrets go to the grave.

But I've got something they don't. A specialty.

I'm not just violent. I'm a psychological menace. With one trick up my sleeve not many others have.

Reggie and Rowan nod and haul the bleeding man out like a broken puppet, leaving me behind in the dark. I stalk back toward the club.

The girl from the first night. It was her. I know it.

That red hair.

Sinful curves.

Plump lips that could make a man lose his soul.

Nothing could beat having Stephanie's lips on mine.

But this woman...

There's a pull. A tension. A question.

Who is she?

And what will I have to do to keep her quiet?

She recognized me. And now she's a threat.

I storm through the hallway, each step heavier than the last.

Stopping outside every door, I wait.

Letting my gut choose for me.

And then, I find it. A gold star on the door. A desperate little warning.

The changing room.

I grin as I grip the handle, but it doesn't budge.

Even better.

I scan the corridor.

Empty.

No cameras.

I made sure of that the first time I came here. No one's watching. Of course they aren't. Everyone knows what happens back here, the naughty things that the world doesn't want to believe still goes on.

What these sick bastards make these women do, dangling wads of cash in front of their noses to push them to make choices they don't want to.

A strip club is not a sex club. In Inferno, we have rules. The women know and willingly play. They are trained, consensually, to do so. It isn't about money. It's about desire. About being able to have your wildest fantasies come to life without judgment.

It is not about a drunk perv getting his dick wet with a barely legal girl for fifty bucks. This is why I go after these kinds of scum.

I don't think a lot of people realize the psychological warfare that goes on in a victim's head for the rest of their fuckin' lives.

But I do. I live it. And I will continue to hunt these monsters down in their sleep.

I pull out a safety pin from my coat pocket and work the lock. I swear I can feel the fear bleeding through the wood.

When the door swings open, my breath catches.

She's perched on the table. Her back to me, it's the mirror that does it.

I see her watching me.

Her profile.

Her eyes.

The stuttering rise and fall of her chest.

I know that fucking face. I know that smell. And those lips. My body reacts exactly how I expect it to.

I shut the door behind me and lock it.

The silence fills the room. Yet, she doesn't move, and neither do I.

Fuck this.

I cross the room, eyes never leaving hers.

Every second closer confirms what my blood already knows.

The curve of her jaw.

The freckles across her nose.

The quiver in her breath.

Familiar. Like I'd spent years studying her for this fuckin' moment.

I stop just in front of her just as she turns herself to face me. Without a word, I close my eyes and breathe her in.

That scent. Floral and innocent, yet underneath it's laced with sin.

Something dark and beautiful that's lived in my bones for six years.

I exhale.

A war between anger and lust battles within me.

Then my hand wraps around her throat. Hard. Not to hurt. Just to hold. To confirm it's really her.

My grin spreads slow and sharp across my face. Our eyes lock. Those brown contact lenses can't hide the true blue beauties beneath them.

I slide my hand along her body, every curve committed to memory.

It's almost as if I'm trying to prove myself wrong. That this cannot be my Stephanie.

And then, right there. The spot where I held her yesterday.

My fingers dig in, and her breath catches.

The shoe fits. Or in this case… the hand fits.

Perfectly.

"So, are you going to tell me what my wife is doing in a place like this?" I ask, keeping my voice low.

She licks her lips as I pull her face closer to mine.

Fuck.

The outfit. Her bare skin, begging to be marked. Those long legs wrapped around my neck. As she moves her hand to place it on my chest, I freeze, snatching her wrist to stop and shake my head.

Don't.

Not there.

The tattoos hide the worst of it. But the scars? They run

deeper than my skin. Beneath the ink, I'm still bleeding. Always will be.

Her eyes widen.

I pin her with a glare.

She doesn't know. Can't know. That even now, I'm still waiting to be hurt again.

Before, back in Vegas, I was drunk. Unarmored. I let her touch me because I wasn't really there.

Now? I'm sharp. I'm clear. I'm in control.

And I don't fucking do touching.

She rips her hand back like I just burned her, but I don't release my grip on her throat.

Not yet.

She's fascinating like this.

Caught. Exposed. Still trying to figure out whether to run or submit.

I run my fingers through the fake red hair and slowly pull it off her head, those dark locks in a ponytail beneath. I pull out the hairband and let it fall over her shoulders.

"Here she is," I mutter.

Her breath catches as I lean in, running my tongue along her jaw, her legs inching wider so I can step between them.

Her head tips back.

"W-what were you doing with that guy?"

I dig my fingers into her thigh.

"Did you see me, really?" I whisper.

She brings her chin down, a darkness creeping behind her eyes. A mischievous smirk teasing her plump lips.

"I did. And you know exactly what I want in return for my silence."

My heart kicks. Slams against my ribcage like it's trying to break out of my chest.

I've never wanted someone this badly.

Not like this.

Not where it hurts.

It's not just sex. It's the fire in her eyes. The challenge. The sharp tongue and brutal wit. The way she fights me without ever actually walking away.

The teasing. The competition. The craving to win her over and destroy her in the same breath.

She's chaos.

And I'm addicted.

On that hospital roof, I let her see it. Just for a second. A flicker of the real me.

I thought it was enough to shake her. Thought maybe she'd finally understand what this is.

An obsession.

A sickness.

But I was wrong.

She still thinks this is a game.

Still thinks she has the upper hand.

I shake my head, the urge to kiss her warring with the need to tear her down.

No.

Not yet.

I've got more work to do.

Clearly.

CHAPTER 30
STEPHANIE

Song- Closer, Kings of Leon.

His hand finally drops from my throat, but the imprint remains. I need more. I've always craved it but never found it.

Everything about him seeps into my dark heart. The way his breath scorched my skin. The way his body boxed me in. The way my thighs trembled around his hips like I belonged there.

I don't.

I won't ever.

He's a disease I should've cut out the second he infected my life. But instead, I married the fucking virus. And now, I want him to ruin every inch of me.

I shove him back and straighten my spine, ignoring the ache between my legs.

"Annul it."

My voice doesn't shake, but my insides are glass. Close to cracking.

He lifts an eyebrow, like I just told him to amputate a limb.

"No."

"Finn," I warn.

He leans in, his palm flattening on the table beside me. "Dance for your divorce. Strip to get your name back."

I blink.

"What?"

"That's the deal, temptress." His voice is low. "You want your freedom? You'll have to earn it. You'll put on a show. For me. Right here. Right now."

The air disappears from my lungs.

My skin burns, not from shame, but from something far more dangerous.

Lust.

This man drives me insane. Makes me feel more alive in five seconds of rage than I've felt in years of medicine.

But I won't give him what he wants.

I swing my legs to the side of the table and hop down, standing chest-to-chest with him in my gigantic heels.

"You think everything is a game, don't you?" I spit. "Marriage. Love. People. Work."

He smirks, teeth flashing like a fucking wolf. "How is it a game when I've already won?"

I shake my head, fury swirling in my throat like acid.

"You haven't won, Finn."

He leans down until his lips ghost my ear.

"Then prove it. Walk away without giving me what I want. Go on, love. Or should I call you Angel here?"

I can't move.

Because deep down, I know I'd rather strip for him than give him the satisfaction of seeing me run.

His palm brushes my waist, and I flinch, not from fear. From the electric, all-consuming obsession between us.

"I like the name choice, but I suppose even the worst of us could be fallen angels," he mutters.

"You came up straight from hell, Dr. Quinn," I whisper.

He chuckles darkly.

"How do you know? Were you holding my hand on the way up?"

I scoff. But he's probably not far from the truth. Is that why I crave him?

Even as I want him gone.

Even as I want my name back.

Even as I want to forget what his hands feel like on my skin.

He pulls back, eyes dragging over my body, slow and possessive. "Clock's ticking, Mrs. Quinn. Want that annulment? Let me see what's mine."

I hate him.

But more than that?

I hate the part of me that's already reaching for the back of my bra.

CHAPTER 31

FINN

She doesn't move at first.

Just stands there glaring at me like I've grown a second head. Like the mere suggestion of her baring herself to me is the most offensive thing I could've said.

But I see the flicker.

The way her pupils flare.

The way her breath catches.

She wants this.

Even if she doesn't want to want it.

Even if it kills her pride.

Good.

We're both dying slowly anyway.

I cross my arms, lean back against the wall, and nod to the space in front of me.

"Go on then. Show me how much you hate being my wife." There's an evil mocking to my tone.

Her fingers twitch at her sides. Rage burns behind her eyes, but that's not all.

She's stalling, trying to convince herself this doesn't affect her.

She fails.

When her bra undoes, she holds it against her breasts; I feel the desire like a pulse in my cock. Her gaze flicks to mine, like she's daring me to blink.

I don't.

I want to see every fucking second of this.

"Fucking beautiful," I murmur, almost to myself.

Her lips purse. She's trying to make this clinical. Rob it of power.

Too bad.

She can strip me of everything but control.

"Next," I rasp.

God, I've never wanted someone to fail so badly.

To break.

To beg.

Because if she does, I'll own her.

"You're halfway there, temptress."

I'm pushing her, wanting her to spiral into insanity with me.

"Take off the bra," I press.

She tosses it to the floor like it means nothing. Her nipples harden instantly, and I almost groan. My mouth fucking waters.

I step forward until I'm in front of her again.

Her breath hitches when I raise a single finger and drag it up her bare stomach, between her breasts, tracing that beautiful snake ink.

And finally to her throat.

I don't squeeze this time.

I don't have to.

She's already mine. It's like she knows what I need, how she has to submit to me eventually. Because this isn't about if or when; it's inevitable.

"I asked you to strip for your divorce," I whisper, brushing my lips against her temple. "Not because I wanted a show."

Her breath shudders out. "Then what the hell do you want?"

I smirk, but my voice is hoarse when I speak. I can't hide my desire. My want.

"I wanted to see how much pride you'd sacrifice… just to walk away from me."

I back away slowly, letting my eyes rake over her once more.

And I see it. Clear as day.

She doesn't want to walk away at all.

Not yet.

Not when she's burning.

Not when we both are. And I don't think I have it in me for her to turn her back on me again. I'm too far gone.

This is a fucking nightmare, against everything I've built to protect myself from harm.

She's crumbling it, second by second.

And I'm allowing it.

She doesn't say a word.

Just stares me down with that sharp, wicked glint in her eye, the one that says she's done letting me hold the reins.

Good.

Let's see what she does with them. Because there ain't a chance in hell she will have them for long.

Her chin lifts as she stalks toward me, still in nothing but her black lace panties. I don't move. Don't breathe. Every nerve in my body is strung tight.

Her fingers graze up the lapels of my grey jacket. She doesn't touch my chest. She's a good girl, listening to my earlier warnings.

She pushes the coat off my shoulders and lets it fall to the ground; it's like she's just tossed another piece of my armor off.

Then she shoves me hard.

I drop into the chair behind me with a grunt, the wood creaking beneath my weight, and before I can even open my mouth, she straddles me.

Fuck.

Heat surges through me, my cock straining, already ready to tear through my slacks. She isn't touching me yet, not properly, but her bare skin hovers just above mine, her breath ghosting over my cheek.

"I'll strip for my divorce," she purrs, "and you be a good husband and watch."

I smirk, even as my pulse hammers. "You think this'll get you out of it?"

"No," she whispers. "I think it'll shut you up for a minute or two though."

Then she starts to move.

Not with hesitation.

With fire.

Her hips roll in perfect rhythm, pure fucking sin that I cannot resist. She trails her fingers through her hair, down her sides, over the soft swell of her breasts as she rocks over me.

It's not just a dance.

It's a threat. A warning. A weapon.

She's marking me, without even touching skin to skin.

And still, I can't bring myself to stop her.

My hands grip the edge of the chair. White-knuckled. Holding myself back, but only just.

"You think this makes you the one in control?" I ask, breathless.

She leans down, her breasts brushing my shirt, her lips at my ear.

"No. I think it makes you obsessed."

She's not wrong.

I should push her off me. Remind her who the fuck I am. Remind her that no one, not even my wife, gets to pull strings on me.

But instead...

I watch.

I admire as she grinds on me, rolling her hips. Her mouth parted. Her hands dragging down her own body like she doesn't even need me, like she's enough for herself. And she is.

She's fucking magnificent in her own right.

It's infuriating. Addictive. Beautiful.

And she has no idea what she's just unleashed.

I grip her thighs hard and drag her forward, pressing her down on my cock that's still painfully trapped behind my zipper.

She gasps, her nails biting into my shoulders.

She can feel how hard I am for her. I want her to know how fucking crazed she makes me, more than anyone else ever has in the world.

"You want to dance, wife?" I growl. "Then fucking dance."

She moves again, slower now, her pussy grinding against my restraint.

But I'm done watching.

"Fuck it," I mutter, not being able to take one second longer of this torture.

I've just found my weakness.

I reach up, grab the back of her neck, and yank her mouth to mine.

And everything ignites.

CHAPTER 32

STEPHANIE

The kiss is everything I never knew I needed.

He leads, I submit. With his hand around my throat, his cock pressing against my pussy as I grind against him.

I want to touch him, to take some control back, but I don't. Because I know the second I do, I'll break the spell.

And I should, because this isn't right.

Married or not, he is not mine. And I am not his.

But right now, it feels like we belong to no one but this moment. His fingers trail along my thigh, and I shiver.

"I knew my wife wanted me," he whispers against my lips.

Then he bites down—hard enough to draw blood.

"Ouch. Fuck." I pull back and wipe the warm liquid from my lip.

He shakes his head, swiping the blood away with the tip of his finger.

My stomach flips.

My mouth drops open as he sucks it clean.

Shit. That was so wrong—and so hot. His hand cups my

aching pussy. Just a light touch, but it's enough to make me almost jump off his lap.

"Did you like that, hmm? A little bit of pain?" he asks, tilting his head, studying me.

"Yes," I breathe.

His fingers slip under my panties, and then he rips them clean off.

"Atta girl."

He grips my throat and thrusts two fingers inside me, making me cry out.

"F-Finn," I moan.

He doesn't let up. There's no teasing build. No slow seduction. Just—intensity.

"Already trembling for me. I fucking knew it."

The sound of my wetness echoes between us.

"I want you to bleed for me, temptress. But before I can do that, I need to break you in. Make you all fuckin' mine. Is that what you want?" he rasps.

I nod, breathless, already ruined for anyone else.

When his thumb presses down on my clit, I jump and moan at the same time.

"You really are sensitive," he says, almost with concern.

He pulls my face to his, stilling his fingers inside me, his eyes locked on mine.

"Fuck. Please tell me you aren't a virgin. I don't have it in me to be gentle with you," he says.

I can't help but giggle.

"You think I'd be brave enough to sit on your lap if I was? No. I was just… surprised," I tell him.

He frowns.

"By?"

I can't find the words right now, my head is fried.

"This is pretty simple stuff you're doing. We haven't even gotten anywhere near the interesting part yet," he continues.

A thrill shoots up my spine.

"Interesting?" I ask.

He smirks.

"All in good time. I don't wanna scare you off just yet."

My mouth drops open just imagining what he could do to me.

"Now, what was surprising about being finger-fucked and choked?" he asks, genuinely curious.

I shake my head with a small smile.

"No. When you pressed down on my clit. You didn't even search for it. You just... knew where it was."

He blinks at me.

"Stephanie… serious question. How many brain cells did your past lovers have? And why couldn't they find the clit? What the fuck were they aiming for?"

I shrug.

"Fuck knows. But I've never had a clit-stimulated orgasm from a man before."

A slow, deadly smile spreads across his lips.

"Never? Fucking hell. You shouldn't have told me that, because I'm about to come in my boxers."

I bite my lip and shake my head. I like that I can make him lose control too.

"Are you accepting this challenge, Dr. Quinn?" I playfully ask him.

His fingers begin to move again, and I lean down to kiss him.

I want to worship him for what he's doing to me. For what he might be capable of.

I want him to feel what he does to me.

"Easy."

I let out a squeal as he lifts me in his arms, then lowers me into the wooden chair.

"Legs open," he says, towering above me.

He slowly unbuttons his shirt, just enough to reveal more tattoos sprawling across his chest. Then he rolls up his sleeves, veins popping. Christ, he's gorgeous.

My heart pounds. My body is burning for him.

Looking around the room, he steps away, only to return with two black and gold belts.

Without a word, he places my arms on the rests and ties them tight.

Then, he drops to his knees in front of me.

And that's when my pulse nearly stops.

My boss. My husband. The man who makes me feel more alive than I've ever felt, on his knees, for me.

Not to propose.

Not to beg.

But to devour.

I never, ever, in a million years, thought I'd have him like this.

Let alone to eat me out in a fucking strip club.

Yet here I am, legs spread, waiting for my husband to put his mouth on me.

And for once in my life, I'm not afraid of being seen. I'm afraid of how good he's going to make it feel.

CHAPTER 33

FINN

Song- The Offering, Sleep Token.

She's strapped to the chair like a fucking offering. Arms restrained. Chest rising in shallow, needy breaths. Her thighs spread wide for me.

I should be ashamed of how hard I am just from watching. But shame left me a long time ago, along with mercy.

The belts tighten against her arms, marking her in ways that will linger long after I'm done here.

She thinks I'm going to be gentle. Sweet. Maybe even a little romantic, because I've kissed her. Let her in.

She's wrong.

Because what I'm about to do?

It isn't kindness.

It's ownership.

I drag the chair forward an inch, towards me. On my fucking knees for my wife. Something I never thought I'd do, but somehow, it's now my reality.

I don't touch her yet. I breathe her in. Her scent, sweet

and intoxicating, wraps around my brain and turns every thought into static.

"You're shaking already, temptress," I murmur, stroking a hand up the inside of her thigh, watching her skin pebble beneath my fingers. "And I haven't even used my tongue."

She moans; it's so desperate. Her hips shifting forward, searching for pressure.

She doesn't get to ask. She gets what I decide she's earned.

"You said no one ever found your clit before," I continue, my voice a low growl as I ghost my mouth over her without touching. "They should've been fucking arrested for it."

I glance up. Her mouth is parted, her brows drawn tight, the anticipation killing her. I grin.

Good.

Because I want her to feel this. To burn for it. I want this imprinted on her soul.

So when I finally lower my mouth and flatten my tongue against her clit, she screams.

Her hips jerk, but the restraints keep her locked in place. I drag my tongue again, then suck her clit into my mouth.

Her thighs clamp around my head, and I welcome the pressure. Let her fucking smother me.

If this is how I go out, it'll be worth it.

"You like that?" I murmur against her soaked pussy. "Fuck, you're drenching me."

She nods frantically, her wrists fighting the belts. Her eyes flutter closed, and I slap her thigh, hard.

"Eyes on me."

They snap open, completely wide and wild.

"There you go," I croon, my lips brushing her. "Now come for me, wife. Ride my fucking tongue, and remember exactly who made you feel this way."

I wrap my arms around her thighs and devour her.

Her body shakes. I feel her losing control. Her breath turns to sobs of pleasure. She's right on the edge, and just when I feel her tighten—I stop.

I pull back, mouth soaked, chest heaving. Her cry of frustration cuts through the air like a blade. I stand and bend over her.

"No," she whimpers. "Please, Finn—"

"Don't beg. Not yet," I whisper, gripping her jaw and yanking her face toward mine. "You think you want release, but you don't. Your body is demanding to submit. You want me to give it to you. And I will. But on my terms. Not yours."

Her eyes fill with tears again. My fingers slide down and tap her clit softly, just enough to make her squirm.

"That's what you are, isn't it?" I murmur against her cheek. "A little desperate slut for me, who gets wet for praise and cries when it's taken away."

She nods, eyes hooded, lips trembling.

"Say it. Who do you belong to now?"

"You."

She doesn't hesitate.

"Damn right, you do."

I shoot her one last look over my shoulder as I untie her wrists.

Then I lean in close, relishing in her desperation for me.

"Next time you want your orgasm, temptress... you better earn it."

And then I leave.

Because I know the ache I've left in her will keep her burning for me.

Exactly the way I want.

I've given her a taste, and if it's meant to be, if the obsession goes both ways, she will run right back to me.

But right now, I have another form of torture to dish out. It's time to see if I can get some answers about The Preacher.

CHAPTER 34

STEPHANIE

Two hours later and my body is still on fire.

I need release, and it turns out, to do that, I need a doctor. Specifically, Dr. Quinn.

But he turned his back on me and walked out.

Shoving on my clothes, I grab my bag and throw on a cap. With my head down, I make my way to the exit.

A shiver runs down my spine as I fast-walk toward my car, tucked away at the far end of the staff lot.

I toss my bag into the passenger seat and slide behind the wheel.

Before I turn the key, I check my phone.

Nothing interesting.

I don't know why I expected something from Finn.

It's not as if that was anything to him other than a damn game.

Shaking my head, I start the car.

But as the engine turns over, headlights flash on across from me.

My heart kicks.

Palms slick with sweat.

After the whole blackmailing saga, I'm always on edge.

Even though I saw what happened to him, I have no idea if Finn let him go.

If that was just a warning.

It's not as if my boss would actually kidnap a man.

Right?

It's so dark I can't even make out what car it is.

Grabbing my phone, I tap his name.

Dr. Quinn.

I might regret this later—but right now, it's better to be safe.

He answers on the first ring, his deep voice filling my car —and making my thighs clench.

"Hello, love."

"Don't call me that," I snap.

He chuckles. Of course he does, which just tightens the knot of irritation in my chest.

"Look, I didn't know who else to call, okay?"

"What's the matter?"

There's concern in his voice, and that eases my anxiety. He makes me feel safe.

"There's someone in the parking lot. At the club," I whisper.

The lights flash in front of me.

My breath catches.

"Flash back, temptress. Don't ignore me."

I scowl.

"What the fuck? You scared the shit out of me!"

"I'm sorry," he says, and for once, it sounds sincere.

"Why are you even still here? You got what you wanted from me."

"Oh, you think I'm done with you? A very bad observation there, wife."

I roll my eyes.

"Well, why are you here?"

"To make sure you get home safely."

My heart picks up speed.

"I don't need babysitting. I'm perfectly capable of making it home."

He sighs.

"And that's why you called me thinking you had a stalker from the club, isn't it? These places aren't safe, love."

He's got me there.

"Fine. Well, as you can see, I got in my car safely. You may go now, bodyguard," I huff.

He chuckles again—and my chest squeezes in a way I don't understand. Or maybe I do.

"I'll follow you home. Watch you get in. Then my job is done. No arguments, please."

Part of me—the independent, abandoned part—wants to tell him to fuck off.

But the other piece?

The piece that's tired.

Tired of fighting. Tired of looking over her shoulder. Tired of doing everything alone.

That piece wants to let him stay.

That piece wants to be protected. I hug myself.

"Thank you, Finn," I say, and cut the call.

I KICK the door shut behind me, dropping my bag in the hallway. The house is silent, just how it always is. It's how I enjoy life, being alone. Or so I thought.

At least I know I will never let myself down.

I peel off my jacket and head straight for the kitchen.

No lights on.

Just the soft hum of the fridge and the sound of my own breathing.

I grab the bottle of red I keep for nights like this, the ones where I feel lost. And in this case, edged to the extreme.

Leaning over the counter, I put on some heavy metal on the speakers and sip my wine, staring at the black boxes in front of me. Taunting me.

After I finish my first glass, I lean over and grab one of them.

The ones I swore I wouldn't touch.

Not until the annulment.

Not until I got rid of him.

But I need to see it.

Taking them, with the wine, to the couch, I sit down and place them down beside me. Refusing to open them, because if I do, it might become real. I might start to believe in this twisted fantasy more than I should.

I don't last two minutes before I peel back the lid.

One that screams money, obscene wealth, and dominance.

The other, quieter, but somehow worse.

It's the kind of ring you only give someone when you plan to keep them.

My fingers hesitate; it's like being a kid and trying on your mom's expensive jewelry when she's out, knowing she will scream in your face if she catches you.

I shake away the memory. That's part of the reason I've never wanted relationships. What if I end up like my parents? What if I fuck up my kids worse than they did to me? It could be genetic.

Fuck it.

I slide on the rings and hold my breath as I hold my hand out.

The engagement ring catches the light.

The wedding band settles too easily on my skin.

Like it belongs there.

Like I belong to him.

I take a sip of wine and sink deeper into the couch. I should take them off.

I should laugh at how ridiculous this is.

But I don't.

Instead, I look down at my hand and wonder, what would it be like to have a life with someone?

A husband.

A home.

Maybe even… kids.

Jesus.

I've never let myself think that far ahead.

There was never a finish line for me. Just survival.

Because how do you dream about a white picket fence when your hands are stained with the lives of men who used you?

Men who thought pain was love.

Men who taught me how to take it and, eventually, how to give it back.

I'm not wife material.

I'm not even human some days.

I'm a ghost with a scalpel and a vendetta.

But still—tonight, on that chair, tied down while he looked at me like I was a fucking prize…

I wanted him.

I wanted him to finish what he started.

I wanted his mouth on my skin, his body breaking me open.

Not just physically.

Emotionally.

Completely.

And that's the part that scares me most.

Because I don't just want the sex.

I want him.

The man who sees all my ugly and doesn't run. Even when I tell him to fuck off.

The one who could destroy me with a single word, but instead, whispers "wife" like it's holy.

I down the rest of my wine and pull my knees to my chest, rings still glinting in the low light.

What does it say about me that the first man who ever made me feel safe is the one most capable of ruining me? What does it say that I want him to?

Maybe I am a monster.

But even monsters crave something real.

CHAPTER 35

FINN

Song- Snake Oil, Foals.

Before I even reach my private torture chamber, disguised as a sterile medical suite tucked inside my own mansion, I stop outside her door.

And I smile.

The soft creak of the hinges as I open it feels almost ceremonial. I cross the threshold and lift the hatch on her enclosure. Then I wait.

She'll sense me soon. She always does.

Eight years I've loved her.

From the moment I found her, half-dead, bleeding, and limp from the hands of her abuser. I knew she was mine. She was small then. Frail. But still coiled in defiance. A force even in pain.

And now?

Now she is death incarnate.

A ripple of black scales emerges from the shadows. I don't flinch. Instead, I lift my bare arm and wait as she glides up it, her weight a relief.

Nyx.

She curls around me, claiming nearly every inch of exposed skin from forearm to shoulder, until she settles in her favorite place.

Around my throat.

A warning and a promise.

They say you can't train a snake. That they act on instinct alone.

That might be true.

But Nyx…

Nyx is different.

She doesn't follow orders. This isn't anything that's spoken between us—it's more.

She reads me. Reacts to my heart rate, my body temperature, the current that pulses just beneath the surface of my skin.

It's not obedience.

It's something deeper.

Bonded in silence, she is the living embodiment of everything they fear in me.

I stroke the top of her head with two fingers.

"You ready to have some fun, girl?" I murmur.

When I'm calm, she's calm. When I strike, she coils tighter.

I don't think she'd ever hurt me, unless I deserved it.

And I would accept that, too.

She's not a pet. She's a reflection. A part of me that crawled out of trauma and learned to kill.

And still, I can't stop thinking about Stephanie's tattoo.

A serpent, etched over her skin beautifully.

Does she see what I see in these creatures?

Or is she another Nyx?

Beautiful and deadly.

I exhale slowly and turn from the tank, stepping into the corridor that leads to the room holding Troy Barnes. Who we know now as the logistics coordinator for The Preacher.

The creep from the strip club. Which, potentially, could be where he was getting girls from in our state.

But he is the man who may hold the answers to the questions burning holes in my fucking skull.

What the fuck does his cult want with me?

And how the hell are they trafficking women across state lines without a trace?

I reach the reinforced door and key in the code. The mechanical lock disengages with a hiss.

As I open it, the stench of sweat and piss hits me first. Then the fear.

Troy's chained to the surgical table in the center of the room. Limbs spread, heart pounding so loud I can hear it from here.

Good.

I step inside, letting the door click shut behind me.

"Hello, Troy," I greet him, full of cheer.

A surgeon's smile cuts across my face as our eyes lock.

I flick the overhead light on, and the white walls glow like an operating room.

Nyx shifts around my throat like she can sense the tension bleeding through me.

She always knows. She's part of me, born from the same quiet rage.

I stop in front of Troy and crouch down, my hands hanging loosely between my knees.

"You know," I murmur, "you logistics boys are the real problem. You're not the preachers. Not the pimps. But you make everything run. The girls, the money. The drugs. You grease the wheels of hell and convince yourselves you're not burning."

He tries to smirk. It doesn't quite land.

"Don't think your silence makes you noble," I continue, slowly standing. "It makes you complicit. You let your hands stay clean while the girls bled. But that is about to change."

I circle him. My fingers trail across the tray of tools, not picking one up yet, just letting the sound of metal taunt him.

"You tried to frame me." My voice drops. "A fellow doctor. A healer."

He says nothing. But I can hear his breathing get louder.

I stop behind him, leaning close. "Why me, Barnes?"

Silence.

"Where did you even get my name from?"

Still nothing.

So I let Nyx slither down my arm.

He jerks when he sees her.

"Are you going to ask the name of my snake? It's rude to be so uninterested, Troy."

He shakes his head and I roll my eyes.

"Meet Julius Squeezer," I say with a grin.

He's shaking, and I can't help but laugh as I approach him.

"Not even going to laugh at my jokes? This is disappointing on so many levels."

He opens his mouth but doesn't say a word. I think Nyx has frightened the words right out of his body.

"Her name is Nyx," I say flatly.

"So many men are afraid of her; I can't work out why,"

Nyx curls across my wrist like a ribbon of shadow, her tongue flicking toward him as she tastes his sweat. I lean in.

"She was tortured once, you know. Starved. Pinned to

walls for entertainment. And now?" I lower my voice to a whisper. "Now she chooses who gets to die."

He pulls against the restraints, but they hold.

"You really want to die for The Preacher?" I ask, softer now, almost intimate. "Do you really believe in his cause? Enough to bleed for him?"

Troy finally speaks, voice hoarse.

"I'd die loyal. They saved me. Just get this over with."

They. Perhaps The Preacher isn't simply one man. I let the words hang between us. I look him dead in the eyes and stare. Seeing what I can read. He doesn't look away.

He isn't bluffing.

He isn't going to give me the answers. It's a shame I can't crack open his skull and get to his brain that way.

Then I reach down and roll up his sleeve. The tattoo's there, the PR that Abigail had, inked into his inner forearm. Poorly done. Rushed. Like a brand, not a choice.

"Pity," I whisper, tracing the edge of it with my scalpel, just enough pressure to make him sweat, not scream. "You didn't even get a good artist."

I use some pressure, enough to break the skin.

"I have a very steady hand; I'll do a better job."

He cries out as I slice around the mark, all the way around, and then cut it clean off and dangle it in front of him.

His face turns grey.

"There. Your alignment has gone. You're a free man, no brand. Now tell me what I want to know."

"Fuck. You. Dr. Quinn."

I let out a dark chuckle.

"Fair enough." I shrug.

Running my palm along Nyx's smooth scales, I give her the permission I know she's been waiting for. "Go on, girl."

Nyx slowly winds her way down his shoulder, across his chest. Her black eyes meet his.

And he cracks, just a little.

"Preacher... said you were too close. Too curious," Troy pants, voice breaking. "Said you needed to be stopped in your tracks. It was meant to be a warning shot, not a war. We didn't know you'd fight back."

I stare at him. "You should have."

Nyx curls tighter around him, squeezing just enough for him to gasp. I don't stop her. She never goes further than I want her to. That's our agreement. Our bond.

"How did you frame me? Who hacked my hospital systems?" I press.

My anger starts to rise, and Nyx curls tighter.

When I finally step back, he's trembling.

"That is all I will tell you. My loyalty earns my place in heaven. I can't."

I let out a laugh deep from my belly.

They really do brainwash these people.

"Loyal even in death?" I echo.

Troy nods.

So I look him in the eye and deliver my final diagnosis. I have his cell to hack. I have confirmation it was them after me specifically.

And I know a war is coming, but they didn't expect us to have a force.

And they haven't even seen half of our reach across the world yet.

"Then die for him," I whisper.

And I step back.

Nyx obeys.

Her body coils. Her muscles flex. And his breath leaves

his lungs in a silent, gurgled prayer to a god that isn't listening.

Troy Barnes dies for the cause that will never remember his name.

And I leave the room with blood on my hands, a snake on my throat, and war pounding in my chest.

CHAPTER 36

STEPHANIE

I somehow, by some miracle, managed to avoid Finn today. Or perhaps, he was doing the same to me. Things have been weird since I had his face between my legs and he walked out like it meant nothing. And damn it, I haven't been able to stop thinking about him since.

And then he followed me home to make sure I was safe. For a few minutes, it felt like more than just a power play for a divorce. It felt comforting. It felt like I wasn't fighting on my own anymore.

I'm now far too close to him, and with the weight of what I did still pressing down on my shoulders, I haven't been remotely interested in killing again. Which is probably a good thing. So as I knock on Paulie's office door at the club, it feels like shedding a skin. But I'm also dreading his wrath. Owners of places like this are known for their violent tendencies. And maybe, just maybe, I've got one last kill in me before I give it up for good.

"In!" he barks.

He doesn't look pleased. His beady eyes roam up and

down my body as I shut the door behind me. It's not my night to work, but I had to get this done.

"Yes? What now?" he says, already irritated.

"Paulie, I need to take some time off. Maybe quite a while."

He scratches his stubble, narrowing his eyes.

"So you're quitting?"

I chew on my bottom lip. "Not exactly. I was hoping you might keep my spot open until I'm ready to come back."

His gaze lingers too long on my chest before he leans back in his chair with a grunt. "You think you're good enough to just hold a space open for?"

I step forward and plant my hands firmly on his desk. "Yes. And you know damn well I am. I bring in a fuck-ton of cash and never cause any drama. So yeah, I think I've earned the right to keep a spot."

What I don't say is that I need a safety net. A cover. A way back in if the itch starts crawling again. If I need to find another target. If my life collapses, which it tends to do with brutal accuracy.

Paulie grins, exposing yellowed gums and a missing tooth. "You owe me."

I cross my arms. "Owe you how?"

"Work tonight and give me all of your takings. Make me more than five grand, and it's a deal."

I swallow the lump rising in my throat. It's a Thursday. The money's never great. Five grand is steep. And I'm exhausted.

"Fine. Done."

We shake hands, and I instantly regret the contact. I want to dunk my arm in bleach.

As I walk toward the changing room, I pass the back door

to the bar and freeze. A familiar Irish accent cuts through the air like a blade.

Peering through the narrow gap, my stomach lurches.

There he is.

Finn. Laughing with his friends. Leaning against the bar with a whiskey in hand like he owns the place. I should've known today had gone too smoothly.

What is he doing here again? I know for a fact he's not a regular. He's here hoping to see me?

By the time I get changed, I decide to leave my snake tattoo on show. What's the point in hiding now? He knows.

When I walk into the main room, his cold eyes are already on me. For some reason, they heat me up.

Another dancer is on stage, so I scan the booths, pretending I don't notice his stare. But I do. I always do.

He's seated with three men, all big, inked, and basking in attention. But it's Finn who makes my stomach twist. One of the girls runs her hand across his shoulder, and he flinches. Subtle. Barely there. But I see it.

And he quietly removes her touch without anyone else noticing.

She leans in, whispers something, and then he smirks. My jaw tightens in response.

A slow burn creeps beneath my skin as another girl drapes herself in front of him, her ass waving in his face. He doesn't stop her. He bites his lip and winks, but right at me.

My vision blurs with rage. He wants a reaction.

Fine.

I scan the room and zero in on a bachelor party nearby. Loud, drunk, and ripe for tips. Perfect. I strut toward them and instantly draw their attention.

"Right, boys. Who's first?" I purr.

They point to the guy at the end, who licks his lips. "Turn around, gorgeous. Let me see that ass."

I fake a sultry smile and do as he says, sliding my hands down my sides.

Out of the corner of my eye, I catch Finn watching. He's not even pretending to enjoy the girl dancing on him. His hands are still on his thighs. He's like a coiled snake ready to attack.

I step between the guy's legs. "Well? Did I pass your test?"

He groans. "Fuck, yeah. Dance for me, whore."

I swallow the bile rising in my throat and push through it, swaying to the beat, hair whipping over my shoulder. There's only one man who can call me that.

"How much for a private room?" he asks.

"I don't do that."

"Everyone's got a price."

"And mine's not for sale."

"Then I'm not paying," he snaps.

"That dance was a hundred bucks, sir," I say politely.

"Take the bra off, then maybe."

I straighten up, forcing sweetness into my voice. "That's not how it works. One hundred. Now."

He stands, like he's reaching for his wallet, but then he grabs my wrist, yanking me forward. His nose almost touches mine, his voice venom-laced.

His fingers trail over my breasts as he shoves a white card in my bra.

"Private room. Now. Don't make a scene. You'll earn your money. Maybe even a tip. And there's my card if you want a big payout later."

I don't hesitate. I lift my heel and slam it into his shin. "No means no, asshole."

Before I can spin away, I slam into something hard. Then a hand is on my waist. The touch doesn't burn, no, it simmers. Like it's meant to be there.

Finn.

"If you'll excuse me for a second, love," he murmurs, his lips brushing the top of my head. "I need to speak to this stupid fucking man. Don't leave this room."

He steps forward, and my heart stutters when I see the gun in his hand, discreetly pressed into the guy's ribs.

"Doors behind you. Now," he says.

No one else in the club notices. No drama. No spectacle. Just Finn Quinn, cold as hell, and completely in control.

And I've never been more terrified or more turned on.

I discreetly trail behind them as Finn shoves the guy into the night, his silhouette sharp beneath the glow of the flickering streetlight.

This seems to be a pattern—me sneaking off to watch my husband beat men senseless. But this time, there's no blade gleaming in his grip. His weapon of choice tonight is his gun, pressed dangerously under the guy's chin.

I'm too far away to hear the words, but I don't need to. The look on the guy's face is all I need to see; he's terrified. Utterly rattled. The kind of fear that seeps into your bones and makes you question every decision that led you to this moment.

I linger at the edge of the alley, watching Finn with a twisted sense of awe. The man isn't some reckless brute. He's calculated. Composed. He doesn't just throw punches; he makes sure you never forget why they landed. Maybe this creep will think twice before threatening another woman again.

But just as I'm about to turn back, the guy does something truly stupid. He swings.

My breath catches in my throat.

Finn doesn't even flinch. He ducks like he's done it a hundred times before, because he probably has, and in that instant, everything shifts. The ice in his expression melts into fire.

His fist cracks against the man's jaw with a sickening thud, and before the guy can even register what's happened, Finn has him by the collar, slamming his skull against the brick wall. The sound echoes down the alley like a warning shot.

And then the man is on the ground choking, and Finn's boot comes down hard on his throat.

"Cunts like you deserve to die."

He spits in the guy's face like it's nothing. No hesitation. No remorse. Just raw, seething dominance.

The man claws at Finn's leg in desperation, and it only earns him a cold laugh. A sound so devoid of humor, it sends shivers through me.

"Pathetic."

Finn eases the pressure, his boot lifting just enough for the man to gasp for air, but the reprieve is fleeting. The gun returns, pressed to his temple this time, and Finn leans in, his voice low and lethal.

I can't tear my eyes away. Do I want him to shoot him? Will that make me feel better about what I do to men like him?

Are me and Finn the same? That's why I'm so drawn to him?

"If you step foot in any club, anywhere in this state, I'll put a bullet between your eyes."

My pulse pounds so hard I can feel it in my ears. My lungs don't remember how to breathe.

And then Finn turns and walks straight toward me, calm as anything, like he didn't just flirt with murder.

I dust off my shirt and close the distance between us.

"You can't just go around attacking people in public places, Dr. Quinn. It's very unprofessional. Imagine if I told the board."

She crosses her arms over her chest, pushing up those full breasts I'm dying to bite. One final step and she's backed into the wall. I press my hand just above her head, inhaling the faint scent of sweat and sweetness clinging to her skin.

I came here on a whim. She didn't speak to me at work, and I had a sneaky suspicion she'd run here after her shift. I think this place is a relief of some sort for her.

"Go ahead," I murmur. "I'll follow up with my own report, temptress. I'm sure they'd love to hear about your extracurriculars. Cardiac surgeon by day, stripper by night."

She inhales sharply.

Too easy.

I tuck a stray strand of her wig behind her ear. "Nothing to say, love?"

Seeing her dance for another man nearly shattered my restraint. I hated it. Hated how much I wanted to rip him away from her. I grab her left hand and find it bare. No ring. Again.

"Keep going out without them, and I'll tattoo them on you," I mutter.

Her eyes narrow into slits. "Don't be a creep. This wedding thing—it isn't real."

She tips her chin up, all defiant. But all it does is bring her closer. Lips nearly brushing. Tempting. So fucking tempting. I know she's still aching for me. Still throbbing from what I didn't finish.

"It is very fucking real, love. Now, I suggest you go straight to Paulie and hand in your resignation. Because my wife doesn't strip. And as your boss, I need you sharp on shift."

That last part isn't the truth. She's flawless at her job. But I don't care. I just don't want any other man seeing what's mine.

I drag my fingers along her tattoo. Maybe it's time she met Nyx. I wonder how she'd react.

"You think I'd quit just for you? You have no power over me."

I nod, breathing in as her hands press against my chest. I brace for recoil. For disgust. But it doesn't come. Her touch calms something in me, and that's what makes it dangerous.

I grab her wrists and lift them above her head, pinning them to the wall.

"You say that like it's a bad thing. You'd be surprised how freeing it is to submit to me. The places I could take you... the things I could make you feel. You give me control, and I'll give you the world. You've already had a little taste."

I tsk, nudging her thighs apart with my own. Her breath stutters. Her chest rises and falls like she's already begging.

"But you're too damn stubborn to see it now, aren't you?"

She licks her lips, and I nearly groan.

"It would be terrible," she breathes.

I dip closer. She tilts her neck for me, and I drag my tongue along her throat.

"So terrible," I whisper, my free hand roaming over her curves.

She parts her legs wider as I hover my mouth over hers. But I don't kiss her. I let the tension simmer.

My hand stops at her panties.

"If I find out you're wet right now, I'll know you're lying. And I don't like liars. One chance, temptress; would it really be so bad to submit to me?"

I pull back slightly, watching. Her pupils dilate. Her lips part.

I slide my fingers beneath the lace. She gasps.

"Fine," she huffs. "I don't think it would be bad. I know it wouldn't."

I grin, cupping her, circling her clit, already soaked.

"Fuck, temptress."

I press one finger into her. "Are you going to be a good girl and quit working here?"

"I—I... fuck. Finn. More."

I growl. "You are not in control. Answer, and I'll give you what you want."

"I already quit. This is my last night. But I need to make five thousand for Paulie before close."

I thrust three fingers deep. Her moan breaks in the back of her throat.

"Done. I'll get it for you. Consider this your resignation bonus."

She squeezes her eyes shut. I curl my fingers inside her, stroking her G-spot until my palm is drenched.

"We could have so much fucking fun, Stephanie. If you'd just stop pretending."

Her eyes snap open.

"This isn't anything," she mutters, but even she doesn't believe it.

I keep going. "Really?"

She moans louder.

"Nothing?" I press, setting a merciless pace.

It's almost amusing how her brain is telling her one thing, yet her body is completely deceiving her. Her body is mine.

"I want to hear you moaning my name. Scream it, and I'll let you come. Right here. In this parking lot. Like the filthy little slut you are."

Her hips rock against my hand. I press my thumb to her clit.

"Finn—"

It slices through me. Her voice. My name.

"Louder."

She trembles, panting, fists clenching like she wants to break free, maybe to run, maybe to stay forever.

"Finn, Finn, Finn—oh my—"

She shouts it as she unravels, and I crash my mouth over hers, swallowing her cries as she comes, her entire body shaking against mine.

Only I get to own the cries of my wife as she comes. *Mine.*

"Not too bad, right?" I ask, pulling back, loosening my grip on her wrists but keeping my fingers buried in her.

She smirks. "Pretty good, I suppose."

I nod. Slowly, I slide my hand out, then grab her jaw and shove my fingers into her mouth until she gags.

"Clean them. Taste how much you hate being my wife."

She bites, but not hard enough. Pain only makes me

harder for her. There's nothing I want more than for her to draw blood from me.

She sucks until I pull away. I reach into my pocket and pull out a wad of cash.

"Here. Freedom's yours. Well earned."

She rolls her eyes and reaches for it. I yank it back and wrap my hand around her throat.

"Say thank you, Finn."

Her nostrils flare.

"Say it."

"Thank you, husband." She smiles through her teeth.

"Good girl."

I press the money to her chest and step back. She just stands there, not moving.

"I'll see you later."

She blinks like a deer in headlights.

"Cool. Bye." She rushes out her words.

She shoves past me, hips swaying like a goddamn challenge. I watch her disappear back into the club.

She has no idea I'll be waiting.

I let her think she's in control now. Let her believe this was her choice.

She'll learn soon enough what belonging to me really means.

But first, I've got to check on the twins and Drago.

And hope to hell one of them didn't light the place on fire in the twenty minutes I've been gone.

CHAPTER 38

STEPHANIE

I have this funny feeling this isn't the end of my encounter with Finn tonight.

But I don't know how much more my body, my mind… or maybe even my heart can take.

He destroys my resolve.

Breaks down the walls I've spent years constructing since I was twelve years old.

If I'm not careful, he'll find my weakness. He'll peel me open and take it.

So, I do what I always do. I go back out there. I dance on stage.

And I watch him with his friends, pretending he's not watching me just as hard.

I have my money; there's no need for me to keep dancing. I'm doing it for him. And I get a thrill out of it, making him squirm in his seat.

Every time I make eye contact, it burns. I can still feel his touch. The way he commands me.

The music blares, yet all I can hear is him calling me temptress.

This is for my husband. Revenge for not giving me what I need.

And once I'm done, I wink right at him and blow him a kiss. Almost dedicating that dance to him. His face remains still, while his friends all whistle. Check. Mate.

Before the night ends, I dash back to the dressing room, change out of the costume, pull on my leggings and black tank, and shove everything into my purse. I race down the hallway and straight into Paulie's office.

He's in his usual spot, cigar burning low between his fingers.

Groaning.

Oh no.

There's a woman under the desk. Fucking hell.

"Out!" he shouts, not even glancing up.

I hold up the cash. "Your money."

He squeezes his eyes shut and moans again.

Disgusting.

I wonder how much money he waved in that poor girl's face to do that.

I make a run for it, slam the cash down on the corner of his desk, ignore the slurping sound beneath, and escape at record speed, clutching my purse like it's a lifeline.

Once I'm outside, I gulp in the cool air.

His Mercedes is easy to spot. Parked way too cockily under the streetlight.

And… I can't feel him behind me.

Good.

I slip the flip knife from my bag and stab it clean into the front passenger-side tire. It hisses, spitting air like it's screaming for help.

I smile. A twisted thrill zips down my spine. It feels good

being bad. Maybe I could lower the severity of my crimes from now on.

I cross over to the back wheel and jam the blade in again.

Then, I move to the front driver's side.

The second the knife sinks in, a hand wraps around the back of my neck.

And I'm slammed down, face first, onto the hood.

"Fuck," I hiss, cheek pressed to the warm metal.

"Fuck, indeed," Finn growls behind me.

His grip is punishing.

Dominating.

Fucking perfect.

He presses into me from behind. His hard chest, thick thighs, and the bulge of his cock resting right against my ass like a silent threat.

"You little fucking menace," he rasps in my ear. "Three tires?"

"I was going for four," I pant. "I don't like odd numbers."

He chuckles darkly. He's not amused. Not even close.

It's the sound of someone losing his last shred of patience. With me.

He drags the flat of his palm down my spine until he reaches my waistband and dips his hand under, digging his fingers into my ass, which drags a gasp from my lips.

"Why are you trying to cause problems for me, love?"

"I don't recall signing a non-destruction clause."

He laughs again. This one deeper, darker. Meaner.

His hand snakes under my top, his palm against my bare stomach. I shiver beneath him.

"You get off on testing me, don't you?" he whispers, lips brushing the shell of my ear. "You want me to lose it. You want to be punished. That's why you went back in and danced, right?"

I smile, even as my breath hitches.

"Y-yes. Why did you go back in? To watch other women dance?" I whisper. I can't seem to hide the hurt inside me.

"I went to get my friends, love. No other woman on this Earth interests me. Only you," he growls against my skin.

My ears ring as I squeeze my eyes shut.

"Now, you've got my full attention, and I want to see if you can handle me," he tells me.

In a flash, he grabs the back of my neck again and grinds me harder against the hood. My pulse pounds. My legs shake. I don't fight back because I don't want to.

And maybe, it's about time he had a taste of his own medicine.

"Are you gonna take your belt off, Dr. Quinn?" I taunt. "Or are you too scared someone might see how desperate you are to fuck your stripper wife?"

He groans. It's filthy and primal and entirely feral. Everything I want. He seems to make my control slip; now it's his turn.

"You don't get it, do you?" His hand slides down and cups me between the legs through my pants, his fingers applying just enough pressure to make me squirm. "I don't give a fuck who sees. When I'm near you, nothing else seems to matter anymore."

I blow out a breath. That's how it's always felt for me. Finn consumes me.

His other hand snakes around to my throat, tilting my head back so I'm forced to meet his eyes in the reflection of the windshield.

Christ.

That look.

Predator locked onto prey. So intense I can't look away.

"Want to know what I'd do? I'd keep you over the hood,

tear your panties off, and fuck you until you cry if it meant making you understand—"

He presses harder against my pussy.

"—that you're mine. You are my wife."

My lips part. A soft moan escapes before I can stop it.

"I'm not crying for anyone," I whisper.

"Not yet."

His hand is suddenly gone, and I'm flipped like a ragdoll, my back slamming into the car as he cages me in. One arm above my head, the other at my throat.

His thigh pushes between my legs. His face, too close. His breath, mint and whiskey and a violence I need.

"The more you push me, the harder I drag you closer, temptress."

His lips graze against mine, but he doesn't give me what I want.

No. Of course not.

He lets go of me and stands straight, leaving me panting on his car. He doesn't say a word, just backs away.

This seems to be how our game is going. Almost breaking for each other.

"Where are you going? Don't you want a ride home?" I ask, standing back up.

He chuckles.

"Nah, I'm all good. Check the license plate, temptress," he winks.

Oh fuck.

I slashed someone else's tires.

Paulie will go crazy if he finds out. So I run.

Heading straight for my car, hearing Finn still laughing as I do.

And that's when I see it. His Mercedes, next to mine. Fucking mocking me.

CHAPTER 39

FINN

Tapping my rings on the table in our office inside Inferno, I listen to the clock ticking in the background, wondering what Stephanie is doing today.

She's close; I can almost taste it—so close to becoming mine.

The fact that she quit her job at the club is another confirmation. And what a good girl for doing it before I even suggested it.

The door opens, and I'm met with Enzo's icy blue stare and his pristine, tailored navy suit.

"Mr. Testa," I greet as I stand to shake his hand.

"Dr. Quinn."

He takes the seat opposite me, and I pour him a scotch and myself one of Dad's whiskeys.

Here he is, our king, looking fucking exhausted. He's quieter than usual. Busy plotting world domination still, I assume.

"How can I help you?" I ask.

Normally he deals with Declan. Him being the boss and all. Mine and Enzo's interactions are usually brief and sharp.

There's always been an unspoken agreement between us—we don't particularly like each other.

I see through him.

And he probably sees straight through me.

"Business already?" he grins, thick Italian accent filling the room.

I shrug. "I don't know what else to talk to you about, Enzo. It's not often we're in the same room on our own."

He chews the inside of his cheek. "And for that, I apologize, Finn."

Fuck. Sincerity?

"It's fine. I get it."

He shakes his head. "You're an important member of the organization. It doesn't matter what your personal opinion is of me—but I'd like to change that."

His gaze locks on mine.

"Why do you care?" I ask, sipping my drink.

"Peace making. And I've underestimated your skill. I'd like to build something better."

So, he has a use for me.

"Look, Enzo. Let's not talk in circles. Just be direct. What do you need me to do?"

He grins. "See? Cunning. Smart." He taps his temple.

"So I've been told."

"Nothing—yet. But I am here with a peace offering. The start of our new friendship together."

"Hmm."

I recline in my chair.

"I've spoken to Mikhail Volkov and Frankie Falcone. Both men have agreed to assist you with manpower when you go to end the Bowens in London."

I nod. "What do I owe them in return?"

"Nothing. This is my point. The Quinns, the Volkovs, and

the Falcones are one family. You may be in different states, but you all have the same goal. United, we can take over— not just here. Everywhere. Decadence has given me invaluable knowledge and leads. You brothers are owed this."

I scratch my stubble. Something doesn't sit right. Mikhail never mentioned London when I saw him in Vegas.

"This isn't about London, though, is it?"

He tugs at his collar. "See? Fucking smart. It is—and it isn't. You'll need backup in London. It's a fucking minefield. But I need the three units ready in case another enemy rears his ugly head."

It all clicks.

"The Preacher?"

He stills. Confirmation.

"Yes."

"I take it you found out that I've already landed on his hit list."

He clears his throat. "I know. That's partly why I'm here. I've been tracking the cult for a long time. It's grown steadily but is mainly limited to Ohio, but also with traces to Russia. But they've started coming out of the shadows, getting braver. It's partly why we needed the Decadence games in the first place. I thought eventually the cunt would start to enter women."

"He is," I cut in. "Well—his men are."

Enzo nods. "Yes. But he has men everywhere now. It works differently than us. It's not mafia—it's a fucking religion. And the one at the top? A ghost. But I'm confident by continuing the games—he'll come out of hiding. And then we'll have a real war on our hands."

I drain my drink.

I knew something was off. Always trust my gut.

"We killed his logistics guy."

He runs his tongue along his teeth.

"I know. I don't think we have long before this explodes. We need London dealt with."

"So, I'm bait?" I smirk.

"In a way, yes. But think of it this way—it's the only way to take down the largest, most unknown sex trafficking ring this country's ever seen."

I take a breath. That's the point of Inferno. Of Decadence.

Our chocolate factory is our sweet haven. Yet behind the gates—it's merely an illusion.

A trap. A weapon. A sanctuary for vengeance.

"We have more games planned for next year. The twins will run one together. Then Drago steps up."

"Keep Drago on your side. Don't let him go back to Russia."

I raise a brow. "What exactly was his role in Russia?"

Drago's past is hazy. But he has his hands in everything. He's lived a hell of a life.

"What wasn't it? He's worked for many families over the years. They saw him as an asset—but he wasn't evil enough. He has morals. Lines he won't cross. That backfired. But, if we're right and The Preacher has ties there somehow. We need him and his contacts."

Makes sense.

Which is why he fits here. Another set of fists to keep our families safe.

"So, my plan—take out the Bowens in London as soon as I can. Hopefully within the month. Once that's done, we'll have allies there too. Then yes—we'll help take down The Preacher. All of us."

Enzo raises his glass. "I like this. I'll keep digging on them. We need to move fast and stay quiet. Let's hold off on any more murders. We keep them alive."

"I agree. But they'll never talk. He was spouting crap about going to heaven for keeping silent."

I check the time on my Rolex. Shift starts in an hour.

"There's one more thing."

"Go on."

"This year's games are ready to go. But with London and now The Preacher—I can't run them and handle the murders too. We've got sway in the hospital, but that only lasts so long before people talk."

He swirls the ice in his glass.

"We don't want you burning out, do we?" he says with sarcasm.

"Not really. I'm not superhuman, Enzo. And quitting my real job? Non-negotiable."

I narrow my eyes. He needs to understand. I'm not stepping away from the hospital. Nor Stephanie.

I used to think it was the only thing tethering me to reality.

But maybe it's not the place.

Maybe it's the person.

My fucking wife.

"So what are you suggesting?"

"I delay the games. Just until we're finished in London. The four rooms are ready. Once we're back—I'll set a date."

He scratches his chin.

"And let's face it, we don't want more of The Preacher's men entering women until we figure them out."

He swears in Italian under his breath.

"You're right."

I grin. I know.

"Don't be so smug," he mutters.

The first time we've ever shared a joke.

"So, we have an agreement? We start fresh?" he asks, extending his tattooed hand.

"Yeah. I'll stop imagining killing you in your sleep once a week."

His eyes widen.

I shake his hand firmly.

"Enzo, since we're friends now—gotta say—you look like shit. You need to sleep. Bad for your heart, working like this. And that's one organ you really want functioning."

He rubs his chest. "Doctor's orders?"

"Exactly."

He pulls a packet of cigarettes from his pocket.

"And these? Do they help?"

He offers me one. I take it and light it.

"Yep. Keeps the stress down."

"Good. So I'm doing something right. My heart's made of steel anyway," he mutters. Almost like he didn't mean to say it aloud.

I frown. I thought mine was too.

But lately…

My heart of ice is starting to thaw.

"Enzo, if I have a heart—everyone fucking does."

He nods slowly, dragging on his smoke.

"Maybe."

My stomach flips thinking about seeing Stephanie today. I hate to admit it, but even before I married her, part of the buzz of work was winding her up.

Now? Still that.

But also seeing how horny I can make her.

I need to do something about it soon. Because edging her is starting to bring out something else. Something lethal.

And maybe she'll actually kill me before I get my dick in her.

Before I die, I need to experience her.

It's my life's fucking calling to explore every inch of her kinks.

I've spent years learning everything about her.

Now, my obsession runs deeper than I ever thought it could.

CHAPTER 40
STEPHANIE

Song- Chokehold, Sleep Token

I knock on the door, holding my breath like it might steady the storm inside me. For days, I've been locked in a mental tug-of-war over this decision. Now that the paper is clutched in my hand, I can't tell if it feels right… or like another mistake I'll regret.

"Come in, Mrs. Quinn," Finn calls, his voice smooth and low. The way it slips through the door and slides down my spine makes me shiver.

I smooth my hair, take a breath, and push the door open, like I'm stepping into a lion's den.

He's smiling when our eyes meet, but the moment he spots what I'm holding, that smile curdles into a scowl.

"Mrs. Quinn. How lovely to see you. You're early for work. Came to see your husband before shift?" His voice oozes sarcasm, his tone so cool it burns. "Seeing as you've been avoiding me like the plague for days. Don't think I didn't notice."

He spins in his chair to face me fully, the movement deliberate enough to make me shiver.

My cheeks heat as he rolls up his sleeves. And just like that, my body betrays me. No. Don't get distracted, Stephanie. You didn't come here to swoon. You came here to end this ridiculous farce before it trashes your career completely.

"I have something for you," I say, injecting as much false confidence as I can into the words.

He extends a hand. I step closer, pressing the paper into his palm. My breath catches as he unfolds it, and then—

A deep laugh bursts from his chest. A sound that should never feel that good in my ears.

"An annulment of our marriage due to intoxication," he reads aloud, lips quirking like I just told him a joke.

I nod stiffly.

"Good try." He winks, then tosses the paper into the trash beside his desk like it's nothing.

That look he gives me now is unreadable. It makes my spine straighten. I plant my hands on my hips.

"Sign it, Finn. Please."

He licks his lips slowly. Intentionally. I need him to sign this, because I'm too quickly becoming intoxicated by him, and I'm scared I'll fall. And if he hurts me, I think that will be worse than anything.

"Please sounds so good coming from your lips, love."

And then he's up. Closing the space between us in seconds, backing me into the wall with the kind of energy that makes me forget why I ever thought this was a good idea.

Fuck, he's dangerous when he's like this.

"You want this marriage to be over so bad…" His voice dips as he leans in, the heat of him invading my skin. "…get on your knees and fucking beg me properly."

A sharp gasp slips out of me, and his grin turns smug. He knows exactly which buttons to press. I swear to God, I'm just a game to him. A puzzle of triggers and reactions, and he's memorized the sequence.

And maybe, just maybe, I'm starting to like the way he plays.

Especially when he presses that button. The one deep inside me that only responds to the curl of his fingers.

Do I really want to walk away from that? Without even getting the full Dr. Quinn experience?

I shake my head, trying to banish the heat building inside me. No. Think with your brain, not your pussy, Stephanie.

This is wrong. I shouldn't be married to my boss. Sleeping with him was one thing; being his wife is something else entirely.

He's not built for relationships. And neither am I.

"You don't want me as your wife, Finn," I say coolly, shifting tactics.

He pulls back just enough to let me breathe. But those sharp eyes stay locked on mine.

"Why not? Give me three constructive arguments, and I'll consider it."

"I'm high maintenance. You won't be able to keep up."

He scoffs, already loading his counterattack.

"I'm rich, remember? You've called me fuckin' rich boy for years. Next?"

Shit. Okay.

"We work together."

"I could fire you. But HR already approved our marriage. Next?"

"Jesus Christ, you're impossible. Fine. Last one. I don't fucking like you, Dr. Quinn."

That smug smile spreads across his face again.

"That's a damn lie."

He grips my jaw, forcing me to hold his gaze.

"I tried to slash your tires. I just handed you the papers. I even begged for you to leave me. How does that scream that I like you?"

He's still smiling. Like I'm the most beautiful contradiction he's ever seen. And maybe I am.

"You just also came all over my hand and had me bend you over what you thought was my car. Your point is what exactly?"

I chew the inside of my lip, searching for a comeback, but—

"Do you believe hate and love can't walk the same line, temptress?"

My mouth opens… and closes again.

Fuck. I hate when he has a point.

"You can hate parts of me and love other parts. It's passion, love. And that's what makes you the perfect wife for me."

He drags his thumb across my bottom lip, and I swear, my knees weaken.

"If you really hated me like you claim, you'd have quit your job years ago. You'd have never woken up with a ring on your finger. And you sure as hell wouldn't be standing this close to me right now."

He leans in again, close enough for his words to settle on my skin like heat.

"And you certainly wouldn't be imagining me spanking and cutting you until you pass out as punishment for your little stunt today. But you are, aren't you? You're soaking fucking wet for me."

When he steps back, it's like the oxygen rushes out of my lungs.

He adjusts his tie, the picture of control again, though I know better.

"All three of your points have been deemed invalid. Therefore, your divorce request has been denied. Again."

I blink at him, stunned, as he settles back into his chair like he hasn't just set my entire world on fire.

"Now, are you staying here to let me show you what it really means to be mine? Or are you running back to your office to finger yourself while you think of me? Choice is yours... wife."

That word. Wife. The way he says it with such possessiveness sends a shock through my chest.

"Who said anything about my fingers? Maybe I'll go back to the club and find another dick to use as my personal fuck toy."

I bite down a grin when his temple twitches, his jaw clenches, and that mask of composure starts to slip.

He sucks in a sharp breath. I know that look. He's about to break.

"Come here, Stephanie," he growls, each syllable bitten off like he's trying not to explode.

"I'm not your property. You don't get to order me around. Sign the damn papers," I snap back.

He nods once, licking his lips like he's tasting blood.

"Ever since those rings went on our fingers, I've remained faithful to you. Because our marriage is real to me. I don't let anyone near me like this."

His words land like fists. I wasn't ready for that. For the brutal sincerity of it.

My heart hammers. I clench my fists, trying to anchor myself. He's catching me off guard at every turn, and it's messing with my head.

"But if that's how you want to play this, then checkmate

to you, *Dr. Miller*. There are plenty of willing women I know who'd be more than happy to be in your shoes once I clock off. Have a good day."

Bile rises in my throat. The image of him with someone else feels like a punch to the gut.

I open my mouth, but nothing comes out. I glance at the papers in the trash.

And weirdly… they look like they belong there.

A soft knock startles me, and I step back.

"If you'll excuse me, I have a meeting with Poppy," he says flatly, not even glancing my way.

I nod numbly and move toward the door.

"Sign the papers, Dr. Quinn, and all of this will go away."

He turns then, and for the first time… I see it.

Not anger.

But disappointment. Maybe even heartbreak.

"Am I really that bad?" he asks quietly.

No one gets me like he does. No one challenges me, pushes me, infuriates me, or turns me on like he does.

We've always been fire. And maybe that's why I can't admit the truth.

Because if I do, it means I've already lost.

So I say nothing. I just walk out and slam the door in his face.

"Good luck," I mutter to Poppy as I pass her. Then I storm into my office and slam that door too.

Not even five minutes later, there's a soft knock.

"Come in," I say, my voice flat.

Poppy slips inside, looking like she's seen a ghost.

"What did you say to Dr. Quinn?"

I frown, spinning the wedding ring in my pocket like it might give me the answer.

"Nothing out of the ordinary. Why?"

She shifts on her feet, glancing back toward the hallway.

"Uh… well, it doesn't seem like nothing. There's a hole in the wall that needs fixing now."

I bite the inside of my cheek.

"Sure it wasn't there before?"

This isn't like Finn. Not here. Not at work.

"Nope. Wasn't there this morning. Showed up right after you slammed the door in his face."

I recline in my chair, the war still raging in my chest.

Part of me wants to storm back in there and demand the truth.

The other part? The part still aching from that look on his face?

Wants to run.

"He didn't seem angry," Poppy says quietly. "He seemed… hurt. If I had to guess. But who knows with him."

I nod slowly. Because yeah… that's the same energy I felt too.

He punched a wall because I asked for a divorce?

What the fuck are we doing?

CHAPTER 41

FINN

Song- Out of the Black, Royal Blood.

"Are we going to be back in time for the party tomorrow?" Rowan asks just as the jet lifts from the tarmac, the engines humming like a prelude to violence.

"We have no choice. Unless we want Conan and Declan to take free shots at our faces in the ring." I don't look at him as I speak, eyes fixed ahead.

Twenty-four hours in London.

One day away from Stephanie, just enough time for her to think about what she's done.

I open the CCTV feed on my phone. Drago hacked into the strip club for me because…well, because I asked him to. Because I need to know if my marriage is really over before it even began. I need to know if she shows up. If she makes good on her little threat.

Because if she does… she'll unleash a level of hell she's never seen from me. Not even close.

This is her test. She just doesn't know it yet.

And if she passes?

Then when I return home, she's mine. No more games. No going back.

But right now, I've got business to handle.

Charles Bowen is finally fucking dead. Seventy years old, a bullet through his skull, and now London bleeds because of it.

War has begun. Theo has taken over territory. It's all falling into place.

And we're here to formally seal our alliance. Me, Reggie, and Rowan, flying in quietly to meet with Theo King and his brothers. Once the handshake happens, the deal is done.

Then we bring our army that Enzo promised. Arthur Bowen and the rest of his men won't know what hit them.

Rubbing my hands together, I lean back in my chair, closing my eyes. I need rest. I rarely get it. My nights are usually haunted by things I can't forget, things I'd rather drown in.

But lately? It's not the past keeping me awake.

It's her.

The thoughts I can't kill. The images of what I'd do to her if she gave me her trust. Instead of shoving fucking divorce papers in my face. I still can't believe how seeing that piece of paper hurt me so much.

"Hey, Finn," Rowan says.

I sigh. Of course. I can't get one moment of peace.

"Yes?" I crack one eye open.

"Are you okay?"

I blink at him.

"Yep. All fine over here." I shut my eyes again, but I can feel it—he's not done.

"It's just…" he trails off, unsure.

I sit up slowly and turn to him.

"Spit it out before you choke on it."

"You seem… more. Or less. I don't know. You don't seem like yourself."

My brow furrows. I glance toward Reggie, the one more likely to understand me.

But he doesn't contradict Rowan. That alone tells me everything.

"Have either of you said anything to my brothers?" I ask.

Because they don't need this right now. Their focus should be on their families. Not on me.

"No. We thought we'd talk to you first," Reggie answers.

I nod.

"What makes you think there's something going on with me?"

Reggie scratches his beard. Always thoughtful, always calculating before he speaks.

"You're showing emotions. You don't seem so cold. Something's gotten to you, and I don't think you've even realized it yet, Finn."

I rub my chest without thinking. That ache. Persistent. Unsettling.

Maybe I am sick.

Or maybe—it's her.

"Have either of you ever been obsessed with a woman?" I ask.

They exchange glances before looking back at me.

"We've had relationships, short ones, but nothing to obsess over," Rowan says carefully.

"So the fact I think about this one every waking second… dream of her every night… and have researched her like a goddamn lab subject for almost six years, writing what could practically be a report on her… that's not normal?"

Reggie's eyes widen, horrified. Rowan bursts into laughter.

"No. You're fucking with us," Rowan chuckles, shaking his head.

I stay silent, unmoved.

"Is there something wrong?" I ask, deadpan.

Reggie shifts, scratching the back of his neck.

"That's obsession, yeah, Finn. Does she even know? Have you asked her out?"

I reach into my pocket, pull out my wedding ring, and slip it onto my finger. Then hold it up for them to see.

"I married her," I say flatly.

Reggie chokes on a cough.

"You are fucking joking, right?"

I shake my head once.

"Married. By accident. She's trying to annul it. I won't let her."

The silence that follows stretches long. I hold up my hand with the wedding ring proudly positioned. How have they missed that?

"Fuck, man. I don't even know what to say," Reggie mutters, stunned.

"Have you had sex with her?" Rowan asks.

I raise a brow at him.

"No. I've tasted her. Given her a glimpse of what I crave. She'll fit me perfectly. I'm waiting for her to break and come to me."

"This is fucked up, Finn," Rowan says, almost amused.

"I'm well aware. I forgot to mention—I'm her boss."

Reggie's jaw drops.

"I have no words, Finn. Sounds like you should take

Con's advice and go see a shrink. Before you end up getting killed by another surgeon."

His comment sticks.

"Why would she kill me?"

"To take half your fortune? Do you really know her?"

I scratch at the stubble on my jaw, staring at the floor.

"Yes."

And no.

I didn't know she was a stripper. I guess it's possible she could be hiding more from me.

"I'm not going to a shrink. I'm fine. It'll work itself out."

Reggie nods, but it's clear he doesn't buy a word of it.

"So, you want to stay married to her?" Rowan asks.

"Is this twenty fucking questions, Rowan?" I snap.

He shrugs.

"That was a lot. I just asked if you were okay. Wasn't expecting a damn confession."

I let out a laugh. Dry and unexpected.

Maybe I am changing.

And maybe… that's not such a bad thing.

"Yes. I want to stay married. I have no intention of marrying anyone else."

"Can you fuck anyone else?" Reggie interjects.

"No. Nor can she."

My blood boils just thinking about our last conversation. That look in her eyes.

She won't.

She'll come back to me. Willingly. She always does.

And just like that, the conversation dies. They know not to push further.

So I close my eyes again, settling into the dark, dangerous quiet.

Letting my mind drift back to the only place it wants to be—

My wife.

Laid out beneath me.

Hooked up to monitors.

A scalpel in my hand.

And all the time in the world to explore her.

There's no way in hell I could ever step foot in the club again. Not after what Poppy told me. It's weighed on me all day.

I don't like hurting Finn.

That little white business card sits in the center of my desk like a taunt. I already have the details for my next victim without even needing to go back to the club. He's an idiot threatening me and still ramming his personal details at me.

Mr. John Avery

Avery & Co. Law Firm

The longer I stare at it, the more pathetic it sounds, talk of acquisitions and mergers, all wrapped in a neat font and false prestige. It's almost laughable.

I open my laptop, fingers flying across the keys as I start digging. My skin prickles as I remember the way his hand dragged across my breasts… how tightly he grabbed my wrist.

Finn beating the shit out of him wasn't enough.

Not for the way he looked at me. Not for the way he tried

to coerce me into giving up something that was never his to take.

It wasn't his first time. It won't be his last.

I check the time: 4:30 p.m.

He'll be leaving his office soon.

I could follow him. Sneak into his home. Wait until he's alone.

But if it was his bachelor party that night, there might be a fiancée. Maybe even kids.

Too risky.

I can't afford to get caught. Not now. Not when I've come this far.

I need a release. A distraction. Something to drown out the endless reel of Finn that's been looping in my head like a punishment.

I can't stop thinking about him. It's driving me insane.

I reach for the burner in my drawer, flipping it open and dialing the law firm.

A soft, overly polite voice answers. "Hello, you've reached Avery & Co., how can I help you?"

I hesitate, a breath caught in my chest. Should I stop?

No. I won't.

I clear my throat and slip on the accent like a mask.

"Hey, I was wondering if I could book an appointment with Mr. Avery. I have a multimillion-dollar company interested in a merger, and, honestly, I inherited it. I don't have a clue what I'm doing here. It's kind of an emergency."

I layer in the panic, just enough.

"Oh, sweetie, don't you worry," the woman croons. "James will be able to handle everything for you."

I sniffle lightly, playing my part.

"Thank you. I feel like I'm drowning. The board members don't trust me. But it's my daddy's name on the line here."

"James is actually on calls until five-thirty, but he has a client meeting at the club in town at seven. Would you be able to meet him around six-thirty there? It's informal. He likes to get to know potential clients over drinks."

Of course he does.

"Sure. What's the address?" I ask, already writing it down.

She gives it without hesitation.

"So, six-thirty. Do I need to bring anything? ID? A deposit?"

She giggles.

"No, his first meetings are always casual. If it's a good fit, we'll schedule something more formal later."

I swallow back the sour taste in my throat.

I wonder if his seven o'clock "client" is also a woman.

"Great. Thank you so much."

I hang up, hand trembling as I toss the burner back into the drawer.

I grab the keys to the safe.

I don't have long to disappear into the skin of someone else—long enough to become her. The kind of woman James Avery would lean into without realizing he'd just kissed death.

Inside the safe, I run my fingers along the neat rows of vials and bottles. My collection.

"Something I can hide in a drink," I murmur.

My fingers stop on the small glass ampoule labeled Digoxin.

A naturally occurring poison. A few drops mixed into alcohol, it'll take its time, meddling with the rhythm of his heart, giving him the illusion of illness. By the time he crawls into bed, it may already be too late. Or maybe he won't make it home. Maybe he collapses on the steps.

I don't care how it ends.

Only that it does.

The thought curls through me, warm and sharp, and I smile.

I shouldn't be doing this.

But then again, there's a lot in this life I shouldn't be doing.

I slip on the rings Finn gave me, letting the weight of them settle around my fingers. They complete the look. A panicked Southern trophy wife, desperate for legal help before her husband finds out she nearly destroyed the family business.

But as the metal touches my skin, the heat in my chest changes.

That ache flares.

I haven't seen him in two days.

Not since I pushed him so far he punched a wall.

I don't like his silence.

It feels like the world is tilting without him in it.

Like I'm back to being alone.

I drop into the chair and slide open the bottom drawer of my desk, the hidden one.

Inside are pieces of the past I've carved into dust.

Little trophies. Memories. Remnants of abusers.

Rings. Watches. Buttons.

And next to them, my journal.

Not a place for worries or tears. Not some healing ritual.

No. This is my ledger.

Every name. Every method. Every justification.

If anyone ever found it, it would put me away for life.

But until then, it's my own kind of therapy.

No one comes to this house.

No one sees this room.

And this drawer? Locked tight.

I open to a fresh page.

James Avery.

I begin to write.

The how.

The when.

And most importantly, the why.

Because someone has to protect the women in this world.

And if the system won't do it…

I fucking will.

CHAPTER 43

FINN

As we step into the dingy little pub on the outskirts of London, a thrill runs through me, like the opening crackle of static before a storm.

I pull my flat cap lower, shadowing my face, and make my way through the haze of sweat and spilled beer to the far corner of the bar. Reggie and Rowan fall into step behind me, their movements loose, but their eyes scanning. We're armed. Alert. We trust no one.

Especially not in a place like this.

The bartender clears his throat, barely meeting my eye. "What can I get you?" he asks, tone flat.

I lift my chin just enough. When our gazes lock, he takes a step back.

"Dog and Duck," I say quietly but deliberately.

His mouth twists into a smirk. Recognition flickers in his eyes.

"He'll be right out. Drink while you wait?"

"Whatever you recommend."

He pours three pints of some dark, bitter beer and slides them over. As I reach for my wallet, he lifts a hand.

"On the house."

I nod. "Thanks."

Behind me, I feel the twins shift, tension tightening between their shoulders just before glass shatters against the wall. Raised voices follow. A scuffle is brewing. But I don't turn around. It's not our fight. Not yet.

I feel him before I see him, Theo King. His presence settles next to me like smoke. He takes the stool at my side without a word.

"Mr. King," I greet, finally turning toward him.

His two brothers, Kane and Ryder, take position behind him, mirroring Reggie and Rowan at my back. A perfect standoff without a single weapon drawn.

"Dr. Quinn." Theo grins, extending his tattooed hand. I shake it.

The shouting behind us gets louder. A man crashes into a table, another bottle smashes, but neither of us so much as blink.

"Thanks for flying over on such short notice," he says, all calm confidence.

"Of course. We want this done as fast as you do."

He nods slowly, glancing past me toward the twins.

"Those your muscle?" he asks, his Cockney twang curling the words.

I grin, just enough.

"No. They're family."

"Good."

Behind him, another man gets slammed into a wall, and I feel the scrape of brass knuckles in my pocket. My fingers twitch for the weight of them.

"Interesting venue choice," I murmur.

"Perfect distraction for us, yeah?"

I meet his gaze; his dark blue eyes are unreadable. Calculating. He's studying me the same way I'm assessing him. Quiet assessments. Who's bluffing. Who'll strike first.

"You're itching, aren't you? To let off some steam," he says, almost amused.

"I don't look for fights. That's more my brother's game. I step in when I have to. I prefer my methods… quieter."

Theo glances at the pub chaos with something close to fondness, that unmistakable glint of violence sparking in his eyes.

"Can't beat a pub brawl though," he says, running a hand through his jet-black hair.

"It's been a while," I admit.

Back in my teens, we used to get into fights in my father's pubs in Ireland every weekend.

He chuckles. We both know the itch never really goes away.

"Shall we get down to business? We have to get back for a family event," I say.

"Eager."

I shrug. I don't like to waste time.

"Well, as Charles is now six feet under, we can, or you can, go after Arthur."

I tense slightly. "When you say 'go after,' you mean…?"

I tilt my head in question. "You aren't planning on capturing him?" The deal was the kill. Not a scavenger hunt through London.

"He's underground. For now. We're working through his men. Someone'll talk."

"Always was a fucking pussy. Running from a fight." My voice drops low.

Theo smirks, eyes scanning the room again.

"Wherever he's hiding, he'll have his best men on him. We track him down, then I'll bring my men. And we've been gifted a few from Mikhail Volkov. And Frankie Falcone."

His words hang. That name.

A grin creeps across Theo's face.

"Oh, it'll be good to see Frankie again."

"You know him well?" I ask.

"Very. Back when he was out to kill his own blood, I helped him out here. So, yeah. He owes me one."

My jaw ticks. That wasn't in the file.

"Helped him out?"

"Hid a girl for him. He finally grew a conscience after taking her. She was pregnant, full of fire. It was a fucking mess. Let her go in the end. He's not been as ruthless since."

"That his wife? Zara?"

Theo laughs, shaking his head.

"Ain't no one kidnapping Zara. Let alone dragging her to another country. She'd have slit my throat in my sleep."

I smirk. I like the sound of her already.

"No. Her name was Maddie. I think she's married to one of his men now."

The dots connect in my head. "Grayson? The boxer?"

Theo holds up a finger. "Yeah. That's the one."

Interesting. Grayson's tight with Frankie now. Whatever went down must've been bloody.

"Are they coming here?" Theo asks.

I grin. "Why, scared Grayson's gonna beat your ass?"

His grin mirrors mine. All teeth. "I'd like to see him try. He's not the only one who likes to fight."

Theo, like Grayson and Keller, is built like a tank. Wouldn't be a bad match.

"Now that we've had a little family history, are we in

agreement on the plan? You hunt, we kill, then we can talk alliances," I ask, taking a long drink of the beer.

"Yes." He doesn't hesitate.

We shake on it.

And that's when the pub explodes into full chaos. The tension that had simmered finally boils over. Tables flip, chairs crash, fists fly.

I wait. Just watch. Let the storm build.

"Now that we've concluded business," I say, ducking as a bottle whistles past my head and smashes into the wall, "can we have some fuckin' fun now? It's been a long day."

I slide on my brass knuckles. The blade fits snug in my other hand. My cap tips low.

Theo's eyes gleam as he surveys the room, carnage in every direction.

"I thought you'd never ask. Show me how the famous Quinns really fight."

"You not joining us?"

He turns toward his brothers. Kane and Ryder are practically vibrating, fists clenched, hungry for blood.

"Might be good to see how well we work together," I offer.

"Fine. Let's clear this fucking place out." Theo slams his hand down on the bar.

Silence.

Every man in the room freezes, the sounds of the fight screeching to a halt. One after the other, they turn to him. Fear widening their eyes. Like they just realized whose fucking pub this is now.

A mistake they can't unmake.

"I thought I said no fucking fighting in my pub," Theo shouts, voice like thunder.

The silence deepens.

"There are six of us. And a fuck lot of you. Either leave…
or fight us. Your choice."

He turns to me, grinning like the devil.

"You know they ain't going to leave, right? These were
Bowen's men. This was Charles's pub before I took it. I'm
not welcome here. And neither are the Irish."

Well, shit.

He walked me straight into the wolves.

And I'm more than ready for it.

Everything in our world is a test. And this one?

We're about to pass with flying fucking colors.

Ryder smashes a bottle on the bar and holds the jagged
edge like a weapon.

The storm's about to break, and I've never felt more alive.

Ryder swings first.

A bottle to the jaw of a man who's stupid enough to lunge
without backup. The crack echoes like a gunshot. Blood
splatters across the bar.

And then it begins.

The room fractures into violence.

I move through it like water, my blade gripped tight in my
left hand, the brass knuckles locked across my right. Precision. Control. No wasted movement.

A man rushes me from the side—beer gut, bad footwork,
fists too high. I duck low, come up under his ribs with my
right, the metal slamming into bone. He chokes on blood and
drops.

Next.

Another one charges; he's bigger and faster. I sidestep,
let him stumble past, and hook my arm around his throat.
The blade presses under his jaw as I drag him back
against me.

"You picked the wrong pub, mate," I mutter, and drive the

blade straight up under his chin, severing whatever was still keeping him upright.

His body drops like a sack of bricks.

Behind me, Rowan is laughing, fully unhinged, a sound that would terrify any sane man. But these men? They're not sane. They're loyal to a dead tyrant and high on bloodlust.

Reggie moves like a ghost. A chair breaks across someone's back, and Reggie doesn't even flinch. He grabs the nearest guy by the jaw, slams his head into the wall twice, then turns to the next.

We're not brawlers.

We're predators.

Kane tackles a man over a table, fists flying. Ryder's knuckles are dripping, face blank as he kicks someone's teeth in. Theo watches for a moment, then finally joins the fight, cracking his knuckles like he's been waiting for an excuse to hurt someone.

I let another man swing at me, let him think he's landed something with his broken bottle, but I pivot, slam my knuckles into his throat, and sweep his legs out. He drops to the floor, gasping like a fish. I don't hesitate. Boot to the neck. One, two, done.

A hand grabs my shoulder. Another reaches for my blade.

Mistake.

I spin, elbowing the first in the nose hard enough to feel the cartilage crack. Then I slice low across the second man's thigh, dropping him to his knees before driving the hilt of my blade into the side of his head.

It's blood and fists and heat and the steady, focused rhythm of destruction.

And I feel alive.

Not because I like it.

Because I'm good at it.

"Finn!" Rowan shouts, tossing me a broken pool cue.

I catch it mid-air, flipping it in my grip. A man stumbles toward me, and I ram it into his ribs, feeling it splinter against bone. He howls. I jab upward into his throat, and he goes silent.

I wipe the blood on my coat and turn.

The pub is wrecked.

Glass everywhere. Bodies groaning and twitching on the floor.

Only a few men still stand, and they're smart enough to stay frozen in place.

Theo grins as he steps over a body, cracking his neck. His hands are bloodied, but he's smiling like it's Christmas morning.

"Well," he says, breathless, "that was cathartic."

Reggie grabs a half-conscious man by the collar and throws him out the front door.

Rowan wipes blood off his jaw and raises a brow. "That all of them?"

One of Bowen's men tries to crawl for the exit. I walk over, crouch beside him, and whisper low.

"You tell Arthur that war's already begun. And next time, I won't stop at your friends."

I let him go, and he scurries like a rat into the night.

Theo claps his hands together once. "Drinks?"

I let out a breath and roll my tense shoulders.

"Only if you've got whiskey that doesn't smell like petrol."

He laughs, stepping behind the bar like he owns the place, which he does now, I suppose.

I glance at the wreckage around us. Broken chairs. Blood smeared on the floor. My brass knuckles stained deep red.

And for the first time in days... I feel something close to peace.

Because the violence silences the noise in my head.

The ache in my chest.

The name I keep biting back.

Stephanie.

And tomorrow, I go home.

And she's going to feel everything I've been holding back.

CHAPTER 44

STEPHANIE

Song- In Your Fantasy, ATEEZ

Another day, another life saved. Balance. I took a man's life last night, and today I saved a woman.

I thought killing James would relieve some of the tension building inside of me. That it would get my mind off Finn. That I'd get that euphoric release that I usually do.

But I didn't.

Because this is different. Finn is so deep in my skin; it doesn't matter what I do, I can't stop thinking about him. I can't stop feeling him on me. I can't stop wanting more.

"Good work today, Josh." I tell him as he appears next to me to scrub out.

"Thanks, Dr. Qui–"

I spin to face him with a scowl.

"Dr. Miller," I correct him with a smile.

He's flustered as he continues to scrub his hands and arms.

"Sorry. I didn't mean… It just slipped."

I roll my eyes.

"It's fine," I tell him as I head out of the door.

As it swings open, I find Finn standing in the hallway, leaning against the wall opposite me with his arms crossed.

My body heats up just with one look.

"Mrs. Quinn." He grins.

Fuck, it does sound good with his Irish accent.

"Dr. Quinn," I say back, full of sugar.

He pushes himself off the wall and falls into step with me as we head to our offices.

"How was your day off?" I ask.

The one that came out of the blue, that wasn't documented anywhere.

"Very nice. London is a favorite of mine."

I nod along.

"Yes. I bet you had lots of champagne and caviar." He comes to a stop, and so do I, spinning to face him.

"Did you miss me?" he whispers, beckoning me over with his finger.

And my feet walk me towards him by their own accord.

Until I'm right in front of him, looking up at him through my lashes.

"Like a hole in the side of my head." I smile with my teeth.

Truth is, I did. I'm not sure who I am without him.

"Ah, so I leave a lasting impression on my wife."

I step back just as some of our colleagues walk past.

"We shouldn't be friendly like this in front of people."

That earns me a chuckle.

"Having a conversation is too friendly, Stephanie? Well, good job no one can see what plays out in my brain every time I see you."

I glance around me, relaxing once it's quiet again. I'm playing with fire.

"And what do you see when you look at me, Dr. Quinn?"

He pulls the stethoscope from around his neck and wraps it around his fist, stepping into my space. He tilts my chin up to him with his finger, his eyes raking over my body as my breath hitches.

Our mouths hover, just inches apart.

Everything around us vanishes; it's just us, like it always has been. My lips part, and all the breath is stolen from my lungs as he leans in.

Then reality kicks in. But I want this. So fucking bad.

My shift is over for today.

So I grab his tie and yank it, making him stumble forward. Grinning as I drag him down the corridor. Not towards our offices, but to the observation wing.

The empty room has hardly been used since the newer rooms were upgraded last year.

As he kicks the door shut behind him, I freeze.

Letting go of him as he locks it without a word.

I don't give my brain another second to overthink this; I launch myself into his arms. With his fingers digging into my ass, his other hand grips my throat.

Our mouths crash. It's urgent and fucking feral.

Our teeth colliding, our tongues dancing.

I fumble with his belt, like I've been starved of him. I'm desperate. And he's letting me.

"See. You did miss me," he murmurs against my mouth.

I bite down on his bottom lip in response.

"Good fucking girl. Make me bleed for you, because you're about to bleed out for me," he says softly, running the back of his hand along my cheek.

He spins me, pinning me to the wall. Pain erupts from my scalp as he grabs a fistful of my hair, tugging my head back to expose my throat.

"You brought this on yourself, Mrs. Quinn."

His grip tightens in my hair, dragging a gasp from my throat as he forces my head back. His mouth is all over me, teeth grazing the column of my neck, tongue chasing the heat he leaves behind.

"I'm counting on it," I whisper, breathless, already arching into him.

His chuckle is sinful, vibrating straight through my core.

He releases my hair and spins me again, pushing me backward with his body until the backs of my thighs hit the edge of the bed. With his lips on me, he drags my scrub top up, pulling away from me as I lift my arms in the air. He tosses it to the ground and grabs my throat again. But his gaze flicks over my breasts.

I work the clasp of my bra and slide the straps over my shoulders, letting that drop down too.

"Oh, fuck yes."

His head dips down, and he takes my nipple in his mouth. My head tips back as he sucks and bites. The perfect amount of pain.

"Fuck, Finn."

He trails his tongue between my breasts and all the way up to my throat.

"Lie down," he commands.

My heart pounds in my chest, a wild rhythm I can't control. I move without thinking, settling onto the padded surface. He heads over to the cupboards behind me. I just lie there, looking at the ceiling as if I am about to be examined.

He drapes the stethoscope across my chest—a tease, a threat, a warning. And then he gently places my wrist on the railings of the bed, securing it with an IV tube. He slowly walks around to the other side and restrains my other wrist.

I tug on them to test the resistance, but they're tight. He grins as I look up at him.

Without a word, the cool end of the stethoscope is back on me.

"Are you just going to listen to my heart?" I pant, every inch of me trembling, soaking for him.

"No," he says softly. "I'm going to make it skip."

He peels my scrub pants down with surgical precision. No time wasted. No hesitation. Just his mouth on my inner thigh, warm breath dragging over skin he knows he owns.

"Let's see what my girl's heart does for me," he murmurs, pointing to the cardiac monitor leads beside us.

He works on attaching the electrodes to my chest. I hear the steady beep as the machine comes to life.

"That's mine now." He taps the screen. "Every flutter. Every spike. I want to see exactly what I do to you."

And God, I want that too.

His fingers trail between my legs, making me squirm.

"You're soaked, Mrs. Quinn. All for me."

"I'm not your property," I breathe, even as my hips chase his touch.

I just hate admitting what he does to me.

He smirks. "No? Then why does your body only respond to mine?"

I don't have an answer for that.

Because it's the truth.

Finn Quinn ruined me.

And he knows it.

I cry out as two fingers slide inside me, curling just enough to hit that devastating spot he's already memorized. My back arches. The monitor beeps harder. He watches it with satisfaction.

"Look at you. Such a good girl for me," he croons.

His fingers keep working me as he reaches for something in his coat pocket.

The glint of steel catches my eye.

A scalpel.

My breath stalls.

"You trust me?" he asks, his tone gentler now.

I nod, chest heaving. "Yes."

I want this. I've always wanted something more like this. Pain tipping the balance with pleasure. But I've never been brave enough to ask, nor trusted someone enough to do it.

Yet with him, it's different. I've seen what he can do with his hands. He can save a life, and he can bring me right to the edge.

He presses the blade flat against my stomach. Not cutting. Just teasing. The cold kiss of metal against burning skin.

"Good. Because tonight, I'm going to take everything from you."

My thighs are trembling as I watch the sharp edge trace the curve of my hipbone. He doesn't cut, not yet.

He's waiting.

Watching my pulse, which is climbing by the second.

And when the moment's right, he presses the tip into my thigh. A small, controlled cut. A droplet of blood wells up, and I moan, because somehow, the pain only makes the pleasure spike.

He leans in and licks it up, his grey eyes never leaving mine. My body shakes around him.

"Beautiful," he whispers. "Bleed for me, wife."

I'm wrecked. Completely. The sound of the monitor echoing my body's betrayal, rising higher with every movement of his hand, every kiss, every cut.

"Say it," he demands, leaning over me, pressing his palm flat to my heart.

"Say you missed me."

"I did," I gasp, on the edge, legs shaking. "I missed you."

Pain sears through me as he makes a larger cut on my hip. The monitor is screaming. Yet I'm feeling on top of the world. Alive and on fire.

"Atta girl. I fuckin' knew it. And I missed you too."

And only then, only when I'm right at the edge, held open for him, dripping, marked as his, does he push his pants down, freeing his huge cock.

"Oh shit." My eyes go wide.

"You weren't joking. That really is massive," I pant.

He curls his hand around himself and strokes.

"Hmm, mm. And it's all yours now, baby. Want a taste?" He bites his bottom lip as I tremble.

I nod.

"Yes, please."

"Please, what?" he asks, moving towards me.

"Sir?"

He nods.

Now beside my face, he pushes the tip against my lip, and I open wide for him. His hand on the back of my head as he thrusts inside, making me gag.

"Good girl, take it."

He glances at the heart rate monitor with a grin. I pull on my restraints, desperate to touch him. But it's clear that isn't what he wants.

"My filthy girl likes her throat being fucked. Good."

So he ups the momentum, no restraint, until tears spill from my eyes. The monitor beeping almost becoming a scream.

"Breathe for me, temptress. Breathe. You're doing a perfect job."

His words only build the fire inside of me faster. I

squeeze my thighs together to stop myself from coming. I know that will get me in trouble. And I'm enjoying the pleasure too much.

When he starts to tense, moans escaping him, he pulls back out of me, and I take a deep breath.

"M-more," I whisper desperately.

"We've got plenty of time. This is about me exploring my wife."

CHAPTER 45

FINN

Song- Creature In The Dark Night- Dayseeker

She's panting beneath me. Her chest heaving, the heart monitor spiking with every breath. Every moan.

All fucking mine.

I slide her black lace panties off and place them on the monitor.

She's strapped to my rhythm now. Her pleasure is being recorded in real time, the final experiment.

But it's more than that. She's finally admitting to herself that she belongs to me.

My wife.

Putting her legs in a better position, her feet flat on the bed and knees bent, I open them up for me.

Her thighs are slick, her lips swollen, her wrists bound to the railings. Stripped down to skin and sweat and submission. Her pussy begging to be fucked raw.

She's perfect like this.

Ravaged. Quietly begging with her body while her mouth still fights me.

God, I fucking missed her. It was one single day too long. I can't deny I've got it bad.

I trace the fresh cut across her thigh with my glove, collecting the blood on two fingers and dragging it slowly over her clit. She twitches violently, the monitor going wild.

"You hear that?" I murmur, ghosting my lips over hers. "That's your heart screaming for me, while your body bleeds for me."

I slide two fingers inside of her, watching in fascination as her back arches off the bed.

Her eyes flutter shut, and her teeth sink into her bottom lip to keep herself from coming.

"No," I growl. "You don't get to finish until I say."

She whimpers, giving in to me. Finally fucking listening.

Submitting to me, just as she was made to do.

"My good girl," I whisper.

My cock's rock hard and aching. But I won't give in until she spills my blood. Not from my hands.

From hers.

I reach into my coat pocket and pull the scalpel free. Her blood is still coating the metal. With my eyes locked on hers, I run the flat edge along my tongue and do the same with the other side.

Ingesting her blood, so I am hers too.

Her breath catches when I unbind her wrists. She shakes them out, her gaze never leaving mine.

I hold out the blade to her.

"Your turn."

She stares up at me, wide-eyed and trembling, but not from fear.

From want.

"If you cut me," I say roughly, "you get to come."

Her lip trembles. Her thighs clench.

"Do it."

This isn't just about me marking her as mine. It's about her owning me too. This is a marriage, a union in blood.

This isn't something any paperwork can take away from us.

Standing beside her, she sits up and takes the blade. I watch the slight shake in her fingers, the movement awkward and hesitant. I've seen her do surgery for hours. I know she can do this. She handles pressure like a pro.

I drag my shirt off, baring my chest to her, forgetting my past for just a second. Forgetting the things I am supposed to hide from the world. Her eyes rake over my body, and she's not horrified; she's not even looking at the scars on my chest that I've covered my best with tattoos. No. She's staring at my shoulders like she wants to sink her teeth into them.

"Something you like, Mrs. Quinn?" I ask with amusement.

It makes my heart flutter seeing her satisfaction with me. Like she wants to tear into me. That this obsession is mutual.

"I knew you were ripped, but damn. Look at those traps."

I tilt my head, amused at her little outburst.

"You mean your leg rests for when I eat you out?"

She licks her lips and nods.

"Not now though, that can be after," I wink.

I tip my head back, offering my skin.

"Make it hurt, Mrs. Quinn."

Her fingers shake. But the blade slices clean and fast across my shoulder. Not deep. Just enough to sting. To satisfy.

My groan is guttural.

Pain and pleasure blur. They always have for me. I need this, and something settles inside of me knowing that she is prepared to give me it. No questions. No persuading her to do it.

She is like me. She wants pain too.

"Nice work, Dr. Quinn," I praise her.

"Now, lie back down."

Blood runs in a thin line, trailing down my chest. I dip my hand into it, smear it between her thighs, and slide two fingers back inside her. Her slickness and my blood mixing into something primal.

Something sacred.

She arches violently, gasping as I stroke her with that unholy blend. The monitor screams. So does she.

But I'm not done.

I yank off the wires from her chest as fast as I can before flipping her onto her stomach so she's on all fours and dragging her to the end of the bed.

She will never comprehend the importance of that. The fact I'm going to fuck her while her hands are free. That this is me giving her power over me.

Something I've never, ever, given away willingly before.

"You earned this," I rasp, lining myself up behind her.

She cries out as I slam into her, slick and hot and desperate. I grip her hair in one hand, the blood-slicked blade in the other. My teeth find her shoulder, biting down as I fuck her deep and slow.

She clenches hard around me.

Her body begs as her screams grow louder.

"Come apart for me," I whisper, pressing the blade flat against her spine. "Bleed and break for your husband."

And she does.

She shatters around me, crying out my name like it's salvation.

I follow her, spilling inside her with a roar. The sight

before me, the most beautiful thing I've ever seen—my blood and hers, on her thighs, on my chest.

A fucking masterpiece.

She collapses forward, chest heaving, wrists limp, skin marked and glowing.

I drop the blade and pull her into my arms.

And for a long moment, we just breathe. Entangled. Covered in our blood. I grip her throat again, bringing her face to mine.

"Everything you hoped and dreamed it would be fucking your boss?" I tease.

She scowls at me, so I squeeze harder.

Her fingers trail up my chest, over the scars, and I close my eyes.

"There is a reason I need pain in my life, Stephanie," I tell her.

The most honest I've ever been with anyone since it happened. I know it's not much. It's not a revelation.

But for me, it is.

It's like she understands the weight of it as she continues to trace them.

"I understand."

My heart stops.

"I really, really fucking hope you don't," I tell her.

She gives me a sad smile.

"I guess we will figure that one out."

If someone has hurt her, I will hunt them down, each and every one, and slit their throats as they sleep.

I stroke her hair away from her face and press my nose against hers, and she smiles.

It's fucked up. All of this.

But so are we. And I wouldn't change a damn thing.

CHAPTER 46

My body hums. Completely overstimulated, wrung out, marked, and used in the most devastatingly perfect way.

My thighs are trembling, slick with blood and cum. My wrists ache where the restraints rubbed raw. My skin stings from every cut and bruise and bite. I can still feel him on me.

In me.

But it's the quiet afterward that unnerves me.

Not the silence of shame.

Not the stillness of regret.

No.

It's him.

The way he holds me.

Like I'm something fragile. Like I didn't just let him drag a scalpel across my skin and fuck me until I saw stars.

His chest is still rising fast, blood sticky between our bodies. But his arms are wrapped around me like he's protecting me from something. Maybe him?

And I don't know what the fuck to do with that.

"You're shaking," he murmurs against my temple, brushing sweat-damp hair away from my face.

I try to say I'm fine, that I don't need his tenderness now, but the words don't come.

Instead, I nod. Just once. Barely a movement.

He shifts beneath me, gently easing away from me, and I wince.

"Sorry," he breathes, like the sound of my pain hurts him more than it hurts me.

The cuts are starting to sting.

Then he's gone. Just for a second. I hear the faucet run and the rustle of a drawer opening.

And then he's back like a professional.

Dr. Finn Quinn, again.

He presses a warm, wet cloth between my thighs and begins to clean me thoroughly. I flinch at first, unsure whether I should stop him or thank him or crawl away and lock myself in a supply closet.

But he doesn't let me move.

"Stay still," he murmurs, dabbing gently at my inner thigh where a line of dried blood clings to a shallow cut. "You're okay. You did so well for me."

His eyes lock with mine.

"I'm proud of you."

No one's ever said that to me.

Not after.

Not with meaning.

"You don't have to," I say, my voice raw.

"I know." His gaze meets mine. "But I want to."

He sterilizes the blade marks with practiced care, cooling antiseptic on warm skin. He bandages the deepest one near my hip and presses his thumb there to hold the gauze in place.

"You're not used to being looked after," he says softly, not as a question.

I shake my head, eyes glassy. "No one ever has."

His jaw flexes. That controlled rage rising again, but not at me this time. For me.

"You should be," he says. "You fucking deserve it."

He tucks my hair behind my ear, then turns to clean himself, grabbing a sterile cloth from the drawer, pressing it over the cut I gave him like it's nothing.

Like it's sacred.

I sit up slowly, reaching for him on instinct. I swipe at the blood on his chest, tracing the line I made with a shaking fingertip.

"I didn't mean to shake like that; you know I'm usually better than that," I whisper.

"I did."

"What?"

"I wanted to shake you. Ruin you. But only if I could put you back together after."

God help me, I believe him.

Finn Quinn is many things. Disturbed, dominant, and terrifying in his control.

But this?

This quiet devotion?

It's the most dangerous part of him.

Because I think I could fall in love with it.

And falling for a man like Finn is a death sentence.

So I lean my head on his shoulder, ignoring the voice in my head screaming at me to run.

Just for now, I let myself feel safe in the arms of the man who could destroy me completely.

And maybe already has.

"What do we do now?" I ask.

My head is a mess, and so is my body.

He frowns, checking the time on his Rolex.

"Well, I have a family party to be at," he pauses, "half an hour ago."

"Oh. Shit. I'm sorry."

He chuckles, leaning in and pulling my lip back.

"I'm not even remotely fucking sorry," he whispers.

"Well, you best get going." I glance at the door.

He doesn't move. He just watches me as I get up and start collecting my clothes and putting them on. And then he does the same.

The silence is deafening.

He unlocks the door and looks down the hallway.

"It's safe, no one will see us," he confirms.

"Cool."

He stops and turns to me.

"Right. Come on, out with it."

"It's nothing. I just want to go home."

He steps forward, crowding my space again so I can't breathe.

"No. You're not going home. You're coming to meet your in-laws."

I blink at him a few times.

"Are you high?"

He takes a deep breath.

"High on you perhaps."

He slides his fingers into mine, and I look down, catching a glimpse of his left hand. There is no ring there anymore.

Something worse. How the hell did I miss this?

"Finn. What the hell is that?"

I hold it up to inspect it. A thick black band inked across his wedding finger, with a delicate 'S' in the middle.

"Please tell me that isn't what I think it is?"

He nods.

"Permanent as fuck, baby. Would you like a matching one?"

I blink at him in disbelief.

"You're a psycho, Finn. Why?"

He grins and holds my hand in his, staring into my eyes.

"Because somehow, I wanted to show you how serious I am about this marriage. That it isn't a game. That you fuckin' own me, love. There's only one way you're getting your last name back, and that's by becoming a widow."

I swallow the lump in my throat. I don't want to lose him. I can't. He's made it clear that he wants this. That he wants me.

"I–I won't be getting a tattoo, but I'll wear the ones you bought me."

He grins like this was his plan all along.

"Every day?" he asks.

I huff.

His eyes form slits.

"Stephanie…"

"Fine. Yes. I'll wear them."

The 'for now' part I leave off. Because right now, I don't want to argue with him over a divorce. I want more of what he just did to me.

Lots more of that.

"Don't you think meeting your family is a bit… soon?" I ask as he leads us out into the hallway.

Hand in hand.

"Too soon? You're already my wife. You've met Conan and Hallie already." He brushes me off.

"I met Conan while in surgery. I haven't seen Hallie in months!"

He tightens his grip on my hand.

"Do they know you're married?" I pull on his arm to stop him.

He chuckles, spinning to face me.

"No. It's now a baby shower and a wedding party."

I pout, shaking my head.

"You are in-fucking-sane, Finn."

He grins wickedly.

"People keep saying this to me." He shakes his head and carries on walking, dragging me with him to his car. Which is neatly parked next to mine.

"I'll go home and get changed. Where shall I meet you?" I ask.

"I'll come and collect you, love."

He leans in and presses a kiss to my lips, taking me by surprise. I don't fight it. I lean into it. Kissing him back with a smile.

His hands cup my face.

"An hour, I have a quick appointment first," he whispers against my lips.

"Okay."

I feel like I'm living in a parallel universe.

CHAPTER 47

FINN

I watch as she drives off, and instead of getting in my own car, I pull out my phone.

"Hey, Fred. I need a favor," I greet him.

Head of Neurology. I suppose I'd call him a friend of sorts. Except, he needs to understand I won't be going to Portugal to play golf, no matter how many times he asks me.

"Of course, Finn. All okay?"

I rub my hands over my face.

"Something's not right. Can I pop down for some scans? I only have an hour."

There's a pause.

"Not right? Do you want to give me some symptoms?"

I let out a ragged breath.

How do I explain to a fucking neurologist that I need my brain scanned because I'm too obsessed with my wife?

That I've been so void of feelings for so long, I now can't stop feeling things.

That I've been laughing, smiling, and lusting over her.

That I care.

And that there is no logical explanation other than a

tumor. Or some kind of brain-eating disease that's causing this.

Because I'm not built to feel love.

And yet, I think I do.

So naturally, to avoid being sent to the psych ward. I lie.

"Lethargic, dizzy, dehydrated, and a constant pounding headache."

"How many days?"

It's been nearly six years since I met her. But I've been in love with her for thirty days.

Obsessed every day since I arrived here.

"A couple of weeks now."

"Alright. Head to my office now. I'll do some assessments and scans."

"Great. Thank you. You sure an hour will cut it?"

He chuckles.

"Head of the department comes with some perks, Finn."

I cut the call and head straight to his office, nerves swirling around in my gut. I haven't thought about what if I am actually sick.

I KNOCK on Fred's door before opening it up.

He turns in his seat and smiles.

"Right, let's get you scanned. You can answer questions as we walk there," he tells me, standing up and holding out his hand to shake.

I look at it. Clean. No tattoos. What a surgeon should look like.

Not like mine. Covered in ink. Blood probably still stained deep within.

"I appreciate this," I tell him and follow him down the corridor.

"Well, I need you alive and well to finally get you on this golf trip," he jokes.

I inwardly groan. Is this the cost of this scan?

I don't answer. I go in silently and let him shove me in machines to scan my brain.

Get this over with so I can get back to Stephanie. I know my family will accept her, because she is mine. I'm more intrigued about how they will react. I've never brought a woman home to them. I've never had someone to call mine.

"I'm sure it's fine, Finn. Don't worry." He claps his hand on my shoulder, and I shudder, turning to him and glaring.

It's enough for him to take his hands off me.

It's not fine either way.

On the one hand, I'm sick.

On the other? I'm falling for my wife.

I'm feeling things.

By the time we're done, I only have ten minutes to get to Stephanie. Fred is sitting behind his desk, pulling up my scan images.

His glasses are on, and he's studying them. But I can see the results clearly.

"You're looking all good, Finn," he mutters, turning to me.

My jaw clenches.

"Do you think maybe it could be stress or anxiety?"

I scoff. Fuck off.

"Why do you look so pissed off?" he asks with a frown.

I tap my fingers on the desk, staring at my healthy brain.

It's not my heart; I already checked that. It's not my head.

Fuck. Is what I feel for her real?

"I just thought I was right."

"We can refer you? More tests? This was obviously quite fast-tracked."

I shake my head.

"No. I know how to fix it."

"Alright. Next month for golf?" he asks.

I refrain from rolling my eyes.

"No."

"One day I'll get you."

He chuckles as I stand. He fucking won't. I couldn't think of anything worse.

"Can you email me those images?" I ask, pointing at the screen.

"Uh. Sure."

A smile tugs at my lips.

Perhaps I'll put it in a card on our wedding anniversary for her.

Or give them to her the next time she tries to divorce me.

Shit. There's that pain in my chest again. Just thinking about her drives me crazy.

That fuzzy feeling in my head.

Her.

She is my symptom.

My cause.

The only fucking drug that will fix me.

How do I get my wife to fall in love with me?

I race back to my car, texting her before I drive, letting her know I will be slightly delayed. I still need to go and get changed.

I DON'T THINK my brothers have clocked that my hand is linked with Stephanie's.

"You're late," Conan grins, then stops cold.

His gaze drops to our joined hands. Back up to me. Back down again.

"Well, well, well, look what the cat dragged—" Declan comes to an abrupt halt beside him.

"Finn?"

I squeeze her hand.

"I'm late because I had to pick up my wife."

Their jaws damn near hit the floor. Perfect timing for Charlotte and Hallie to walk up behind them.

Stephanie nudges closer to my side. The room goes still. I lean down—feeling like she's going to say something.

"I feel like we're animals in a zoo being viewed. Say something," she whispers.

So I straighten and clear my throat. But she surprises me and beats me to it.

"I'm Stephanie, or Dr. Miller, you may know me as," she says to Conan.

Conan steps forward, offers his hand. She takes it, smiling.

"You saved my life," he says.

Fuck, my chest tightens.

"I did. But you did most of the hard work yourself. It's good to see you looking well, Conan."

I release her hand and slide my arm around her waist. My

eyes find Hallie's; she's already glassy-eyed. She steps forward and wraps Stephanie in her arms.

Stephanie freezes, just for a second, then hugs her back.

"I always knew you two didn't really hate each other," Hallie says, looking directly at me.

"Is that so?" I ask.

She nods. Hallie's been under my wing since her father died in my O.R. Great nurse. Better wife to Conan. She's perfect for him, and everyone can see it, including me.

Declan and Charlotte are both sizing us up. Declan's got that disappointed dad look, like he's about to start lecturing.

"How long have you been married?" Charlotte asks carefully, biting her lip and avoiding my eyes.

"Charlotte," I warn, "spit it out."

She's a trained assassin with a heart too soft for this world, until someone threatens her family. Then the darkness resurfaces.

A slow smile spreads across Charlotte's face. "I think you're fucking with us."

My turn to grin. I pull my arm from Stephanie's waist and hold up my tattooed ring finger.

"Finn," Declan hisses.

Not sure what reaction I was expecting from them, but this whole thing's turning into a circus.

"Vegas. A few weeks ago. We were slightly drunk, yes. But now she's come to her senses and stopped begging me to annul it."

I feel her glare burning into the side of my head.

Conan scratches his jaw. "So… are you a couple? Or just fucking? I'm confused."

Hallie smacks his arm.

I glance down at my wife. She's fighting a smile.

"What are we, wife?" I ask.

"We're something not many people can comprehend," she says, her voice confident.

I like that answer.

We *are* different.

"Are we done with the grilling? I'd like a drink and to see my nephews."

"Steph! Come sit with us, we have a lot to catch up on!" Hallie links arms with her, dragging her away from me.

I stay put, hands in my pockets, watching as the three of them head over to Lily with the kids. I've never seen Stephanie with friends outside the hospital—she's a lone wolf. Like I'd be without my brothers.

But that smile on her face? She likes this. It looks natural. And fuck… when Hallie hands her baby Liam to hold, my heart skips.

I need to start tracking her cycle. Because I want that.

Declan holds out a whiskey in front of my nose. "What the hell's happened to you?" he asks low.

I take the glass. "What do you mean?"

I don't take my eyes off her.

"Since when do you fall in love? You didn't like her five minutes ago; now you're married? Looking at her like you're about to drop to your knees for her."

Conan barks a laugh. "Why'd you say that like it's a bad thing? Fuck, I get on my knees for Hallie most nights if she calls me a good boy."

I nearly choke on my drink. "Good boy? Like a dog?"

Conan glares. "Don't knock it 'til you try it. Letting her take control is hot as fuck."

I hold up a hand. "Don't. I don't want that mental image burned into my brain."

He rolls his eyes.

"Everyone's got their own kink," I mutter.

I'm not sure my brother needs to know I have to bleed just to feel anything.

Conan narrows his eyes. "What's yours then? Something to do with the medical shit you've got at home? Or nurse role play? Fuck, it's so hot when—"

I chuckle and tap his cheek to stop him from finishing his sentence. Hallie is my friend, I don't need to know.

"Be a good boy and shut the fuck up."

His jaw tenses. I grin wider. "And I'm not sure a brotherly fistfight's the right move at a baby shower."

Declan steps between us. "You didn't answer me. Is this serious? Is she part of our family now?"

"Yes. And yes."

"Do you trust her to know the truth? About the Decadence Trials?"

I scratch my stubble. "Eventually. Trust takes time. As you well know."

My gaze pins his. His wife once tried to kill him, betrayed him, and lied to him. He forgave her. Trusted her again.

"Are you happy?" he asks.

I chew the inside of my cheek. Happiness isn't something I've ever truly claimed. Any time I thought I had it, the memories came back and poisoned it.

But since marrying Stephanie? I've been so distracted, the darkness hasn't found a way in.

"Yeah. As happy as I can be."

Declan relaxes. "Then congratulations. She seems good for you."

I tilt my head. My brothers believe in this fairytale love shit. And maybe they have it.

But my life isn't built for that. I know, deep down, Stephanie won't accept all of me, not the truth. Not the part I don't speak aloud.

I haven't even told my brothers. The only people who know are all dead, including my own parents.

The mafia? The killing? She could handle that. I see the dark in her too.

But what happened to me as a kid? The hatred it left me with? The way I can turn off my emotions like a switch? That's different.

She deserves better.

"We should have confirmation from Theo in a few days to head to London," I tell my brothers.

Conan grins, but he's looking at Hallie.

"You don't have to leave them. I can do it for you," I tell him.

He shakes his head.

"We do this together." He claps his hand on my shoulder.

"I'm protecting my family; I have to."

I nod in agreement. They're safe here, and we won't be gone long. I don't have plans to leave Stephanie either.

Still… for now, I'll let myself pretend. Live in the fantasy my brothers swear by.

Just to know what it feels like.

CHAPTER 48

STEPHANIE

olding a baby in my arms while feeling Finn's stare burn into me does something dangerous to my body.

Is this the kind of life he wants?

Is this the kind I want?

I've never entertained the idea before. But here I am, married, at his family gathering. I suppose anything can happen when you least expect it.

I shift in my seat, and the cut on my thigh stings, a sharp reminder of who I really am. Of how his blade made me come alive.

"This is crazy, you being here with us. It's cool, though," Hallie says, lifting her diet coke.

"Yeah. It's a lot to wrap my head around. Finn is… a force I can't seem to keep away from."

Both girls laugh.

"These Quinn brothers are built differently. Once they get under your skin, you can't get rid of them," Charlotte says, glancing at her husband.

I look across the room. The three brothers are deep in

conversation, their similarities obvious, but each one carved by their own edges.

"Oh, I'm Lily, by the way." The blonde smiles warmly.

"Stephanie. Are you with anyone here?"

She giggles, lifting her champagne. "God, no. I'm Hallie's best friend. I'm too busy to date."

I nod. "Yeah, I thought the same thing a few weeks ago."

"We should do a girls' night soon. Something fun," Hallie suggests.

I've never had this. In medical school, I kept my head down and studied. Growing up in foster care, I never trusted people enough to let them close.

At work, I have acquaintances—nothing more.

This… might be good for me.

"That sounds good. Just let me know when, and I'll work around my schedule," I tell them.

The doors to the restaurant fly open, and two massive men walk in—identical twins, both wearing thunderous expressions.

They're terrifying.

They remind me of the men Finn was speaking to in Vegas.

"Who are they?" I ask.

"The twins. Reggie and Rowan. The brothers' right-hand men, really."

I frown. These are the same men from the strip club— alongside an older blond man I've seen before.

"Right-hand men… for what?"

Hallie bites her lip. "Just work stuff. They're all in business together."

I nod, not believing her. I already know there's another side to Finn. I've seen it.

But I let it go. He can keep his secrets. I'll keep mine.

After greeting them, Finn makes a beeline for me. His hand lands on the back of my chair as he leans down.

"You holding Liam is doing things to me it really shouldn't," he murmurs.

My cheeks flush. "Oh yeah?"

He drags his lips across my cheek. "I think it's time I showed you another kink of mine that I've just suddenly decided I have."

I swallow hard, my thighs pressing together. "Now?"

"You wanna go?"

I hand baby Liam to him, watching as he cradles the baby with practiced ease. And damn… it suits him.

Daddy Finn.

Hot. As. Fuck.

I can't stop watching him fuss over his nephew. And that smile—it's the realest I've ever seen. Pure happiness.

I wonder how he would look at his own baby.

"Does that make you broody?" Hallie whispers.

"I think so?"

"Did I pass your test?" Finn asks.

I nod. "Let's go."

He hands Liam back to Hallie and offers me his hand. Standing, I take it.

"You know this is crazy, right? All of this? Us?" I say, my hands resting against his chest.

The room stills.

His brothers watch, like they can't believe what they're seeing. Finn covers my hands with his own, pressing them harder into him—making a point.

He doesn't usually allow touch. The flinches, the faint scars beneath his tattoos—I've noticed them.

But now? He's letting me in.

"I am crazy, Stephanie. You've told me that for years. Turns out you're crazy like me," he says, grinning.

"You really want to stay married to me?" I ask softly.

I've pushed him away so hard because deep down, I was terrified. Terrified of caring enough that he could leave me.

"Yeah, I really fucking do, Mrs. Quinn. I rather like you."

A smile spreads across my lips. "Love and hate can walk the same line, I suppose."

"There was never any hate, was there?" he murmurs, brushing his lips against mine.

I shake my head. "Annoyance and jealousy, maybe."

"Admitting it is the first step."

"Are you going to show me this new kink or…?"

"New?" His brow arches.

I narrow my eyes. "You better not be doing that with other women, Dr. Quinn."

His finger presses to my lips, making my eyes go wide.

"You drive me insane, wife. Do you honestly think I have the time or patience to entertain anyone else?" He leans in closer. "You're the only woman who's ever had her hands on me like this. The only one who's felt me fill her and drip down her thighs. The only one who makes my heart skip a beat. And you're about to be the only woman I've ever let touch me back—look me in the eyes—as we both break for each other. So no, temptress. You're the only one who gets this side of me. Understand how rare that is."

Holy. Fucking. Shit.

I slide my arms around his neck. "I understand, sir," I whisper.

His body vibrates against mine. "Fuck, we gotta go."

We say our goodbyes in a blur; he's practically dragging me to his car.

He fastens my seatbelt before sliding in behind the wheel.

"I feel bad we weren't there long," I tell him.

He laces my fingers through his and pulls my hand up to his mouth, pressing a gentle kiss there.

"They know I'm a busy man. There will be plenty of time for you to get to know them all. I'm selfish when it comes to you, love. Now I have you, I want to know everything there is about you."

My eyes start to sting with tears. The weight of this whole relationship crashing down on me. How this man knows how to say just the right thing to settle everything inside of me.

"I think you know more about me than anyone else in my entire life, Finn."

He smiles and places another kiss on my ring finger.

"Ditto," he whispers as he turns on the engine.

"Now, I need to feed you before I feed on you," he says with a grin.

"What kind of food do you like? Other than my pussy?"

"Caviar?" he teases.

I wrinkle my nose. "No, rich boy. Burgers?"

His tone shifts. "What have I told you about calling me that?"

"But you are rich," I tease.

"Very. Obscenely. And it means nothing to me."

I take a breath. "You know my money from the strip club? I donated every cent to women's shelters."

His hand lands on my thigh, squeezing. "Particular reason?"

I swallow. "I have a past, Finn. When I said I'd made sacrifices to get here, I didn't mean studying instead of going out. I had nothing, and I did some… things."

He grabs my chin, making me face him. "Things you do

to survive aren't mistakes. Our pasts make us. They can ruin us if we let them."

That sadness in his voice tells me enough. I don't press.

Between breaking his no-touch rule and these cracks in his armor, I know one day he'll tell me what happened to him.

"So… burgers?" I say, changing the subject.

I take the booth in the far corner, the one with a clear line to every exit. Always. She slides in next to me, crossing her legs, lips glossed and begging for trouble. The waitress drops menus we don't need.

"You said burgers," I remind her, leaning my forearms on the table.

She bites her bottom lip. "That was before you got me worked up in the parking lot. Now all I can think about is you bending me over this table." She bats her lashes at me.

Fuck. She knows exactly what she's doing.

The waitress comes back, takes our order, and leaves us in the low hum of clinking cutlery and soft music. My eyes never leave hers, even when she tries to look away.

Under the table, my hand slides across, over her knee, and up her thigh.

Her breath hitches.

"Finn—"

"Wait for your food like a good girl," I murmur, my thumb stroking the soft skin just above her hemline. "You will finish every last bite, while I get you nice and ready for me."

The corner of her mouth lifts. "Yes, sir."

I push her legs apart, heat radiating from her through thin fabric. Already wet. My fingers trace her pussy, slow enough to make her tremble.

When the burgers arrive, she picks hers up, trying to look casual. First bite, she closes her eyes, so I slip two fingers under the edge of her panties and into her.

She jolts. I hook my foot around her ankle to keep her steady.

"That's it, love. Take another bite," I coax, curling my fingers just right.

One of my observations over time has been that Stephanie doesn't really eat. At work, it's barely a snack all day. And now that I know about her second job, I struggle to see when she has time to cook.

So, I've made a note to make sure my wife eats. Her body is perfect. But I don't want her getting sick. I need to make sure she's healthy. That she makes time for herself. I need to look after her.

She takes another mouthful. Sauce clings to her lips, her cheeks flushed as she tries to chew when every nerve in her body is telling her to moan.

The waitress sets my whiskey and her fries down. Stephanie thanks her without breaking eye contact with me. Good girl.

I work her slow, then faster, keeping her right at the edge. She grips her burger like it's her lifeline. Every shift of her hips presses her closer into my hand.

"You look beautiful like this," I murmur. "Trying so hard to be good for me. But, you're being very, very naughty letting me do this in public."

Her breathing grows uneven. Her eyes glaze. I pull my fingers free just as she's about to tip.

She drops her burger onto her plate and glares at me like she's ready to climb on me and ruin me.

I'd let her.

Then I'd throw everyone out of this place and bend her over the table to remind her who's in charge.

"Your place or mine?" I ask, hoping she says hers. Most of mine is locked down for the Decadence Trials. And I want to see how she lives. How she decorates, what she owns. Whether it matches what I've imagined for her.

"Mine isn't anything special, but I have booze and food. I don't have any kinky stuff you probably own."

I smirk. "I can get creative with anything, Stephanie. But tonight… I'd like to do something different."

She sips her milkshake through a straw, eyes narrowing. "Different?"

"Less distractions. Just us. I'll still cut you. Spank you raw. Fuck you until you pass out. But I want to try it gently, too."

I rub at my chest. I've never done it. I've never let a woman roam her hands over me, touch me back. After what Conan said earlier, maybe she could have some power in that. I'll never be a good boy on my knees; that isn't in me. I can't strip myself of all of my control. But I'd like to fuck her with eye contact. Let her choke on my cock with her hands on me.

Fuck, I'm getting hard just thinking about it.

"You mean… like making love?" she asks.

My heart kicks hard. The word is alien to me, but she's right. I nod, not trusting myself to say it aloud.

She smiles. "I've never done that either."

I blow out a breath. "You've never been in—?"

She giggles. "My god, you can't even say it. I'm in a loveless marriage."

My jaw twitches. Is she? Am I loveless?

I can do this. It's just a word.

"I'd like to make love to my wife," I say. And to my own surprise, the words don't make me sick.

Her eyes light up.

I glance at my glistening fingers and bring them to my mouth, licking them clean. "My dessert."

Her blush deepens.

"You're cruel," she whispers.

"Only because I want to watch you squirm until we get home. Then, Mrs. Quinn, you'll learn what cruel really means."

"So my place?" She grins, finishing the last bites.

I nod. "I'd love to see your lair."

CHAPTER 50

STEPHANIE

Song- Die With A Smile, Lady Gaga, Bruno Mars.

By the time we reach my apartment, my pulse is a slow, heavy thud in my ears.

It isn't nerves.

It's something worse.

Because I'm expecting the same thing I've already experienced with Finn. Fast, rough, no room to breathe, or being left on the edge of frustration. The kind of sex that feels like a fight we both lose and win at the same time.

But when I unlock the door and step aside, he doesn't touch me.

He looks.

His gaze moves across every inch of my living space, lingering on the things I never thought twice about. My mismatched coffee mugs left on the table, the pile of medical journals on the counter, and the old blanket draped over the couch.

"This is… you," he says finally.

I can't read his tone.

"Nothing special." I shrug.

It's not that I don't have the money, because I do. I just don't want a lavish lifestyle. I work long enough hours to kill me.

This is simply a place to sleep. It's not a home.

I've never truly had one of those.

He tips my chin up to him.

"You simply have no idea, do you?" he whispers.

My body tingles against his touch.

"About what?" I ask, my voice breaking as I suck in a breath.

"There isn't a single soul more special than yours, temptress."

I try to look away, but he keeps me in place. This is too raw, too vulnerable. What if he leaves? Who will be there to pick up the fractured pieces of my heart then?

"Want a drink?" I ask, taking a step toward the kitchen.

He catches my hand before I get two steps in.

"Later."

That one word, it's quiet but loaded, and it roots me to the spot.

He walks me backward, slow enough that my heart has time to speed up with every step, until the backs of my knees hit the couch. His hand comes up, not to grab my jaw or wrap around my throat like I expected, but to tip my chin up with the gentlest pressure.

"You've never done this before," he says, almost to confirm it as a fact.

"And you have?" I challenge.

The corner of his mouth curves. "No. I haven't."

"I've never had sex where the woman hasn't been restrained. I've never had them facing me, looking into my soul. I've never trusted anyone to give even the smallest piece of me to them. There is no other word for my past encounters than simply "a fuck". But you're different. I want to change that, for you."

I bite down on my lip. I want to kill whoever hurt him enough to make him this closed off. I thought I was bad, but he is really, deeply in pain.

"You can trust me, Finn. I won't hurt you. I'm yours."

He blinks at me and grins.

"All mine?"

I nod as we just stand there, watching each other, like whoever moves first will lose. I break, curling my fingers in his tie and pulling him down. The kiss starts soft; it's strange for us. My lips brushing his, testing, tasting.

Then it deepens. His mouth claims mine, slowly at first, his tongue sweeping deliberately like he's cataloguing me.

When he pulls back, his forehead rests against mine. His breathing is unsteady. Mine's worse. We're a hot mess. But it's beautiful.

His hands move to my arms, sliding down over my ribs, like he's memorizing me by touch alone. The slow drag of his fingers makes me shiver. I expect him to pin me. He doesn't.

Instead, he says, "I want you to touch me."

My brows knit. That's new. It feels so powerful. A moment where he breaks for me. Not in a harsh way, in the most perfect way. Chipping off another layer of his armor.

I place my hands on his chest, feeling the solid muscles beneath the shirt. No flinch. No tightening in his shoulders.

I slowly work on removing his tie and unbuttoning his shirt. Sliding the fabric over his shoulders, I see them—the faint scars beneath the ink. My fingers hesitate over one near his ribs.

He wants to hide them. Yet, not from me. He is allowing me to get under his skin, his scars, and into his heart.

He catches my wrist, his grip warm. "Go on."

So I do.

I trace every inch over the planes of his chest, across the dips and rises of his abdomen, and around the swell of his shoulders. His breathing changes. Not rough, but heavier.

Like he's on the edge of falling, and I am the anchor he needs. Dr. Finn Quinn is vulnerable to my touch.

"You're dangerous like this," I whisper.

He smirks faintly. "Not half as dangerous as you."

I unbuckle his belt and push the waistband of his pants down just enough to slide my fingers along the hard line of muscle there. His eyes go darker, pupils blown wide.

When I slip my hand under his boxers and wrap my fingers around him, his breath leaves him in a slow, shaky exhale.

"Is this okay for you?" I whisper, searching his face.

He nods once. Not rushed. Not barking orders. Just... letting me.

I keep stroking him, feeling every twitch and pulse under my fingers, until I slide his pants and boxers down fully. He helps me, kicking them off without looking away from me.

With my free hand, I thread my fingers through his hair, tugging him down until his lips are on mine.

"I want you in my mouth, Finn," I murmur against his lips, tasting whiskey and heat.

His voice drops. "Get on your knees then, wife."

I lick my lips as I sink to the floor in front of him. The carpet brushes my knees.

A thought flickers. Has he done this before? This breaks his rules. No touching. No eye contact. Those boundaries he's kept like a wall between him and the world.

Does that mean I'm the first one to suck his dick?

But then he smiles; it's soft, almost shy, and he strokes

my cheek with the backs of his fingers. Like he's reading my damn mind.

"Just you."

Those two words settle deep inside me.

I hold his gaze as I take him into my mouth. His hand slips into my hair, not to force me, but to anchor himself.

And I don't look away. Not once.

Because for the first time, I think we both understand exactly what's breaking between us.

I hollow my cheeks and take him deeper, letting my tongue trace every ridge and vein. His breath catches, like it surprised him.

I drag my mouth back slowly, my lips slick around him, then swirl my tongue over the sensitive tip before sinking down again. His jaw flexes, eyes locked on mine, his control starting to fray.

"Fuck, you're... perfect," he breathes.

I hum around him, loving the way his hips twitch at the vibration. My hands wrap around the base, stroking in rhythm with my mouth, each movement deliberate.

He's watching me like he's memorizing the sight. Me on my knees, mouth full of him, staring up like I can see straight through him. Like I'm meant to be here for him.

"You know what you're doing to me, don't you?" His voice is strained.

I nod without breaking my pace, my lips stretching around him as I take him deeper still. His hand slides to my jaw, tilting my face up even more so he can see every flicker of expression.

It's not just about the pleasure. It's about him letting me in.

I speed up, alternating pressure and angle, until I feel the tension coil hard in his thighs. His breathing is ragged now, every muscle drawn tight.

"Stephanie…" It's half a warning, half a plea.

I grip him tighter, work him faster, sucking him deep until his control shatters. His hips jerk once, hard, and he comes with a low, guttural sound that sends heat flooding through me.

I swallow, never looking away.

When I finally release him, I swipe the corner of my mouth with the back of my hand, and he's still staring, like I've just done something far more dangerous than make him come.

"Fuck," he murmurs. "If I'd known it would feel like that with you, I'd have broken my rules years ago for you."

CHAPTER 51

FINN

My chest is tight in that way it gets when something bigger than pleasure has just ripped through me.

It's like a light went off in my head, and I felt everything. The desire, the surrender, the ache of giving control away and taking it back, all at once.

She looked me dead in the eyes and sucked the soul out of me.

But she didn't just take, she gave something back. She healed a part of me without even realizing it.

I drag my fingers through her hair, fist at the base of her skull, and tug her head back.

"Open your mouth."

She does.

My cum still coats her tongue, and my cock already aches to go again. I bend down, collect the saliva pooling in my mouth, and spit it straight into hers.

"Such a good fucking girl for me," I mutter, hauling her to her feet.

She bats her lashes like the menace she is.

My hands roam her curves, tracing them like I'm committing every inch to memory for the rest of my life.

I crash my mouth onto hers, reclaiming some of the power, and she gives it up so easily. My tongue explores, my hands grip her ass.

"Strip for me, baby," I whisper against her lips.

Her eyes light up, and she runs her tongue along her perfect white teeth.

"Are you paying me, sir? I don't dance for free," she purrs.

That tightens something in my ribs. Her dancing for other men. Fuck. No. Mine.

I grip her throat.

"You only ever dance for me now, wife," I growl.

She nods slowly and backs away with a naughty smile, peeling off her black dress until she's standing there in just her lace panties. She lets her hair down from the bun and shakes it out, her black hair framing her beautiful face.

Her hands roam seductively down her sides, and she moves her hips slowly, causing me to groan and my cock to twitch for her.

I close the distance between us again.

"Now…" I lean in, my lips grazing her ear. "How about you test out that leg rest you've been eyeing up?"

Her hands roam up my chest, heat radiating from her touch. She grabs my traps and digs her nails in.

"Finn… You are so fucking hot. It isn't fair for any other man. You're smart. You're sexy. You're funny—sometimes. And you're just fucking insane in every way. I love it," she beams, and it guts me in the best way.

I can't help the smile that tugs at my mouth. I love her unfiltered thoughts, especially when they're about me.

I wrap my hand lightly around her throat, and she grins like she's been waiting for it.

"That's what I thought," I murmur. "You like a little risk, don't you? You want me to push you. Keep you balanced on the edge. Pleasure and pain, life and death. You like knowing my hands can give you everything… and take it away just as fast."

She nods as I nudge her legs apart with my knee.

My fingers find her soaked slit, and she moans.

"Yes, Finn. Fuck… I want it all with you."

I push two fingers inside as her reward, curling them just right.

"We're making love, baby," I tell her. "Remember that. But, after—" my mouth brushes hers, "—I can choke you, cut you, and edge you until you scream."

She sucks in a sharp breath, eyes locked on mine.

"Right now though?" My grin turns wicked. "I just want my wife to soak my face before I stretch her on my cock."

I drop to my knees in front of her, spreading her legs wider with my hands on her thighs.

Her skin is warm and flushed, her breathing already uneven.

"Sit," I tell her, guiding her down onto the couch so she's right at the edge.

I hook my hands behind her knees, pulling them over my shoulders.

She shivers when my mouth hovers an inch from her, my breath ghosting over her slick heat.

"You're dripping for me already." I drag my index finger over her glistening pussy, holding it up so she can see how wet she is. "And I haven't even started."

Her eyes are locked on mine. I want to keep it that way.

I lower my head and lick a slow line from her entrance up to her clit, tasting her, groaning into her like I've just been given my first hit of oxygen. She gasps, her hips twitching, but my grip tightens on her thighs, pinning her exactly where I want her.

"That's it," I murmur against her. "Stay open for me."

I work her with my tongue. Slow circles, teasing flicks, watching every reaction play across her face. Her head tips back.

"Eyes on me," I growl.

She forces herself to look, and fuck, the sight nearly undoes me. Her pupils are blown, her lips parted, and her chest rising and falling fast.

I suck her clit between my lips, adding two fingers inside her, curling them until she's panting. Every moan vibrates against my mouth, spurring me on.

Her thighs start to tremble, the muscles clenching around my head. She's close. Too close.

I pull back just enough to speak, my lips brushing her. "Soak me, Stephanie. I want every drop."

Her body bows, the sound she makes is half a sob, half a scream. The gush hits my tongue, and I drink her down, holding her through it until she's shuddering and gasping my name.

When she finally collapses back against the couch, I lick my fingers clean, keeping my eyes on her the whole time. I can't stop watching her. Studying her. Being fascinated by her.

"You taste like sin," I murmur.

Her gaze drops to my cock, hard and aching.

"Now," I say, stepping between her legs, "let's watch how well my wife takes every inch of me."

At the hospital, that was too fast, too rough. This time, I want to watch my dick slide in and out of her. Really see how well she takes me.

Song- Masterpiece, Motionless In White

He stands up, teasing me with his dick in my face; I'm desperate to lick that pre-cum away. But I don't. I wait for my instructions, because I want him to make love to me.

"Lay down."

I do as he says, my legs falling open for him like they were made to. He climbs onto the sofa, between my legs. His cock in his hand, the head brushing against my sensitive clit, sending a shiver through me.

"Look at me," he says. It's not loud. It doesn't need to be.

I do, holding his gaze as he presses forward. The first inch burns in the best way, stretching me slowly, my body trying to accommodate him. My breath catches, my nails digging into the cushions on either side of me.

This is different from our first time. Because I really have time to feel him, adjust to him. Let him fucking consume me.

"Breathe, wife," he murmurs, sliding deeper. The stretch

is exquisite, filling me until there's nowhere else for him to go.

"Oh, fuck," I gasp.

"That's it," he murmurs. I cry out as he sinks deeper inside of me.

"That's all of me. Every inch."

He bends down, resting himself on his forearm, his other hand settling around my neck. With just enough pressure to make my head fuzzy.

He starts to move, like each thrust is deliberate, like he's carving himself into me. There's no frantic pace, no tearing urgency, just him watching me take him, feeling every squeeze, every flutter inside me.

Our eyes locked on each other.

It's intimate in a way that feels dangerous. Like he's seeing parts of me I don't even show myself. Sparking something inside of me I didn't even know existed.

My hands find his shoulders, sliding down his back, gripping hard when he changes angle and hits something that makes me cry out and my entire body shake.

"You're doing a perfect job, love. You were made for me."

His eyes darken, but his touch stays steady, each movement sending heat coiling tighter in my belly. "You feel that, love? That's me and you, there is nothing else between us."

I nod, my voice caught somewhere between a moan and a whimper.

"Say it," he orders, his thumb finding my clit.

"It's just you and me," I breathe.

His control slips then, the thrusts growing harder and faster, his forehead dropping to mine. I can feel the tension in him, the fight between staying here in this slow burn and chasing the edge.

Our lips collide brutally. I'm clawing at his back, my breath burning in my lungs. I'm letting him take me. Own me. And ruin me for any other man.

"Come with me," he growls.

The heat breaks first in my chest, then everywhere at once. My walls clamp down around him, pulling him in deeper as he groans and spills inside me, holding himself there while my orgasm milks every last drop.

He stays buried in me, his weight grounding me, our breaths mingling in the silence after. I feel his heart hammer against mine, the sweat cooling between our skin.

When he finally pulls out, the loss makes me whimper, but then his fingers are there, catching the slick mess of him inside me.

His eyes meet mine as he pushes it all back in with a grin.

"You keep it," he says softly, almost like a vow.

"I told you I wanted to show you what I wanted with you."

It's a silent truth, and one I want too. That future probably neither of us ever pictured for ourselves.

"I'm not on the pill," I admit.

Everything messes with my hormones too much and sends me crazy every month. Nothing ever worked. And it's not as if I make a habit of having sex. Usually it's a drunk one-night stand.

"Good. Makes the risk even greater." He grins.

"You'd want a baby with me? You're serious?" I ask, tilting my head, trying to assess what's going on in his brain.

"You pregnant with my child would send me over the brink to insanity." He twists his fingers inside of me, and I cry out.

"And it's now all I can think about."

I shake my head.

"This is crazy," I mutter.

"Is it? Says who? Who makes the rules? We're married. I'm not a stranger, I am your husband. I've stayed and fought your every attempt to get rid of me. So yes, I am confident that I want you to have my babies."

My eyes go wide.

"More than one?"

He licks his bottom lip.

"You need your head checked. What have you done with Dr. Quinn?" I joke.

His eyes darken and his jaw goes tight.

"I haven't done anything to him. You have, though. You've made me into this man, just for you…"

My heart flutters in my chest.

"Mine," I tell him.

He nods.

Then he slides his fingers out, glistening, and brings them to my lips. "Clean them, Mrs. Quinn."

I open my mouth, sucking them deep, tasting both of us. His groan is low and guttural, his eyes fixed on me like I've just healed something in him he didn't think could be touched.

And maybe I have.

"We've done the pleasure. Now can we do the pain?" I ask sweetly.

He tuts and shakes his head, looking up to the ceiling.

"Perfect for me," he whispers.

"Who are you whispering to up there?" I ask.

He brings his head back down to face me, offering a sad smile.

"This sounds ridiculous, but you already think I'm crazy. But, my mom. She always said I'd find the perfect person, that I'd just fuckin' know. And I think she might just be right."

"Aw, Finn."

I leap up into his arms, wrapping my legs around his waist. He holds me tight, smiling against my lips.

"I wouldn't say 'aw' too quick, love. I'm about to raid your kitchen to find some knives appropriate enough to cut your wedding ring into your finger with."

I pull back and search his eyes; he's not fucking around either.

"How about… You mark your initials on my ass and then take my virginity there?"

He stops in his tracks. I want to give him a part of me back. I want it to hurt. I want to feel him break me.

"Is that seriously what you want?" he asks, reading my face.

"Yeah. I do."

"I'm starting to get suspicious this is too good to be true. Are you sure you're real? You aren't a robot? Or a demon sent from hell to fuck with me?"

I giggle, grinding my pussy against him.

"All real and all yours, Mr. Quinn."

He groans and tips his head back, so I lean in and sink my teeth into his throat.

"Mark me, psycho. Put your name on my ass and fuck me there."

He grips my cheeks.

"You're so fuckin' naughty, love. It would be my pleasure."

CHAPTER 53

FINN

Song- Sin, Ash to Eden

I carry her to the bedroom like I own her.

She's still wrapped around me, grinning like she just dared me to do my worst.

She doesn't know how far I'll take it.

"Face down, ass up, love," I tell her quietly, but it lands heavy.

She slides off me and crawls onto the bed, arching her back, looking over her shoulder like the little tease she is.

"You got a knife in here?" I ask.

If she thinks like I do, she will have supplies in her bedroom.

Her lips twitch. "In my closet, my medical bag."

Of course she does.

I stalk to the closet, find her bag, and pull out the slim leather case. When I open it, the light catches on the stainless steel. The kind made to cut with intent, not force.

I hold it in my hand for a second, feeling its weight.

This will do.

"Last chance to change your mind," I say as I kneel behind her. My hand spreads over the swell of her ass, thumb pressing into the soft dip.

"Do it," she breathes.

"This is very permanent, love."

She giggles. Fuck, I'm obsessed with her.

"Like I'm getting rid of you, Finn. I think we've established that isn't happening. So mark me."

I like that answer. I like it a lot.

I press the flat of the blade to her cheek and let the cold kiss linger before I start. The first shallow slice curves into the F. It's sharp and neat. To me, it's beautiful. Her breath hitches, but she doesn't pull away.

"Good girl," I murmur.

The Q follows. Two letters marking her mine.

But I'm not done.

I flip the blade in my hand and press it into my own palm.

Her head jerks up. "Finn—"

"Shh." The sting barely registers as I draw a short line across the thick muscle of my hand. Blood wells immediately. I drag my fingers over the fresh mark and then begin painting her skin with my blood.

"Now you're mine," I tell her. "And I'm yours."

Before she can answer, I offer her my bleeding hand. "Taste it."

She takes my wrist without hesitation, her tongue dragging over the cut, her lips sealing around it. The pull of her mouth there does something savage to me, something that feels like worship and war at the same time.

When she lets go, her mouth is stained red. She's breathing harder, and so am I.

I bend, licking along the fresh FQ carved into her, tasting her blood under mine. Then my mouth moves lower, between her cheeks, my tongue circling the other entrance I'm about to claim.

She gasps, gripping the sheets.

I keep working her with my mouth until her muscles loosen under me, then slick a finger and press it slowly inside.

"That's it," I murmur, pushing deeper, curling slightly. "Relax for me."

She likes the pain; that's why she is so desperate for me to claim her here. But I want to make sure the pleasure is still there. So I keep working her, one hand deep inside her pussy, the other in her ass, until she's dripping all over me.

"Please tell me you have lube?" I groan.

"Bedside drawer with my toys."

I quickly open it up; I will need to test these on her thoroughly as part of my Stephanie Research Journals. But now, I need my dick in her ass like I need air to breathe.

I grab the rose toy and hand it to her.

"Use that while I fuck that virgin ass of yours," I tell her as I lean in and kiss her.

Once I coat myself, I press forward, just the tip against her ass to see how she reacts. I grin when she pushes back. The hum of her toy fills the room.

"Mmm, good girl. Does that feel nice?"

"Finn, please, I need you," she cries.

I slap her unbranded ass cheek, admiring the redness forming.

I slide in, inch by inch, her moans mixing with screams, until I'm buried to the hilt.

The heat and tightness are a punch to the gut, but I hold still, stroking her hips, brushing my mouth along her spine.

"Breathe, wife."

When she gives me that first shaky moan, I start to move

—slow, deep—pushing down on her upper back so her ass stays high for me.

"Look at you… taking me in your ass so fuckin' well. Made. For. Me," I grit out, watching every inch of my cock disappear inside her tight heat.

"Oh my god, Finn," she screams.

I slide two fingers in her pussy, and she tightens around me. Her body shaking.

"That's it, baby, ride me. Remember who owns you."

My free hand slides up her spine, fingers threading into her hair. I grab a fistful and yank her head back so her cries and panting fill my ears.

"Say it. You are mine." My voice is raw, teeth clenched.

"I'm yours!"

She tightens around me, giving me a virginity I have no right to take, and yet she's giving it freely. And easily, because my girl wants pain.

I've handed her parts of myself tonight I never meant to. Parts I keep locked in the dark, and here she is, doing the same.

This isn't just sex.

This is a ritual.

A binding.

"Come for me," I command, my thrusts turning relentless.

The sound she makes when she falls apart is burned into me, her body gripping me like she'll never let me go. I spill inside her, holding her there until she's wrung out and shaking.

Only then do I pull free, flipping her onto her back, settling my weight on top of her. I grab her toy and turn it off. Tossing it to one side.

"Thank you," I whisper against her swollen lips.

Her arms stretch above her head, hair wild, eyes glistening.

"No. Thank you."

"Let's get you cleaned up."

She nods, lids heavy, but when she starts to sit, I push her gently back down, shaking my head.

"No, love. I look after you, remember?"

A lazy smile curves her mouth. "Can you stay with me tonight?" she whispers.

I freeze. The request sits heavy in my chest.

This isn't a good idea. There's a reason I don't sleep. A monster under my skin that could ruin everything.

I am poison.

But I nod anyway.

My body betrays me.

Fuck.

Song- Specter, Bad Omens.

I relax into his hold, my back against his chest, his warm breath hitting against my shoulder.

"This is nice," I whisper.

He kisses my back.

"Very. Get some sleep, temptress."

My eyes flutter closed. This feeling of safety wrapping me up and keeping me warm.

"Night, night, Finn."

He strokes his fingers through my hair.

"Night, love."

Before I drift off, he hugs me tighter. I can feel him relaxing too.

"I think we should do more of this, maybe it might be time for my wife to live with me."

It isn't a question.

"Oh, I can't wait to see where my rich boy lives," I tease him.

His arms tighten around me, his teeth sinking into my shoulder.

"What's mine is yours, love."

I smile as I drift off in his arms, with a happiness I haven't felt for a long time, if ever.

HIS SCREAMS RIP through the room, and I startle awake. Sitting up, I turn my bedside light on, creating a warm glow.

My heart is in my throat as I watch him scratching at his chest, as if he's fighting something off of him.

"No. Get off me. Don't touch me," he cries out. It's desperate and painful.

His voice is like a knife through my skin, piercing me.

Fuck. He's having a nightmare.

"Finn, it's me," I whisper, trying not to wake him up too abruptly.

He could hurt me. Worse, he could kill me with one hand.

"No!" he screams.

I scoot closer, holding my breath as I reach out to his hand. He slaps me away, the contact brutal. I wince but stay where I am.

"Finn, baby. It's just a nightmare. I'm here," I say softly.

His eyes flash open, and I don't recognize him; he's dead behind the eyes. Evil.

A scream rips through me as he launches himself at me, pinning me on my back, his hand squeezing around my throat like he wants to take my life.

"Fuck you," he spits.

"Finn!" I scream.

But I don't fight him. I just need to get through to him. Wake him up.

"Finn, it's me. Your wife," I say harshly.

His body slumps, his grip on my throat less deadly, but still there. He blinks rapidly, focusing on me.

His face pales as he realizes what's just happened.

I reach out to him, and he bats my hand away, shaking his head. He rolls off of me and onto his back, gasping for air.

I sit up, taking a shaky breath.

"Finn, are you okay?" I ask.

"I need to leave." His voice is cold and cruel.

"No."

I scoot closer, and he flinches.

He sucks in a breath as if it's his last one.

"I could have killed you, Stephanie. Fuck." He rips the duvet away and starts pacing the room, pulling at his hair.

"Get away from me, Stephanie. Don't let me hurt you. Please."

I don't move. I'm not scared of him.

He's desperately clinging on to reality, but something is haunting his dreams, and it's slowly killing every part of him.

"I don't want you to see me like this, Stephanie. This is my burden to deal with, not yours. I can't be trusted around you."

Tears start to burn in my eyes, but I hold them back. He won't want my pity, my sympathy. He needs me to be strong for him. He needs me to help fight his demons, just like he does for mine.

"I'm your wife, Finn. Your problems are mine now, remember? I'm here, and I'm not going anywhere."

His eyes lock onto mine.

"I'll annul it as soon as my lawyer is awake."

Shaking my head, I jump out of bed, closing the distance between us.

His breathing is still shallow, his eyes wild.

And all I can think is that this man needs me.

This is more than a rivalry. More than a wedding gone wrong.

This is about the man who pushed me to be better. Who studied me to know me better than I know myself.

Who listened to me.

Who showed me who I really am. And gave me things I never knew I needed.

He never gave up on me, and I won't ever do that to him.

"Baby, it's okay. Whatever it is you're fighting, you can tell me. I am your wife. I'm your friend. You can trust me."

He runs a hand over his face, letting out a ragged breath.

"Love, I think there is a point at which a person becomes too broken to fix."

I shrug, taking another careful step towards him.

"Did I say I wanted you to be anyone else but you? If you changed, I'm not sure I'd like you so much."

I grin, hoping to tease him back to life.

"I always knew you were fucking insane, Dr. Quinn. It's part of the attraction here."

He tilts his head to the side, that spark returning in his dead eyes.

Sliding my arms around his neck, I drag him down to me.

"I trust you. You're the only man I've ever trusted. Please come back to bed."

He shakes his head, brushing his nose against mine.

"I don't want to go back there. It's been so long since my last nightmare. I thought maybe I'd gotten better, that I'd finally get over it."

I suck in a breath. The more he speaks, the more it resonates with my own past.

"Maybe it's a sign to finally set it free. We gotta work through it to come out on the other side, Finn," I whisper.

Stroking his cheek, I wipe away a tear, and the last part of my heart that I was protecting from him—just became his.

"I'm scared, love." He speaks so quietly.

My own stream of tears is set free.

"I know, baby. I know. But by holding onto it, letting it live in your brain, you're letting that memory win. You're giving it power that it doesn't deserve from you."

"I just want to forget."

"And one day, you will, I promise you. We can make new memories to replace the evil. We've got this. Come back to bed? Don't let it win."

He swallows but shakes his head.

"I really could have killed you, Stephanie."

I nod in understanding.

"But you didn't, Finn."

"Not this time. But what about if it happens again? Sleeping with you in my arms is the calmest I've ever been, and it still happened. I can't escape my nightmares. I can't trust myself around you."

"I'm aware of it now, we can take precautions." I pause. "Like a gun in my nightstand maybe?"

A slow smile spreads across his lips.

"Temptress, this really isn't a joke. I can't lose you."

I shrug.

"Sometimes you have to make light out of your trauma. I'm still standing. You choked me in your sleep, that's all. You have my consent to do whatever you want to me any time of the day, awake or not."

He chokes on a cough.

"Don't give me that kind of power over you."

I place my hand on his bare chest.

"I can give you whatever the hell I want. It's only mine to give. Now, why don't you go and get some water and have a cigarette, I've got some stashed in my cupboard with the mugs. Clear your head under the stars, and when you're ready, slip back into bed, cuddle me, and pretend it never happened."

His finger strokes along my cheek, and he leans in, stealing a kiss from me.

"I'll do that."

"Good. And don't go disappearing on me and running away, because I will chase you down, Dr. Quinn. You wanted me, you've got me, now you can't leave me."

I mean this more than he will ever know.

And as his face softens, it's like he understands my silent plea. Don't leave me.

"Never," he whispers.

And then he's gone.

Song- Worst In Me, Bad Omens

By the time I take my last drag, my head feels clearer, but my chest is still tight.

I hurt her. Even if I didn't mean to, that's not the point. I could've killed her.

I knew the risk and still took it selfishly. And if anything ever happened to her because of me, I'd never be able to forgive myself.

I shake my head, lock the door, and down a glass of ice-cold water.

Falling asleep with her in my arms was the safest I've ever felt. The most at home.

Maybe I should talk to someone about my past. Omit the parts I can't share. But what would it even achieve? I can't undo what they did to me. Can't change the fact I sacrificed everything to save a friend and failed.

She died anyway.

And I was ten years old.

Now I'm not even sure I can save myself. And it's not

Stephanie's job to fix me.

I rub my hands over my face. I saw the way she looked at me earlier—pleading without words for me not to leave her. That silent plea hit straight to the bone. She's been abandoned. Hurt. Afraid.

So have I.

What we have is too strong to just let go.

I head for the bedroom. But as I pass the bathroom, I see it, a soft glow leaking from the room next to it.

Curiosity hooks me by the throat.

She never mentioned this room. The door's locked. I frown. She hasn't left my sight all night. She didn't lock it while I've been here.

A slow grin pulls at my mouth. You only lock something you don't want found. I know, half my house is locked down for a reason. The Decadence Trials. Although, delayed or not, the games haven't been part of my thoughts for a while.

She's just like me.

I find something small and thin in the kitchen and jiggle the lock until it clicks open.

The light comes on to reveal a plain, windowless office. The glow is from the computer monitor. No photos. No art. Just a desk and a cupboard. It's bland and boring.

I try the computer. Password protected. Figures.

First drawer: empty except for a small key.

Second drawer: locked. The key doesn't fit.

My gaze shifts to the cupboard. This is like a puzzle.

Inside is a metal safe. The key slides in perfectly.

My breath stops when I open it. There are rows of vials. All hospital stock. All lethal in the wrong hands.

My pulse climbs. This isn't shit you take recreationally. That's not what she's doing.

I know exactly what I'd do with them.

At the back, a second key. I try it on the locked drawer. It works.

Inside is a red leather box.

I set it on the desk and open it. Jewelry. Men's jewelry.

Silver and gold rings. Watches. Chains. At least fifteen pieces.

One watch freezes me cold. A vintage silver watch with emerald stones on the face and a marbled back. Rare. Worth a fortune.

I've seen it before. Complimented the old guy wearing it… before I took him into surgery.

My stomach knots.

I pull the drawer out further, revealing a slim black notebook. My gut tells me not to open it. My hand ignores me.

First page: a date from two years ago. A name I know.

The sex trafficker Stephanie saved. I remember cunts like that.

And in her handwriting:

He took something from me when I was eighteen, so I stole it back.

My chest tightens.

I flip through. More men. More dates. Short, brutal notes.

He paid to have sex with me when I was a teenager.

Is this a kill journal?

She understands me because she's like me. No, because she's been doing the same damn thing.

And her past aligns with mine in a way. I hate that for her.

I'm glad she kills these motherfuckers. Because if she didn't, I fucking would for her.

Except she's reckless enough to keep it written down.

I keep going until I hit the last entry, only days ago. The bastard from the club. He had his hands on her.

If she wasn't there, I would have shot him in the head.

I go back one page. My blood runs cold.

That name. That date. That fucking expensive watch.

Right before I was arrested.

My hands are shaking when I pull out my phone. I call Drago, not caring it's three in the morning.

"Finn?" His voice is thick with sleep.

"I need you to get the file from the Commissioner, tell me the exact name and date of the patient I was accused of murdering."

I want to be sick.

"Uh… yeah, sure, one minute."

"I don't have a minute."

I pace, jaw tight, rage boiling under my skin but kept on a leash. It's the hurt that's killing me, not the anger.

Drago finally reads out the name and date.

I stare down at the identical entry in her journal.

My chest seizes. I can't breathe. I can't speak.

"Finn? You okay?"

"No."

I hang up and pinch the bridge of my nose.

She fucking did that.

Is that all I've been to her? A pawn? Was she working with The Preacher this whole time? Is that why she's here, why she suddenly fell for me?

It wasn't trust. It wasn't love.

She still hates me.

She's worse than a traitor.

She broke my black fucking heart.

And with that, the last sliver of hope I'd been holding onto dies.

The empathy goes with it. So does every trace of feeling.

I close the book. My mind goes still.

The man I used to be slides back into place with the ease

of muscle memory. The one who feels nothing, who hurts for no one.

I am dead inside. Again.

And she's to blame.

Putting everything back into its perfect place, making sure it looks untouched, I rifle around the kitchen drawers until I find it. The key to lock the office door.

And then, I slip back into bed beside her.

Watching the steady rise and fall of her chest.

The way her lips part and little soft moans escape.

Is she dreaming about me?

About that future we started to plan together?

Or is she dreaming about taking me down?

A smile spreads across my lips as I stroke her hair away from her face.

"You're about to enter into your own nightmare," I whisper and press a soft kiss to her cheek.

She turns to face me, wrapping her arms around me and snuggling closer.

While I just lie here.

Calculating my next move. All whilst being fucking dead inside.

CHAPTER 56

STEPHANIE

Song- Euthanasia, NXW TIME

I wake to find Finn staring at me.

A faint smile curves his mouth as I blink against the light. He looks like he's been awake for hours.

"Good morning, love," he whispers.

"Morning," I croak, my voice still heavy with sleep.

Sliding my hands up his chest, I feel him flinch. His fingers curl around my wrist, not rough, but firm. The smile doesn't fade.

Weird.

"Are you okay?" I ask.

He nods. "Would you like to play a game with me, Stephanie?"

I blink, trying to read him. "What kind of game?"

"I like to call it more of a trial. A way to unlock our truths. Find our kinks. See what we're really made of." His voice is steady, almost too calm. "It will reveal a lot about us. Are you in?"

I swallow. It's too early for this. "Uh… yeah. Sure. When?"

"Now. I'll need to blindfold you for the drive. I'd like to keep everything a surprise for my wife."

"Okay… Can I have breakfast first?"

He rolls on top of me, and I instinctively hook my legs around him. His eyes dart between my lips and my gaze, something shadowed moving behind the grey.

I can't name it.

"You pack a bag, I'll make some pancakes."

His finger runs up my snake tattoo, sending shivers down me.

"This is beautiful," he whispers.

"Thank you," I smile, leaning up to kiss him, but it lands flat. No hunger. No spark. Just a press of lips.

Then he's off me, already pulling on his clothes. A switch flipped, and I don't know why.

Was it last night? Did we push too far, too soon?

His footsteps fade down the stairs, and that familiar wound opens in my chest—that jagged thought that there's something wrong with me. That maybe he doesn't want to keep me.

And it hurts.

I drag myself out of bed and pull on my favorite black lingerie set, the one with silver skulls, then hide it beneath a loose black dress. A little winged eyeliner, a comb through my hair. I'm ready.

The smell of pancakes pulls me downstairs. My stomach growls as I toss a few clothes in a bag and hurry into the kitchen.

"Finn?" My voice is cautious.

"Yes, love?" He doesn't turn, focused on flipping the pancake.

I perch on a stool, watching him. "Are you mad at me? Was last night too much?"

He takes a breath, slides the pancake onto a plate, then turns with a smile that loosens my chest. "Last night was perfect."

He sets the plate in front of me, passing the syrup.

"Are you not having any?"

"No, I'm not hungry."

Something is gnawing at him.

"You sure you're okay?"

"I'm always fine, love. Don't worry about me." He turns his back to wash the pan.

I take my first bite, and a soft moan slips out without thinking. His head whips around, eyes locked on me, burning.

I grin; I'm pushing and tempting him, hoping he'll break and come over here and wrap his hand around my throat.

Nothing.

I finish in silence. He grabs my duffle bag.

"You ready to go, love?"

"Yeah. So… What's the game?"

He taps the side of his nose. "Where we're going is going to either make us or break us, temptress."

A shiver slides down my spine. Break us?

"I—I don't like the sound of that." I stop walking.

"If something crumbles so easily, it was never meant to be. This is about revealing our true selves. It's important to me."

His face softens. I step forward, palm brushing his cheek. "I don't want to hide from you."

But the truth is coiled deep inside me. And I know exactly who I am.

A murderer.

A victim.

A woman who let men take from her to pay for medical school.

I'm not even sure I like myself.

"Secrets only kill you in the end, Stephanie. Remember that."

He kisses my temple, then guides me out to his Mercedes.

As soon as I settle in the passenger seat, he secures his tie around my eyes, blocking my vision.

"All good?" he asks.

"Yes."

Maybe the truth will set me free.

Or it'll burn me alive.

CHAPTER 57

FINN

Song, Counterpart, take luck.
https://takeluck.komi.io/

This morning was harder than I imagined.

I never anticipated her slipping past my walls so fast.

How did she know something was wrong? Am I that easy to read?

I shouldn't be. Not when I'm this numb inside.

But the worry etched into her face cracked something in my chest.

Just for a second, it stole my resolve.

No. I can't afford weakness, not when I want answers.

Not when this could be nothing more than her game. A way to fuck with me.

She could be my enemy.

I might have delayed the Decadence Trials this year, but this trial… this one matters more than any other.

This one decides if she's worthy of my heart that she stole.

We're both on trial here, and I don't know which of us will break first.

Because if she answers wrong… that's game over. For both of us.

I lead her through my home, straight to the back of the mansion, punching in the code until the lock clicks.

That familiar chemical tang hits my nose.

No one needs to know about this, as it's not an official Decadence Trial.

"Finn, are we at work?" she asks.

I grin. "No."

Short answers. Keeping myself controlled. I won't give myself away again.

The second door on the right yields to my code, and I guide her inside.

White walls. White floors. It's clinical and instantly instills fear in most people.

Chains hang from the ceiling, ending in a leather collar designed to wrap snug around a throat. The chain has just enough give for her to complete tasks, but not enough to roam.

A constant reminder I'm here; there's no escape from me.

To my left, three metal trays wait. Each one holds part of the trial. I go to the second and pick up a scalpel.

I never planned for Stephanie to be my one and only contestant. And each game is usually pre-planned to each contestant that Enzo selects for me. Now, I'm going to have to think on my feet. I had all night to get some ideas together.

I've also never had a contestant with any medical knowledge. That is usually my advantage to spark the fear in them. The women truly believe what a doctor tells them.

That any drug they take will have an effect. That there are no illusions. We make it look as real as possible here.

The Quinn brothers are masters of letting the world think we are evil.

But, deep down, especially in my brothers, there is a good heart. My mom always said we all did. Yet, when she looked at me, all I saw was sadness. Regret. It must have hurt her, knowing what happened to me and that she couldn't protect me.

It hurt my dad too.

It's what escalated the war with the Bowens. Because I didn't learn until I was in my twenties, my abusers were cousins to Charles Bowen.

Which makes wiping out every single one of them even more fulfilling to me. They are the true evil, it's bred into them.

That is who they are. And that is why they need putting the fuck down.

I circle around Stephanie, and it jolts me back into the present. If anyone would ever understand, looking at her little murder journal, it would be her.

I know Stephanie and how her brain is wired. She will see through that in no time. That won't get me my answers. That will just break her trust in me.

She knows me… better than anyone outside of my family.

The contestants never even know who I am. They never get to see my face or hear my voice.

This is different in every way. And yet, it's the trial with the most risk on the line. There is no going back from this.

"Stay still," I order.

The metal kisses her skin. Her breath hitches, her pulse beating against the blade's edge.

"Welcome to Decadence, wife," I say, my tone cold.

She freezes, and there is a pause. A grin tugs at my lips. "As in… the chocolate factory?" she whispers.

"The grounds of," I correct. "I live here. We own Decadence. And now, I own you."

The scalpel slips under the straps of her dress and slices. Fabric pools at her feet, leaving her in black lingerie. I trace her tattoo, pressing my finger to the silver skull in the center of her bra.

"That's kinda cool," she says lightly.

I frown. None of this is how I pictured it. She isn't scared of me—yet. She hasn't met the side of Dr. Quinn that she will meet today.

The one I've hidden from her. The most evil part of me that was born out of abuse. I wonder what she will think of me once she learns more about the man she married.

I step back and look at my wife, my only contestant this year. Disappointment fills me.

The Trials usually take in women given to me, each one here to earn freedom from her abusive family. It's a cleansing ritual, a way to hunt down the filth in our world. Whoever sacrifices a woman is ended quietly, in their sleep, once the game is done.

These men believe it's their ticket into Inferno, to the largest mafia network across the world. When in reality, it's their demise. It shows us exactly who they are and what they will sacrifice for power.

But this trial? This is for me.

To discover why my wife has lied to me. Betrayed me. Used me.

And maybe... a trial for myself.

How did I let this happen?

How did I give her my heart?

"There's a lot to learn about the family you married into, Stephanie."

I know to get her to open up, I have to sacrifice some of

my own truths. My fingers trail along her collarbones before I reach for the collar above. The leather fits perfectly around her neck. I buckle it tight enough to keep her aware of its pressure.

"Keep the blindfold on until I tell you otherwise. There are rules in Decadence that must be followed. Do you understand?"

Her mouth opens and closes. The air in the room chills.

"Y-yes. I understand, sir."

That's a kick to the gut. She could have been so perfect for me. A killer, just like me. A woman who craves pain alongside her pleasure.

Yet, here we are, on the brink of losing everything.

"I have some paperwork for you to fill out shortly. Take a seat while you wait."

I guide her to the metal chair, tipping her chin up so I can look at her.

My chest aches.

What will I do if she's working with The Preacher?

Am I really that much of a monster?

I have to be to protect my family. That always comes first. My brothers, my niece and nephews, the damn unhinged twins. They mean more than what my heart wants to crave.

I step back slowly.

"Will you be long?" she asks, a flicker of fear in her voice.

A grin tugs at my mouth.

Good.

Fear will spark the truth.

I don't answer. I just walk away from her, feeling the ache in my chest with each step.

As soon as I leave the room, I take a deep breath and head to the control center, calling Drago's cell as I do.

"Finn. How can I help?"

I close the door to the office and sit behind the desk.

"Well, I'll need you to email me over a blank contract of the Decadence Trials. I will need to adjust some of the wording accordingly. I need it now if possible?"

He clears his throat.

"Now? I thought the Trials were delayed?"

"They were. But I'm starting them today, with one contestant."

I can picture the confusion on his face. So I clear it up for him.

"My wife, Drago. She's chained up in Room One. And she's about to experience a new version of the Trials to give me my answers."

"Finn…" There is a warning in his tone.

"Yes?"

"She's your wife. Why not just ask the questions? Do you really need to do this? If you're wrong, there is no going back from this."

I rub at my chest.

"I'm not wrong about what she's done. I just need to know why, to decide if it's forgivable or not."

"And you think she will forgive you after?"

I chew on my lip.

"I don't care."

As soon as I say the words out loud, I know that isn't true. But this is the only way I know how. The only way to make her see the true monster I am.

Because even if I can forgive her, I'm not worthy of keeping her. I'll wreck her just like she's wrecked me.

"Fine. I'll send them across. Just be careful."

"I always am."

He takes a breath.

"I'm not just talking about her. I mean you. You're invested in her, clearly. You're hurting about something."

He has no fucking idea.

"She framed me for murder, Drago. I think she's working with The Preacher. If that is the case, none of it matters because none of it was ever real."

"Fuck. I'm sorry, Finn."

"Not as sorry as I am. But, look at the bright side, we might get closer to The Preacher and can take him the fuck down," I reply flatly.

"Do you want me to send one of your brothers over?" he asks.

"No. Don't breathe a word of this. If you're concerned, either you come here or send one of the twins. I don't need my brothers being wrapped up in my marital problems. But this probably isn't something any of you need to witness. This is between me and her."

They'll see right through me.

They might see my hurt.

I can't let them. I deal with my pain the only way I know how. By inflicting more of it.

"Okay. Email is sending now."

"Why do you need the contract? If she's part of The Preacher's organization, she won't be walking back out of here, will she?"

That thought makes me feel sick. Because even if this was a lie, my feelings weren't. I'm not sure either of us will be walking out of that room at the end of the trial.

There isn't an illusion of survival like in my brothers' games.

No. With this one, the threat is real.

Neither of us are ending up as a widow. But I don't tell

him that. If that is how it needs to go down, I'll say a proper goodbye to them all first.

"No. She won't. But I'd like my wife to sign it so I have it. A reminder of why I will never trust anyone ever again. And she might start to understand more about me by reading it."

"Let's think about that if we reach that hurdle, Finn. She might just surprise you."

I click my tongue against my teeth. I doubt it. I know what I saw.

"I have one more favor for you or the twins. I need you to get me some evidence."

I have one game planned where there will be no escape from the truth.

We end the call, and I pull up the contract, making a few tweaks, especially for my wife.

Because this is a different circumstance.

The girls that normally come here don't enter themselves; they have no choice but to play the game.

We make them believe it's a game of survival. When in fact, we never hurt them; we give them new lives, new identities, and no ghosts to haunt them any longer.

They have no idea who the Quinn brothers are.

But Stephanie is different.

Because she is here willingly. And she's not being chased by any monsters. No. She's the one haunting me.

And the game of survival isn't an illusion for her.

This trial really is life or death.

Our enemies don't survive in Decadence.

And she's going to take part with me right there with her. No hiding who I am.

She's unleashed the monster.

CHAPTER 58
STEPHANIE

Song- Madness, Ruelle

The room is cold, the kind that seeps through skin and straight into bone.

Clinical.

Too much like work.

But the worst part isn't the temperature. It's Finn.

He's turned to ice.

I'm tempted to sneak a peek beneath my blindfold, but I don't. I know him well enough to understand his rules aren't suggestions. Breaking them would be failing before we've even started.

The door unlocks and I hear his footsteps. His aftershave cuts through the sterile air as he re-enters. Metal scrapes across the floor.

My breath hitches when his fingers graze my cheek. The blindfold slips away, and light floods in, sharp enough to sting my eyes.

When I focus on him, my heart stumbles.

His grey eyes are glazed, manic, just like the night his brother was rushed into the hospital.

He's hurting.

And that makes no sense. What happened to the Finn who made love to me a few hours ago?

"Finn," I whisper.

He takes the seat opposite me, leaning back, arms folded. "Stephanie."

From his jacket pocket, he pulls out folded papers and a pen. He pops the cap off with his mouth, spitting it onto the floor.

"Before the games begin, I need you to sign something. A formality." His smile is thin.

He passes me the papers. His face stays hard, unreadable.

"Read it. Then you'll sign in pen… and blood. I'll do the same."

It has to be part of the trial. Another push, to see how far I'll bend before I snap. This whole setup suits him. Exerting the power he has over people. Organized and clinical, yet probably sadistic.

"I'd rather not bore myself with legal documents and just get on with the games," I say, forcing confidence I don't fully feel.

His thumb drags slowly along his bottom lip.

"You're already ignoring my rules. Not a great start, is it, Stephanie?"

I sigh and look down at the page headed with *"The Decadence Trials of Dr. Stephanie Quinn and Dr. Finn Quinn."*

Everything is a blur of words on a page as I skim through. Formalities. I know how contracts work. And it hurts that he doesn't just accept my consent. That he needs it in writing.

It covers everything. From cutting to spanking to taking

trial medicines. It even covers the death of both parties. Listed like it's nothing.

I trust him. I know the risks with anything in life. I could walk out in front of a car and die. I take risks every single day with other people's lives.

This doesn't faze me. And it's not telling me anything about what is in the trials. It's not telling me what happens when I win or lose. It's pretty basic with terrifying wording.

But then, my eyes catch on the final clause. The part that is a kick in the teeth.

If I fail the games, this document will annul our marriage.

"You want this marriage to be over?" My throat tightens, heat threatening my eyes.

He reclines in his chair, ankle over his knee. "I never did. You did. Here's the out you've been wanting."

His eyes are shards of ice.

"I–I don't want that. Not anymore."

"I wouldn't be so confident, love. I'm not the man you think I am. Sign it, and I'll reintroduce you to the real Dr. Quinn."

A shiver runs down my spine. My fingers shake around the pen.

It's a game. It has to be. He wouldn't actually hurt me. Not really.

But the contract says death.

A game of survival.

And if I don't sign, I fail.

"You wouldn't really kill me, would you?"

His smile blooms, and somehow he becomes more dangerous.

"That's a risk you take, love. Do you trust me with your life?"

He leans forward, elbows braced on his thighs, gaze steady and unblinking.

He's always been a mindfuck. This is just another one.

"Yes," I say, honestly.

So I sign. *Mrs. Quinn.*

I hold the pen out. His fingers brush my wrist, and a jolt sparks through me.

He signs beside my name, then reaches for a scalpel from the tray.

"Anywhere in particular you want me to cut?" he asks, completely void of emotion.

"I… kinda preferred it with the whole pleasure part."

His brow lifts. "You won't sign without that?"

I shake my head.

"Fine. One hand for me to cut, the other you can use to pleasure yourself."

My stomach dips. Not what I'd meant.

"I want you to do it."

He stands, towering over me, his hand clamping my jaw.

"I am in control of your pleasure. Your pain. Your whole fucking life in here. You don't make requests. You don't make demands. Do you understand? You're lucky I'm being this nice."

"Nice? You think this is nice? Chaining me in a cold medical room, waving a creepy contract in my face like some kind of—"

He lets go, stepping back and placing the signed document neatly on the tray.

"This isn't a game, love. It's a trial. The man you think I am and the man I actually am? Not the same. You're lucky to have this much grace. Men in your position wouldn't. But you—" his voice hardens— "you took part of my heart."

My pulse thrashes.

This isn't theater. This is real.

"If I've pissed you off, I'm sorry," I breathe.

His laugh is low, humorless.

He kicks my legs apart and steps between them, his voice almost gentle now.

"Now… are you going to give me what I want?"

"Do I have a choice?"

His jaw tightens. He doesn't answer.

I place my hand in his. He takes my ring finger, slicing the tip. I hiss at the sting.

He presses the paper to my blood. "Atta girl."

He does the same to himself, then tucks the document away in his pocket.

"Are you ready to play?"

"Yes."

He grins. "Game one comes with a choice. Choose right, and I'll tell you who I really am. A little bonding session before we continue."

I've always known there's a dark streak in him. That something carved him into this cold shape.

What else has he hidden from me?

He rolls the first metal table between us and sits. Two pills rest in the center—one red, one white.

The collar around my throat tightens when I shift.

"Is there anything you could learn about me that would change your opinion of me?" he asks, tapping the table.

"Not unless you abuse children… or women… or animals. Then I'd leave you."

He studies me for a long moment. Then nods.

"Let's play."

His hands clap together, sharp in the silence, and I flinch.

I can smell her fear, but under it, there's arousal. That, I didn't brace for.

She still hasn't grasped the seriousness of this.

Even with the contract in front of her, she's too busy trying to work out why I'm pissed off to put two and two together.

I doubt she ever thought I'd uncover her secrets.

But she's throwing me off.

She's not playing a game to push me away.

She's dead serious about staying. About being my wife.

You can't fake emotions like that. She's no actress. I've studied her long enough to know the difference.

That flash of sadness in her eyes when she read the annulment clause—I put it there to test her. She passed.

It was a pointless clause, because neither of us gets to become a widow.

I shake my head. I need to get back to the game. I know she's itching to learn more about me. About the scars on my chest. About my past.

I fascinate her as much as she does me. And that is my leverage here.

"In order to learn about me," I say, keeping my tone even, "I need to know you understand there are always choices in life. One leads to the truth—happiness, let's call it. The other brings pain and destruction."

She nods.

I gesture to the two pills on the table. "But sometimes you don't know which choice leads where. Sometimes the truth can hurt. Sometimes doing the wrong thing leads to happiness."

Every word is measured.

I know she kills men for revenge.

No different than me.

I kill those who deserve it. And those kills… they feed something in me.

"And sometimes," I continue, "you have to be brave and make a choice into the unknown."

Her voice is soft. "Okay."

"Are you brave, Stephanie?"

"Not always."

I nod slowly. "Do you want to be brave now? Make a choice into the unknown? Put your trust in your husband?"

She exhales. "I guess so."

"Good." I lean forward, voice dropping lower. "One pill will make you violently sick. A venom with an antidote I hold. Your life will be in my hands. The other will make you… unbearably horny, in this dose. Relief will also be mine to grant—if you earn it. Either way, it'll make the rest of the trial harder."

She blinks at me, flicking her gaze between my face and the pills.

"Which one is which?"

A slow grin spreads across my mouth. "Fate decides. Pick one, and you'll get your reward."

I glance at my Rolex, watch the second hand tick.

When I look back, she already has the red pill in her fingers.

The trust in that choice twists in my chest.

If she had even the slightest inkling I knew the truth, she'd be resisting, pressing, panicking.

But she's not.

Her body language says something else entirely—that she trusts me.

"Do I get to ask you a question once I take it?" she asks.

I clench my fists.

"Yes."

She smiles, looking down at the pill between her fingers.

"Happy with your choice?"

She shrugs, pops the pill and swallows.

"Open," I order.

She parts her lips and moves her tongue to show me.

I push back from the table and head for the door.

"Finn!" Her voice cuts sharper now.

I smile with my hand on the handle. "Yes, love?"

Another slip. Calling her love.

"W-what if it's the poison? You need to monitor me."

Finally—real panic.

"I'll be back." My voice is casual, dismissive.

Then I walk out, letting the silence close in around her.

Part of this trial is going to be about letting her think. Assessing from afar her reactions to see if we're going in the right direction.

I want the truth. Not a half-truth. Not bullshit.

I need to know if any of this was real. Or if it's all part of a bigger scheme.

I know The Preacher is out to get me.

But the question is, whose side is my wife on?

It's clear she framed me, and my first guess is them. There is no way Stephanie tampered with the CCTV. There is no way she'd risk her career for this.

There is someone above her pulling the strings.

That I can find out later. But, this trial is more about her. Was it fucking real, what she felt for me?

That's all I need to know.

CHAPTER 60

STEPHANIE

B eads of sweat drip down my temple, before sliding over my cheek.

I can't tell if it's from stress or because I've just swallowed poison.

And the one man who claims to hold the antidote walked out like it didn't matter.

Like I didn't matter.

His words still itch under my skin, pulling at the threads of who I am, what I've done. But as I glance around the room, I start to wonder what all of this is set up for.

Is this something he does regularly with other women?

Or is this something he set up for me? To test me?

I don't know how long passes before I start to doubt the pill was anything but a placebo. Time seems to stand still here.

Maybe this is part of the game, to make women spiral, to watch them fake sickness or lust, to see how far they'll degrade themselves for him.

This can't be the first and only time he's done this.

Does he do this with all of them?

Is this his ritual?

The thought twists in my stomach. Not because I'm scared, but because I hate the idea of being reduced to just another player on his board.

I force myself to lean back in the chair, crossing one leg over the other. My nails scrape against my palm.

The door opens.

My head snaps up, eyes locking on his.

There's conflict there, a flicker that doesn't match the coldness he wears like armor.

He sits across from me, deliberately further away this time.

"How do you feel?" he asks.

A smile tugs at my lips.

"Absolutely fine and no hornier than normal around you. So, I suppose my body just didn't react to whatever it was."

He runs his thumb across his lip.

"Hmm. I didn't think it would take you long to see through that one."

I grin.

"Placebo test. Very good." I wink.

His fists clench at his sides, and I stiffen. He's unamused.

"Do you play this game with other women?" My arms fold over my chest. My voice is steady, but my pulse ticks faster.

"Game? This is just a game for you?" he counters.

I chew on my lip.

"Well, that's what you called it earlier? I just want to know if I'm just another woman to you."

His eyes form slits and he sits upright.

"Oh, is that how this is going? You get to interrogate me?" His smirk is all teeth.

"What? Are you interrogating me?"

"Testing," he corrects.

"Do you?" I press softer now.

He nods.

Something tugs in my chest.

I'm not special.

I always assumed he wasn't the type for a string of women, especially with his strict rules about no looking, no touching.

I thought what I'd seen of him—the softer edges, the cracks—were mine alone.

I turn my head, letting my hair fall forward as I reset my expression.

Maybe to him, everything is a game.

"Does that hurt?" he asks.

My eyes snap back to his. "No."

"Awful liar, love." He looks pleased.

"The women who attend my trials," he says, "are part of a competition me and my brothers host here at Decadence. Entered by their families or husbands. They compete... to survive."

My mouth parts.

"What the fuck are you talking about? You're lying."

"I don't lie, Stephanie." His face doesn't move.

"Why? How? What the hell?" I'm speechless.

I know he likes to play games. But actual trials on people? No. I don't see it.

"This is where I introduce myself."

He extends his hand. I hesitate, then take it.

"I'm Dr. Finn Quinn. Son of Seamus Quinn. Irish mafia— born and bred. We deal in arms and drugs. This chocolate factory? It's our front. Inferno hosts the elite of the under- world—alliances that span the globe. You were right, you know?"

One word sticks in my mind.

"Inferno." A place I've only heard whispers about. A sex club.

"You own Inferno?"

His smirk deepens. "Is that where you wanted to end up with your side career?"

"I—I don't know. I've just... heard of it. Stripping was only ever a way to feel powerful, just for an evening, when in the day, I just go back to being no-one." The words fall from my lips, a revelation I wasn't ready to give.

I shake my head to recompose myself.

"What was I right about?" I ask.

He crosses his arms, looking completely casual about this entire situation.

"That I bought my way to the top. I did. But not with high-class family money. With blood. From an empire built on the bodies of our enemies. Do you want to know my role?"

He leans in, and my breath catches. Not out of fear, but because the heat between us spikes, even as the words coming are laced in violence.

"I kill people. Bad, bad people." His voice ghosts over my cheek.

His hands run down my arms, and my skin prickles.

"These hands you've felt inside you? They're the same ones I kill with. I have no remorse, temptress. In fact, I enjoy it. Finding new, inventive ways to end a life. While at work, I dedicate myself to saving them."

My heartbeat is fast but steady. He's not telling me anything I didn't already suspect.

The shadows in his eyes were always there.

This just gives them a name.

And he's just like me.

"Are you scared of me now?"

No.

I should be, maybe. But I'm not.

What I am is watching, measuring him the way he's measuring me. Because now I know exactly what kind of man I married. And I still want him.

"Do you kill the women that compete?"

He shakes his head.

"No. I don't. I let them think their life is at risk so they fully immerse themselves in the trial. You see, the assholes that send them here, they're the ones who actually lose their lives. The women, they all get their freedom. A new life. We like to balance the good and the evil in Decadence."

I close my eyes, trying to compute what he's telling me. How everything he's saying is striking me as a reflection of myself. Of how my brain works.

How I try to balance the good and the bad.

"No. I'm not scared of you," I tell him.

"You should be."

I sit up straight in my chair. His words slice through me.

"Are there any dark secrets you'd like to tell your husband?" he asks, running a finger along my lips.

I answer in a way to play the game. The lines are blurring, and I'm not sure what is real between us anymore.

And he seems to thrive with the illusion, with bringing out fear.

I have to keep myself safe.

"No. You know me," I say.

He nods, slowly.

"On to the second trial then, wife."

A mix of dread and hurt swirls in my stomach.

Perhaps I've got this all wrong. Him all wrong.

Her first fuck up. Lying to my damn face.

That was a perfect setup for her to come clean, at least to some of her wrongdoings. I admitted who I am.

But, if I'm going to suck the truth out of her and she wants pleasure… Maybe I can start to coax it out of her.

I have to think fast and calculate my next move.

Because the next trial I would have done is pointless.

She's already branded for me, on her ass. But I have four other rooms to play with. And a new toy I've never gotten to use.

"Stand," I command.

And she does, her eyes never leaving mine. Her blind trust in me is a problem here.

Her failure to see how serious this is.

I unstrap her collar, and the moment I take her hand in mine, electricity shoots up my arm, making me tense.

"Are we done already?" she asks.

"No, love. This is just the beginning."

Fuck, I need to stop calling her that. But I can't stop. It's instinct now. No matter what, she's woven her way into my fucking heart.

The brain scan proves that.

This was real for me and I cannot change that.

I lead her out of Room One and down to Room Five.

"You said this is part of your house? How big is the house?"

I chuckle.

"Rich boy size."

She smiles, and it stabs me through the heart. I want to believe this is all some fuck up, that she hasn't done what I believe her to.

And Drago's words run through my mind, she might surprise me. Maybe there is another alternative; there always seems to be in my world.

Putting the code in the door, I open it up and guide her through.

There it is. A wooden structure made to look like a real guillotine. Of course, it isn't fully functional. It's the threat, the illusion that it's real, that sparks the fear.

"What the hell is this?" she asks.

"Never read a history book before, Stephanie?" I ask, shutting the door behind us.

She lets out an annoyed huff.

"Shut up. I don't want my head chopped off. Do you have the Henry VIII fantasy or something? Chopping your wife's head off?"

The sass in her voice makes my cock twitch.

I turn to her, grabbing her throat and pushing her against the wall, my restraint lifting for a second.

"I told you, I'll only be married once. That's the difference here. I only wanted you."

Her mouth parts and I lean in.

No matter how angry I am with her, I still want her. Fucking crave her. An addiction I can't be without.

But then I remember that she is my enemy right now. Until proven otherwise. So I release her.

"Are you ready for the rules?" I ask.

"Go ahead."

Her confidence is equally infuriating as it is a turn on.

"Three minutes. During that time, the blade will move up the guillotine and into position. You have three minutes to prove to me you're worthy of an orgasm. If you pass by answering my questions, you'll come and the guillotine will stay at the top."

She swallows against my palm.

"And remember, I know you well enough to detect a lie."

I glance down at the slight shake in her hand; the nerves from her are exactly what I need.

"T-that thing doesn't actually fall though, right?"

There is no slot for the blade to go through; it doesn't fall with enough power to slice through the solid wood that is simply covering a metal block. She is safe. But she doesn't need to know that.

"Don't let it fall, love."

She blinks at me. Confusion on her pretty face. She's trying to get a read on me. I only allow her to see what I want her to.

I've spent what feels like my entire life mastering this art. Be who you need to be. Show them only what they need to see.

And it's worked well, up until Stephanie.

And I want her to trust me. I know she doesn't want to fail.

"Do you want to play the game?" I ask, dipping my voice lower.

I trail my hands along her sides, gripping her hips.

She pushes her hand under her panties, and a little breathy moan escapes her; then, as she withdraws, she presses two fingers against my lips.

I suck them clean, fuck. I shouldn't be doing this.

"Does it taste like I do?" she purrs.

Her eyes sparkle.

"Good girl," I mutter.

I've never been intimate with a contestant before. I've never wanted to sink my cock in one so badly to punish her for betraying me.

I've never wanted not to like someone so bad either.

It's a switch I can't figure out how to turn off.

Any other feeling is easy, I've spent years perfecting it.

But the switch for my wife? It's fucking jammed on. It won't turn off no matter what I try. And even if I do, just slightly, she flips it herself.

Grabbing a fistful of her hair, I drag her over behind the mechanism.

"On your knees for me, wife," I grunt.

And she does. It's a relief for a second, not having her beautiful eyes burning into me.

She gets in position without needing to ask. Her head in one space, her wrists in the other. I lower the wood to secure her in.

The FQ branded into her ass taunts me and makes me hard.

Mine.

No matter what. She is mine.

I don't want to go straight in for the blow, the big questions. We have to start small not to rattle her. Because if she closes up on me and refuses to speak, she will unleash a Finn that neither of us can ever survive from.

It seems the way to get to her is by being Finn. The one she was falling for. The one she trusts and doesn't want to let go of.

But the more frustrated I get, the less sure I am how long I can be that version of myself for her.

Dragging her thong to one side, her glistening pussy has my full attention.

I drop down to my knees.

The timer on the wall begins to count down from three minutes, and I press the button on the wood to start the blade's slow journey to the top.

"Is this what you need?" I ask, sliding my fingers across her wetness.

"Y-yes."

As I sink two fingers inside of her, she gushes all over my hand.

"So, the fear of death really does make you soaked, doesn't it?"

"Y-yes."

Fuck. She's so perfect for me. It's such a shame we've ended up like this.

I get her close to the edge, her moans filling the room. And then I stop. But I don't withdraw.

"I'd like to know about your parents, Stephanie."

She freezes up.

"W-what? Why?"

I slowly start to pull them out. I've hit a nerve with her.

"This is part of our trial. Learning about each other. Pasts are very important, and time is of the essence."

Although, I have no intentions of revealing more about myself to her. I thought she deserved that part of me.

"Fine. Fine!" she cries out.

"My parents are in jail for murder. They got life. I haven't seen them since I was twelve. I was in the foster system. I moved around a lot and finally settled here when I got into med school."

I push my fingers back in and curl them on her G-spot as a reward.

"Fuck," she cries out.

"Good girl."

I know that's the truth. Because I know all about her parents' murder spree. A case of desperation. Her father was being sued and on the brink of losing everything. So they poisoned the claimants and got caught.

I feel for her. And this is where her abandonment wound shows. Why she pushes herself so hard to be independent.

The career, being top of her class, never having a boyfriend. It all is her attempt to keep her heart safe.

It's exactly how I've protected myself too.

Circling her clit with my thumb, I give her a few seconds of pleasure.

"Now. I'd like to know why my wife is a stripper. You have the money, the career. Why did you start, and why do you still do it now?"

I keep gently gliding in and out of her, making her legs start to tremble.

"You're so close to a relief, temptress. Answer this and I'll give it to you with my mouth."

She sucks in a breath and pauses. The timer is ticking away.

"I had to pay for school. I had scholarships, but that didn't cover everything I needed to live. It was quick and easy cash."

Makes sense, but I know there is more. I'm close though.

"Just dancing alone gave you enough cash? You must have been something special."

She shudders.

But she is special.

"Well, to start with, yes. I was young and dumb. I let the manager at the time convince me to give up more; for money that meant I never had to worry. I let them do things to me. It makes me sick. If I didn't, I'd lose my job. I was only eighteen. I thought if I sacrificed my dignity then, once I'd made it in my career, I'd forget about it. I was wrong. So wrong."

My stomach sinks at the pain in her voice. The regret. The disgust. It's all so raw and real.

I understand her pain.

"Why were you still doing it?"

I up the tempo to distract her from her pain inside.

She doesn't answer immediately.

So I spank her, hard, on her branded ass. That might spark something inside of her to talk.

"Sixty seconds left, love."

She lets out a breath of defeat.

"To feel. I told you. That power—I'm not that scared and desperate eighteen-year-old girl anymore. I look after the girls. I stop predators from getting to them like they did me."

A grin tugs at my lips.

Almost. So fucking close.

I know she stops predators, but it's the how I'm interested in.

One fucking name I'm interested in.

She is primed and ready for the next game.

Spreading her legs wider, I move myself between them, spreading her open with my hands. And I feast on her.

She's earned this.

"So fucking good for me, love."

Her hips roll against my face and my fingers dig into her ass.

With twenty seconds left, she's passed this test.

"Come for me, wife."

The wood cuts into my skin as I writhe in this guillotine. I scream out his name. And as I do, the blade crashes against the wood on top of me.

My body goes into a mode of shock. I'm shaking and trembling, and I can't breathe.

Pure confusion. Terror and pleasure.

He keeps his mouth on my pussy, reminding me he's there. My heart is racing so hard my head goes fuzzy.

"Finn, fuck," I cry out.

My body is on such high alert, every swipe of his tongue sends a jolt through me.

As I ride my climax out over his mouth, my body starts to get a grip of itself.

My breathing steadies as he lets me out, helping me to my wobbling legs.

He spins me to face him, saying nothing. Just looking into my eyes.

"How did that feel?" He grins.

"Fucking terrifying, but I nearly passed out I came so hard."

He nods and strokes my cheek.

"Did you enjoy it? The fear? The trust?"

"I did." I smile.

But there is one burning question I wonder if he will answer. The other girls did this to win a new life. I'm doing this for him. To unlock things about myself and him.

"Finn, what do I get if I pass the trials? If I win?"

"If you pass the next trial, I'll tell you. You have to earn your answers, remember," he says bluntly.

I wrap my arms around his waist, and he moves out of my hold.

"Have I done something to upset you?"

I can't ignore this nagging feeling in my chest that he's mad at me. Or is this part of the game? Playing his part to test me.

He tips my chin up.

"I never get upset, love. I'd need to have feelings for that," he says coldly.

"You're not a robot, Finn. I've seen you."

His stare hardens.

"I sometimes wish I was," he whispers.

I place my hand on his cheek.

"You don't need to be, not with me," I tell him.

He lets out a breath.

"That's what I thought too," he mutters, and without another word, he takes my hand and drags me out of the room, back down the hallway to the room opposite the first one.

He stops before putting in the code and turns to me.

"I'm giving you one hint to come out of this room unscathed."

I nod, swallowing hard at the seriousness of his tone.

"I've studied you for years, Stephanie. I have a notepad full of observations. Never lie to me."

My heart hammers, the weight of the world falling on me.

There is no way he can know who I am.

He opens up the door and nods for me to go in. I stop and take in the room. Set up exactly like his office at work.

A desk with a chair and a bed, but this one has chained restraints. Next to it, an ECG machine. No windows.

Just white walls and floors and a fucking sink.

"On the bed, please," he asks.

My feet don't move.

Something feels different about this room. A shift in the energy. It's colder, it's more serious.

His words playing heavily on my mind.

I close my eyes; I don't have time to figure a way out. I don't think there is.

There is only one explanation for this.

One reason why he is torn between hating and loving me.

Finn knows the fucking truth.

It hits me like a ton of bricks. What if he broke into my office at home? I was asleep by the time he came back to bed.

The whole needing the truth.

Doing the wrong thing.

He's been teasing this moment this entire time.

He knows what I do.

But does he know what I did to him? Does he know I framed him?

He kills people.

He is part of the mafia.

If he knew, would I still be alive?

Bile rises up my throat. I have to play the game to survive. This wasn't a joke or a test.

This is really fucking real.

He leads me over to the bed, and I blindly follow him and get up on the bed.

I'm numb.

As his fingers trail across my chest, removing my bra, a tingle of life jolts through me.

He fixes my wrists into the chains on the bed railings. He places the pads on my chest for the monitor.

The ECG whines to life, filling the room with the steady, loud thud of my heartbeat. Too fast. Too revealing.

I stare at the ceiling, my pulse hammering against my ribs.

The game is over for me. I lose no matter what.

Because when I tell him the truth, he'll leave.

And that will hurt more than anything.

I've spent my life pushing people away, clinging to my independence because I'm the only person I can count on.

And now? All I want is to grip my husband and beg him not to go.

Being with him is the first time I've felt safe in my life.

Giving him my heart was never a decision.

But it is his to crush.

CHAPTER 63

FINN

Song- Control, Halsey

I blow out a breath as I attach the nipple clamps to her rosy buds. Part of me wishes we were just playing this for fun.

That I could have my wicked way with her in these rooms and see how many times I could make her scream for me.

She cries out a little once they're attached. I drag my chair over, watching the monitor get faster as I sit beside her and pull out my phone. I hesitate over the video before pressing play.

Our wedding day.

A moment she doesn't remember.

A day that I will never forget.

I look down at my tattooed wedding ring, and it hurts. A pain I've never felt before. It's so fucking alien it makes my skin crawl. Yet, it's not something I want to stop.

She takes in a shaky breath.

"I didn't know you had this," she whispers.

"I have secrets of my own, temptress. Just like you do."

Her eyes fill with tears as if she's finally figured this out. I let it play out, our drunken laughs as we say our vows.

And then the kiss. The way she looks at me. The way I'm looking at her, like she's the most important person in my life.

Fuck. I think she was.

Our first kiss will forever be etched into my memory. I instinctively brush my finger over my lips. Watching how she touches me, and I don't back away, I don't freeze up. It's like her touch was meant to be on me.

"Til' death do us part—those were the vows we said to each other, correct?" I say coldly.

She nods, tears streaming down her cheeks now. I take in a deep breath. This is it. The real Finn she gets to see.

I lean in closer.

"So that means you either tell me the damn truth or this room becomes a morgue for both of our bodies."

She flinches away from me, tugging at the chains on her wrists.

"Finn. What do you mean? What's going on?"

I chuckle in response. She will soon realize her mistakes.

"I mean, if I have to kill you, temptress, then I won't be able to live with myself. So, we either both survive here, or we both die."

Death doesn't scare me.

But loving Stephanie does. That petrifies me.

I said this marriage would be my first and my last. It seems I can predict my future better than I thought.

"Say it with me, love. Til'. Death. Do. Us. Part."

She whispers it back to me and I pull away from her.

"Would you like to hear the rules of this room?" I ask.

She closes her eyes and I shake my head, grabbing her jaw.

She doesn't get to hide from this. From me.

She pushed me this far. Let out the monster I never wanted her to fucking see.

"No. You will not take your eyes off me," I growl.

I'm stern, but it's important.

This is our make or break.

My make or break.

I pick up the remote and press the button that sends shocks to her nipples. Her back arches, and she lets out a scream.

"I said, do you want to hear the rules of this room?" My voice is louder. Harsher.

My patience is wearing thin.

"Yes!" she cries out.

I push my chair away, and it clatters onto the floor with a crash as I stand.

Her heart rate is screaming.

And everything inside me is raging.

"I ask questions, you answer. For each lie, your punishment gets worse. There are no limits here. Life or fucking death. It's only the truth that can save you." I lean over her, gripping her throat so we're nose to nose.

"Remember who you're talking to now. I'm not your husband anymore. I'm the decider on whether you go straight to hell. This isn't a fucking game, there are no illusions. You should never have trusted me. Now, you get to see the man you really married, and I want you to show me who you really are, Stephanie Miller."

"Finn, please."

I squeeze her throat tighter, stopping myself from taking it too far.

"Begging for mercy won't work now. Play the game."

I release her and stand, straightening my shirt and shrugging off my suit jacket. I turn slowly back to face her.

Panting, petrified. Looking at me like I am a fucking monster.

Good. She's understanding that she hurt me.

"Question one. Tell me about your first murder," I say bluntly, not mincing my words.

Her eyes go wide, the tears slipping down her cheeks.

"You're punishing me for doing the same thing you do?" she spits back.

I let out a laugh that echoes around the room.

"No, love. That isn't it. Answer the question."

She closes her eyes, and I hit the button, shocking her again.

"Fuck. Fine!"

"He was my first boss at the strip club. The one who groomed me into being his prized possession. The one who ripped everything from me." She all but screams the words.

The pain ripping through her.

I nod with a smirk.

"Good girl. Keep going, I want all the details."

She lets out a shaky breath. The monitor is screaming and only fueling me to push harder. How far can I go?

At what point will I switch out of this? She can't save me from myself now.

No one can.

"I saved his life on the operating table; I knew who he was. And then, I saw you in the locker room, and you said something along the lines that he was a sex trafficker and I let him live. I couldn't stop thinking about the other girls he's hurt or will continue to hurt. So I went back in, and I put air in his line."

She's speaking so fast she's almost out of breath.

"How did it feel?" I ask.

"Freeing. Liberating. Really fucking good."

Her eyes lock onto mine.

She's just like me.

It's haunting.

"And that's why you didn't stop? You like to play God? Is that what it is?"

She shakes her head.

"You think the justice system would care about a stripper? Really? And something from years ago? These men are more powerful than that. They're like you. I let them manipulate me, I was stupid for that. I was desperate to be better than my parents."

I grit my teeth, her words jabbing me in the heart.

That desperation is real, it's fucking raw. I get it. None of these deaths bother me.

Except the one that put me in a cop car.

"They're nothing fucking like me," I spit back.

"You're a fucking monster, Finn."

Now that really gets me laughing.

"Coming from our very own resident Doctor Death."

I shake my head, picking up the scalpel from the side.

"Tell me about the others. How many more have there been?"

She sucks in a breath as I brush the blade along her throat. I assess her, the way her body is trembling in fear.

"Ten?"

She says it as if it's a question.

"You don't keep count? Don't lie to me."

"Ten," she says more confidently.

"The others, who were they?"

I continue to drag the metal along her skin, down her stomach.

"Either men I recognized from my past or assholes like the one who you beat the shit out of at the club. Men who don't understand the word no."

I bite back a grin.

I like this side of her. This murderous one. Who strongly believes what she's doing is right.

And in my book, it is. I'm fully behind it.

I'd encourage it.

It's everything I would want in a wife.

But the betrayal—that is what is fueling me.

"Tell me about the man you killed in the hospital recently. I've never killed at work, Stephanie. Ever. It's too risky. Yet, you did it again. Why?"

She pauses, her heart rate dramatically climbing.

There is no rhythm to her kills. Her first one was in the hospital, yet it seems she then went back to the strip club to find the other victims. She's clever enough to know not to do it at work.

That she would get caught. Yet something made her be reckless. That isn't my Stephanie.

"I knew him from before," she says quietly.

I arch a brow, turning the dial up on the remote and pressing it. Her back arches and she screams out.

My cock fucking twitches, and my heart breaks all in one.

"Do you remember the fucking rules?" I spit.

"Y-Yes."

"You didn't know him, did you?"

Backing away from her, I go to my jacket and pull out the watch that the twins have recovered from her house.

I hold it up in front of her face with a wild smirk.

"This man was not part of your history. Was he?"

She shakes her head.

"W-why do you have that? Are you trying to blackmail me?"

Interesting. She knows I'm rich. I don't need money. Yet, that is her first instinct to assume.

"No. That isn't my style. I like to extract the truth. So tell me. This is the one opportunity to save your life."

I stare into her soul, letting her know I'm not bluffing.

"I didn't know him."

I pick up the chair and turn it around to straddle it.

She watches nervously as I run the flat end of the blade across my hand. Processing. Making her wait.

Letting her think about her next move.

Slowly, I bring my gaze back to hers. Those blue eyes full of fear, full of sadness and regret.

"W-what do you know, Finn?" she asks quietly.

I shrug.

"You tell me what you think I know."

I drag my finger across her lip.

"Life or fucking death, love. I'm prepared to fucking lose it all if you are."

I already have.

There isn't any going back from this.

My mask has slipped. She's seen the real me. She knows too much.

I am unlovable.

I am a fucking psychopath.

And I don't see a way back from this.

He knows.

I fucking know he does.

And right now, he believes I am the enemy here.

I might be the woman he thinks I am. The murderer. But that, I don't think, is his issue.

After what he's revealed. After what I've seen.

It's the betrayal. He's made it clear that he let me in, that he started breaking down his walls for me.

And now, he thinks I'm a monster.

This whole facade is to hide his hurt. He's acting out. Trying to show me the worst version of himself.

Do I believe he would kill us both? Yes.

He's dangerous.

He's unhinged right now.

And he believes his wife is a traitor.

What do I do?

If I reveal everything, he might not even believe me. How do I make him believe that I was forced to frame him? When I have no evidence of who was behind the phone call.

Only a hunch it was that sleazy guy in the strip club.

I'm screwed whatever I decide.

"I can sit here for as long as you want, love. I have no plans. We can sit in silence and starve to death if you really want."

I chew the inside of my mouth until I taste blood, my hands trembling despite my attempts to keep them still.

He's going to hate me. He's going to leave me.

"Finn, please, just stop this. I can't even think properly like this."

His eyes snap to mine, sharp as a blade.

"Think about what? How to fool me again? Figure out how to get rid of me for good this time?"

He stands, nostrils flaring, the tension in his jaw flexing as he unbinds my wrists, and I rub at them instinctively before tearing the ECG patches from my chest, then carefully unclipping the nipple clamps with a hiss.

"Finn." My voice is low, wary.

"I always said you were a terrible actress. Fucking got me though, didn't you?"

I push off the bed, my legs unsteady, but I plant myself in front of him. I'm not backing down. I'm not running scared.

"What are you talking about? This is real!" I shout, pointing between us.

He shakes his head slowly, eyes shadowed. Then he reaches into his waistband, and I gasp, stumbling back as the gleam of metal catches the light.

He doesn't point it at me. He holds the gun out in his palm.

"Do you want me dead? Is that the next step of your plan, huh?"

I shake my head quickly, the fear curling hot and heavy in my stomach.

"What? No? Why would I do that?"

My voice is trembling, my eyes blurry from the tears I'm trying to keep from spilling. What have I done?

A dangerous laugh slips from his lips. He presses the barrel to his temple like it's nothing.

"Will I still make it in your little book of murders if I shoot my own brains out?" His voice is quiet, almost gentle. That's what makes it terrifying.

Psychotic.

I take a small step forward, hands outstretched. I can get through to him. I have to.

"Well, wife? Tell me? You clearly want me fucking dead. What happens to your plan if I do it myself?"

I blink, throat tightening.

"Or does your boss not care?" he adds.

"My boss? You're my boss. Are you going crazy?"

He flicks off the safety.

"Stop!" The word rips from me in a sob.

"No. You stop fuckin' lying to me. Tell me why."

He slams his hand down on the metal tray beside us, the sound sharp enough to make my body jolt.

"You've got this all wrong, Finn."

He steps in, and before I can react, his hand is around my throat, shoving me back against the wall. The gun digs into the soft skin beneath my jaw.

"That's what traitors always say." His whisper burns hot against my ear.

"I'm not. I swear. Finn. Listen to me."

I push both hands against his chest, but he doesn't move.

I force myself to look into his eyes. Pleading with him the only way I know how.

"I'm not scared of you," I tell him. "You can show me your crazy, and I'll show you mine. Shoot me. Do it. I've got nothing anyway. I'll just be another statistic. And I'm sure you know how to hide a body."

My eyes narrow, chin tipping up in defiance.

"I'm clearly fucking crazy for falling for a psycho like you." I let the words drip with a sweet smile.

He grunts.

"Ditto."

"You never fell for me, temptress. I was just a pawn in your game. Tell me why. You wanted my job that bad? Or have you been working with them this whole time?"

A laugh bursts from me.

"You really are full of yourself, Dr. Quinn. You seriously think I'd do all of this, for what? Get a job? Is that what you think of me? Why did you even want to stay married to someone as pathetic as that?"

His chest heaves. I can feel the shift—he's listening. So I keep going. Keep prodding.

"I didn't do it out of choice, Finn. I was blackmailed. Again, my hand was forced by a man. It was my life over yours. I couldn't say no. So I'm sorry. I'm so fucking sorry some asshole is coming after you and dragged me into your orbit."

He jabs the gun harder, forcing my chin up.

"Why didn't you tell me? I thought we'd gotten closer. I let you in."

The words cut deep.

"I didn't tell you because I was scared."

"Of me?" His brow furrows.

"No."

I inhale deeply, the air shaking in my lungs.

"I was scared you'd leave me. And now I'm scared you'll do that anyways. I assumed since you got away with it, you wouldn't care. That it was done," I quietly admit.

He pulls back, leaving me panting against the wall, my throat throbbing where his fingers were.

"You were wrong. Who blackmailed you?"

I twist my thumbs together, avoiding his gaze.

"There was a note left on my car. It was after that same guy you had a knife to, that wanted to speak to me. He had an accent not from around here. Then it was a phone call, a distorted voice. They gave me the warning and the details. Nothing else. But they knew about my first murder. They knew enough to ruin me."

My stomach twists. Everything is collapsing, and it's my fault.

I always knew I'd end up alone. I just didn't think it would be this soon. And I didn't expect my husband to be the one to kill me.

My ears ring as he watches me, silent, calculating.

"And they didn't say who?"

I shake my head.

"All I had was that stupid bit of paper with a PR in a fancy font at the top."

He stills, scratching at his jaw.

"You're sure. PR?" he asks.

"Yes. I can read, psycho."

He grunts under his breath. I'm getting agitated with this now too.

"And did they say exactly why it had to be me?" he asks, tilting his head.

"Nope. Nothing. And I haven't heard anything from them since. I'm waiting for them to either kill me in my sleep or try to use me again."

He blows out a long breath, his eyes diverting away from me. Reality must be setting in.

His eyes snap to mine.

"They won't fucking touch you, Stephanie," he grits out.

"I didn't mean to hurt you," I whisper.

His cold eyes snap back to mine.

"I'm not hurt. I'm disappointed you couldn't confide in your husband. That I still wouldn't have known. It's only because of that stupid fucking nightmare that I even found this out. I could have protected you—and myself."

I nod slowly, stepping closer to him.

"You know the truth about me now, Finn. You know who I am. I have nothing more to hide. I'm still not scared of you, though."

His head tilts.

"You really are as crazy as me, aren't you?" He grins, and my heart pounds.

"I think that might be the case." I pause, thinking back to some of our previous interactions.

How, for years, he's been making notes about me. Analyzing me. Yet, he missed all of this. This whole other side to me.

"Did you have any of this in your notepad about me?" I ask, rubbing my sore throat.

He shoves the gun back in its holster on his waistband, and I let out a slow breath. But then as his fingertip runs along my snake tattoo, tracing every line, my stomach flips.

I might be fucking crazy, but even after this stunt, my feelings towards him haven't changed. I just want him to understand, not just what I've done, but who I am.

No one ever has, but he could. If he'd stop shutting himself off. Trying to prove he's a monster, when really, he's just staring right back at another one.

"No. I had no idea my wife was as bad as me," he whispers.

"Now what?" I ask, swallowing hard.

"I guess you passed this room. I'll be back shortly for your final trial. And this one, even I have no control over. There is nothing you can say or do. It's either in you to pass or it's not."

I frown, taking in his words. What the hell does he mean?

"And what if I win?"

A small smile tugs on his lips.

"You'll get a shot to prove your loyalty to me again. But winning shouldn't be your concern. Think about what will happen to you if you lose."

My mouth drops open and he releases me.

"Do we have to do this trial? Can't we just talk?"

He shakes his head.

"Love, when you've lived the life that I have, you learn never to trust what someone says. Even if that person owns your fuckin' heart. There is only one way for me to fully believe you. To know you're completely in. I believe you. I do. But what I feel for you could cloud my judgment. I can't risk that, not when it comes to our enemies and protecting my blood."

I swallow the bile rising in my throat. The guilt is eating me alive. I blink back the tears.

"I don't want to lose you, Finn. I'm not bothered about dying. About paying for my sins. I didn't want this to happen."

He lowers his gaze to the floor.

"Have you ever heard of The Preacher?" he asks.

"No? Is that what the PR stands for?"

He nods.

"I believe so, love. I believe so. And they're exactly the kind of people we would both murder."

So they're abusers. Traffickers, perhaps?

"And they know who I am," I whisper.

Finn sighs as he steps towards me.

"Our plan is to take them down. To stop the cult in their tracks. But it's harder than we ever imagined. It's going to take time, manpower, and a lot of skill."

"I can help," I cut in.

"If you'd have told me before this point, perhaps. Let's see how the next trial goes."

As he goes to leave, I grab his hand.

"If I fail the next room, can I ask one last thing of you?" I ask him.

He chews on his lip and nods.

"That you don't let me free. Just fucking kill me. I can't live my life running from some cult. I won't have my job. I won't have my husband. I've got nothing left but a death sentence. So if anyone gets to do it, it's you."

His face pales and he squeezes my hand.

"Let's just hope it doesn't get to that, yeah?" I can hear his pain.

This is killing him too.

He releases my hand and storms to the door, not even a glance back, and slams it shut behind him.

Leaving me standing here, tears streaming down my face as my heart cracks in two.

I've hurt the only man who made me feel. The only man I've ever loved.

CHAPTER 65

FINN

I swear I can't see straight by the time I get to my office. Every step feels heavier, my head pounding with the leftover adrenaline. I want to throw everything against the wall. Hell, I want to throw my own fucking head against it just to quiet the noise.

But the second I open the door, I freeze. My brothers are inside, both staring at me with looks I've only ever seen at funerals.

My eyes flick to the monitor. The camera is off, but the sound is on.

They heard it all.

"Get out." My voice is sharp enough to cut glass.

They don't move. My jaw clenches as I slam the door behind me.

"How did you even get back here?" I head for the liquor cabinet and grab a whiskey. "Wait. Don't tell me. Drago?"

They stay silent, watching me like I'm a live grenade. I drop into my chair, twist off the bottle top, and drown myself in liquor.

"You okay?" I ask, like I'm the one checking on them.

They glance at each other.

"We're fine, Finn. Are you?" Declan steps closer, careful, like I might snap his neck for breathing too loud.

"I'm doing grand. Never better."

I knock back another mouthful, letting the burn fight with the rage. The hurt. The betrayal.

And the worst part—the gnawing, unshakable thought that she's telling me the truth. And that she's scared. That she needs protecting.

That I let my mask slip. That she saw the real me. The version that should have stayed locked away. The evil side never meant for her.

I'll never be fucking normal.

"Finn, I think we need to talk about this," Conan says.

"Talk about what? It's a marital matter. It doesn't concern my entire family."

Declan scratches at his stubble, unimpressed.

"You're fucking wrong. It does concern us because look at you. Threatening to end it all? You think your wife wants you dead? Is she a risk to you? To our kids?"

I push to my feet, the chair scraping back hard.

"No. She's fucking not. She's lied to me. She's caught me off guard, yes. But she's not working with The Preacher."

"You believe her?" Conan's eyes narrow.

I don't hesitate.

"Yeah. I fuckin' do."

"So what are you going to do about it? Now she knows what we are—what you are? What if she runs to the cops? Or worse, The Preacher?"

I laugh, the sound dark and humorless.

"She won't. We're way past that."

"You're in love with her?" Declan's voice is a whisper.

My eyes snap to his.

"Who says she's walking back out of here?" I smirk, dropping back into my chair.

"Finn, come on. Clearly you have feelings for her, and you believe her. She stood up to you. She's not running anywhere." Conan's glare cuts at Declan.

"I'm glad I've got both of your psychological assessments of my wife." My rings tap against the glass in a deliberate rhythm.

"You're wrong. Both of you. She was scared; she hides it well. But the way her breathing changed, her pupils dilated— she fears me. Hence why she lied to me in the first place. There's only one way I'll know the truth."

Conan shakes his head.

"She's scared of losing you, brother."

I scoff.

"The next trial will decide our fate. There's only one thing I trust to coax her real intentions. My girl will work her out."

"Nyx?"

I nod, a slow smile forming.

"She tells me she accepts my crazy. That she's scared I'll leave her. Let's see what Nyx thinks of her. Let's see what she really accepts of me."

I lean back in my chair and look at the ceiling, letting the weight settle. I thought I'd shut it all off. But every time I'm near her, she cuts straight through the glass.

She fucking sees me. And she knows exactly how to pull me back to her.

"You're putting your future on a snake?" Declan asks.

I shrug.

"Trust me, it's better than any truth serum."

"You could just talk to her?" Conan suggests.

"Would you sit down with a coffee and talk to your enemy? To someone who has betrayed you? Shall I call

Theo and ask him to book us a table for lunch with Arthur?"

Conan's jaw flexes as he steps forward, eyes darkening.

"That's different. I did nearly die. Your wife just threw you to the cops to save herself. Everyone makes mistakes, Finn. Even you. I'm sure there are things in your life you wish never happened. I wish I never killed James Bowen and that our father would still be alive."

I pinch the bridge of my nose, dragging in a breath.

They have no idea. No idea what happened to me. No idea what I'd take back if I could.

I wonder who I'd be if I never let them do the things they did. If I didn't try to save my friend by taking her place.

But I can't change the past. I can't even change what I've done today to Stephanie. It's too late.

She's seen me, and I've seen her. And she didn't crumble. She still pushed back—even with a gun to my temple.

But how the hell do we move past this?

"There are many things I regret, brother. Today might be one of them. But I am who I am."

I stand, rounding the desk, and clasp Declan's shoulder.

"We need you, Finn. Theo called," Declan says sharply.

"When do I go?" I ask.

"They're setting up a meet with Arthur. So, as soon as you can get there, it's game on."

I nod slowly, glancing to Conan.

"Are you ready to leave?"

"Yeah. Hallie is fine with it too, she understands."

"Good. And you, Declan? Are you joining your brothers?"

He takes in a breath.

"You know I'd never fucking leave you both. We're in

this together. Always have been, always will be," he tells me, his eyes narrowing at me.

"And someone has to stop you from putting loaded guns to your damn head," he continues.

"Let me deal with this, and then I'll pack a bag. Get the jet ready; let's end this once and for all," I tell him.

As Declan runs a hand through his dark hair, I can't help but think how much he is like our father. Trying so hard to hold this family together. I can see how worried he is, just by the way he's looking at me. At the way he's speaking to me, everything is so careful.

"I know you care about me, but stop worrying. I've survived this long. Nothing has changed. I'll see to this, and then we go."

I don't wait for their reply. I head out, down the hall, and straight into the part of my mansion where Nyx waits.

She is my judgment day.

CHAPTER 66

STEPHANIE

Song- over me, Camylio

The heavy door opens again.

Finn steps inside, and he's holding something. I see the ripple of muscle beneath midnight-black scales, the slow movement as the snake coils lazily around his tattooed forearm.

My breath catches.

"Meet Nyx," he says, his voice low but holding that edge, the kind that makes the air too heavy to breathe.

My feet stay rooted in the spot. I can't move. I can't breathe as he closes the distance between us.

"Please, take a seat, love." He motions to the medical chair behind me.

But it's the way he's still calling me love that makes my heart race. That electricity between us is still there.

My gaze fixes on the beautiful creature sliding up him.

She's exquisite. Her scales catch the faint light like polished obsidian, each ripple moving with a grace I can't look away from. Her head lifts slightly, tongue flicking the air.

"Black snakes have always been my thing," I mutter without thinking.

He smirks faintly.

"I did wonder whether that tattoo was just for aesthetics or something deeper. I was always hoping it was the latter."

He moves closer, letting the snake's body rest higher on his arm. She winds herself around him like she owns him.

"H-how old is she?" I ask.

"I found her around eight years ago, back in Ireland," he begins, his tone turning darker. "She belonged to a man I was... dealing with. He didn't just hurt people. He hurt her. Starved her. Used her as a threat in his little games." His jaw tightens. "When I got to her, she was weak. But she was still a fighter. Everyone else was too frightened of who she could become. But I wasn't. I saw past that. So I took her. Nursed her back to strength."

Nyx moves up toward his throat, coiling loosely around it. He doesn't flinch, doesn't tense. His hand rests over her body like it's second nature.

"She kills for me now. Doesn't take orders like a dog would. She just... knows. Reacts to me. To my breathing. My body temperature. The state of my pulse. She's an extension of me." His pale eyes find mine. "She knows what's mine. And she knows what to do if anyone tries to hurt me."

The image is hypnotic—this man standing there with a lethal predator draped like a crown around his throat. Not a hint of fear in him. Just trust. A deadly, intimate kind of trust. Snakes can't be trained, and yet, somehow, he's gone beyond that with Nyx.

He stops in front of me. "Do you know why I keep her here?"

I shake my head slowly.

"Because she's my last line of truth. People lie. People break. Nyx doesn't."

His gaze hardens as he reaches into his pocket, pulling out the handcuffs.

"I thought I told you to sit down," he says sternly.

I obey, my skin prickling. He cuffs my wrists to the arms of the chair, then crouches to secure my ankles to the legs, each click of the lock echoing in the quiet. My pulse thunders in my ears.

When he's done, he steps back, studying me like he's imagining the next move.

"You're going to sit here with her," he says finally. "We'll see what she thinks of you. She gets to decide our fate, temptress. You may have fooled me, but you won't fool her."

The room turns to black as he slides a blindfold over my eyes.

"And I'm taking away your sight. The eyes can deceive. She doesn't need the light, and neither do you."

Then I feel it. The cool, smooth slide of scales against my bare arm.

He's placed her on me.

"She won't harm you unless she feels a reason to," his voice rumbles from somewhere in the dark. "And if she does... you won't have time to scream."

"Finn,"

"Yes, love?"

"If I'd have known how hard I'd fall for you, I'd have told you the truth at the start. I fucked up, but I really didn't mean to hurt you."

He lets out a chuckle.

"It's funny. People keep saying I'm hurt. Like I'm not already dead inside."

My chest aches for him.

"You aren't. I've seen that," I whisper.

"Maybe, if you pass this test, you'll find out more about me, and then you'll figure out how wrong you are."

The door shuts. I'm alone.

Alone with Nyx.

I keep my breathing slow. She's heavier than I expected, and the warmth of her body seeps into my skin.

I should be terrified. But instead, I'm captivated.

The darkness presses in, swallowing everything except the sound of my own breathing.

Nyx shifts against my arm, her scales cool and impossibly smooth, muscles tightening in a slow wave as she moves higher. Every ripple feels deliberate, like she's studying me with her body.

Her head brushes my shoulder, tongue flicking, tasting the air around my neck.

I fight the instinct to flinch. Any sudden movement feels like a challenge, and I'm not stupid enough to test her.

My wrists pull lightly against the cuffs, a useless reflex, and the steel bites back. I force myself still.

I've always loved snakes. Their silence. Their elegance. The way they move without apology. It's why I inked one into my skin, coiled in black between my breasts. But loving them from afar and sitting handcuffed in the dark with one draped over me are very different things.

Nyx slides across my collarbone, the shift of her weight making my pulse spike. She's not heavy enough to crush, but she's strong enough to remind me she could. Her tail winds loosely around my forearm, not trapping me, just holding me.

Her head lifts, and I feel her presence more than I see her.

The warmth from her body bleeds into mine, almost intimate, her movements unhurried.

Nyx shifts again, this time gliding down over my chest. Her scales whisper against my skin before finding the curve of my hip.

I swallow hard. My breaths are so slow now they're barely there, like I'm trying to trick her into thinking I'm part of the furniture.

But she knows.

She knows my heartbeat doesn't match my stillness.

I can feel her reading me the way Finn said she reads him —temperature, pulse, the rhythm of breath. Every tiny shift in my body is hers to interpret.

And I can't decide if I want her to find me worthy… or if part of me wants her to decide I'm not.

CHAPTER 67

FINN

Song- Wires, The Neighbourhood

I never leave the room. I stand with my back against the door, watching them. I'm not even sure I'm breathing.

Nyx is measuring every part of Stephanie. Dragging herself effortlessly along pale skin that almost glows in the dim light.

A fucking picture.

Stephanie's holding her breath, every muscle tight, ready to snap. But the longer Nyx moves over her, the more I see her start to give in. Shoulders loosening. Breathing shifting. That subtle surrender when fight or flight finally lets go.

She's feeling what I feel with Nyx.

The calm. The stilling of a racing mind. The way danger can feel like safety when it's in the right hands.

Nyx lifts her head, turning her gaze on me. She stays like that, unblinking, her body still.

She's not just reading Stephanie. She's assessing me.

My true feelings for Stephanie are laid bare to her.

There's no point in hiding them. Nyx sees in ways no human can.

I don't move. My body loosens, my breathing evens. I let her decide.

Her head lowers again, and she glides back up Stephanie's body. When she coils around her throat, my eyes close for just a second.

Fuck.

Fuck. Fuck. Fuck.

I take a deep breath and step forward, working on instinct.

I can't lose this woman. Maybe that was fate all along, dragging us through this chaos just to shove the truth in my face.

She's not just my wife on paper. She's mine to defend. Mine to fight for.

I believe her.

When she told me she was blackmailed, my anger wasn't truly at her. It was at them. At the men who thought they could use her to get to me. At the fact they pushed me to the brink and forced her into the line of fire.

I would never have let Nyx harm her. Not for a second. But now… now it's gone further than that. It's in my chest, aching like an old wound that never healed right.

Stephanie hasn't just seen my pain, my anger, my darkness.

She's embracing it. Right now.

That snake around her throat isn't a threat. It's a seal.

We're not just bound. We're fate.

Two people fighting against each other until we finally recognized the truth—that it was never a trial, never an obsession, never a test.

It was always this. Our ending. Our future.

I needed her to heal the parts of me I buried so deep they nearly killed me. And she's letting me do the same for her.

"Hey, Nyx. You're kinda heavy around my neck there, girl." Stephanie's voice is soft, almost teasing.

Nyx's head tilts, and she rubs her face against Stephanie's cheek, and fuck, my heart explodes.

She doesn't tighten. She doesn't coil. She just rests there, peaceful and still.

She's made her judgment.

And so have I.

CHAPTER 68

STEPHANIE

**Song- can you see me in the dark? Halestorm,
I Prevail.**

I feel his presence without needing my eyes.

His breathing. That sharp, controlled rhythm I've learned to read like a language. The way my body reacts to him without permission.

Nyx has loosened even further around my throat, her body heavy but no longer threatening.

That moment she settled there, I thought it was over, that she'd keep tightening until there was nothing left.

But she didn't.

She accepted me. And I accepted her.

I understand now why Finn trusts her. She's like him, calculating, reading every detail, and assessing in ways most people could never comprehend.

"Finn," I whisper.

I flinch when his fingers brush my cheek, but the instinct fades, and I lean into his touch.

"You passed."

The air leaves my lungs in a long, shaky exhale, as if he's just cut a dead weight from my shoulders.

"H-how did you know she wouldn't kill me?"

I can feel the grin in his voice without even seeing it.

"Because I wouldn't have let her."

My heart thunders as he pulls the blindfold up. Light floods my vision, making me blink until my eyes lock on his.

There's life there again. That cold, brutal mask is gone.

"How does it feel?" His fingers trail slowly down my arms, tracing the edge between comfort and possession.

"Perfect," I answer. And it's the truth. Not to win his forgiveness, not to impress him. I would make the same choices again.

Maybe in hindsight, I'd have told him sooner. I'd have stopped trying to figure out everything by myself and let him in, instead of fighting him. But I don't want him to love some fake version of me.

The truth is a relief. His acceptance is all I want. Not to be boxed in as the perfect wife. Not to be fixed.

I'm not broken.

I've been hurt. I've been hunted. But I fought my way to here.

"Is the trial over?"

He bends down on one knee, removing the chains on my ankles. When he stands, he kicks my legs apart and steps between them, heat radiating through me. Nyx's weight against my neck keeps me rooted in the reminder that she's still there.

His hands slide up my thighs.

"Do you want it to be over," he murmurs, "or do you want a final trial?"

His palm stops at my hip.

"Do you forgive me?" I ask.

He leans in, dragging his tongue along my cheek. The sound I make is half-whimper, half-need.

"Do you forgive me, love? I can't take back what you've seen. What you know about me. What I do. The evil under my skin. Can you forgive the man who could have killed you?"

I breathe in, the air shaking in my chest.

"I always saw your darkness. That's what drew me in. Now, it just makes sense. We're not too dissimilar, Dr. Quinn."

His fingers tighten on my thigh, claiming me.

"That is my fear, temptress. You can still count your kills on your hands. I could own an entire graveyard. There is nothing good inside of me, Stephanie."

He grips my chin, forcing my eyes to his. My body shivers under the pressure of his touch.

"There is only goodness in me when you're inside of me, Finn."

I bite my lip and bat my lashes, watching the smirk climb his mouth.

"I'm deadly serious."

"I know. So am I." My voice is sweet as I open my legs wider.

"You think maybe we could forgive each other?"

His gaze moves over my face, deliberate and heavy.

"I think that is possible, love. Only if—" he pauses, sliding his hand beneath my panties "—you pass this last test."

I lift my hips in answer, and he chuckles low.

"Remember who's around your throat, Stephanie. Remember what she can do. The risk. The pleasure."

I suck in a breath.

Nyx shifts against my skin, her body flexing with slow,

deliberate power. Each movement is a whisper of scales, a reminder that one wrong signal from me—or from him—and this moment could end in death.

Finn's fingers stroke over the edge of my panties, dragging the thin fabric against my skin until my breath hitches. His other hand rests on the arm of the chair beside my cuffed wrist, his weight caging me in completely.

"I can feel your pulse from here," he murmurs, his mouth hovering over mine. "It's racing, temptress."

"Maybe I like the risk, or maybe it's just you," I breathe.

His eyes darken, and for a moment I can't tell if it's lust, amusement, or that lethal edge that has always lived inside him.

Nyx adjusts her coil, the pressure feather-light along my throat, and my heart rate spikes again. He notices, of course he notices, and his lips curve into something dangerous.

"That's the thing about fear," he says softly. "It sharpens everything else. Every touch. Every sound. Every taste."

He presses his mouth to my jaw.

"She knows you now," he continues, his voice low, his fingers slipping beneath the lace. "But, you haven't earned her trust yet. So she is still a threat to you; she will be reading my reactions, going off my cues to keep you alive. "

My thighs tense, but I don't pull away. If anything, I push into his touch, the cuffed restraints biting into my wrists as I strain toward him.

"Do you want me to stop?" he asks, his lips brushing my ear, the question nothing more than a taunt.

I shake my head. "No."

Nyx's tongue flicks against my skin, tasting my accelerated pulse, and my breath stutters. The combination of the deadly caress of her body and the claiming roughness of his fingers is overwhelming, blurring the edge between panic and pleasure.

"Good fuckin' girl." His mouth finds mine in a hard, consuming kiss, swallowing the sound I make when his hand moves lower.

Every muscle in my body is taut, caught between the cold thrill of knowing she could end me and the heat of knowing he never will.

I like being choked. When Finn wraps his hand around my throat, I come alive.

But this? This is a whole new dimension.

A snake coiled around my neck. A fucking snake necklace. All while my crazy husband is on his knees, eating me out like he's starved himself all day just for me.

And it's kind of perfect. Walking that line between life and death. Pain and pleasure. Fear and desire.

I don't know where the trial ends and the surrender begins.

And maybe that's the point.

I surrender to him only.

CHAPTER 69

FINN

Her pulse is a drumbeat I can feel through my fingertips.

Nyx feels it too. I can tell by the subtle twitch of her muscles, the way she adjusts her coil so she's settled high. She's reading Stephanie's body like I am. Watching the changes, gauging the intent behind them.

Stephanie isn't frozen anymore. She's leaning into me. Straining against the cuffs to close the space I deliberately keep between us.

Good.

The only truth that matters is what happens when there's no safe distance left.

I let my fingers work deeper, slow enough to keep her on edge, hard enough to make her gasp. Every sound she makes is a confession. I'm not sure who is more vulnerable here. Because with each second that passes, she's clawing more and more back from me.

Nyx's head lifts slightly. I don't move. I don't speak. My breathing stays steady, my heart rate controlled. Telling her that it's okay.

And then I see it—Stephanie's eyes flutter closed, her mouth parting in a sound that isn't fear. Her body isn't tense for escape; it's tense for release.

She's not fighting me. She's not fighting Nyx.

She's giving herself over to both.

My chest tightens, and it's not lust that hits me hardest. It's that I know exactly what this means. Nyx has judged her, and so have I.

She's mine. Not because she survived this. Not because she passed some fucking test. But because she's sitting here, cuffed and collared by fate itself, and still choosing me.

I press my mouth to hers, claiming the sound she makes as if I'm sealing it inside me.

This is what it is to be accepted for every truth and every lie I've ever carried.

And for the first time in my life, I'm not just trusted.

I'm seen.

I keep exploring her mouth, tasting the surrender in her kiss.

Then I drop to my knees.

Her eyes widen, her breath catches, but she doesn't speak. She doesn't have to.

Nyx shifts slightly with the change in my height, her body still coiled loosely around Stephanie's throat.

"You're going to come on my tongue, love. You're going to give the last pieces of yourself that you've been keeping from me. I want to see you break so I can piece you back together," I tell her.

I push her knees wider. My hands grip her thighs, firm enough that she can't mistake this for anything less than ownership.

And I bite down on the flesh inside of her thigh, making her cry out.

When my mouth finds her, she gasps, the sound vibrating through me. I keep my gaze locked on hers, refusing to let her look away.

"Finn, she's getting tighter," she breathes out.

That panic flickering in her voice.

"Just relax for me, baby. She won't hurt you, I won't hurt you," I tell her.

Every flick of my tongue is deliberate, every draw of breath from her chest a mark I'm burning into memory. She tugs against the cuffs, not knowing what to do with herself. All her power has been stripped.

And yet, she's never had more control over me than right now.

I want her helpless like this. Not from fear. From need.

Her eyes hold mine, even as her breathing stutters, even as her body trembles. I see the exact moment the wave takes her. Her pupils blown wide, her mouth parting in a sound she doesn't try to hide.

"Keep your eyes on me, love."

She obeys my command, and a jolt stabs me through the heart. Not in a painful way. In a way that makes me feel whole.

"Come for me, temptress."

And she does, bound and crowned in Nyx, and she doesn't look away. Soaking my face, I drink her in.

It shreds something in me I thought was indestructible.

Every barrier, every defense I've built to keep myself untouchable—it's gone.

Because this woman doesn't just take my darkness.

She makes me want to give her everything I've been guarding all my life.

And for the first time, I know it with absolute certainty.

I'm in love with her.
I don't need scans and tests to know that.

He carefully removes Nyx from my neck before settling her around his. It's almost as if they calm each other, like two predators that only breathe easy in the presence of their own.

"What happens now, Finn? You know everything. I've played by your rules, your trials. You know everything, yet you're still hiding from me."

His stare doesn't falter. Not even a flicker.

He simply nods, then moves behind me. I hear the faint rustle before he returns without Nyx. Without a word, he unbinds my wrists. I shake them out, blood rushing back in sharp pins and needles.

My whole body is wound tight.

When I stand, I lay my hands flat against his shirt, feeling the rapid thud of his heart under my palm.

"See? You aren't a robot. I can feel it right here." I look up at him.

"My heart only beats for one person, love."

My breath catches in my throat. I slide my hand down and capture his, guiding it over my own chest.

"So does mine."

He leans down, his lips crashing over mine. I hook my arms around his neck, pulling him closer and closer until there's no space left.

I want him to consume me. Poison me.

We bleed from the same wounds. He knows what haunts me. I want to know what terrorizes him.

"It's not always a bad thing to put your trust in someone else, Finn," I whisper against his lips.

"Your blind trust nearly killed us both."

I shake my head.

"I trusted your heart would win over your head, that's all. It's in there, and it beats for me. This is real, Dr. Quinn. Whether you want to accept it or not. We found each other for a reason. Let me in. Please?"

His breath is warm against my skin.

Then he pulls back, unbuttoning his shirt and sliding it off his shoulders. My eyes trace the ink etched into his skin, but they linger on the scars. They're small and scattered. I step closer, fingertips brushing over his shoulders.

On closer look, they're not random. Scratches. Deep ones. From nails. My heart twists, remembering the way he clawed at himself in his sleep.

The nightmares.

"I won't be able to tell you," he says quietly.

I bite my tongue. Maybe it will take time. Maybe I'll never know what haunts him.

Then he retreats into the chair, muscles flexing as he sets both wrists on the arms.

"I won't be able to freely say it. But you can force it out of me. You can hurt me enough for me to tell you."

My mouth parts.

"Stephanie, hurt me until I tell you the truth."

He locks one wrist into the restraint with a sharp click.

"It's the only way I can let you in."

There's almost fear in his voice, but his face is carved in stone.

I step forward, bend down, and secure his other wrist.

"I can't hurt you back like this. You're safe from me," he whispers.

"I never was worried about myself with you."

"Grab one of the metal trays. They have a variety of instruments. You have my permission to do what you want. I'm on trial now. Extract what you can. This is your one and only opportunity, love."

I turn toward the metal trays, my pulse pounding in my ears. Stainless steel glints under the light. Forceps, scalpels, clamps, and tools that could break a body down piece by piece. God, the fun I could have here with the right victim. I always do my kills quietly and cleanly.

I wonder how it would feel to kill like Finn? To have blood really on my hands.

My fingers hover over the choices, and I feel his eyes on me, tracking every move.

"You're hesitating," he says. I hear the undertone; he's daring me to prove him wrong.

I pick up a scalpel; I don't want to leave more scars. But maybe he needs new ones to remind him of something better when he looks at them.

When I face him again, his head tilts ever so slightly, like he's curious to see which part of him I'll touch first.

I move in close, the chair creaking under the shift of his weight as I straddle his thighs. My free hand grips his jaw, holding his gaze steady.

"I could make you bleed," I murmur. "But you already bleed for me in ways you don't realize."

The scalpel's edge kisses the side of his throat, just enough to let him feel how precise my hand is. His pulse flutters beneath the blade, but he doesn't flinch.

"Do it," he says.

I shake my head, dragging the cold steel across his chest instead until it rests over his heart.

"This isn't about hurting you, Finn," I say softly. "It's about making you understand you don't have to hide from me."

His breath deepens, but he stays silent.

So I press the blade down just enough to break the skin. A thin red line blooms against his tattooed chest. His muscles flex beneath me, his eyes locked on mine.

"What made you want to become a surgeon?" I ask.

His jaw works, but nothing comes out.

I lean in, my lips brushing his ear. "Do you think anything you tell me at this point will change how I feel about you? It won't."

I set the scalpel aside, my hands gripping the arms of the chair as I kiss him hard, taking his mouth like I'm claiming it. His wrists strain against the restraints, his body pushing into mine.

When I pull back, his breathing is ragged.

"This is your trial, Dr. Quinn," I whisper. "And I'm not stopping until you let me in."

With a wicked smile, I lean down and lick up the blood dripping down his chest.

I could hurt him by not allowing him access to me.

It doesn't need to just be physical wounds. What we have is more than that.

Sliding one hand behind me, I cup his growing dick in my hand, and I squeeze.

"What made you want to become a surgeon?" I press.

"My first kill," he says bluntly.

Okay. I have an answer. That makes me smile.

"Who was it?" I ask.

He swallows as I remove my hand from his dick and instead, grip his throat.

"My best friend's parents. I was ten."

My eyes go wide. Ten years old. Murdering? I knew the mafia was bad; it's engrained into their kids from a young age. But that seems absurd.

"Why did you kill them, Finn?"

His face pales. His body jerking beneath me. I quickly make another cut on the other side of his chest, and he grits his teeth.

But it calms him down. The pain distracts from the carnage inside his brain.

Fuck, this is breaking my heart watching him.

CHAPTER 71

FINN

Song- Drag Me Under, Sleep Token

I shake my head. The words are there, but they're burning me from the inside out.

The memories flooding my brain.

The way the father would hold my arms behind my back. The things she would do to me for praise from her husband.

My wrists crash against the restraints, but Stephanie delivers another cut. And like that, it severs the memory.

I can't see their faces anymore. I can't feel them on me.

All I can focus on is my wife.

I open my mouth to say it, but the words don't follow. I'm so fucking close. But I can't. It feels like I'm choking.

Like I am in my nightmares.

"I can't," I stutter.

"You can." Her words are sharp.

She grabs my face, forcing me to look into her deep blue eyes. Dragging the blade along my nose, she doesn't cut. She tilts her head, watching me.

There isn't pity there. Just strength.

I keep my eyes fixed on hers.

"They abused me."

The words come out like fire, making me cough after. Stephanie goes still on top of me. Her eyes close, just for a second. I just need to get it out of me. Rid me of the fucking horrors they left me with.

"They had a daughter, who was a year younger than me at school. They lived near us. We used to play out on the road on our bikes together. I started to notice her bruises, and I got inquisitive. So I started going around to their house for dinner. The more time went on, the more I noticed. The more I saw her fear. I felt her pain, and I wanted to take it away from her. So, I went around more and more. They were very kind to me at the start. I thought perhaps I was wrong."

Stephanie lets out a ragged breath, stroking her thumbs along my cheeks.

I can't stop now, because if I do, I won't have the guts to open up again.

"But then, it progressed very quickly into more. And I stupidly thought, if I took her place, they wouldn't hurt her."

"Oh, my god, Finn," Stephanie whispers.

The shock in her voice is what hits me the hardest.

"W-what did they do?"

"It wasn't just violent. It was everything." I pause and swallow. "Sexually too. They'd make me watch them, they'd try and involve me. They would beat me if I didn't comply."

I swallow down the bile in my throat, that sickness I always feel. Disgust. Pure fucking agony. The visions of her, in her room, blood pooling out of her.

I close my eyes and squeeze them shut, but when I do, I'm just transported back there. So I jolt them back open, trying to focus on my wife. On my fucking anchor to the real world.

CHAPTER 72

He's looking at me as if I am his only lifeline.

I can feel it—how when he speaks, he transports himself back to being a vulnerable ten-year-old.

I can't imagine how painful this is.

"I'm here, baby. I always will be. You can do this." I keep my voice calm.

When inside, I'm breaking for him.

"I—I need more fucking pain, love. Please," he stutters.

I suck in a breath, trying to stop my fingers from shaking. He tips his head back, and I drag the blade along his left shoulder.

The blood spills, and he doesn't even flinch, like he's numb.

I hate this for him. I can't ever take this away from him. But I hope I can help him heal in some way.

That he can realize he isn't evil. He's not a cold-hearted monster.

He's everything to me. Regardless of his past. No matter what made him who he is today.

I love him no matter what.

"Better?" I whisper.

He brings his head back to mine; I can see the tears threatening to stream from his eyes, but he holds them back.

I press my forehead against his.

"Just let it all out, let me take some of this pain from you. Please, Finn."

I pull back and swipe up some of the blood dripping down his skin and swipe it between my breasts.

"I'm yours. Nothing can ever change that."

He nods, and tears stream down his cheeks.

I chase them away and kiss him gently.

"It's always going to be you for me, Finn," I whisper against his lips.

This woman is fucking perfect. I don't deserve her. Not after today.

But I want to somehow be worthy enough of her without letting my damage ruin her too. She has that dark streak, the same as I do.

Yet, there is still light in her that hasn't been dimmed. I don't want to be the one who does that to her either.

"They killed my friend. And so, I killed them," I say harshly.

There is no sugarcoating what I did. Or how brutally I did it.

She nods. I'm waiting for that look of pity, but it's not coming. So I keep talking. I'm only doing this once.

I take a deep breath.

"That is the day I realized I wanted to be a surgeon. I went there for dinner but heard her parents screaming at each other, so I looked in through her window, and that's when I saw her fucking murder scene. She was just lying by their feet in a pool of blood while they argued about what to do with her body." I say it with such anger my body shakes.

"Fuck," Stephanie hisses.

"So, I snuck back in while they slept that night. I killed them in their sleep, and then I cut them up. I was fascinated, and I finally, after weeks of torture, felt alive again. Covered in blood. Organs all over the floor. I got my revenge. I ended it, but it was too late. I couldn't save her. But I realized I wanted to cut people up, both for good and bad reasons."

I close my eyes as they start to sting. It wasn't good enough. *I* wasn't enough.

"You did what you could, Finn. I'm proud of ten-year-old you. But, and I'm only going to say this once, I'm so fucking sorry that happened to you, baby. No one deserves that."

She presses her lips against my cheek, and we just stay there in silence. My heart is hammering, and my body is exhausted.

That dark place I try to shut out consumes me, and Stephanie is that light at the end of the tunnel, grounding me back with her rather than letting me rot with my abusers.

I keep my forehead pressed to hers, letting her steady my breathing until it matches hers. The restraints bite at my wrists, but I don't move. For once, I'm not fighting the hold.

She knows now. All of it. And the world hasn't ended.

I open my eyes and study her. There's no calculation in my gaze now. No test. Just the knowledge that this woman has crawled into my darkest place and refused to leave.

My hands flex uselessly in the cuffs. I want them free. I want to hold her like I'm never letting her go.

"I've never told anyone that," I say, my voice low. "Not my brothers. Not anyone. You're it, Stephanie."

Her eyes soften, but she doesn't try to fill the space with words. She just nods, like she understands exactly what it costs me to say that.

I love her because she's looking at me right now, knowing everything, and she's still here.

I swallow the ache in my throat. "Take these off."

She unbuckles the restraints, and the second my hands are free, I pull her to me. Not rough. Not a claim. Just an anchor. My arms lock around her, and for the first time, I let her feel all of it. The fear, the relief, the desperate need for her.

Her fingers slide into my hair, and I bury my face in her neck.

"Do you still want me now?" I murmur against her skin.

She nods against me. "Always. In fact, more than ever."

And for the first time in my life, I believe it.

But there is still that nagging feeling in my chest that I'm dragging her into hell with me. My evil can't be healed or tamed. All it's going to do is take hold of her.

Yet, for the first time, my past doesn't feel as heavy. And that is thanks to her. There is nothing stopping her from making a run for it once she really digests what I've told her.

I guess that's a chance I have to take. Maybe my wife really means she isn't going anywhere. That she isn't scared of me.

CHAPTER 74

STEPHANIE

I sit in silence trying to comprehend the last few hours while Finn goes to fetch my bag. Even this moment is a test. The doors are open. I could attempt to run from him.

But I don't want to. Not now. I want to wrap my arms around him and tell him everything is going to be okay.

My husband is part of the mafia. I've been blackmailed by his enemies. Yet, none of that bothers me. I've never felt safe, not until I fell for Finn.

When he returns, he gives me a soft smile as he hands me my bag. I pull out another sundress, this time red, and slip it on while he gets Nyx, and she settles around his neck.

"No panties?" he asks.

"More for you to rip off me? I'll end up with none if you carry on."

He lifts me up to my feet and laces his fingers through mine.

I follow Finn's lead out of the room and down the hallway toward the main set of doors.

"One chance to leave, temptress."

I squeeze his hand tighter.

"I'm not going anywhere without you."

He turns, really looking at me this time, his eyes searching mine like he's trying to burn the truth out of me.

"I don't want to ruin you, too," he sighs.

I tug him closer, my grip catching on his chin until his face tilts toward mine.

"I was broken a long time before I met you, psycho." A grin curls at my mouth. "You just gave me the freedom to be myself."

His tongue drags along his teeth as he smirks.

"Freedom to be yourself, huh? You mean you want me to facilitate your murderous ways?"

I nod slowly, biting back my smile. It feels good to not just be seen but to be accepted.

"Yeah. That's what a good husband should do, right? Bury the bodies for me?"

He chuckles, and his fingers circle my throat like a warning.

"Are you burying mine too? Or am I going to need a bigger cleanup crew?"

I press a finger to his lips, shaking my head.

"Not if we make them look like accidents." I wink.

"Fuck, you're a menace, aren't you?" he whispers.

"Only to those who deserve it."

I rise onto my toes and press my lips to his.

"Let's keep it that way, eh?" he says, a seriousness flashing in his pale eyes.

"I'm not crazy, Finn. I'm not someone they're going to make documentaries about."

"I know. Although I can't say the same about myself. We do have to be careful. There are rules in my world that you'll have to follow. Do you understand that? The mafia is different."

I blow out a long breath.

I'm sure I have a lot to learn about his way of life, but I want to. I want to know everything there is to know about Finn. I want to be part of it in every way. With him I have a purpose, that little spark I was missing this whole time.

I love my job, yes. But there was always something missing. Life was always a little dull. Until I fell madly in love with Finn. The pieces are finally fitting together. We make each other whole.

"I understand, sir."

"Good girl."

He opens the metal door and leads me through a dark corridor. Then it's like stepping foot into another world.

A mansion that's elegant, with glittering chandeliers, neutral tones, tasteful wallpaper, polished wood, and plants thriving in corners.

He has fucking plants.

Not just a house. A palace. A home.

We stop at one door, and Finn carefully unwinds Nyx from his throat, placing her into a room that looks like paradise, with glass tanks, heat lamps, and no way for her to escape. She's safe. She belongs here.

We head down the grand staircase into the living room.

"Wow. Finn. This isn't what I expected."

He strides to the kitchen and puts coffee on. I'm still spinning, taking it in. The air smells divine. The place is spotless.

I'd pictured a cold bachelor pad. A shell. Not this.

"What did you expect? Zebra print walls and some inspirational quotes? Something like, *Only you can be the one to make it happen*?" he mocks.

I bite my lip to keep from laughing.

"Yeah, something like that. Or a gold toilet. Rich boy," I tease.

He chuckles.

"Who says I don't have that? Gotta waste my money somehow."

My mouth drops.

"Shut. Up. No, you do not."

He hands me my coffee, and I smile; it's perfect, oat milk and a sprinkle of sugar. Exactly how I take it.

"Thank you."

He nods, then gestures with his cup.

"Go on, explore. This place is your new home."

I nearly choke, almost spitting onto his pristine rug.

"Excuse me?"

He tugs me into his chest, his fingers biting into my waist.

"My wife will live with me. You want this, right?"

I stare into his eyes, the fight bleeding out of me. We are a team. That's how it was always meant to be.

"Sounds fun. Roomie." I wink.

A growl rumbles from his chest, his grip on my hip hardening.

"That isn't how this is going. You're mine, love."

My heart flutters wildly.

I slip from his hold and wander down the hallway until I find his office. Shelves climb high with books and medical journals, leather-bound volumes older than either of us. Wooden desk, polished floor.

His footsteps follow close behind.

I trail my hand across the desk until he spins me to face him.

"Does this feel like home?"

I set my coffee down on his paperwork, placing both hands on his chest, feeling his heart pick up under my palms.

I smile. "Anywhere you are is now my home, Finn."

His expression darkens as he nods. "I feel that way too. But, I do have to go away for a little while, love."

My smile falters. "Where? Not prison, I hope."

He runs his fingers through my hair.

"To London. There's a man there, the one who tried to kill Conan. The one who killed my father. The family who fucking ruined me." His jaw grinds, rage simmering in every muscle.

"You're going to kill him?"

He chuckles low.

"Kill? We're going to make him wish he was never fucking born. We're going to torture him and every one of his men until they're begging for death. It's not just a kill, love. This is ending a war that's gone on for decades."

I wrap my arms around his neck, pulling him down to me.

"That's hot, hearing you speak like that. I bet your enemies are petrified of you."

A shiver runs through me. My husband is terrifying.

"I'd like to think so. Conan is the one they fear most because of his size and his fury. I'm the quiet one they know will slit their throats."

I drag my finger along his neck.

"Oh yeah? You like it messy?" I bite down hard on his skin, tasting him.

"Sometimes. Depends on where the mood takes me," he says with a menacing grin.

He lifts me onto the desk, spreading my legs open.

"I really should get some more clothes delivered here." I flutter my lashes.

"Already one step ahead of you," he says with a wink.

"Good. Because I'll need outfits for London."

His expression shuts down.

"No." His voice is firm.

"No? You're telling your wife no?"

I snap my legs closed, but he growls and yanks them back apart with a sharp tut.

"Temptress. I am not taking you into an active warzone to watch me torture a man."

I pout.

"I want to watch. I want to see how you work. I want to learn from you."

His hand clamps around my throat.

"And it'll really turn me on," I whisper.

"No. Stephanie. You do not want to see me like that."

"Yes. Finn. I do. Take me with you. Please."

He shakes his head.

"You have work."

"You're my boss. I'd like to request vacation for a few days," I counter.

His grip tightens, lips brushing mine.

"It's dangerous."

"More dangerous than what you just did to me?" I spit back.

"Low blow," he whispers.

"I can look after myself. You won't have to babysit me. I just want to be there for you."

He steps back, studying me with a predator's patience.

"You can fight?"

A grin tugs at his lips.

"I—uh—may have taken some self-defense classes. You know, being a young stripper, I had to have some kind of protection."

He nods once, then straightens, his gaze sharp.

"Punch me."

"Pardon?"

"Did I stutter, love? Hit me. Show me you deserve to join me."

He's not joking. I slip off the desk, clenching my fist. As I step in front of him, I'm torn with a mixture of excitement and nerves. But I want to prove myself.

"In the time you've taken to contemplate the punch, I could have killed you already," he mutters, completely unamused.

I pull back my fist, and it lands square on his jaw.

He doesn't move. Doesn't even blink.

Fuck.

"Finn." My voice is cautious.

"Again. Harder," he barks.

I grit my teeth and swing again, with a lot more power this time.

His head goes back with the impact, and he rubs his cheek as he looks dead at me. And my fucking psycho husband smiles.

He smirks. "Atta girl."

Then he surges forward, slamming me back against the bookshelf.

"What now?" His voice drops to a whisper, heat and threat tangled together. "How are you getting me off you?"

A thrill shoots through me.

I fight him, straining against his hold, knowing this is only the beginning. He's strong; I know I don't really have a chance in hell. But I'll try.

CHAPTER 75

FINN

Song- Put It On Me, Matt Maeson

Her body writhes against mine, fighting me like she means it.

Good.

I press her harder into the bookshelf, the wood rattling under the force, and pin both her wrists above her head with one hand. She's small, but she's all fire, thrashing with enough strength to make most men stumble. Not me.

Her knee snaps up, aiming for my crotch. I catch it with my thigh, grinning as her eyes flare.

"Clever girl," I murmur, my breath hot against her ear. "Always aim for a man's weak spot."

She bucks against me, trying to twist free, her nails digging into my arm. The scratch only fuels me.

"Show me more," I taunt.

She shifts her weight and drops low, managing to slip one hand free. Her fist flies, catching me in the cheek. My head jerks to the side.

And I laugh.

That dark, dangerous sound that always makes people flinch. Not her, though. It just fires her up more.

"That's my girl. Keep fuckin' goin."

Her chest heaves, her eyes wide but burning with determination. She doesn't know it yet, but this is exactly what I wanted. To see if she'd strike me and keep going or fold the second she tasted resistance.

She swings again, but this time I catch her wrist midair and twist it behind her back, spinning her so her chest slams against the bookshelf. Her breath leaves her in a sharp gasp.

I cage her there, my body pressed to hers, my lips brushing the shell of her ear.

"You're quick," I whisper. "You'll never beat me, though."

"Maybe I don't need to beat you. Maybe I just need to keep you on your toes. We're a team. I can distract them while you deliver the killer blow. See?"

Fuck, she's lethal when she's like this.

I press my mouth to the curve of her throat, dragging my teeth along her skin until she shivers beneath me. My free hand slides down her hip, anchoring her to me. My cock is aching to take her.

"This is why you can't come to London," I growl. "You'll distract me. And when I'm distracted, people I love could die."

She twists her head just enough to meet my gaze, her eyes sharp. "Then maybe you should let me be the one watching your back. Ever thought about that? You don't have to take on the world on your own. And neither do I."

The fight in her voice and the heat in her eyes punch through me harder than any blow she's landed.

My resolve cracks.

She's not just my wife. Not just my temptress. She's my equal.

And God help anyone who thinks they can take her from me.

"I'll think about it," I tell her and pull away.

Could I really take her with me? Let her see this other side to me and my family? She was never meant to just be a wife.

But I think she's right. We might be better together in all aspects.

"For now, let's get your closet done, shall we?"

She turns and scowls at me, like she might pounce on me for another attack.

"When do you leave?" she asks.

"Tomorrow night."

I still need to speak to Theo and see what this plan is. Them saying they have Arthur and actually having him are two different things. I expect there will be more to this than just simply killing the cunt.

CHAPTER 76

Song- Him & I, Halsey, G-Eazy

Finn is still sleeping, his face almost peaceful, as I admire my new walk-in closet. Not only did he have everything important moved over from my house, but he filled it with new additions. Expensive ones.

And that makes me feel bad. I've spent years teasing him about being the rich boy, but I never wanted him to spend it on me. That isn't who I am. Yet here I am, staring at clothes and shoes that are to die for.

One red dress in particular catches my eye. It's fit for a gala, with a low-cut back and sapphires stitched into the bust. It's breathtaking.

Except, I have no idea when I'd ever wear it.

My trophies, the souvenirs of my kills, Finn has locked away, protecting me even from myself. Keeping me safe.

I glance back at him as he shifts in his sleep, broad shoulders stretching against the sheets.

My heart is set. I want to go with him today. I don't want to be left here, wandering this mansion alone. I know this place will feel empty without him. That isn't the wife I want to be. Waiting on the sidelines for him to come home.

I've never been that girl, and I never will be. And I don't think that's what he wants either.

And I want to see it end. For him. He deserves that after everything.

More than that, I want to prove myself. Prove that I'm worthy of knowing his deepest truths. Prove I can carry them, keep them safe, and never betray them.

I'm not just his wife. I'm his partner. At work, at home, and in every shadow his world demands.

I can be useful. I know I can. And I can look after him, because deep down, he needs it.

My hand brushes over his silk ties, and an idea sparks. A way to make my case.

Grabbing two black ties, I tiptoe back to bed. The second the mattress dips, his eyes open and lock on me.

Caught.

"Stephanie." His voice carries a warning.

"Morning, hubby," I chirp, pulling the blanket back and swinging one leg over him.

He stretches, arms folding lazily above his head, and lets them rest there. Perfect.

I shift higher up his body, straddling his chest.

"What are you doing?" His voice is full of hunger.

"Fucking some sense into my husband."

I grab one of his wrists, tying it to the headboard with a neat, hard knot.

"I really, really wouldn't do this if I were you, love," he warns.

I grin down at him, nudging my pussy against his chin.

"Oh, yeah?"

I fasten his other wrist. His words are saying one thing, yet he's not fighting back against what I'm doing.

"Yeah. Really. Whatever you think this will achieve, you're sorely mistaken. I'm not a man you tie up without consequence."

A shiver runs down my spine at the promise in his tone.

"You don't like me being in charge?"

I roll my hips, dragging my aching pussy across his mouth. His groan rumbles against me.

"No matter what you do, you'll never be in charge. Not really. And we both know that isn't what you need, really."

I nod with a teasing grin.

"So… you don't want your breakfast now?"

I lift myself, hovering just above him.

"Stephanie." His growl sends sparks through me.

"That's a shame. Breakfast is the most important meal of the day. Didn't they teach you that in med school in Dublin, Finn?"

I lower slightly, just enough for his nose to brush against me, then pull back. Sliding my hand into my red lace panties, I spread my legs a little wider so he can see what he's missing.

"Just think—if I come to London with you, I can provide relief whenever you need it. Stress relief. You can tie me up, bend me over, and fuck every frustration out on me. Or…" I moan softly, circling my clit. "You can leave me here. And I'll come on every surface of this house without you. That would be a shame, wouldn't it? Missing out on all of that. Missing out on me."

His groan is feral, torn from his chest, and I smirk at him.

"I suppose you did get all my toys delivered. Nothing like reading a good book with one of those. Hmm. Maybe that will be fun."

He yanks his hands against the restraints.

"All you have to do is agree to take me, Finn. Say the words, and I'll sit on your face and let you taste what's yours."

"This is cruel, baby." His breath is hot against my thigh.

"I know. But you love me this way."

My heart stutters. He hasn't said the words—not yet. But I feel them. And I know. I love this man.

"Oh, Finn…" I moan, sliding two fingers inside myself, tipping my head back, picturing the punishment he'll unleash once free.

His body bucks beneath me, his resolve slipping. Good.

"Stephanie. Pull those panties to the side and sit the fuck down," he growls.

Sparks shoot through me.

"Does that mean I can come?" I ask, looking down at him.

His eyes burn into mine.

"You can come on my face, yeah."

I lift away, making him groan, dragging out his torment.

"Fine. Yes. My demanding wife. You can come to London with me. But you'll follow every damn instruction. You won't leave my side. And I'll be taking you up on that offer of fucking every ounce of frustration out on you, even if I'm covered in blood. Do you hear me?"

My smile is so wide it aches.

"I understand." I pause, savoring it.

"Sir."

"Good. Now sit the fuck down," he growls.

And I do. Riding his tongue, knowing the second I release him, I'm in serious trouble. As he sucks on my clit, my toes curl.

"Finn. I'm close."

"I know. But you've been a bad girl, and you don't deserve to come like this, do you?"

I shake my head. My eyes locking on his. He swipes his tongue along me, and I tremble. Holding onto the headboard for support.

"I–I can't hold it."

He ignores my plea, and I squeeze my eyes shut. If I come, I know my punishment will be torturous. So I hold it back, fighting every nerve in my body.

"You can, and you are. Because you're my good girl," he praises.

And that nearly sends me over the edge.

"Let me loose, and you can come as hard as you want, temptress."

As fast as I can, I begin undoing the knots. I have no idea what I'm in for, but I can't fucking wait.

The second my wrists are free, the beast inside me snaps loose.

I hurl her across the bed like she weighs nothing, her back hitting the mattress. I'm up on my feet, and I drag her down and pin her to the floor. Before she can even blink, I'm on top of her. My mouth crushes hers, teeth clashing. She tastes like sin, like victory, like the one thing I'll never let go of.

I rip her panties away in one savage pull, leaving her bare and writhing. She claws at me, but I catch her wrists, slam them above her head, and bite down into the soft curve of her throat. Her cry echoes through me, spurring me on.

"You tied me up?" I growl against her skin, biting again at her collarbone until I feel her shudder. "You thought you could trick me into getting your own way?"

And she can. Because she won. But she won before this little stunt. That's why that gala dress is hanging up in the closet for her.

I flip her, forcing her up on her knees so her chest is

against the wall, my hand fisting in her hair, yanking her head back until her throat arches.

"I don't get restrained, temptress. I do the restraining."

This is the man she wanted to unleash.

Her laugh is breathless. "Maybe I like the punishment."

That noise fucking undoes me.

I bite down on her jaw, marking her cheek, tasting the heat of her skin. My hands grip her hips hard enough to bruise, grinding against her ass, my cock straining through thin fabric.

"You'll wear me," I snarl. "Every mark, every bruise, every bite. You'll carry them until you can never forget who you belong to."

I pull her back, bending her at the waist, her palms flat against the wall as I tear my boxers down. My hand snakes around her throat, squeezing just enough to remind her of Nyx, of what it means to surrender to me completely.

"Beg," I order.

Her moan vibrates through my hand. "Please, Finn. Please fuck me."

I slam into her in one brutal thrust, burying myself to the hilt. Her scream rips the air, half pleasure, half surrender.

I pound into her, driving her against the wall. My teeth sink into her shoulder, marking her as mine. I can't stop. She drives me fucking insane.

My free hand drags down her stomach, finding her clit, rubbing rough and fast as I fuck her harder.

She writhes, moans, and begs, but I don't ease up. She wanted this. She deserves this.

"Is this the man you wanted?" I grit out, biting her ear.

"Yes—fuck—yes, Finn!" she cries, body trembling.

Her walls clamp around me, and I feel her shatter,

convulsing against me, her orgasm ripping through her like a storm. Her scream is raw, my name broken on her lips.

I don't stop. I fuck her through it, claiming every inch until her body can't take more. Only then do I let myself go, slamming deep, spilling into her with a noise so feral I don't even recognize myself.

I collapse against her, both of us heaving, drenched in sweat, her skin a canvas of red marks and teeth prints.

My arms wrap around her waist, pulling her tight against me even as my cock still throbs inside her.

"You're mine," I whisper against her hair. "And I'll never let you go. Even if I ruin you."

Her answer is a whimper, but her body melts back into mine.

"I'm yours to ruin, Finn. Do your worst," she pants.

And I know, with bone-deep certainty, she doesn't want saving. And that she wants me—exactly as I am.

And that is what terrifies me.

This woman is perfect just as she is. I don't want to taint her with my evil. I just want to love her how she deserves.

That is why she's coming to London with me. Not as a test of loyalty. Not to see me kill a man. But she is there as my anchor.

Because I fucking need her by my side. All the years I've spent believing I was better off on my own, she's proven me wrong.

I never found anyone else because I was waiting for her. My soulmate.

"We better get packed then, don't you think?" I whisper in her ear, pushing her hair over her shoulder.

We board the private jet, and Finn squeezes my hand so tightly my rings cut into my skin. His grip is almost painful, but it steadies me. Everyone else is already on board when we step inside.

"I thought you were taking an army with you?" I whisper.

"We are. We just have separate jets. You don't take a whole army on one plane."

Oh. Right.

His brothers sit together on one side, the twins on the other. The tall blond guy from the strip club is hunched over a laptop, fingers moving quickly across the keys. His eyes lift briefly to mine, and I offer a smile.

"Hi. I'm Drago." He stands, offering a tattooed hand, his Russian accent thick.

"Uh. Hi. Stephanie." I give it a firm shake.

Finn's brothers greet me too, though it's clear Declan is less welcoming than Conan. Conan's easy smile softens me, but Declan's sharp stare makes it obvious that he doesn't want me here. He's worried about Finn, I assume. It's up to me to prove to them all I can be trusted. The twins are too wrapped up in their own argument to notice anything at all.

"Declan isn't angry with you, love. He's worried about me bringing you, is all. I promise he doesn't usually behave like he's got a stick up his ass," Finn whispers.

I cover my mouth to stop the laugh.

"Finn," I hiss, jabbing my elbow into his ribs.

Then there's another man clearing his throat, with dark brown hair and piercing blue eyes, snapping something vicious in Italian into his phone. His voice is low but deadly.

"Who is that?" I murmur.

"I'll introduce you." Finn smiles, leading me further down.

The man looks up, cuts the call without a word, and rises to his feet.

"Enzo. Meet my wife, Stephanie."

Enzo's gaze drops to our joined hands, then flicks back to Finn.

"I didn't get invited to the wedding? I thought we got past this," he says dryly.

Finn chuckles, completely unbothered.

"Hey! His own brothers didn't either!" Conan calls from the front.

"It was a spur-of-the-moment wedding," I add quickly.

"Nice to meet you," I offer, and Enzo gives me a smile that softens him, but not entirely. There's still an edge there, like a blade hidden under silk.

None of these men feel quite as frightening as the Russians I saw in Vegas, though. Those men wore their violence like armor. And now… it makes sense. The tattoos. The danger. The way Finn blended seamlessly among them. These people, this life, are the real Finn Quinn.

And I like him this way. More than I ever expected.

We slip into the back row near Enzo as the jet takes off. I rest my head on Finn's shoulder, grounding myself in him.

"What's your favorite food?" I ask softly.

"Your pussy," he answers flatly.

I smack his arm. "No. Seriously. I want to know everything about you."

"You already know all the important things. More than anyone else, ever, in my life." His voice is low as he presses a kiss to the top of my head.

"Yeah, but I want to know the trivial stuff too. Like what I can do for your birthday. Date nights. Fun stuff."

He rests his head against mine. "Fillet steak. Rare. Skin-on fries. A brandy-based sauce. Finished off with a glass of my dad's finest whiskey."

I smile. "Yum. And no caviar in sight?"

"No." He smirks. "What about yours, love? What should I cook for you?"

"I love seafood. But I really, really love melted chocolate on strawberries."

"Ah. A sweet tooth."

"Yep. That's why I have to run, so I can have my extra treats."

His arms tighten, and suddenly I'm in his lap, straddling him. My cheeks flame as I glance around, but no one bats an eye. His grip on my ass is firm enough to make me squirm.

"You're perfect exactly how you are," he says. "Don't you dare say anything otherwise."

I chew my lip. He's deadly serious, though, his eyes burning through me. Almost as if he's angry I'd think otherwise.

"So, you don't want me to be like one of the models you probably jerk off to?" I tease.

His hands slide over my hips, and he squeezes. "Baby, I

need something to grab hold of to fuck you thoroughly. These are staying. Your ass is staying. I want you exactly how you are."

I squint at him, trying to read the truth. I've never been content in my skin. Stripping kept me disciplined, but I was never the most toned girl on stage. Never enough compared to the others. And now I'm in my thirties, it's even harder to feel good about myself.

I open my mouth to argue, but he digs his fingers into my skin harder.

"If you even contemplate arguing with me on this, I'll feed you every damn meal myself. Mouthful by mouthful. Got it?"

I nod and can't help but smile. Just that alone has made me feel better about myself than any other man has.

"So you do jerk off to other women?" I ask.

His expression hardens like stone. "No. I don't even touch myself. I have no need. And now, the only time I will is if I've got a front-row seat of your ass so I can paint my cum all over your cheeks."

My face burns hot at the crude promise.

"Noted. Want me to spread them apart, or…?"

He groans low in his throat. "Not here, love. Not here."

I press a kiss to his jaw, softer now. "Okay. Where do you see yourself in five years?"

He smiles. "Easy. You, me, Nyx, and a couple of little hellions running around." His hands slide over my stomach, lingering there.

"Oh yeah? You still want to be Daddy Finn, huh?"

His mouth finds my ear. "I've already started tracking your cycle, temptress. It's not an if, it's a when."

My eyes widen. "You… what?"

"I'm a doctor. And I know you very, very well, Stephanie," he says, grinning at me.

I gape at him. "So you know when I need extra chocolate strawberries, right?"

"In approximately four days," he tells me with a smug grin.

He's right. Of course he is.

"You better get all the action in before then, doctor."

His fingers curl lightly around my throat. "Nothing can stop me from having you, love. We've established that the blood doesn't faze me."

I melt into him, shutting my eyes, listening to the steady rhythm of his heart. For the first time in my life, I feel safe. Like I'm not in complete survival mode anymore.

After a beat of silence, his voice lowers. "Do you want kids with me?"

"Yes. But can you promise me something?" I lift my head to meet his eyes.

"I can try."

"That our kids will always be safe. That if something awful ever happens to us, your family will protect them. I don't have anyone. I was abandoned, and I can't face the idea of that happening to them."

Finn takes my hand, pressing a kiss to every finger, his gaze never leaving mine. His answer is silent but unshakable.

Tears sting my eyes.

"Family is everything to me, temptress. I'd die for them. I'd die for you. And for our children? I'd rip my own heart out for them. You'll never have to worry. Here, we stick together. Always."

My breath catches as his fingers brush my cheek.

"And now you're part of the family too. You might've

been alone for a long time, but not anymore. We've got you. I promise." He leans closer. "Till death do us part, right?"

My tears spill over, sliding down my cheeks.

"You'll always be safe with me," he whispers, sealing it with a kiss.

"And your heart is safe with me, Finn. I swear."

I press my palm against his chest, right over his steady beat.

"I know, baby. I know. Get some rest. We've got a lot to do once we arrive, and it's not going to be pretty."

I nod, eyelids heavy. "I still get to wear my pretty dress, right?"

"Yes. My killer in red heels. You get to wear the dress." His mouth brushes my ear. "And then I'll rip it off you the second it's over."

His arms tighten around me, locking me in, and I fall asleep to the sound of his heart.

CHAPTER 79

FINN

Song- Outro, M83

Stephanie is busy getting ready for the gala, leaving me and Declan to finalize our plans for this evening.

"Are you sure you don't want to leave Reggie with her here?" Declan asks, sliding his Rolex over his wrist, his eyes flicking up at me.

"Her?" I echo, my irritation bleeding into my voice.

"Steph," he clarifies.

"Stephanie. My wife, you mean?" My glare sharpens as I correct him.

Declan scoffs under his breath.

"Come on. After what we saw the other day, it isn't a real marriage. This is just another game to you, isn't it?"

My jaw tightens, but I force myself to shake my head.

"That was a misunderstanding, brother." I take a step closer, closing the space until the tension between us crackles like a live wire.

I don't often want to smash his skull into a wall, but right now I do.

"Your wife not only had a hit out on you twice, but she was also prepared to shoot Conan. I don't think you are in any place to talk shit about my fuckin' wife, Declan. Choose your next words very carefully." My voice is low.

Declan draws in a breath; he's battling with what to say to me next. I know him too well. "I'm worried about you, Finn. You've changed recently."

"And that's a bad thing? You want me to be a fucking robot that just kills people on your command? Is that it?"

He blinks, shaking his head quickly. "What? Fuck. No. I didn't mean that. It's just… different. I've never seen you in love. Never seen you trust someone, let alone forgive."

"Sit down." My order cracks like a whip as I point at the grand dining table.

Conan appears in the doorway, skidding to a halt.

"Shall I leave?" he asks.

"Do you have any concerns about me?" I fire back.

His mouth opens, but his eyes dart straight to Declan. Guilty.

"Sit." My tone leaves no room for refusal.

I love my brothers, and I would die for them, but Stephanie is my wife, my equal, and now a part of this family. They need to understand that I will protect her the same way I'd protect them. And that I need them to protect her the way they would protect me.

We will give Stephanie the family she deserves. She will never be abandoned again.

They both take their seats opposite me. The room is tense; the only comfort is the glitter of Tower Bridge in the night sky through the floor-to-ceiling windows of Theo's penthouse.

"Stephanie is my wife and will remain my wife until I

fucking die. Do I make myself clear?" My stare shifts between them.

"Yes."

"Nothing you can say or do will change that. She makes me…" I pause, searching, grinding through my chest for the right word. "…happy. Happier than I've ever been in my entire fucking life. She is part of our family now, and she will be treated as such."

Conan scratches at his stubble, glancing at Declan. "Finn, we have no problem with her. We're happy for you both."

"Then what is it? Why are you concerned about me?"

Declan leans forward, voice quieter. "We know something happened, Finn. When we were kids. I remember. I remember you before and then the version of you after. I remember Dad screaming, Mom crying. But the married Finn? He's neither version. It's like something happens in life, and you just respawn as a new person."

My throat closes up. They saw more than I ever wanted them to. All this time I thought I'd hidden it, locked it down so tightly my brothers never had to know. But they did. They've respected my silence, but they've always known.

"Stephanie has taught me how to love. How to heal from my past or, at least, begin to."

Sweat beads on my forehead. My hand twitches toward the whiskey, but I hold back. Could I tell them? Saying it aloud to Stephanie took the weight off my chest. Maybe telling them will kill what's left of the shame.

"Finn. You don't have to tell us anything. Just know we are here if you need us." Declan's voice is steady, but his eyes flicker with something soft.

I glance toward the stairs, silently begging for Stephanie to come down and anchor me with her hand in mine.

Maybe this part of my past needs to die tonight too.

"Let me grab more whiskey. We're going to need it," I tell them as I stand. My hand trembles as I reach for the bottle, my fist clenching before I carry it back.

I pour slowly, deliberately taking my time. "Remember the little girl I used to play out on the bikes with? When we were younger?" My voice is cracking as I direct the question at Declan.

"Yeah… the blonde one. You used to sneak her snacks from our house. Penelope?"

The name stabs through me like glass. I nod.

"I did that because her parents were abusing her. Starving her. Beating her. And…" My voice fractures. I can't say it. Fuck. "Doing everything to her."

I'll never find the words to express in detail what they did to us both. That never needs speaking out loud. I need them to understand, not live my trauma with me.

Declan pales. Conan's fists clench white.

"Fuck. That's awful. What happened to her? She just disappeared, didn't she?"

I swallow hard, nails digging into my palm. Pain. I fucking need pain.

"Her parents murdered her."

Conan hisses through his teeth. Declan presses his lips together, holding back the curse I know is on his tongue.

"It gets worse," I whisper.

They lean in, but I can barely get the words out. "I found out about her abuse long before she died. And I… I decided to take the brunt of it. For her."

Declan's jaw drops. "You mean?"

I nod. Shame floods me, burning down my spine. I close my eyes, fighting tears, fighting the memories of their hands on me in that house.

"I thought I could handle it better than her. That I could

find a way to save her. I was ten. Ten. I didn't know what to do, just that I had to try."

Conan wipes at his cheek, and the sight of his tears twists my stomach. I don't want pity. I don't want their grief. I just want to be heard.

"But one night she didn't come out. I snuck to her window, and I saw her. Throat slit. Bleeding out on her pink rug. The one with the ballerinas on it."

That was the moment my soul turned to ash.

"The lights went out in me that night. And they didn't come back until Stephanie."

I grip the glass so tight I'm sure it'll shatter.

"I made the decision then to end it. So while her parents slept, I snuck into their room, and I repaid the favor. Brutally. And then I cut them up. I made them pay."

Silence. My brothers stare, stunned and horrified, hands over their mouths.

"That's when I knew I wanted to be a surgeon. The only good thing to come from it. I found a purpose. I got revenge. But I failed her."

They're both out of their chairs in seconds, arms wrapping around me in a bear hug. My tears fall freely. I fucking hate it. This weakness.

That's why I am the way I am. That's why I cut my heart out and locked it in a box. Why I fucked, fought, and killed instead of feeling.

"Finn, why didn't you tell us? You've carried this for twenty-five years," Declan's voice breaks.

"Because I didn't want my cuts to bleed into you. I didn't want you to become like me."

Conan's grip tightens. Declan's jaw works as he tries not to break. Conan doesn't even bother to hide his. I've always been jealous of him in a way, being able to just feel. Even if people think it's too loudly. I've kept my emotions locked in a prison inside my brain, and now that I've unlocked it, I'm not sure which way to turn anymore. I've gone from feeling nothing to everything all at once.

"Did Dad know?"

"Yeah. He caught me mid-surgery. He covered it up. Hid it from the authorities. That was the last time I spoke of it… until recently."

Conan looks at me sharply. "You told Stephanie?"

"I did. And she made me see that keeping it inside is killing me. She makes me want to be better."

Declan gives a small nod. "Crazy what a woman can do."

"She's the best thing that ever happened to me. From the moment we met at the hospital, even when we were sworn rivals. She was keeping me alive, and I didn't even realize."

"I'm happy for you, Finn," Declan says softly. "This is the start of a new life for you."

I pray to God he's right.

"There's one more thing."

Conan leans forward, mouth falling open. "She's pregnant, isn't she?"

I chuckle, shaking my head. "I fuckin' wish. But no. Penelope's parents were cousins of the Bowens. That's why the war started when we were kids. Dad blamed all of them."

"Those motherfuckers," Conan growls.

"So killing Arthur is the end. Revenge for her. Revenge for Dad."

"And revenge for you, Finn," Declan adds.

Conan's fist clenches. "I'm glad I smashed James' skull."

"You're not to blame for Dad's death, Conan. That was his sacrifice. Don't carry that weight," I tell him.

Tears fill his eyes, but he nods.

I lift my glass. "To Mom and Dad."

"They'd be proud of us," Declan whispers.

"And Dad will be watching as we skin Arthur alive, whiskey in hand, smiling." I smirk.

The energy shifts in the room. My heart slams against my ribs.

I turn, and my lungs seize.

"Holy shit, love. You look breathtaking."

I stride toward her, her smile growing with every step. That smile is what my heart beats for now.

I tilt her chin up, drinking her in. "Absolutely beautiful, temptress. Gorgeous. Stunning. A masterpiece. Perfection." My lips hover over hers. "All fuckin' mine."

Her blush rises, heat radiating between us. Her hands smooth over my chest as she straightens my bow tie.

"I'll look good as an accessory on your arm, Dr. Quinn."

"No. You're the main event."

The dress hugs her like it was sewn on her body, red fabric sculpting every curve. The snake tattoo between her breasts captivating me. My fingers run through her curls, my gaze locked on hers.

"I want to kiss you, but I don't want to get red lipstick on you," she whispers.

I ignore her, crashing my mouth onto hers.

"Nothing gets between us. Remember that."

A knock sounds at the door. Conan rushes to answer, leaving Declan chuckling.

I focus back on her, softer now, and she reaches up, wiping the lipstick away from my lips.

"I told them," I say quietly.

Her eyes widen, then she gives me a soft smile as she cups my face. "I'm proud of you. Was it okay?"

I nod. "It's done. Now we have one more task to complete. Then I'll be free."

She wraps her arms around my neck. "And then what's the plan?"

"World's ours, love. Whatever we want to do. Just as long as we're together."

CHAPTER 80

STEPHANIE

A stream of men enters through the door. One after another. Each one bigger than the last, like some twisted parade of giants.

I'm frozen on the spot.

Then she arrives. A woman with a razor-sharp bob of jet-black hair and a smile that could kill. She's draped over the arm of a man in a navy suit who radiates power, the kind of man who doesn't need to speak to own a room.

"I think you'll like her," Finn whispers into my ear.

"Who are they?" My voice is low.

"Frankie and Zara Falcone. They run New York. She's the commissioner."

My jaw nearly hits the floor. "Pardon?"

"Corruption at its finest," Finn murmurs, almost amused.

Declan and Conan move forward, greeting the men like old allies. My stomach knots as I recognize one of them—the masked man from Vegas. Those dark eyes would haunt anyone, and when they lock on me, every instinct in my body screams to hide behind Finn.

He feels it instantly. His arm tightens around my waist, iron and protective, pulling me flush against him.

The door swings again, and another beast of a man steps in. He's followed by a woman just as stunning and dangerous as Zara.

"Nikolai and Mila Volkov, and their leader, Mikhail," Finn says. "Again, you'll like her too."

My head snaps toward him. "Why do you keep saying I'll like them?"

He chuckles, tapping the tip of my nose. "Just a hunch."

I scowl, but heat blooms in my chest at the way he says it —like he sees every hidden part of me and doesn't flinch.

We all spill into the dining room, Declan already pouring drinks like it's another night at Inferno. But Frankie and Zara cut straight toward us.

"Dr. Quinn." Frankie's Italian accent rolls thick and heavy.

"Good to see you again, Frankie. And Zara." Finn greets them easily, offering Zara one of those rare smiles he saves for people who matter. "This is my wife, Stephanie."

The room stills. It's subtle, but I feel it. Eyes drag to us. To me.

Zara's gaze softens as she steps forward, her smile disarming. Almost like she sees the nerves cracking under my surface.

"It's a lot, isn't it?" she whispers.

I exhale, the breath shaking out of me. "Yeah. I'm used to stressful situations at work, but this… this is topping it."

Her brows lift, intrigued. "What do you do?" She plucks a glass of champagne from Frankie without breaking eye contact.

"I'm a surgeon in cardiology. I work for Finn."

Her grin widens knowingly. "Nice. Married the boss." She winks.

"That wasn't my initial plan."

"No. She wanted to kill me, really," Finn's voice cuts in dryly.

Frankie chuckles, joining the conversation. "Most of our women do want to kill us. That's how we know they really love us."

Nikolai and Mila drift closer, catching the tail end of the exchange.

"That's how we met too, wasn't it, d'yavolitsa?" Nikolai rumbles, looking down at Mila like she hung the stars.

Her lip curls, eyes full of adoration. "It worked out for us eventually."

She steps toward me, hand extended, black nails like claws. "I'm Mila. Nice to meet you."

"Stephanie."

Finn presses a kiss to my neck, murmuring something against my skin before excusing himself to join the men. My body instantly misses the cage of his hold, but Mila and Zara close in on either side of me.

"You're new to this world, aren't you?" Mila asks.

I nod.

Zara smirks like she's already seen my future. "But you're going to be one of us. I can feel it."

I glance around at the room full of predators and power. My lips twitch with something dark. "I'm not your typical surgeon. I guess you could say I have a past. And... some interesting pastimes."

Their eyes light up. "Tell us more," Mila presses, leaning in.

"Well," I lower my voice, "up until recently, I had a part-time gig at a strip club. So I could hunt down men from my past… and kill them in their sleep."

"Wow," Zara breathes, genuine awe in her tone.

I blink. Wait. She's a cop.

But her smile only widens. "Welcome to the family." She slings an arm around my shoulder like we've known each other for years. "Whatever you have to do to survive, you'll never catch judgment from us. We stick together in this world —especially us women."

Tears sting unexpectedly in my eyes. I've never had women like this in my corner. Never felt the weight of protection that wasn't transactional, wasn't false. Just… fierce and loyal.

"Has Finn given you your instructions for tonight?" Mila asks.

I nod. "I–I kinda forced him to bring me here. I don't really have a role, just that I have to stay with him at all times."

The girls sip their champagne, perfectly poised.

"We came under the pretense of a date night in London," Zara says lightly, though her eyes glint with steel. "But we're here if we're needed. Honestly? I think this will be an easy night for them. Precaution, more than anything."

The door opens again, pulling my attention. Enzo. The twins. Drago. And three men I don't recognize, their accents giving away their British roots the moment they speak.

"Should I be more prepared for this?" I whisper.

"Just trust Finn," Mila says. "He knows what he's doing. The Quinn brothers are well respected by our husbands."

My gaze finds Finn across the room. He's in deep discussion with the newcomers, the masked man listening closely.

And then those pale eyes of my husband cut to me again.

This time, he smiles.

I wonder what the world will hold for us once this is over.

The next thing I know, the men are carting guns, knives, throwing stars—every weapon you could imagine—straight from the adjoining room and dumping them across the dining table like it's nothing more than a buffet spread.

"Come and pick your weapons," the British one announces with a grin, like this is his idea of hospitality.

I watch as Finn's pale hand hovers, deliberate, before he plucks a small handgun from the pile. The way he tests its weight, the way his eyes find mine—it's not just a choice. It's a lesson.

"Ever shot someone?" he asks casually, but I feel the weight of the question in my bones.

I shake my head. "No. But I know how to use one."

I reach for it, fingers brushing his, but he doesn't let go. Instead, his hand tightens over mine, holding it there, eyes boring into me.

"Think you could shoot someone?"

"Yes," I answer without hesitation. Because I've thought about it. Lived it in my head a hundred times over.

The corner of his mouth curves, wicked and proud. He dips close enough that only I can hear. "Good girl."

The whisper slithers through me, hot and sharp. His lips brush mine in a fleeting kiss before he finally releases the gun into my hand.

"Keep it in your purse," he instructs. "Just a precaution."

My stomach twists with nerves as I slide the weapon into the depths of my bag. Precaution. Nothing about this night feels like precaution.

Finn's arm circles around my waist, pulling me into his side as though he can feel the thoughts racing in my head.

"We've got a quick meeting with Theo now to cover all

the bases before we leave." He tilts his head, watching my face, reading me the way only he can. "Want to listen in?"

"I'd love that." I fake a smile. I can't show him how nervous I am deep down. I want to be here. I want to see this side of him.

His smile is sharp and feral, full of something only I get to see. "Then stay close, temptress. Tonight, you'll see everything."

I nod and follow closely behind him into the living room.

CHAPTER 81

FINN

The room sharpens when Theo enters. His presence has that effect; every conversation dulls, every glass stills on the table, and all eyes shift his way. The man doesn't need to raise his voice to command an army. He's been doing it his whole life.

And that's what makes him the perfect ally now.

"We go in separately," Theo starts. "The guest list is tight, and they'll be checking every name. You'll use the covers provided." He glances at Enzo, who nods once, sliding slim envelopes across the polished oak table.

I catch mine before it hits the edge. My alias stares back at me in bold letters. A name that isn't mine, but tonight it will be.

Amy Beck and David Beck.

"The second Arthur steps foot inside," Theo continues, "I'll give the signal. Then it's over to the Quinn brothers—" His gaze cuts like glass, locking on me, then Declan, then Conan. "He's yours."

A low burn settles in my chest. Mine. Ours. The bastard's

life has been circling this drain for decades, and now it ends. Not quick, not merciful. Justice, Quinn style.

"The rest of you are on standby," Theo says, sweeping the table with his eyes. "No unnecessary theatrics. No heroics. If it goes loud, we'll adjust. We have already taken down the majority of Bowen's army here. But as Finn has informed me, they seem to respawn. So keep your eyes peeled. He's been in hiding for weeks; this is our first solid lead to get to him."

I tap my rings on the table.

"What brought him out of hiding? What does this gala mean to him?"

Theo gives me a menacing grin, and I already know what he's done.

"Me. He thinks he's getting me delivered on a silver fucking platter with a cup of steaming hot tea."

Ryder's face scrunches up, and I can feel the anger radiating from him. And I smile. I can imagine that's exactly how my brothers would react too. But sometimes you have to do what you need to do to gain power.

The Kings are close to a takeover now. Arthur is the only one standing in their way. Once they can establish their empire here, they will form their alliance with us. They're set for life.

"How did you manage that?" I ask, tightening my hold around Stephanie's waist.

"He actually reached out to me. Wanted to have a civil discussion around a ceasefire. Clearly a trick. So, I played along and suggested the gala. It's hosted by one of the companies our elders own. No links to us directly, though. He thinks he's walking into neutral territory," Theo tells me.

I glance at Declan and know he's thinking the same as me.

That does not sound like Arthur. He's greedy. Power hungry. A ceasefire is not in his vocabulary. But, I guess, maybe all of his close relatives being six feet under has changed him.

Desperation can change a man.

"And what if he brings an army? What if he's already planted bombs there?" Drago asks, his voice like ice.

"We own the building. Twenty-four-hour security. You think I wanna get blown up? No thanks. Arthur knows he will not be granted access to the building with a bodyguard. He accepted the terms."

I scratch at my jaw. I don't like this. I lean in closer to Declan.

"Do you think Arthur would walk into his death this easily?" I whisper.

Declan shifts in his seat.

"It ain't the Arthur we know, is it?"

The purpose of my fucking life is sitting on my lap, walking into this with me. And that puts the stakes that much higher. The Finn before her? He would have loved the idea of walking into a war zone, just for the fucking thrill.

The Finn now?

I'm worried. Something deep in my gut is telling me to tell her to stay here. But the thought of leaving her in a country I have no real power in?

I can't do that either.

"She's safer with us, Finn," Declan says quietly, as if he can read my fucking mind.

He probably goes through this with Charlotte, our little assassin. Even though we know she could chop us up if she wanted to, he's still worried about her. I think it's natural when you love someone with your entire being.

Part of me wants to lock Stephanie up, keep her safe forever. But, that isn't my girl. That isn't what she wants or needs from me. She wants to be a part of something. She deserves to be beside me.

And it's on me to keep her safe.

Enzo pulls a slim black case from his briefcase and flicks it open. "Earpieces," he says simply. One by one, he drops them onto the table, each delicate curve of metal and wire looking harmless enough, but they'll be the thread keeping us together tonight.

He meets my eyes as he passes mine over. "I'll be watching from here. Every camera, every feed. If anything shifts, I'll see it first."

"Thank you," I reply, sliding it into my palm. The weight feels too light for what it means.

Enzo has come through on his promise. We've got the manpower. The technology. And it is all thanks to him. Hell, he even bothered to join us in London. Perhaps our new alliance together will work out after all.

Stephanie stiffens in my grip, her gaze darting over the table, memorizing every detail. I can see the questions forming on her lips, the way her hands grip her purse where the gun sits hidden. Brave little temptress. In over her head, yet she refuses to sink.

Theo's eyes catch her for a beat before returning to me. He doesn't question it. He knows better.

"This is precise work," he reminds the room. "We don't get a second chance. And we never trust our enemies."

A chill runs through the air.

Arthur has his own revenge plan. Conan murdered his brother in the cage. Brutally.

I lean back in my chair, pulling Stephanie's back tight

against my chest. My pulse is steady, but my mind is already there—at the gala. Arthur's pale face already appearing in my mind. My fingers itching for the moment I wrap them around his throat.

Tonight, the war ends.

I can't believe I'm driving a Rolls Royce. In London. The skyline is sparkling as we make our way past St. Katherine's Docks. I've always dreamed of visiting this city.

"It's beautiful here, Finn."

"Hmm. It is," he rasps.

A blush spreads up my neck as I glance at him. He isn't looking anywhere else other than at me.

"Smooth," I tease.

We've all taken separate cars. Each of us with our own time slot to enter the party from different entrances.

It feels like a military operation, and I am the rookie with no experience.

"How are you feeling, Stephanie?"

I tap my nails against the steering wheel as I stop for the traffic.

"Uh. Nervous. But still kind of excited?"

He gives me a sharp nod.

"The plan seems good. I'll be relieved once it's over," he tells me.

I frown, placing my hand on his thigh.

"Why? That doesn't seem like you."

"I've never had to worry about the safety of my wife before. Or my own life, really. Now, I have something to live for; it feels heavier. I'm not sure what to feel."

That raw honesty in his voice makes me smile.

"I promise I won't get in your way. But I do like that you have concern for your own safety now. Because you're important too, Finn. I need you."

He glances at me and grins.

"You need me? Huh? Or just my dick?" He plants his hand down on my thigh and squeezes hard.

"You are more than just a big dick, Dr. Quinn."

He leans in, and I suck in a breath.

"I did tell you in Vegas you were missing out on him."

I let out a giggle.

"You did. But I'd still have to try out alien dick if I ever get the chance."

He tuts and removes his hand.

"Look, if my wife really, really wants it, I might let it slide, just once."

"Aw. That's so sweet of you, letting me go after my dreams."

His eyes darken.

"I don't share, love. Please don't ever ask me to. My only fucking hard limit here."

I smile and run my fingers along his cheek.

"I don't want, need, or desire anyone else other than my husband. You complete me."

The cars start to move ahead, and I shift into gear. Driving on the wrong side of the road feels weird, but I'm getting the hang of it.

I take a left, and the huge, very old-looking building is in my sights. Almost like a royal estate like you see on TV.

"Keep going round the building and park around the back," Finn directs me.

Once I find a space, I cut the engine.

"The man you're going to see me be in there, he's the one who has to protect his family. Okay?"

I thread my fingers through his.

"Finn, I want you to show me every version of you there is. I'm not scared."

His gaze meets mine, and his face softens.

"Perhaps we will have time to get a dance in," he says.

My heart races.

"I thought Dr. Quinn doesn't do dancing?" I tease.

"I don't. But, for you, I will. If it makes you smile."

I lean over, and his lips capture mine.

"I've never been happier, Finn," I tell him honestly.

"Me neither, love."

The second Finn opens my door, the cool London night cuts into me. I place my hand in his, expecting the same warmth from the car, but what I get instead makes me falter.

His grip isn't tender now. It's firm and commanding, like he's guiding me into enemy territory. Which, I guess, he is.

I step out, my heels crunching against the gravel, and my chest tightens as I take in the scene. The mansion looms like something out of a gothic fairytale, grand and lit to perfection, but its beauty feels like a trap. Like every chandelier inside is waiting to shatter to pieces.

Finn closes the door behind me, his shoulders squaring as he straightens to his full height. And in that instant, he changes.

The husband who teased me about chocolate strawberries and alien dick is gone. His face hardens, his eyes turn to ice, and I can practically see him slip into his role. The cold, calculating, and untouchable version of him is here. And I love him just as much.

My pulse stutters because I realize this is what he meant. The version of him that has to exist to keep me safe.

"Temptress." His voice is dangerous. "Do not leave my side. If anything feels off, it probably is. And, remember, every single one of my men is there to protect you."

I nod, my throat too tight to answer.

He leads me forward, his presence radiating like a shield and a warning all at once. I hold my purse tighter against me; knowing what I've got in there makes me nervous too.

And as the grand doors open, spilling gold light into the night, I understand something better than I have before.

My husband isn't just a man. He's a deadly weapon.

CHAPTER 83

FINN

Song- As The World Caves In, Sarah Cothran

There is no relaxing when it comes to events like this. No matter how much you prepare, no matter how many people stand on your side, you never know when shit will go south.

It's how I've lived my entire life.

Coiled. On edge. Waiting for everything to fall apart.

And no matter how many times Theo or Enzo try to reassure me this is a clean in-and-out job, I know better. Nothing is clean when it comes to the Bowens.

Our father lost his life to these men. Conan spilled the blood of Arthur's younger brother in the cage. We've hunted each other across oceans, each strike leaving scars. Even after we moved to the States, he found a way back to us. To hurt Conan.

And now I'm meant to put my trust in Theo. Not a man I give my faith to lightly. He has a long fucking road ahead before he earns this alliance.

As we enter the room, it's a sea of bodies. A woman brushes into my side as she walks past and stops.

"Excuse me, darlin', we need to get past," I say.

"Oh, sorry." She steps back, flustered, and moves to the side and keeps walking.

Stephanie's hand slips from mine, and I immediately turn to face her. Her nostrils are flaring, her eyes are daggers as she crosses her arms over her chest.

"What?" I ask, raising an eyebrow.

She steps closer and pushes against my chest so my back is against the wall.

"Call another woman darlin' again, and neither of you will be walking out of here alive," she says with a straight face.

It makes my cock twitch, her being possessive like this.

"I hear you. No problem. Never again."

She blinks at me. I think she was expecting me to fire back. But I understand. To me, it was being polite. Life is different now. Stephanie is the only woman who has a nickname.

"Well," she smiles.

I curl my fingers around her throat and lean in.

"I wouldn't threaten me with death again though, love," I whisper in her ear, and she shivers against my touch.

"Why is that, Dr. Quinn?" she whispers back.

"Because that makes me hard as fuck," I tell her, feeling her skin heat.

"Noted." She winks and smirks back at me.

I press my lips firmly against hers. Fuck. She's perfect.

"That was easier than I thought," she mutters as she pulls away and puts her hand in mine like nothing happened.

I lead Stephanie straight to the bar. The air is thick with cigar smoke, laughter, and the sound of money being thrown around like it means nothing. A string quartet plays to Polish the Illusion of Elegance, but underneath it all this room reeks of predators in expensive suits.

My brothers are already in place, posted on either side of the bar, scanning the crowd with eyes that miss nothing. The Volkov men are scattered strategically around the floor. Frankie and Zara waltz on the dance floor like this is any other Saturday night date.

"Champagne?" A deep British voice cuts in behind me.

"Sure," I mutter.

The flute is in my hand a second later, but Stephanie goes stiff beside me. Her body jolts against mine.

"What is it?" I lean down, my mouth close to her ear.

"I—uh… I don't mean to be rude, but that guy's face was a mess."

A mess?

She swallows, her voice dropping lower. "Like… broken. Like he took a heavy beating and walked away without an eye."

I frown. That doesn't fit with the kind of staff they hire to work these floors. My gaze flicks to the man, but he's already moving—disappearing through the double doors into the kitchen, back turned before I can get a good look.

"Maybe he's part of one of the families that run this place," I tell her, though the unease prickles my skin.

I wish I'd seen his face for myself.

Stephanie takes a sip of her champagne, a soft moan slipping from her lips. My eyes follow the drop that spills down, sliding from the corner of her mouth along her chin.

I put my glass down, curl my hand around her waist, and pull her flush against me. My tongue sweeps over her skin, licking the champagne from her chin.

"Don't moan like that in public," I growl against her mouth.

"Why not?" Her eyes spark with challenge, blue fire burning me alive.

Because she doesn't understand. I'm obsessed. Addicted. Every sound, every look, every part of her is mine, and mine alone.

"Because your moans belong to me," I mutter, stealing a kiss.

My hand grips her ass hard enough to make her breath hitch. She sets her glass down beside mine, her smile lighting her face until everything else in the room falls away.

She's the center of my fucking universe.

"Dance with me?" I whisper against her lips.

Her mouth tips into a grin, teeth catching her bottom lip. "My husband wants to dance with me? In front of everyone?"

"Careful," I warn. "Keep pushing and I'll fuck you in front of them too."

Her mouth falls open, shock and heat clashing across her face, and I smirk. We both know I couldn't. I wouldn't. She's mine. Only mine.

Her hands slide slowly down my chest, her touch a brand. "I'll dance with you, rich boy."

A growl rips out of my chest as I duck my head, sinking my teeth into her neck hard enough to make her gasp.

"Whatever my wife wants, she gets," I murmur, pulling back just enough to see her smile.

She tilts her head, still looking at me like I'm the only thing that's ever mattered. "I just want you."

That does it.

She grabs my hand, dragging me right into the center of the dance floor, under the chandeliers, and pulls me into her orbit.

The music slows, the swell of strings drifting through the air as I wrap an arm around her waist and pull her in. Her body fits against mine like it was always meant to be there, like the universe has been carving us into each other piece by piece.

I've danced in operating rooms. With death. With blood. With the silence of failing heart monitors. But I've never danced like this. Never with a woman pressed so close, her heartbeat tangled with mine, every breath she takes pulling me deeper into something I swore I'd never feel.

Stephanie tilts her head up, her eyes locking on mine. "You don't even know how to waltz, do you?"

"No," I rasp. My hand tightens at her lower back, and I lead her anyway. "But you'll follow me. You always do."

She gives me a coy smile. "Well, neither do I. Looks like we're perfectly paired."

Her laugh is soft, breaking me open. Her palm presses against my chest, right over the heart I've kept buried from the world. The heart I've told myself doesn't exist. And fuck, it hurts. The pressure of it. The weight. Because I can feel it hammering under her touch, beating just for her.

"Finn…" she whispers, like she knows. Like she feels the storm tearing me apart inside.

I close my eyes for a second, pulling her in tighter, because the past is bleeding into the present. Just like it always does. I see Penelope's face. I see every patient I've lost. Every kill I've made. Every grave I've filled. A life built on precision, violence, and walls I swore would never crack.

I can feel Conan's blood on my hands again. See my father's grave. Feeling the world fall apart when my mom died.

And yet here I am. Cracking. Splintering. Bleeding right into her hands, and she doesn't falter.

She fucking grounds me.

When I open my eyes, she's still watching me, her eyes shining, her lip caught between her teeth like she's scared to breathe too loud and shatter this moment.

But this is it. Our fucking moment. The one my mom always promised me I'd have.

I never believed her. She always saw the good in me, too. Even when I screamed at her that she was wrong. She never gave up on me, not until the world ripped her away from me.

I can't fight it anymore.

I open my mouth to speak, but she beats me to it.

"I love you," she breathes out.

She truly is a fuckin' menace.

"That's great, love." I keep my tone neutral.

She frowns, licking her lip.

"That's all you have to say? Seriously?"

I can't help but grin.

"You're the one who stole my line, temptress. Now, are you gonna let me say my whole declaration properly?"

I tilt my head and she blushes.

"I get a whole speech?" she whispers.

"I'll give you the whole damn world if you'll let me. So, yes."

I cup her cheeks and take a deep breath.

"Stephanie Quinn. I love you," I tell her quietly so only she can hear.

The words are a raw confession, ripped straight from a place I didn't even think was alive anymore.

Her mouth parts, her breath catching, tears flooding her eyes as though she's been waiting for this, needing it as much as I've needed to say it.

"I love you, temptress. More than I can stand. More than I ever thought I was capable of. I thought love was a weakness.

I thought it would destroy me. But you—" My voice fractures, my throat burning as I press my forehead to hers. "You're the only thing that's ever made me want to fucking live."

Her palm rests on my cheek as she whispers back.

"Finn…" Her voice trembles, it's broken and beautiful. "I've loved you since the second you terrified me into noticing you. And I'll love you for the rest of my life. I want to be your wife for as long as you'll have me."

I can't breathe. My chest aches like it's collapsing in on itself, but her arms come around my neck, holding me together, and it's the first time in my entire fucked-up existence that I believe I'm not beyond saving.

"So, forever? Does that sound okay? In this life and the next," I whisper.

"Yes." She hiccups. "I'd love that."

The world blurs around us. The chandeliers, the music, the predators circling the room. It all fades until it's just her and me. My temptress. My wife. My salvation.

And when I kiss her, it isn't the kiss of a man who's claiming. It's the kiss of a man who's surrendering.

I might as well be on my fucking knees.

Because I've finally fucking found the one thing stronger than the darkness inside me.

Her.

As I rest my head on his chest, we sway to the music. But with each step, his heart rate is getting faster and faster.

"Finn," I whisper.

"Hmm?"

I pull back and look up as he wipes the sweat from his forehead. And the color in his face—it isn't right.

He blinks heavily.

"Something's wrong," he tells me.

His arms drop from me and he shakes his head.

"Fuck," he hisses.

Grabbing my hand, he weaves us through the couples dancing and straight to the bar.

"Water. Please. Now!" he barks to the bartender.

I keep my hand tightly in his, grabbing a container of salt. He glances down and half smiles. He takes the water, and I follow him to the side of the room; he nods over to the twins, and they join us.

"I've been fucking spiked," he tells us.

My heart is racing. He rests his hand on my neck, feeling my pulse. Looking into my eyes.

"Do you feel okay, love?"

I nod.

"Yes."

"Okay. Reggie, get through Enzo. Find out who the fuck touched my drink. Steph, I need you to go to the car with Rowan. In the trunk, there's a bag of medical supplies. I'm going to the bathroom to get this shit out of my system. Meet me in there." He points to the door behind us.

I hand him the salt and he crashes his lips over mine.

"Don't let Rowan out of your sight. I'm going to be fine." My bottom lip trembles as he turns to Rowan.

"Protect her with your fucking life. Be quick."

I link my arm through Rowan's as Finn stumbles into the bathrooms with Reggie close behind.

"Pass me your purse," Rowan tells me.

"There's a, um, gun in there," I whisper, eyes wide.

He nods as I slide the chain off my shoulder and hand it to him, and he shoves it under his armpit and pushes open the double doors to the stairwell with the side of his body.

My head is spinning from fear, nerves, all of it. Everything is unfolding so fast, and I can't catch up.

CHAPTER 85

FINN

I brace my hands on the porcelain sink, my chest heaving. The salt water I forced down is clawing its way back up, mixing with bile as I shove two fingers down my throat. My body convulses, retching until my ribs ache, until sweat is dripping down my back.

Poison. Fucking poison. Whoever slipped it to me knew what they were doing. I spit again, rinse my mouth, and look at the stranger staring back from the mirror. Grey skin, pupils blown, jaw tight enough to snap.

Not tonight. I'm not dying tonight.

"You good, Finn?" Reggie asks from behind me.

I spit again. Fuck. There are stars in the corners of my vision.

The door creaks open, and my hand goes straight to my gun before I see Theo step in, his expression unreadable, tailored suit pristine against the filth I'm dragging up out of myself.

"Jesus Christ, Finn—"

"Save it." My voice is hoarse. I slam the tap off and grab

the edge of the sink again as another wave of dizziness slams through me. "Where the fuck is Arthur?"

Theo stiffens. "Enzo said he's only just arrived. He ain't even in the building yet. This wasn't him."

This doesn't make sense. My head is pounding. I check my watch. It's been four minutes since Stephanie left with Rowan.

"Someone else is here." My throat feels scorched, but I force the words out. "Man with a scarred face. One working eye. I barely saw him—Stephanie did. Tell me you clocked him."

Theo's frown deepens, and for a second, he looks like he's about to lie. Then his jaw works and he shakes his head.

"No one that matches that description is on my guest list."

"Exactly." I spit into the sink, my hands shaking, fury burning through the weakness in my veins. "Then find him. Now."

"I'll get my brothers on it. Arthur's gonna be here any minute, Finn. There's no one on our list that would try and hurt you," Theo tells me.

This anger might keep me alive long enough. Whatever I've been spiked with wasn't to kill me. It was to throw me off.

I slam my fist against the counter, the crack ricocheting off the tiles. "I don't give a fuck what game Arthur's running or how clean you think your list is. Someone just tried to put me in the ground. I want that man with the mangled face found and in front of me before this night ends. You hear me?"

The only thing I've ingested was that champagne. This is no coincidence.

Theo hesitates, then nods once. "Consider it done. Our plan is still in motion; it's going to be okay."

He turns to leave, and I drag another mouthful of water down, forcing my body to obey me. My chest burns, my vision tunnels, but the rage steadies me.

"Finn. Arthur is parking up now at the front of the building. Two guards. Arthur is in the passenger seat," Enzo confirms in my ear.

I tap my earpiece. We try not to talk back to Enzo often so we don't clog the feeds. But, I can't rely on anyone else, not when Stephanie is here.

"Theo, wait!" I call out.

Fuck, I feel awful.

He stands in the doorway as I talk back to Enzo.

"I've been drugged, Enzo. Help Kane and Ryder find the cunt who did this. Theo is going to bring Arthur to me now. Get Conan and Declan to me."

"Copy that," Enzo replies.

I look to Theo, who nods.

"I'll bring you Arthur," he confirms and storms out.

Where is Stephanie? Fuck. I need her by my side. Out of harm's way.

I don't like how Theo faltered. What if this isn't just about Arthur? What if it's something bigger than this?

The Preacher has tried to let me rot in jail. Blackmailed my wife. What if this is more than just the Bowen war?

What if I really did bring my wife into a fucking war?

I'm going to be sick again.

"Wait. I'm unlocking the car back here," Rowan orders as we step outside.

"Uh. Okay."

He clicks the button and the soft chirp of the Rolls Royce makes my chest tighten even further.

Rowan positions himself behind me, his gun angled low and discreet, his eyes sweeping left and right like we're already under fire. "Stay close."

He guides me to the trunk and I pop it open. The cool night air hits me with the faint scent of oil and metal, and there it is—the little black bag Finn insisted on packing himself. Seeing it now feels like a lifeline.

I grab the handle, clutching it to my chest. "Got it."

Rowan's jaw clenches as he takes the gun out and shoves my purse in the back of the trunk before shutting it quietly.

"Take this. Keep it discreet." Rowan grunts.

As I take it, I take a deep breath. Fuck.

The parking lot looks empty, but it doesn't feel empty. My skin prickles with the sense of being watched, like eyes are on us from every corner.

Someone tried to hurt Finn.

"Back inside. Quick." His tone is calm, but I hear the steel underneath. He places a hand at my back, moving me forward, his body a barrier between me and whatever threat he sees in every shadow.

My heels crunch on the gravel, my heart slamming with every step. All I can think about is Finn, pale and sweating, forcing himself to stand upright. Poison crawling through his veins.

Everything was perfect. The dance. Hearing him say those words. I can't lose him.

I tighten my grip on the bag. He's still alive. He's still fighting. And I'll drag him back from the brink with my bare hands if I have to.

As Rowan opens up the emergency exit to the stairs, a bang makes me jump, the blood draining from me.

The world fractures with the crack of a gunshot.

Rowan jerks beside me, his hand flying to his stomach. For a split second, I can't even process it. Then the wet warmth of blood seeps through his fingers, and my scream rips from my throat.

I bring my hands to my mouth to muffle the noise.

"Go!" he snarls, his voice raw with pain as he bundles me forward, shoving me into the side entrance before another shot can follow. The door slams shut behind us, and the silence on this side is deafening compared to the ringing in my ears.

We stagger into the stairwell and his legs buckle. He collapses hard against the wall, sliding down until he's sitting on the concrete, breath ragged.

"No, no, no, stay with me." My hands shake as I rip his jacket off, pressing it against the hole in his stomach; the blood is soaking through too fast.

"Let me look."

I peel away his shirt carefully. It looks clean. But he needs help.

"Move, Stephanie. Finn needs you." His voice is steel, even now.

He keeps tapping on his ear.

"Fuck. I've lost it," he hisses as he tips his head back.

His back slides down the wall and he sits on the floor.

"You need medic—"

"Phone," he cuts me off, grimacing. "Pass me my phone from my pocket."

I fumble it out of his jacket with slippery fingers, thrusting it into his hand. He dials with a grunt, his jaw clenched against the pain.

"No fucking signal." He squeezes his eyes shut.

I want to stay, to keep pressure on the wound until help comes, but his hand clamps over mine, forcing me back.

"Up the stairs, Stephanie. You don't stop. You hear me? Get me help. And don't be afraid to shoot anyone that gets in your way." His words are a command, not a request.

He hands me my gun and the medical bag and I shake my head.

"What if they come for you first?"

He waves me away. "I can fight anyone except your husband and I'm loaded up." He tries to grin.

A chill runs down my spine.

Tears blur my vision as I nod, trembling, and scoop up the black medical bag again. My legs feel like lead, but I run, each step pounding with panic.

At the top, the hallway stretches before me. The door to the bathroom looms only feet away. Finn is inside. Relief and terror twist together in my chest.

I reach for the handle—

And a hand clamps over my mouth, yanking me back before I can scream.

The bag slips from my grip, hitting the ground with a heavy thud. I fight against him; my arm smashes against the wall, and the gun clatters to the floor before the world goes black.

CHAPTER 87

FINN

"Go outside and wait for Stephanie and Rowan." I point to the door before dry heaving again.

Reggie storms out.

Tapping my earpiece, I patch through to Enzo again.

"Enzo. Where are they?" I hiss, my stomach cramping.

"Finn. I've been thrown out. The systems are diabolical. I can't see shit inside right now. Only the outside cameras."

"Fuck," I hiss.

The door crashes open and a concerned Declan and Conan arrive.

"Finn. What the fuck is going on?" Declan grabs my face, forcing me to look at him.

I'm struggling to focus properly.

"We need to find Stephanie. Rowan."

Am I slurring?

I push Declan away and shove my fingers back down my throat.

"Finn. We have a problem," Reggie says.

My heart is beating so fast I can feel it pounding all over my body.

I take a breath, wiping my mouth. And my heart nearly stops when I see Reggie holding my black medical bag and Stephanie's gun.

My knees threaten to buckle under me.

"Where are they?" I roar with every bit of energy I have.

Grasping onto the basin, I take a breath.

"Finn. You need to calm down," Conan tells me.

"No!" I push myself upright.

My eyes are heavy. Fuck. I don't have time to sleep.

"Reggie. The bag." I motion for him to come over.

I need to be okay so I can get to my wife.

"I need to find my brother," Reggie says, full of pure anger.

I grab it from him and open it up on the side, grabbing the Flumazenil. It's the only thing that could help. Depending on what the fuck I ingested. But, it's worth a shot, on top of purging it out of my system.

I take the shot and release any air, stretching out my arm.

"What the hell is that?" Declan hisses.

"Something that might work. I need to find her, Dec."

I tap on my veins and inject the drug. A small dose for now, just in case.

Between all of this and the adrenaline, I will get through this; I can die later.

Just not now.

Running the cold tap, I splash my face a few times and look at my bloodshot eyes in the mirror.

Please fucking work.

"Theo has Arthur, they're outside the main entrance. Meet him there. Theo says it's clear to do as you wish," Enzo says through the earpiece.

My hands are fucking trembling. The result of the adrenaline mixing with the drugs. I wipe the sweat away from my forehead.

"Go!" I order Reggie. "I'll follow. Grab as many of our men as you can on the way. Have the Volkovs sweeping the building for her and Rowan."

I stumble through the door, my vision still hazy but better than it was.

It's working. It will be enough to see me through this and get Stephanie back.

If I fucking collapse after that, then so be it. I'm not going down without a fight.

I'm not leaving this life without telling my wife that I fucking love her again.

Without kissing her one more time.

As I open my eyes, the room is hazy. Red carpets. Cream walls. I don't think I've left the gala.

My body aches everywhere. Panic rips through me as I try to move my wrists, but they're bound tight to the chair. The rope cuts into my skin like it's alive, digging deeper every time I shift.

I try to scream, but it comes out muffled, suffocating me.

A deep man's voice booms from somewhere beside me, but the ringing in my ears makes it hard to make out the words.

Shit.

Finn. I need to get to him.

I turn my head slowly, and there he is. My attacker. The disfigured man from earlier, except now he's dressed down in sweats, a navy T-shirt, and a black baseball cap shadowing the ruin of his face.

That smile he wears makes my stomach turn.

With each step closer, I thrash against my restraints.

"I'm not going to hurt you," he whispers, leaning in until the stench of his breath coats my skin.

I squeeze my eyes shut, fighting the urge to gag.

"Yet. Can you behave for me? Be quiet. It will all be over soon."

Bile rises in my throat as his finger trails lazily down my neck. I can't fight back. I can't even speak. This—this helplessness—is my worst nightmare.

But I won't cry. I won't let him win. Finn will find me. Someone will. They have to. This can't be how it ends.

"You should've picked a better husband," he murmurs, tapping the diamond on my finger.

I bite down hard on the gag.

"Aw. You really do love him, don't you? Do you even know who he is? He's got fewer screws up here than me." He taps the side of his head, eyes gleaming with madness.

I shake mine violently. Rage surges hotter than fear.

He checks his watch, muttering, then looks back at me with that grin that makes my skin crawl.

"That's if he's still even alive."

The words slam into me like a bullet. My chest caves. I need to get to him. I need him. He's all I want in this life.

I try to shout, but the gag swallows my voice.

"I'm not letting you go. Not yet." He starts pacing, restless energy snapping off him. "I just need my brother to get here."

His eyes turn to slits; he's shifting so fast into anger.

"But, he's always so fucking late," he hisses.

This isn't just about me. This is about Finn. His family. The war that never ends.

I yank against the restraints until I feel the burn of skin splitting, until blood slicks down my wrists. Pain be damned. I'll tear myself to shreds if that's what it takes.

Because if Finn's heart stops beating… so will mine.

I wait until he leans close again, his scarred face inches

from mine, and then I snap my head forward with every ounce of strength I have.

Bone cracks against bone.

He reels back with a snarl, clutching his face. I can't do much more damage than what's already been done to him. It looks like he fought a bear.

For a fleeting second, victory surges through me.

But it's gone in an instant.

His hand whips across my cheek, the impact so sharp it rattles my skull. My vision explodes with stars, the world tilting and dimming.

The last thing I hear before the blackness drags me under is his laughter.

And all I want is for my husband to burst through the doors and save me.

I burst out into the night, lungs heaving, the cool air doing nothing to soothe the fire burning in my chest. My gun clutched in one hand, the other trembling like it can't hold me together. Every step without Stephanie tears another piece of me away.

I can't breathe knowing she's in this place and I'm not with her.

Enzo is confident she hasn't left the building. He's back in the feeds, or most of them. Which means she's here. Somewhere. My wife. My everything.

Theo drags Arthur toward us, the bastard's face twisted in defiance, but I only see red.

"Where is my wife?" My roar cracks the air. "Where the fuck is she?"

Arthur shakes his head, but it's too slow, too calm, and I lose it. My fist collides with his jaw, the crack satisfying, the blood better. He staggers, and I hit him again and again, until Conan's iron grip clamps onto me from behind.

"Finn! Stop! He'll be no good to us dead!"

I thrash against him, my blood boiling. "He took her from me! He knows where she is!"

Arthur spits blood onto the ground, smirking through his broken lip. "I don't. I don't even know who the fuck you're talking about."

"Bullshit!" My voice shreds from my throat. I surge forward again, Conan holding me back by sheer force. "Tell me who told you to come. Who are you working with? Tell me who gave the fucking order! Who has my fucking wife, Arthur!"

Arthur's smirk falters. For the first time tonight, his mask slips.

"Finn. This ain't me. This has nothing to do with me. I'm here to meet."

He stops. His face drains of all color.

"Who?" I grab his throat and slam him against the brick wall.

"The one person in my life I never thought would betray me," he mutters, eyes flicking to the ground.

Silence falls heavy. My stomach twists. Whoever he means, the weight of it crushes the air from all of us.

The disfigured guy crashes into my mind, and I release my hold.

No. There's no fucking way. We're not just dealing with our ghosts of the past.

We're fighting the dead, literally.

"Say his name, Arthur." My tone is deadly.

This is going to kill Conan.

Our father's death was for nothing. A fucking setup that's lasted years.

"James," Arthur says quietly. Almost like it hurt him to say it.

I press my hand against Conan's chest to stop him from

killing Arthur with his bare hands. New rules have just come into play.

"You fuckin' cunt!" Declan smashes his fist into Arthur's nose.

I clearly tried to tame the wrong brother here.

"Our father fucking died as penance for Conan killing James. If James never died, you motherfuckers set this up. You murdered our father for no reason. You've gone against everything," I seethe, coming nose to nose with him.

"If I didn't need you to save my wife, I'd cut your head off your shoulders and fucking stomp your brains out. But that can wait. Because you're going to get my wife back to me," I tell him, my voice deadly.

"O-okay. Okay, fuck." His voice shakes.

There's a bang on the door behind us; Drago grabs the scruff of Arthur's neck, and he looks like he might piss himself.

I shove the door open, the creak echoing through the stone halls.

And then I freeze.

Rowan.

He's sprawled on the floor, pale, blood soaking through his shirt. My stomach drops, the world narrowing.

"Fuck!" Conan rushes forward, dropping to his knees.

Declan takes hold of Arthur as I watch this play out. I'm fucking frozen.

Reggie and Drago are already moving, working fast.

"We're getting him to the hospital. Now," Reggie barks.

Rowan groans weakly, his eyes rolling back.

I can't even breathe. Seeing someone in my family bleeding out again, my wife is still missing. Every failure crushing me like bricks. This... this is why I need to get

Stephanie back. She is my anchor. She is the only one who can help stay sane through all this.

I grip the gun tighter, my vision tunneling.

Shit just got a lot more serious.

Bending down, I remove the jacket he's clutching to his wound, finding the entrance and exit holes. "It looks clean, but he needs to get out of here. You're going to be fine, Rowan." I tap his cheek to try and keep him with us.

They lift him carefully and rush him out and I hold myself up against the wall.

My voice doesn't sound human anymore. "We find her now."

I turn to Arthur, pointing my gun straight between his eyes. I'm fighting a battle within myself, and I have to find her before I lose. I might have stopped the drug from taking me over, but the side effects are still trying to knock me on my ass.

"If you want any chance of walking out of here alive. Call your cunt of a brother," I order.

Blood drips from my nose and I bite down on my tongue. My whole body throbs, but I don't dare let him see the weakness. He's unraveling—his temper a live wire—and I know with every bone in my body that if Finn doesn't find me soon, this man will kill me.

I'm not alive because he wants me alive. I'm alive because I'm a pawn. A piece in his game for power against the Quinns. That's the only thing keeping me breathing.

He drags a chair across the carpet and straddles it backward, leaning his arms against the top. Just watching me, wearing that wicked grin like he's already won.

"You're pretty," he says.

I scrunch my nose, glaring at him as he rips off my gag.

"I can see why the doctor went for you." He props his cheek against his hand. "Open your legs for me."

I shake my head sharply. "I can't. My dress is down to my ankles, dickhead."

He bursts out laughing, the sound manic.

"And she's sassy. Fuck, Finn did hit the jackpot."

My stomach knots as he pulls a flip knife from his pocket, the metallic click echoing through me.

"I can cut you out of it. Make you more comfortable?"

"I wouldn't." My voice is sharp.

"Why? Because your husband's going to kill me?" He runs a finger along the blade.

"Probably, yeah."

He shakes his head. "No. Because if my plan works the way I want it to, I'm not getting the blame for this."

A chill rips through me. "What is the plan?" I ask sweetly, trying to buy time.

His dark eyes snap to mine. "It involves you dying. Someone else holding the gun. Just long enough for me to swoop in and hand them over to your husband. Play the hero. Win their trust. And then I'll take London back piece by piece as a ghost again."

I nod slowly, masking the fear that claws at me. He's going to kill me.

"Or," I counter, forcing a smirk, "you could not kill me. And I just keep my mouth shut, pretend this never happened."

He chuckles. "Good try. But I need the dramatics. Wait—what's your name?"

"Angel," I lie, voice steady despite the thundering of my heart.

His eyes narrow, and he presses the knife point into the chair between us. "My cousin, Ben, ran a strip club in America for me while I was pretending to be dead. He used to talk about an Angel that worked for him. Red hair. Fine ass. But he was always fucking some blonde chick. Until he got himself caught and I got his head delivered back to me."

Ice crawls through my veins.

Holy shit.

Ben. The sleazy asshole who employed me. The club. All

of it is tied to this. And here I am—back in their orbit. It was always leading me to Finn.

"I'm sorry about Ben," I say quietly, my voice trembling in spite of myself.

"Yeah?" His lip curls. "Ask your husband how he died."

Good. I think viciously. At least one of them is gone.

Tears prick at my eyes. What if I don't even get the chance to ask Finn about it? What if I never get to tell him I love him again?

He said it once. Those words. They meant everything. Enough to bury all the pain in me. Enough to make dying feel almost worth it, if it comes to that. Because I was loved—fiercely, completely. The kind of love people search a lifetime for.

I just wish I'd had more time. To see him as a father. To see the life we could've built.

"What's the matter, Angel?" he mocks.

Before I can answer, his phone rings. His eyes light up like a kid at Christmas.

"It's almost showtime."

My throat tightens as he stands abruptly, pacing like a madman.

"Arthur. We have a problem. Has anyone seen you come in yet?" His tone carries just enough fear to be convincing. "Good. Good. I'm in the systems room behind the cinema. Left door before you go in. Code is 4-5-2-3. First door on the left. Don't be seen."

He pauses, listening, then laughs. "What have I done? I'm getting us our empire back, brother. Like I've been doing for years. But I need your help, okay?"

His hand trembles, a vein bulging on his forehead as rage flashes in his eyes. "Just get here now." He snaps the call shut.

The breath shudders out of him. He slams his fist into his laptop keyboard, the crack of plastic echoing.

"These motherfuckers," he mutters.

"W-what?" My voice cracks.

"They've locked me out of the security feeds."

His eyes close, his chest rising and falling as he fights for calm. Then his lips curve into that grin again.

"But it's okay. Arthur's coming. It's going to work out."

Relief flares in my chest. If they've hacked the systems, it means they're onto him.

And if I know my husband, he'll already be hunting for blood.

This bastard will pay for taking me.

"You're not going in there alone," Declan hisses, pulling me back by my arm.

I wrench free, teeth grinding. "And you think charging in with an army will save her? If he feels cornered, she's dead before we even breach the door. James needs to believe he has a chance. That's the only way she walks out alive."

Theo folds his arms, expression grim. "That man's lost in his own head. You don't bargain with crazy."

It turns out, Theo has been talking to James, not Arthur, this entire time. James came here to kill me and my brothers. And I think Stephanie has been caught in the crossfire.

If she's hurt. It's all on me.

A humorless laugh rips out of me. "You're wrong. Crazy understands crazy. I've been training for this my whole life."

Conan steps forward, his fists clenched. "Then let me go in. I'm the one he wants revenge on. I'm the one who disfigured him."

I square up to him, nose to nose. "And leave Liam without a father? Not a fucking chance. Don't you dare."

His jaw flexes, but he doesn't move.

"Listen to me," I exhale, lungs burning as the words tear through me. "This isn't a fight. It's a trial. Just like Decadence. James thinks he's the game master, but he isn't. He's the fucking prey. He needs to believe there's a way out, and I'm going to let him think that—until I take his head off."

Declan swears under his breath. "You're walking into the lion's den unarmed."

I raise my gun, sliding back the chamber with a metallic click. "Not unarmed. Just calculated."

They exchange a look, both of them knowing what this means. There's no pulling me back from this.

Theo's men shove Arthur forward. His face is pale, sweat sheening his brow, but his eyes don't leave mine. "He's not bluffing," he mutters. "James will kill her if he sees any of you. He ain't right, not since the way Conan left him. My father tried to keep him at bay, but, clearly, I couldn't."

His gaze lowers to the ground.

"Then you're coming with me." I jam the gun against his temple, dragging him to the keypad. "You open that door. You walk me in. And you pray to whatever god you still believe in that she's breathing when we get there."

Arthur swallows hard but doesn't resist. He knows this is the only way.

I glance back once at my brothers. Their faces are carved from stone, but I see it—the fear.

"I love you both, so fucking much. But I love that woman in there too." My throat tightens as I say it. They'll understand. Because both of them would do the same for their women.

"If you hear a gunshot," I tell them, "that's your signal. Breach it. End it. But until then—you stay the fuck out."

Conan's fists flex, but he nods. Declan drags a hand through his hair, muttering a curse.

I turn back, pressing the gun harder into Arthur's skull. The keypad beeps. The lock releases.

And I step into hell.

"Arthur," I murmur as the heavy door clicks shut behind us. "I don't know if you've ever been in love, but just know, I'll kill us both to save her. Alright?"

He nods stiffly. "I get it."

I'd get down on my knees and say a prayer if I could— that when that door opens, my girl is still alive. She has to be. Because there's no life for me without her. She is what my heart beats for. Her and only her.

We start our ascent up the stairs until we reach the door. I open it slowly, bracing for the worst. For my life to be over.

And there he is. The ghost. Half-blind, face carved with scars, a monster dragged out of the grave. Pressing a gun into the side of my wife's head.

The rage that tears through me is near blinding. I shove Arthur inside and kick the door shut.

"I'm just here for a friendly discussion, James. Let her go," I say, keeping my voice calm.

He bursts into a fit of laughter, sadistic and broken. "Oh, finally the psychopathic brother is here. Just a little bit early, but it's fine, we can adapt." His eyes flick between me and Arthur without a flicker of care.

"James," Arthur hisses. "Just fucking listen to him. It's over. We're done."

James sneers, his face twisting. "There is no fucking we. You fucked this whole family up. I had to do this all by myself. And yet, you still couldn't even stick to my plan. All you had to do was come up here unnoticed."

"And then what?" Arthur spits.

James tilts his head. His gun digs deeper into Stephanie's temple. I could blow Arthur's brains out beside me, and James wouldn't flinch.

"You wanted us to kill your brother," I say coldly, "so you could swoop in, save my wife, and crawl to Theo with your hero act. Right? Is that what this is all about? This isn't revenge, this is a power trip."

I can't look at Stephanie. If I do, I'll fucking break. I have to play the role. I have to be the man who feels nothing.

"Almost, Dr. Quinn," James purrs. "Almost. Except I planned on blowing her brains out and letting Arthur take the blame. Then I swoop in and hand him to you to take revenge, all the while I reclaim my empire. I've worked hard behind the scenes for this. It's been a long time coming. Would you like to hear more?"

My blood runs cold and I take a step closer. "Please. Tell me. I'd love to hear."

He smiles smugly. "I set Dad's trap so Theo's men would kill him."

Arthur's whole body jerks with fury and I dig the gun harder into him, stopping him from lunging.

"I knew he was softening to your pathetic cries for surrender," James sneers. "Talk of working with the Kings? No. Bowens don't work with anyone. We rule. You lost our territories, Arthur. You were too weak. And so was Dad. I needed you both out of the picture."

"You piece of fucking shit!" Arthur roars, voice breaking with pain.

I lean in, whispering, "Hurts, doesn't it, when someone murders your father?"

James smiles, the scar on his cheek pulling taut. "Ah, yes.

Seamus' death was a necessity. You all had to believe I died, that revenge had to be taken. And Conan—oh, Conan will have his turn."

My fist clenches at my side. Nothing will happen to my brothers.

"Why did you take my wife, James? There's no need to keep her here, you've got me and your plan is fucked."

I risk it and steal a glance at her. And it shatters me. Blood streaking from her nose. Tears trembling in her eyes. Bound to the chair, and I can't fucking do a thing about it yet.

I failed her. Just like I failed Penelope.

"I didn't care who showed up," he admits with a shrug. "My plan was drugging and capturing you, turning your brothers on Arthur. But the second I saw her on your arm, I knew I had the stronger hand. You showed me your weakness."

I nod slowly, letting a grin creep across my face. "Good game, James. I'll give you that. But you know, I'm not going to let anything happen to her, don't you? And now I know your weakness."

I shove Arthur forward, releasing him.

James tilts his head. "What's that then?"

"That I could kill your brother, and you'd thank me for it. Power is your weakness."

He glances at Arthur, the tension twisting between them.

"So. Tell me what the fuck you want to let her go. Your hero act has gone out the window, so it's time we made new rules to this game," I tell him.

James scratches his scar, eyes glittering. "Easy. Your life for hers. I gotta see one Quinn brother suffer."

"James. Enough," Arthur snaps.

And James just laughs.

I know what I have to do. There's only one way to level with someone like this.

It's to let them believe they have the upper hand.

That she is my weakness.

When in reality, he couldn't be further from the truth.

She's my strength in this life.

CHAPTER 92

The words hit me like a sledgehammer.

"Your life for hers," James repeats.

And then Finn nods. He doesn't even hesitate. He nods.

"Is that all? Easy," Finn tells him.

"Gun on the floor first Quinn, kick it away and get on your knees." James orders.

"No, Finn!" The scream tears from my throat, shredded and broken. My whole body thrashes against the chair, wrists tearing at the restraints until the rope slices into my skin. "No, no, no!"

He looks at me then, his pale eyes finding mine. And his lips move.

"I love you."

He does as James says. The moment his gun slides across the floor I fight the urge to throw up.

It wrecks me. I shake my head so hard it hurts, tears pouring down my face, my chest heaving as panic claws up my throat. My whole body is convulsing with the need to break free, to put myself between him and the bullet.

Because I would.

"Stop it!" My scream is hysterical, my voice nothing but cracked glass. "Finn, don't you fucking dare! You can't do this! Please!"

But he doesn't flinch. He doesn't look away. He lowers himself to his knees, his whole stance that of a man who has already made peace with dying.

James watches me unravel with something close to amusement.

"Touching, isn't it? Almost makes me believe in love." He strides over to Finn and presses the barrel harder into his chest, his smile venomous. "But love makes men weak. And weakness gets you killed."

Arthur's voice cuts through.

"James. Enough. This isn't how we win."

James tilts his head toward him, his scarred face twisting into something even more grotesque.

"Win? You really think you still have a side, brother? You've been bleeding us dry for years. Surrendering scraps like some lapdog." His good eye burns into Arthur as he steps closer to Finn. "You should be standing with me. We could take it all back. Every territory. Every throne that was stolen from us. I couldn't even trust you enough to bring you in on this scheme."

Arthur doesn't answer. His chest heaves, hate in his eyes. None of it matters because all I can see is the gun aimed at Finn's heart.

"Arthur," James pushes. "This is your chance. Prove your loyalty. Prove you're still a Bowen. Kill this Quinn scum and then shoot his wife."

"Don't you dare," I choke out, thrashing until the chair rattles against the floor. My skin is raw where the rope bite, but I can't stop. I can't let this play out. "Arthur, please."

Everything in me breaks.

And the world stops.

James turns his head to me, grinning like he's savoring every second. "You're about to watch your psycho husband die for you, Angel. Must feel special."

My stomach twists.

But then I catch it. The tiniest flicker in Finn's face, the subtlest edge to his smirk. He's not surrendering. He's baiting him. He's playing James the way he plays everyone else.

It's Decadence all over again. A trial. A game.

And James has no idea he's already lost.

CHAPTER 93

FINN

This was the biggest risk of my life. Years of games. Years of sacrifices. All of it leading to this moment.

I'd put my trust in the very man I came here to slaughter. Arthur Bowen. My enemy. My father's executioner's son.

But I've studied the Bowens since I was ten years old.

I know their tells. Their quirks. Their brand of cruelty. And Arthur's reaction earlier told me everything—that this wasn't him. Taking my wife would never be his play. He knows what I'm capable of. He knows better.

And something in my gut is telling me to trust him. Worst case, as soon as the bullet rips through me, our army will be in here quick enough to save Stephanie. That's what I'm telling myself. That she will be saved.

A shot fires.

Stephanie's muffled scream rips through the room, drowning out everything else. My pulse hammers, my body braces, waiting for the bullet. For the ripping pain. For the end.

But it never comes.

When I open my eyes, James is already crumbling at my feet. His gun clatters uselessly to the floor. He's clawing at his chest, his ruined face twisting in disbelief before his knees slam against the carpet.

And Arthur stands over him. Chest heaving. His own weapon still smoking.

For a split second, I can't move. Relief and suspicion collide inside me. Because Arthur Bowen doesn't save lives. Not unless it feeds his own survival. But this is different. He's been betrayed by his own blood.

Our eyes lock. His grief is naked, his fury at the truth of betrayal written all over him. But I don't let myself soften. I can't afford to.

I lunge forward, grabbing James's fallen gun just as the door bursts open and chaos explodes in. Declan and Conan, weapons raised, rage burning in their eyes. Frankie right behind, Zara at his shoulder. All of their weapons pointing at Arthur.

"Don't!" My roar tears out. "No one touches him! Not yet!"

The whole room freezes. Every muscle wound tight, every barrel trained. But I keep my gaze on Arthur, but I'm well aware James is still alive.

"I'm giving you one chance, Arthur," I growl. "One. You hand me James, and I will offer you a chance to live."

Every gun shifts, the tension balanced on a blade's edge. But Arthur just exhales, the fight bleeding out of his shoulders. He lowers his weapon.

"He's all yours."

He spits in James's bloodied face, the sound harsh in the silence. "You're no brother of mine."

I turn to Conan, who is seething.

"Con. Take Arthur. You get to decide if he lives or dies.

Give him the opportunity to fight back. Have Declan go with you."

Conan nods, and Arthur freezes. The chances of him surviving are slim, but so were Jame's. A shot to live is better than a bullet in the skull.

And he understands that. This is me giving him grace for saving my life. I give him a nod. Behind me, my family parts just enough to let him through, Conan grabbing him by the arm with a snarl. Arthur earned the right to fight for his life tonight. He's lost everything else; that punishment is heavier than any bullet.

And now, he must fight with everything he has left. But to me, it's done. My brothers will make their judgments.

I have something far more important.

Stephanie.

My temptress. My wife.

"Grab him," I order, jerking my chin at James as I cross the room. Frankie and Zara get to work moving him.

Then I'm on my knees in front of her, the world dissolving into static. My hands shake as I tear at the restraints, cursing when the rope bites deeper into her wrists.

"Easy, love. I've got you. I've got you now." My voice breaks, but I don't care.

I'm not a robot. I do have so many emotions when it comes to her. And I'm no longer afraid to show them.

The second she's free, she launches into me. Her body slams into mine so hard I lose my breath. She clings to me, sobbing into my neck, as though if she lets go I'll vanish.

"Finn—" Her voice shatters against my ear. "I thought—I thought you were—"

"I know." My arms lock around her, crushing her to me. My chest splits wide open as I bury my face in her hair. "I'm here. You hear me? I'm fucking here. I'll never leave you. I'm sorry."

Her hands find my face, dragging me back until I'm staring into her eyes—wild, terrified, glistening.

"I can't lose you," she cries. "I can't—"

"You won't." My thumb brushes the tears from her cheek. "Not now. Not ever. You're mine, Stephanie. Always."

And when I kiss her, it isn't desperate. It isn't frantic.

It's a vow.

One I'll burn the entire world to keep.

CHAPTER 94

STEPHANIE

Song- The Drug In Me Is Reimagined,
Falling In Reverse.

I shake in Finn's arms as he carries me over to the corner of the room.

That moment the gun went off.

I thought my life was over.

Because when his heart stops beating, so will mine.

"I love you, Stephanie. I love you with every single part of me. I'm sorry I let you down."

I rest my forehead against his.

"I love you, Finn. Fuck, I was so scared that I'd never see you again."

He pulls back and cups my face.

"I was always coming to get you, baby. Always."

I smile.

And one thing rests heavy on me. Something that I know I want to remember this time.

"Finn?"

"Yes, love?"

"Will you marry me? For real this time?"

A slow smile spreads across his lips as he brings my left hand up to his mouth and kisses over my rings.

"You stole my line again, temptress. I even had a new ring ready."

Tears stream down my cheeks.

"You did?"

He nods.

"I did. I want a wedding that we remember. Something that could never be forgotten. Our moment for everyone to see. You deserve the world, love. And I want to be the man to give you that."

I lean in and kiss him with everything that I am.

"But I asked first. Will you marry me, Finn Quinn? Will you make me the happiest woman in the world?"

He laces a finger around my throat, staring into my eyes.

"Yes, Stephanie. I'll marry you. We can do it every year if you want to. Whatever makes you smile like you are right now."

James's groan from behind us burst our little bubble.

"Do you want to end this with me? By my side as we get our revenge?" he asks quietly.

I can barely process Finn's words. My body is still trembling in his arms, but when he pulls me closer and I follow his gaze over his shoulder, my stomach twists.

James.

Bound to the same chair that held me captive. His ruined face glistening with sweat, the ugly curve of his mouth curled into a smirk like he doesn't give a single fuck what's about to happen.

"You said you wanted to learn. You wanted to know every side of me. That includes this."

The part of me that's still the surgeon, still the girl who

believed in mercy, hesitates. But the part of me that bled, that begged, that thought I'd lost the man I love forever—that part burns hotter.

"Do you want me to…?" My voice wavers.

Finn cups the side of my face again, grounding me with his pale eyes.

"Only if you want to, love. You don't owe me this. You don't owe him a damn thing. But I'll give you the choice. You can walk out that door and never see what happens. Or you can stand beside me and know exactly what it means to be mine. To be one of us."

My throat tightens. He's not asking me to cross a line for him; he's asking me to decide who I am.

I want to be his wife. His partner. His fucking everything.

I glance back at James. He sneers, even with blood dripping from the corner of his mouth.

"You think she's got it in her? She's weak. Pathetic. Be a man and torture me yourself!"

My hands curl into fists. Every nerve in my body screams with rage. Weak? No. He's wrong. I survived him. I survived all of them. And I'll never let anyone call me weak again.

I lean in closer to Finn, my lips brushing his ear.

"Show me."

His hand slides to the small of my back.

"Good girl."

When he pulls away, his smile is dark. The kind of smile that promises blood.

I step forward, my pulse hammering as James's one good eye watches me. He's still smirking. Still convinced I won't follow through.

But this time, he's going to learn just how wrong he is.

Finn's voice cuts through, not leaving any room for argument.

"Out."

I glance behind at Finn's family as they hesitate. One word, and still, no one moves. His pale eyes sweep the room.

"I said out. This isn't yours. This is ours. It's for me and my wife to end. Leave us."

Something about the way he says *ours* sends a shiver down my spine.

Finn's eyes fix on Conan. "Do what you feel is right, brother," he tells him.

Conan's face is stern as he nods, dragging Arthur out. Declan lingers, but one look from Finn has him bowing his head and leaving. Frankie and Zara exchange a glance, and then they leave.

The door shuts. The silence swallows us.

It's just Finn, me, and James.

My pulse hammers as I take in the sight of him tied to the chair. Finn moves behind me, his hand settling on my hip, grounding me with his touch.

"This is your moment, love. Not his. Not mine. Yours."

"I don't know what to do," I whisper.

I want to make this hurt.

"You don't need to." He presses a kiss to my temple. "I'll talk you through it. You just follow my voice. You trust me."

James scoffs, spitting blood onto the floor.

"She's not like you. She's not a killer."

My jaw clenches. I don't look at him. I only look at Finn.

"Yes, she is," Finn says softly, and his lips brush my ear. "She's better than me. Stronger. She's survived things I couldn't." His hand tightens on my hip. "Show him that, temptress. Show him who you are."

I nod, breath shaky. "Okay."

Finn pulls out a blade from his pocket and presses it into my palm, his hand folding around mine.

"Start small. You don't need to rush. Just touch him. Let him feel how steady you are."

I step forward. My knees are trembling, but my hand doesn't shake. I trail the blade against James's cheek, over the puckered scar tissue. His smirk falters.

"That's it," Finn murmurs, his chest against my back. His voice is dark, reverent. "Look how perfect you are. Even with a blade in your hand, you're still calm. Still in control."

James tries to laugh, but it comes out strangled. "You're turning her into you."

Finn's mouth curves against my ear.

"No. I'm letting her be herself."

The words crack something open inside me. I drag the blade down James's neck, light enough to draw a bead of blood. His hiss makes my pulse pound harder.

I glance back at Finn. His eyes are locked on me like I'm the only thing in existence. Proud. Possessive. Mine.

"Good girl," he breathes. "Again."

So I do. A slice down his arm. Another over the top of his hand. Shallow, but enough to make him flinch, enough to remind him he's the one tied down now.

I find myself breathing heavier, my body pressed against Finn's, my hand guided by his. It's terrifying, it's intoxicating, and it feels like freedom.

This is where I was meant to be.

I was always bound to find the other half of my soul in Finn. Two halves that complete each other.

"Beautiful," Finn praises. His lips find my throat, his words a brand against my skin. "Every cut you make is a promise that no one will ever touch you again. That you are untouchable."

James spits blood again, glaring at me with his one good eye. "You're pathetic."

Before I can think, I drive the knife into his thigh. His scream rips through the room. My whole body jerks with the sound, but Finn's arms are around me instantly, holding me steady, whispering against my hair.

"That's it. Look at him. He bleeds for you now. He suffers for you."

My chest heaves. I glance down at James, sweat rolling down his face, his arrogance slipping into something uglier—fear. And I realize I like the sight of it.

I lean back against Finn, my voice low.

"What now?"

Finn's lips brush my ear again. "Whatever you want, temptress. You can walk away. Or you can end him."

I look into James's eye. His smirk is gone. The monster who held a gun to my head is nothing but a broken, bloodied shell.

And when I answer, my voice is steady.

"I want to end him."

Finn smiles against my skin. "My perfect girl."

CHAPTER 95

FINN

Taking the bloodied knife from her, I throw it down on the floor and pull out the gun instead.

I study her for a moment. My wife. My temptress. The woman who stormed her way into my blackened life and now stands here, trembling but unbroken. The most powerful woman I've ever met. Her chest rises and falls like she's been running for miles, and still she hasn't looked away from the bastard in the chair.

"Stephanie." I tilt the gun in my hand, then offer it to her grip-first. "This one's yours."

Her eyes widen. I can see the war inside her. The part of her that still wants to heal people and the part that wants to burn every monster to ash. But her hand doesn't hesitate. She takes it.

James lets out a rasp of a laugh, blood slicking his teeth. He doesn't have long left anyway, that bullet hole is killing him.

"She won't do it. She doesn't have it in her to kill me."

I step behind her again, my palms bracketing her hips, my mouth brushing her ear.

"Prove him wrong, temptress. Show him what I already know—that you're stronger than both of us put together."

Her shoulders tense, then square. She raises the gun, two hands around the grip. She doesn't flinch when James spits at her feet, doesn't shake when his one good eye burns into hers with hate.

I've never been prouder in my life.

"Breathe in," I whisper. "Breathe out. Let every memory of what he did to you, of how he touched what's mine, flow into that trigger finger."

Her finger curls. A single squeeze.

The blast is deafening in the enclosed room.

James's head jerks back, and then he's nothing but dead weight slumped in the chair, blood painting his ruined face. Silence follows, broken only by her ragged gasp as the gun clatters from her hand to the floor.

I catch her before she can collapse, wrapping her in my arms and pulling her tight against my chest. She's shaking, but she's here. Breathing. Alive.

And forever mine.

"You did it," I murmur, kissing the crown of her head. My throat burns, but my voice stays low. "My clever girl. My fearless temptress."

Her fists curl into my shirt, wetness soaking the fabric where her face hides against me. "I'm scared, Finn."

I tip her chin up until her tear-soaked eyes meet mine. I want her to see the truth.

"Why?"

"Because I have no remorse. I just shot a man dead and felt nothing but happiness. That isn't normal, is it?"

I let out a small chuckle.

"No, love. He hurt you so he deserved to die. Don't ever feel guilty about that. That man causes nothing but pain, you should be happy, you probably saved a lot of lives by killing him."

She sobs once, and I kiss her mouth like I can pull every broken shard of her into me. Her hands tremble on my jaw, but there's fire in her eyes.

The kind of fire that tells me she's mine forever.

I've never been so proud.

"Shall we get out of here?" I whisper against her lips.

She nods slowly and I hear the door creak open.

Conan and Declan are the first two in, with Frankie and Zara behind them.

"Theo is holding Arthur, we wanted to wait for you to be done here," Declan tells me, looking at Jame's corpse.

I nod.

I look down at my girl and tug her tighter against my side.

"My wife did the honors," I say proudly.

Conan smirks with approval.

Her head tilts up, meeting every single pair of eyes in the room. She doesn't hide. Doesn't shrink.

Conan's fists unclench at his sides. Declan drags a hand over his face, muttering something about Quinn women always being terrifying. Frankie grins, that sharp Italian approval glinting in his eyes, and Zara moves a step closer, pride written in every line of her face.

"She's one of us now," Zara says simply.

I look down at my wife, at the fire smoldering in her tear-soaked eyes, and my chest aches with something I've never felt before. Not just pride. Not just love. But certainty.

Stephanie straightens at my side, her arm wrapping around my waist. Even covered in blood, her body trembling with adrenaline, she radiates power. Not the kind I gave her, not the kind I shaped. Her own.

Conan lets out a low whistle. Declan shakes his head with

a half-smile that almost looks like respect. Frankie raises his glass like we're at a wedding toast instead of standing in a slaughterhouse.

Because tonight wasn't just about vengeance. Tonight, Stephanie proved she belongs right here, beside me, in the dark, with blood on her hands and her crown forged in fire.

And I've never loved her more.

"Now, if you don't mind us. I've got a private suite booked to celebrate," I joke.

"No. You need to go to a fucking hospital, brother." Declan steps forward, his brows furrowed deep.

"You're forgetting my wife is also a doctor, Declan. I'll be fine."

Stephanie looks up at me, and I can feel the heat of her stare burn into the side of my head. She doesn't buy my bravado for a second. Truth is, I'm running on fumes, every muscle shaking, and tomorrow I'll probably feel like death warmed over.

"If I was going to collapse, I would've by now. Stop worrying," I mutter, forcing the grin back into place.

She slides her hand discreetly onto my wrist, and I can't help but smile as I bend down toward her.

"Are you seriously checking my pulse?" I whisper.

"Yeah. You're my husband. My responsibility to keep alive." She smiles sweetly.

"I like her," Conan chuckles, folding his massive arms.

"Have you heard from Reggie?" I ask Declan, my throat tight as the question slips out.

"The little shit is going to live to see another day. Reggie is going to stay here with Drago until Rowan is fit to fly home. But he's fine. Theo has offered hospital protection as a precaution."

A breath I didn't realize I was holding tears from my chest.

"Thank fuck."

"Are we really letting Arthur live, Finn? Or am I killing him?" Conan asks, his tone sharp as a blade.

I step forward, clasping his shoulder, grounding him. His own anger scares him, I know that. That's why they waited for me before he let himself loose on Arthur.

"What do you want to do? He saved my life. He saved Stephanie's. He was being played by James. We've killed the real Bowen threat to us now. But, it's your call."

Conan scrubs his hand over his face, torn. I know deep down he wants to rip Arthur apart piece by piece. But when his eyes flick to James's corpse, to the mangled face of the man he once beat so savagely we believed him dead, I see the war in him settle.

We're not angels. We're monsters with second chances. Maybe Arthur deserves one too. For now.

"Let me get my anger out on him and see if he's still standing. If he does live, the second he steps one foot out of line, I will be on that jet back here."

"Agreed." I nod, turning to Declan. "Are you happy with that?"

"As long as I can watch Conan in beast mode on him, I'm good for now," Declan mutters.

A low chuckle escapes me. The tension breaks, just a fraction.

Arthur is a problem for London. Not for the Quinns anymore. We've battled enough. The Bowens are done.

He isn't a threat to us any longer.

The Volkovs arrive next, Mikhail's voice muffled through his balaclava.

"We've swept the entire building. You're safe to leave.

We're going to stay behind and help Theo's guys with the clean-up."

My chest swells, warmth cutting through the blood and chaos. When we came to America, it was just a dream. An idea. We bled for it, killed for it, built every brick of our empire in the shadow of our father's ghost.

And here we are now. Not just working for the most powerful mafia families in the world, but standing alongside them. As equals.

We've earned this. We've carved our place into history.

I've always had my brothers at my side. But now, we've got family everywhere.

Because that's what this is.

Not just business. Not just vengeance.

Family.

And we protect our own—fiercely.

Song- My Demons, STARSET

Before I open the door, he spins me around, pinning my back to the wall. One hand curls tight around my throat, the other braced beside my head, his body towering over mine.

"I need you," he breathes, voice rough.

"I know you do. You'd be lost without me." I smile, trying to cut the weight of the moment, but his face doesn't soften.

His stare is serious. "How do you need me, Finn? What do you want me to do?"

"I need you to remember how much I love you. Because once I open that door, it might not seem like love. But it is. It's my way of showing you."

I press both hands against his chest, the erratic pounding of his heart rattling through my palms.

"You better not overdo it and die fucking me, Finn. I swear to god."

He grins, a wicked flash of teeth. "I did say I'd die for you, love. Dying inside of you doesn't seem so bad."

"And you nearly did die today, psycho. I vote we shower and nap first."

"You might change your mind when you see what I've done."

He swipes the keycard and pushes the door open, pulling me in with him.

The skyline pours glitter through the windows, city lights glittering like stars. He flicks on the lamps, bathing the room in warm gold. A four-poster bed waits in the corner, covered in black rose petals. A table beside it holds a plate of chocolate-dipped strawberries and an ice bucket cradling champagne.

"Oh, how romantic of you," I tease, waltzing closer.

And then my heart slams against my ribs when my eyes land on the bed.

"The annulment?" I whisper.

Tears sting as I step closer. Both our signatures are scrawled across the page, mocking me, promising an end I can't survive.

"You signed them?" I can't hide my hurt.

"Not for the reason you think, love. Turn around."

I spin around to face him, my throat burning, only to find him on one knee.

"You're a brave man." I shake my head, choked between a sob and a laugh. "I was about to punch you in the balls. I never want to see those papers again."

"Me neither, love. Me neither."

He chuckles, opening a velvet box in one hand, covering his crotch with the other. My gasp echoes through the room.

A massive diamond, twined with a black-diamond snake wrapped around the band. Deadly. Beautiful. Ours.

"Finn—"

"Stephanie Quinn." His voice is steady. "You might have proposed first. Said you love me first. But, I want to do this properly and get down on one knee with a ring you deserve. Will you do me the absolute honor of marrying me a second time? Only this time, we both remember saying our vows?"

My head nods frantically before the words even leave me. And when he rises, I launch myself into his arms with a squeal, clinging tight.

"Is that a yes?" he asks, his voice husky against my ear.

"A million times over—yes, yes, yes. Always yes, Dr. Quinn."

Our lips crash together, his smile pressed into mine as he drops me down on the petal-covered bed.

"Stephanie." He brushes the back of his hand against my cheek.

"Finn." I copy his tone.

"Our future, it might be a little messy to start with. We're entering a war with The Preacher, I can feel it in my bones. And I need you to know, that I will fucking die to keep you safe. I'll protect you until I take my last damn breath. They got to you once, and that was a grave mistake from them."

I slide my hands up his chest and grab his throat.

"I want you safe too, Finn. I'll be by your side however you need me, okay? We are a team now. And those assholes need to pay for what they've done."

A slow grin spreads across his lips, his grey eyes lighting up.

"Fuck. I love you, baby. I love you so much."

I grab the annulment papers, holding them up between us.

"I love you, Finn. More than you could ever imagine," I whisper.

He glances down at the paper and bites his lip.

"What are we doing with these? I don't want to end our first marriage. I think this next one is just more of a vow renewal. That first wedding—it made us," I ask.

His brow arches, a smirk curling like sin.

"We fuck over it and then rip it up?"

A grin spreads across my lips.

"Yes."

He yanks me toward him, bending low until his breath is hot on my shoulder, fingers dragging the zipper down the side of my dress.

"You really thought I was going to leave you? Even after I told you I loved you? That's punishable behavior, love," he whispers against my bare skin.

"My first reaction was that, yes. It's what I'm used to people leaving me," I tell him, voice breaking.

His teeth sink into me and I moan, the annulment sliding from my hand to the sheets.

"Not me, temptress. Never me."

The papers crumple beneath me as Finn pushes me back up the bed, the sound of them crackling under my spine as he strips the dress down my body. His hands are desperate, tearing at fabric like it's the thing standing between him and oxygen.

"Finn—" I gasp, arching into him as his mouth latches onto my throat, biting and sucking hard enough to bruise.

"You're mine," he growls against my skin, sliding my panties down my thighs and tossing them aside. "No annulment. No escape. You're mine until they bury me in the fucking ground."

I rake my nails down his chest, catching on buttons until they scatter across the floor. "Good. Because I'll be buried right beside you."

He leans back and unbuckles his belt, freeing his cock. He

grips my hips, pinning me down on the petals and papers, his eyes burning into mine like he's sealing this with fire.

"You want this vow, temptress?" His voice is dangerous. "Then take it."

He slams into me, the breath ripped from my lungs as pleasure crashes through me. The annulment paper shifts under us, crinkling with every brutal thrust, ink smearing with sweat as we destroy the words meant to break us.

My nails dig into his shoulders, his name torn from my throat. "Finn—oh god, yes—"

He hisses through his teeth, fucking me harder, deeper, until there's nothing but the sound of our bodies colliding. He drags his thumb over my clit, watching me unravel with his cock buried inside me.

"That's it, love. Vow to me. With your body. With your fucking soul."

Tears sting my eyes as I cling to him, every thrust branding me with his devotion. "I'm yours forever. No papers. No games. Just us."

He kisses me hard, swallowing my sobbed moan as my climax rips through me, soaking him, shattering me. And still he doesn't stop. He fucks me through it, holding my gaze like he's daring me to look away from the truth.

And I'm at one with it. He owns me.

"I love you," he rasps, forehead pressed to mine. "I fucking love you, Stephanie Quinn. And I'll say it every day, every time I fuck you, every time you breathe, until you never doubt it again."

I come again at his words, my body trembling, breaking open under him. And when he finally lets go, when he spills inside me with a guttural roar, I know that every horrible thing that I've ever gone through was worth it because it all led me to Finn Quinn.

He collapses against me, both of us shaking, panting, clinging like we're the last two people alive.

And maybe we are.

Because in this moment, nothing exists but him and me. No annulment. No past. No future without each other.

Just a vow written in blood, sweat, and love.

"It's my turn to look after you, Finn," I whisper against his lips.

He smiles softly and doesn't fight me this time.

CHAPTER 97

FINN

Two weeks later...

The room falls silent as I lead Stephanie into the meeting chamber at Inferno. My hand is linked with hers, and we take our seats beside Declan and Charlotte. Conan plants himself to Stephanie's left, Drago is on the other side of Charlotte. At the far end of the table sit Reggie and Rowan—because today concerns them most of all.

I nod toward Theo and his brothers, a curt greeting. Enzo is beside them, an unlit cigarette between his fingers. At the end of the day, whatever decisions are made here will rest on Enzo's final call.

I know what my brothers want. I know what my future with Stephanie looks like. Now we just need the nod.

"Well, London was a shit show." My voice cuts the silence.

Theo exhales, tugging at his collar. "We had no idea we were dealing with a ghost. Everyone believed James was dead. I'm sorry."

I understand his point; none of us had a clue James was alive, pulling the strings from a grave.

"It's done with now," Declan snaps, cutting him off before sparks can fly. "What matters is how we move forward with this alliance."

The truth is, with the war on the horizon here, we need Theo's men with us.

"We've spoken to our elders," Theo says. "We still want it. We have permission to agree to terms today."

I glance toward the twins. I'm not sure how much Declan has filled them in, but they'll find out soon enough. Old school. A vow of loyalty.

"Then here's the deal. Your sister, Bella, will marry Reggie. She moves here, marries him, becomes one of us. Once that's done, we begin working together."

Theo looks to his brothers. Kane coughs. Ryder grins like this might actually be a relief.

"You clearly haven't met our sister," Ryder smirks.

"This might be the best thing for her," Kane says. "She needs the real world."

"I'll deal with her," Reggie cuts in, his voice deeper than usual.

Rowan frowns. "Why do you get to—"

Reggie silences him with a stare sharp enough to cut glass. "You've had enough shit to deal with recently. You're still recovering. Let me take this one."

Rowan opens his mouth, but Reggie raises his brows.

"I'm the eldest. It's my duty. I'll marry Bella."

The words sound like poison on his tongue, but he doesn't flinch.

"We'll make it happen," Theo agrees, though unease shadows his voice.

I've got a funny feeling Reggie has no idea what storm is about to land in his lap.

"And Arthur?" I ask. "Keeping quiet, I assume?"

After Conan went ten rounds on him, my brother let him walk, well only just. Even Conan knows sometimes death is too easy. Conan hasn't lost his spark. No. He saw that Arthur saved me, and even my beast of a brother has a fucking heart.

We will never, ever, forgive Arthur. But, it's not his time to die. He's earned a few more years to survive. Or maybe months, who knows.

Theo nods. "We've got eyes on him. Man can't take a shit without us knowing. Not that he can physically move much right now."

I chuckle darkly. "Good."

"So. A union through marriage. Old school." I smirk.

Theo returns it. "Yeah. But it's not the elders I'm worried about, Finn."

I shrug. Their sister will adjust. Maybe she'll even like her grumpy new husband.

Declan rises, offering Theo his hand. They shake, sealing the deal.

"This is also a good time to tell you—we're going after The Preacher," Declan announces.

Theo blinks. "As in… the cult?"

Kane and Ryder exchange confused looks. Drago shifts in his seat; I need to know more about his past. I like him. He's a great asset. But he has secrets that are buried in Russia.

"I thought that was all bullshit," Theo mutters.

"It's real," Declan says flatly. "They're spreading into new territories. Inferno might've been on their list. That's not who we are. Not what we stand for. They already tried to have Finn locked up and blackmailed Stephanie."

Stephanie's hand squeezes mine under the table. Forgiveness is one thing that came easy with her. But I still enjoy punishing her for that slip.

"What the fuck," Theo mutters again.

"So, we'll need men. Intelligence." Declan glances at Ryder.

"Ex-army," Theo says, pointing at his brother. "He'll help."

"Whatever you need," Ryder agrees. "We're in."

Rowan clears his throat. All eyes snap to him. "So, uh… what about our Decadence Games?"

I pinch the bridge of my nose. "Not here, Rowan."

Stephanie straightens her spine beside me, that spark in her eye lighting me up inside. I grin. She knows what's coming.

"Decadence Games?" Theo frowns.

"It's Inferno business," Declan says. "We'll explain another day."

Theo shrugs. "Alright. I'll be in touch soon about the wedding."

Once they leave, Enzo leans forward,a grin curling his lips. "Out with it, Dr. Quinn."

I nod at the twins. Declan catches it. "Reg, Rowan—bar."

They leave, bickering as they do and I chuckle. Enzo lights his cigarette.

"Let me guess. The Trials are done?"

"Wrong." I smirk.

"Oh?"

I glance at my wife. She beams, though nerves flash across her face. I squeeze her hand. She deserves this seat at my side.

"We'll keep the Trials," she says, her voice steady. "But we're changing the rules. Husbands or families still sign up the women… But the women never step inside. We put the men who entered them into the Trials there instead. And help the women from the outside."

Enzo raises a brow. "And the winner?"

"There isn't one," I answer.

"They'll believe there's a chance. That's enough," Stephanie finishes.

I can't hide my pride. Whiskey and strategy, nights spent with her planning this out. My perfect partner.

"And you'll both host?" Enzo asks.

"Yes," I say. "It's the twenty-first century. Women kill too."

Enzo chuckles. "Fair enough. We'll iron out the logistics."

Stephanie shivers when I lean in, lips brushing her ear. "Good girl. You did perfectly."

Enzo exhales smoke. "Think Rowan's ready to host on his own without Reggie?"

"He'll manage," I answer. "Reggie will be busy. And Rowan needs something to keep himself entertained."

Conan cracks his knuckles. "Bella's marrying the wrong twin. Reggie'll take this too seriously. Rowan would've been better."

I glance at Drago, who's been silent. "Or maybe Drago should marry her."

His face is a picture of horror. Charlotte bursts into laughter.

"He'd terrify the poor girl," she says. "And he's double her age."

I wonder what Drago's real thoughts are. He, to me, seems like a guy who already has his heart set on someone.

I grin. "Then it's settled. Reggie is the choice."

I press a kiss to Stephanie's temple.

"Speaking of weddings. One month from today."

Declan and Charlotte smile.

"I'd like to invite you all to wedding number two."

Conan smirks. "About time. Can't believe we missed the first one."

"Did you forget to send our invites to your Vegas wedding?" I shoot back.

He raises his hands. "Fair. Continue."

I wouldn't have it any other way. My brothers. My wife. My family. And the fact they accept her as theirs too? That's everything.

I'll die a happy man. Having everything I never knew I needed.

Well, minus one thing.

But I'm sure that will be coming soon.

I check the time on my phone. Finn is late.

He's never late. Like, ever.

We're supposed to be cake tasting tonight, and I need him there so I don't end up ordering us a ten-tier chocolate monstrosity. Because I would. My sweet tooth has no shame.

I grab my bag and make a beeline for Finn's office.

"Steph!" Poppy calls.

I turn, smiling. "Hey!"

"I wanted to ask…" she trails off, twirling her thumbs.

"Go ahead."

"Now that you're… with Dr. Quinn. Like, officially. Does that mean you're leaving?"

The question knocks me off balance. I hadn't even thought about it. Technically, dating your boss isn't a great look. But quitting? The thought makes my chest tighten. I love this place. I love my job.

Still—logistics? That's another thing. We want kids. Vacations. We have the Trials. God.

"No, I won't be," I tell her, though the weight of it settles heavy in my chest. It's something I'll need to talk through with my husband. Maybe even move hospitals. Later. Not now.

Because right now all I can think about is chocolate cake and wedding dresses.

"I need to pop in to see Finn. Coffee tomorrow?" I offer.

She nods, smiling. "Have a good evening, Steph. It's good to see you happy."

I wave and push through Finn's door. His voice fills the office, deep and commanding. A smile creeps across my lips.

He's behind his desk, in front of the computer, on a video call. The hospital director, Bruce's clipped voice filters through the speakers.

I slip the door shut quietly and drop to my knees.

Finn's eyes snap to mine. One brow arches, and he crooks a finger.

Heat licks through me. I crawl to him, palms against the polished floor, until I'm under his desk.

"Yes. I understand," he says smoothly, gaze never faltering on the screen. "I'm more than happy to assist with any transition process. I'm not leaving the state."

I settle on my knees, hands gliding up his shins. He doesn't stop me. My grin widens. Higher, higher, until I reach his belt.

"What timescale are you thinking, Dr. Quinn?" the director asks.

Finn clears his throat. My heart pounds. I free him from his trousers, my mouth watering at the sight of his cock heavy in my hand.

"My wedding is in three weeks," he answers evenly. "So let's say… two months?"

Two months? My brows knit in confusion. What the hell is he talking about?

His hand fists in my hair, tugging me up until my lips part.

I take him in my mouth.

And Finn Quinn doesn't miss a single beat.

His fingers tighten in my hair, guiding me into a rhythm that has my throat burning and my core aching. His voice stays smooth, collected, like he isn't buried halfway down my throat.

"Yes… two months is workable. I'll ensure a clean handover."

My eyes snap up to him. Handover? My pulse spikes, but I don't stop. I take him deeper, hollowing my cheeks, desperate to draw out the cracks in his mask.

"Thank you, Director. That's all for now."

He ends the call with one hand, the other still tangled in my hair. His head drops back against the chair, a hiss tearing through his teeth as I swallow around him.

Then his hand tightens, pulling me off him with a wet gasp. My lips are swollen, my eyes glassy, but he doesn't let me move. His pale gaze pins me like steel.

"I quit," he says simply.

My chest caves. "What?"

"I quit the hospital, love." His thumb brushes across my mouth. "You keep your job."

The floor tilts beneath me. "Finn, you can't—"

"I can. I did." His jaw is set, but his voice softens. "I've watched you bleed for that career. Work every shift you could grab. Fight tooth and nail for respect in a world that tried to take it from you. I'll never be the man who steals that from you. If we want a family, and all the other things we have planned, we both can't work here."

Tears sting my eyes. My throat tightens.

"You don't need to sacrifice for me, we can make it work," I whisper.

His hand cups my cheek, rough and tender all at once. "I'm not sacrificing. I'm choosing. And I finally realized—" His voice cracks. "It was never the job I was obsessed with. It was always you."

The words hit like a blade to the chest.

"I want children with you," he continues. "I want nights where I'm not buried in surgeries or charts. I want mornings where the only thing I'm studying is the rise and fall of your chest while you sleep beside me. I want our family. And I don't need this fucking hospital to prove who I am. I only need you."

I can't breathe. Can't move. My hands clutch his thighs like I'm holding myself up with the last strength I have left.

"Finn…" My voice breaks. "You'd give that up for me?"

"For us," he corrects softly, tipping my chin up until my eyes lock on his. "Because all the control, all the precision, all the power—none of it meant shit until you walked into my operating room and lit me on fire. You're my obsession. You always were. The rest was noise."

And then he pulls me up onto his lap and his mouth is on mine, swallowing my tears, his kiss bruising and claiming all at once.

I straddle his lap, clinging to him like he's oxygen, and in a way, he is. He always was.

"Finn Quinn," I murmur against his lips, "I think you just became the perfect husband."

His smirk is wicked. "And I haven't even fucked you over my desk yet."

His smirk fades into something darker as I shift against his lap. His cock is still hard and pressing against my thigh like it owns me.

"Desk." His voice is gravel.

I shake my head, clutching his jaw, my tears still wet between us. "No. I want you to look at me while you claim me, Finn."

His breath catches, his eyes narrowing, and for a beat I think he'll argue. But then his hands snap to my hips, dragging me closer, grinding me down over his cock through my panties.

"You'll get every fucking part of me, temptress. You'll take it all until you can't move."

I gasp as he yanks my dress up; little does he realize I only changed into this in the hopes he'd do exactly this. He tears the lace panties clean down the middle. My legs are spread wide across him.

His mouth finds mine again as I sink down on him.

"Oh, fuck," I choke, nails clawing at his shirt. He's so deep, my body stretching to take him, to hold him.

His forehead presses against mine, sweat beading at his temple. He isn't in control now. His thrusts are erratic, desperate, each one harder than the last.

"You feel that?" he pants.

"That's me. Not the surgeon. Not the psycho. Just the man who would rip the world apart to keep you."

Tears slip down my cheeks again and he kisses them away, his hips snapping up into me so hard the desk behind us rattles even though we're not on it.

"Finn—" My moan tears from me as my orgasm builds too quickly. "I love you. God, I love you."

His head falls back, throat straining, and for the first time I see him let go. No control. No precision. Just wild, devastating need.

"I love you, Stephanie." His roar vibrates against my lips

as his release crashes into me, mine unraveling right after, my whole body convulsing around him.

We cling to each other in the aftermath, shaking, breathless, ruined.

His face is buried in my neck, his voice muffled and wrecked. "See? You don't need a perfect husband, love. You just need me. Exactly as I am."

I thread my fingers through his damp hair, holding him tight. "Exactly as you are, Finn. And I'll never let you go."

CHAPTER 99

FINN

Song, Take Me Back To Eden, Sleep Token.

My breath catches in my throat the moment those double doors open. My entire fucking world steps through, Nyx coiled up her arm, a bouquet of red roses clutched in her hand.

Her dress is everything I imagined. Sexy and elegant, with just enough sin at the neckline to show the edge of her tattoo.

With every step she takes, my chest tightens. The sting of tears presses against my eyes.

I remember our first wedding. I was tipsy, but I knew exactly what I was doing. I knew I wanted her.

But this… this is different.

Because Stephanie is walking toward me with purpose. To become mine. And I'll become hers. For eternity.

This time in front of our family and friends. This isn't just about us anymore—it's about Stephanie finally finding the family she's fought so long without. She won't fight alone again. She has all of us now.

Even Frankie and Zara, wide-eyed, are watching her come down the aisle.

The mafia life might break you down. Sometimes destroy you. But it's ours. It's what we live for.

Behind the gates of Decadence, we've built something powerful. Something worth bleeding for.

Our dad's death wasn't in vain. It led us here. To this. To her.

To my wife.

When Stephanie stops in front of me, the tears break free, slipping hot down my cheeks. I reach up, brushing away her own.

"Hi, beautiful," I whisper.

"Finn. You look so handsome my panties are wet."

The priest clears his throat, but I can't help the smile tugging at my mouth.

I lean in, lips brushing her cheek. "I'm disappointed you're wearing any, love."

Her blush blooms against me.

"Not for long, I hope."

Hallie slips Stephanie's bouquet from her hands so I can lace my fingers with hers. The priest starts his speech, but all I see is her. The way she lights up the room, the way she's always lit up my fucking life.

I pull my vows from my pocket, and Conan steps up, handing me the notepad.

"I'd like you to read out loud the very first page. My first ever observation about you."

Her brows rise. "Is this the book? I get to keep it?"

I chuckle. "It's one of the books, yes. I have four."

Her jaw drops.

"I'm really that interesting?" she teases.

"To me? The most fascinating person on the planet, love."

She flips open the little black book, and her breath stutters into a sob. My collar feels too fucking tight as I tug at it.

"Stephanie Miller. This is our second interaction. She scowls at me, a lot. I think she might find me attractive. I'm not sure. I will observe her behavior further. Note. Her smile is infectious, and so is her scowl. She's the brightest person in the room, including myself."

The crowd breaks into soft coos. Stephanie's sobs rack her chest, but she steadies herself and reads on.

"I'm fascinated. I need to be in a room with her on my own to assess further."

She flips through more pages until she finds a folded piece of paper. Her face pales as she unfolds it.

"What is this?"

Her voice trembles.

"Finn. Tell me what this is."

Fuck.

"No. No, it's all good, love. It's healthy. Just the scan results. When I was falling in love with you, I had brain scans done. I needed to be sure I wasn't sick. It all felt so alien."

Her lip trembles. "You thought loving me was making you sick?"

I shake my head, firm.

"Loving you is the only thing that makes everything in here okay." I tap my temple. "That day was confirmation of what I already knew. That I love you."

She folds it carefully, tucking it back into the book before pressing it into my palm.

"So you were obsessed with me from day one."

A grin pulls at my mouth.

"It would appear that way, temptress." I wink.

The priest clears his throat, carrying on, but pauses when

we give him our request. He wasn't thrilled, but a few thousand dollars softened the blow.

Declan hands me two gold scalpels. I give one to my wife.

"Dec. I need you to take Nyx," I murmur.

He freezes. "You never fucking mentioned that. You know how I feel about it."

"It?" I growl.

He sighs.

"Put your arm next to Stephanie's, and I'll move her over, okay? Just… breathe normally and relax," I tell him calmly.

Christ, they're all such pussies when it comes to Nyx.

I move her carefully, and Declan looks like he's about to piss himself before dropping into the front row with Charlotte. I spot Reggie, who is looking more stressed than usual.

Perhaps it's pre-wedding jitters for his own big day coming up. If Theo can find his runaway sister, that is. I was right. She's going to be a complete handful. And I cannot wait to watch this unfold.

Stephanie and I press our palms together, blades poised.

"We bleed for each other."

We cut a shallow line across our skin. I take her hand and lick the blood from her palm. She does the same to mine.

As the priest announces us husband and wife, I crash my lips to hers. One hand locked around her throat.

I kiss her with everything I am. Everything I'll ever be. Everything she's healed inside me.

A love like this burns eternal.

And I vow to spend every day of my life making sure my wife knows she saved me. That she brought me back to life. And that I would die for her.

She is my purpose. My fucking world.

Our love is intense. Some might say it's crazy. But, it's perfect, and it's ours.

Forever.

THE END.

EPILOGUE

STEPHANIE

I know he's behind me before I even look. But I can't. Because before I can even turn, my stomach wrenches and I'm throwing up into the toilet again.

This time, when it's over, I actually feel lighter. I sit back on the cold floor, breathless, and Finn is already there, rubbing slow circles into my back.

"You okay, love?" he asks, lowering himself beside me on the tiles like he belongs there.

"I've been better. Do you think it was the fish? But you aren't sick?"

I press the back of my hand to my forehead. I'm not sweaty. Not feverish. Just… off.

Finn chuckles, that dark sound that always carries a secret, and lays his palm against my stomach.

"No. I don't think it was anything you ate. I think it's something I put inside of you."

I swallow hard, fighting the sting of tears.

"You're late, temptress. Three days, if my calculations are correct."

"I'm pregnant?" The words come out broken, almost a hiccup.

I shoved that thought so far back, I almost convinced myself it wasn't possible. I didn't want the disappointment. I should have known better. I should have trusted Finn. His obsession with tracking me, my body, my cycles. When he wants something, he always gets it. And what he's wanted—what we've both wanted—is a baby.

He pulls me up from the floor, steadying me with his hands around my waist, grounding me in his arms.

"I hope you're right, Finn." My voice is barely a whisper.

His face softens, that hard mask of his cracking, and he presses a kiss into my hair.

"So do I."

He grabs a bottle of water and presses it into my hand. His eyes flicker with that dual edge of care and control.

"Are you well enough to host the Decadence Trials? I can start without you."

I gasp. "How dare you even suggest that!"

He smirks, eyes glittering with mischief.

"There she is." He chuckles, holding out his hand.

"Wait—let me brush my teeth first."

"Why? Just adds more to the torture methods. Vomit breath."

I laugh, shaking my head. I love seeing him like this— lighter, uncoiled, less haunted.

When I've cleaned myself up, I take his hand, and he leads me into the trial chamber.

It looks different now. Deadlier. Sharper. More refined. Finn and his brothers worked through the night while I slept, bringing in the five men now waiting. We even set up pre-recorded videos, calculated perfectly to unravel their nerves before we ever step inside. They think they're on trial for survival.

The truth? None of them are walking out of here.

They'll burn. Their ashes scattered with their sins. And the women they tried to throw into this hell? We'll pull them out. Between me and Charlotte, we've crafted a plan to reach them. To save them. To remind them that monsters can be stopped.

And if we succeed, then maybe—maybe—I won't carry the weight of guilt anymore.

We stop outside the first room. Finn hands me my mask. Mine glows red when I switch it on, eerie and blood-soaked in appearance.

"We can do a test after we've finished with the first trial," he tells me.

"Okay."

Finn slides his gold skeleton mask over his face, and the sight steals my breath.

"Fuck. Finn. That's hot. Don't get it dirty, I wanna use that later."

He tugs me flush against him.

"I bought a spare just for you. I had a feeling you'd say that."

I punch in the code. The door clicks, and the stench of urine and raw terror spills out.

Inside, a man is chained to a wooden chair, skin pale, eyes darting with wild panic.

"Please. I can pay you. Just let me go," he begs.

Finn laughs, cold and sharp, like ice cracking.

"The only way you can save yourself is by doing exactly as we instruct you. Welcome to Decadence."

Behind my mask, I'm smiling. I pick up the blade from the counter and press it into Finn's waiting hand.

This moment—this darkness—shared with him? It's everything I never thought I'd have. A husband who sees me. Who accepts me. Who loves me fiercely and without flinching.

To the world, we're monsters.

But we're not.

We're the ones who fight the battles others won't touch. Who've bled and sacrificed pieces of ourselves no one should ever have to give.

And maybe that makes us dangerous. But it doesn't make us evil.

Because I know the truth.

We love with good hearts. For each other. For the family we built in blood and fire.

For the ones worth saving.

DO YOU WANT MORE MR. & MRS. QUINN?

This couple deserves more than just a bonus scene… So they will be getting their own murder spree short story.

Want to be the first to receive it, **FOR FREE?**

Sign up to my newsletter here and it will drop in your inbox as soon as it's ready.

https://bit.ly/3SShFuW

Are you ready for the first Luna Mason MFM?

It's Reggie and Rowan's turn next in Indulge. What happens when Reggie's arranged marriage to Bella, our sassy British mafia princess, gets extremely complicated?

Get ready for all the spice. All the angst. And all the twists and turns. And of course, a why choose situation.

These brothers will be bringing it all.

Releasing November 2025!

Pre-Order is live now on Amazon: https://mybook.to/RPF3C

The series doesn't stop there. Our grand finale will take place in early 2026 with DADDY DRAGO AND LILY in **INSTINCT.**

A dad's best friend, age-gap, body guard romance.

Pre-order it here: https://mybook.to/vK40

MORE FROM LUNA MASON IN THE BENEATH UNIVERSE

Start the Beneath The Blaze Series with Finn's brothers, Declan and Conan! Both are available now on Amazon & KU!

INFERNO: A black cat assassin FMC that falls for the mob boss, and ends up in a kinky game of survival in a chocolate factory.

https://books2read.com/u/4DBg9Q

IGNITE: A cage fighting good boy and the nurse he calls trouble. A dark Irish Mafia Rom-Com with a primal game of survival.

https://mybook.to/cEm7

Back to where it all began in SERIES ONE, Beneath The Mask, which has been picked up by Kensington and **TRADITIONALLY PUBLISHED!!!**

You saw Frankie and Zara in Intense and you can read their explosive story in Detained.

You can read all four online (all platforms including KU) and they will be releasing in bookstores throughout 2025:

You can find all the details for Distance, Detonate, Devoted and Detained here!

https://www.kensingtonbooks.com/pages/beneaththemask/

Some of the characters from Beneath The Secrets made an appearance in Intense. You can read their stories in Beneath The Secrets.

A Dark and spicy Russian mafia romance set in Vegas.

ALL ARE LIVE ON AMAZON and KU!

Chaos (Jax 'The King of Chaos' Carter and Sofia)

An ex-husband's brother romance, where the MMC is a boxer, biker and has a vibrating tongue piercing.

https://mybook.to/QaGijx

Caged (Nikolai and Mila)

An explosive enemies to lovers, with a sexy single dad and assassin FMC.

https://mybook.to/Fc18uiK

Crave (Alexei and Lara)

A childhood best friends to lovers, that is also a brother's best friend romance. (This is the one where he puts a lollipop in her ass, and owns a pet flamingo)

https://mybook.to/rTb4

Claim (Mikhail and Ana)

A masked mafia boss and his step sister. Full of kidnapping, a sassy mafia princess, and a Cane Corso that steals the show.

https://mybook.to/6Nyh